Faraway Hill: Book One

Gold Editon

This book is a work of fiction. Names, characters, places and incidents are either the products of the author's imagination or are used fictionally.

Any resemblance of any of these fictional characters to an actual person (living or deceased) is entirely coincidental.

ISBN 978-0-9963134-0-7

Dedicated to the good people of a great state who host my silly story and to the pioneers of early television who had to make it all up as they went along.

AUTHOR'S INTRODUCTION

Like many writers, I am always looking to craft something new or a little different. My first novel, *Summer Club and the Creatures*, was inspired in part by the film "Shortbus," which included actual (not simulated) sex in a character-driven, non-pornographic story. *Summer Club* attempted to do something similar, with graphic sex scenes in a literary context. Obviously many people feel that my experiment worked: the novel was nominated for two Lambda Literary Foundation Awards and was the finalist in a web magazine's book award program.

This left me to wonder what should be my next project. I decided to tap into my television background and re-imagine one of TV's least known but historically important shows.

Alfred P. DuMont was one of television's pioneers, and not just as a manufacturer of TV equipment and sets. He started his own little network and brought the world everything from "Captain Video" to Jackie Gleason. But a series of cascading circumstances --- both economic and regulatory --- forced the DuMont network to go black in the mid-1950s. Very little is left of any of the DuMont programming because the person who eventually came into procession of the kinescopes decided in the 1970s to destroy most of them. The move angered a lot of TV historians and aficionados. It also turned out to be a stupid business decision: less than a decade later the home video industry would begin.

One of these lost shows is called "Faraway Hill," credited as network television's first prime time soap opera. There only a few scraps of information remaining. All of the scripts and kinescopes are gone. We do know that it aired as an experiment for 13 weeks in 1946. It was a live show, with a few filmed segments depicting things like place or travel. The actors apparently would stand in front of the camera each week to remind viewers of whom their characters were, and update them on the story. The series centered on a wealthy widow named Karen St. John who returned to her small home town of Faraway Hill where she got involved in a love triangle.

For my purposes, that lack of information turned out to be a blessing. It freed me up to craft a brand new *Faraway Hill*. As a bisexual man, I was also able to modernize the tale with lots of GLBT elements. One of the most important changes involves Karen: I have begun the story <u>before</u> her move back to town and she is now a very different kind of protagonist. This allowed other characters to move to the forefront without sacrificing Karen's importance.

The television series was vague as to where the town of Faraway Hill was ocated. In my research, I concluded that New Hampshire would be ideal. Although predominately rural with many small towns, New Hampshire has a certain amount of sophistication, a well educated population and a city in

Manchester that has many cultural amenities. I did make one important rule: that any references to the real New Hampshire are presented in as positive a light as possible. The good people of this state are the hosts of my story and my characters --- and I wish to be a gracious guest.

Out of respect to the legacy of the TV "Faraway Hill," I have labeled each chapter an "episode" and end all of them with a cliffhanger, revelation or climax. There is also a cliffhanger at the end of this book, which will be resolved in *Faraway Hill: Book Two*, the second installment of this trilogy.

Faraway Hill is a much lighter and less serious story than *Summer Club and the Creatures*, and I hope that you enjoy it.

James A. Richards, author
Faraway Hill: Book One

EPISODE ONE

There is something special about Central Park in the morning. It's as if the park and the city around it are waking from a long, sound slumber. A spring chill is in the air. The birds can be heard chirping overhead. Fresh dew is on the grass. All kinds of people are roaming about, starting their day at a coffee cart or by reading the *New York Times* on a bench near the pond.

Karen St. John seldom sees the park like this. She normally sleeps in, having spent the prior evening at a museum or charity event with people like the Bronfmans, Perelmans or Bancrofts. But this morning she has a meeting, an unwanted and unavoidable meeting. They agreed on the park's Belvedere Castle, a delightful folly that never fails to make her smile. So Karen pulls her mink coat closer and strides toward her destination.

Standing outside the castle is a woman, about Karen's age and wearing her own mink. She is not smiling, not even in greeting, as Karen approaches. "Good morning, Madeline."

"Never mind that," the woman answers contemptuously. "Are you going to accept our offer?"

Karen smiles; it's a practiced, elegant smile that either enchants or infuriates other people. It all depends on what they know about her. "I'm sorry, Madeline, but your father wouldn't want me to."

Madeline shakes her head in frustration. "Why am I not surprised? What the hell do we have to do to get you out of our lives?"

"Nothing," Karen smiles again and again that smile angers Madeline. "I'm going home for awhile, to visit family."

"You're leaving?"

"Yes, dear, I'm returning to Faraway Hill."

✳✳✳✳

Summer is nearly here and the town of Faraway Hill, New Hampshire is slowly waking to what will be a warm and pleasant day.

Faraway Hill's downtown --- which is so small it barely qualifies as a "downtown" --- is filled with quaint little shops and inns that primarily serve the tourist trade. It's fairly quiet these days, but in a matter of weeks it will be bustling with visitors.

The central point is its historic town square, with a small flowered park in the middle. The park features a charming old fountain bubbling with fresh water and a statue of John Halloran, one of New Hampshire's most famous men. More than two centuries ago he was the top aide of Josiah Barlett, a member of the Continental Congress. He used that position as the starting point for building the family fortune. The statue presents the figure of a handsome, confident, capable and ambitious man staring down on the town he and his descendants have built.

One of these descendants is jogging around the square this morning. Never a jock, Greg Halloran nevertheless enjoys a morning run. It keeps the 23-year-old fit and trim, but more importantly, it helps clear his head. His mind has been reeling lately: going from his new career at the family company, to his impending wedding --- and especially the arrival of a certain wedding guest.

He turns and crosses the street, passing a couple of antique shops, a restaurant and a dollar store. No one is inside any of them; it's still too early in the day. Faraway Hill has been his family's home for generations, but Greg feels like a stranger, an outsider. That comes from spending most of his life at boarding schools and college. Faraway Hill has always been the place to visit for summers and holidays. But now it's his place to live.

Greg makes another turn to cross another street. He isn't sure how many times around the square constitute a mile, but at least he can work up a sweat.

He can see the family home a short distance away. First built in the post-colonial period, it has been rebuilt and modified several times. Its elegant portico and imposing presence can be felt all over town. Despite his brief times at the house, Greg has fond memories of the huge garden in the summer months and of festive Christmases each December. But even then he felt more like a guest than a resident. His parents had little time for him, choosing to live their own lives instead. The few times he saw his father were always formal and seldom warm. That hasn't changed. But with his mother's death coming just after graduation, his father insisted that he come home. He is needed here.

Greg didn't cry at his mother's funeral and everyone commented on how brave he was. He wasn't being stoic. He was sorry that she had died, of course, but she was so distant with him that it seemed more like an aunt had passed rather than his mother. Greg was sad, but sad for a very different reason: he had just broken up with the love of his life. They agreed to "remain friends" and have had a few friendly emails and calls but have not seen each other since.

Another turn and Greg is again jogging past tourist-friendly shops. Just off this street are two of the town's most popular B&B's. One more turn and Greg is back on the street where he started. The sweaty shirt is clinging to his flat chest. He will need to quit soon and go back home.

Going back home means going back to the subject that has him the most concerned. When Greg proposed to Julie and wedding plans began, Lewis asked: who would be his best man? The question raised a difficult issue, since all of his school friends are now scattered across the country and he really doesn't know many people in Faraway Hill. There was only one man to ask, and Greg was surprised and anxious when he said yes.

And that's the problem.

****

A few miles away, Manchester is beginning its day in the same way it does every morning. Streets are being swept. Workers are cleaning office buildings. City buses are starting to roll and trucks are delivering today's edition of the *Union Leader*.

The city has transformed itself in recent years. Most of the textile mills have been shut down, and Manchester's citizens are now more likely to wear a suit to work than a blue collar shirt. This is a city of corporations and college students, of tourists and teachers. A few mills still operate in and near the city, including one owned by the Hallorans. But most of the old factory buildings that used to churn out bolt after bolt of fine cloth are now used for offices, stores and condos.

Some of those copies of the *Leader* are dropped off at King's Corner, a recent addition to downtown. Despite the popular Mall of New Hampshire, the city center remains almost as vibrant as it was a century ago. Located just off Elm Street, King's Corner is an eclectic store selling books and gifts with a coffee shop. At this moment Julie King is restocking the counter. She and her mother started the little shop about a year ago not long after she graduated college. So much has happened since then, especially with Greg Halloran. Her wedding is coming up soon and every so often she stops to admire her engagement ring. Life is moving faster and better than she can almost believe.

Sitting at the counter is her best friend, Ann Gale, who rode in with her today. The two have known each other since grade school, having both grown up in Faraway Hill. Julie isn't the only one with marriage on her mind: Ann's own wedding is coming up in just a few days.

"I can't believe what a cheap bastard Munroe is," Ann complains between sips of decaf. "Do you realize that I had to buy my own wedding dress at a clearance store? A clearance store! How embarrassing is that?" Munroe is Ann's father and it's a sign of her contempt that Julie can't recall the last time Ann called him Dad. *Probably months, maybe a year,* Julie thinks.

"No offense Ann, but is the farm really doing that well? I mean if it's just the three of you working it, it can't be making that much money."

"Its making enough for a decent dress, trust me."

A few early morning customers come in and get Julie's attention. The college girl they just hired is running late so it is up to her to sell the coffee, muffins and newspapers. When she returns, Ann picks up the conversation like there was no interruption. "By the way, how are things coming with *your* dress?"

Sometimes she doesn't like to talk about the wedding. Her whole life has been wrapped up in it for the last few months. It's been overwhelming. "Not bad. The alterations will be done in a couple of days." She and Ann normally tell each other everything. But there is something that Julie is keeping to herself, something connected to the wedding, something important. She has been avoiding anything and anyone connected with this something especially Greg. He is obviously frustrated but this something is so big and unexpected she has no idea how to tell him.

"Marrying Greg Halloran," Ann shakes her head in amazement. "Damn you are lucky."

Julie starts brewing a fresh pot of coffee. She doesn't like it when Ann compares the two weddings. Ever since she was a little girl, Ann has never been happy with her life in Faraway Hill. She always dreams of something better and never tires of saying so. That habit often annoys people. Julie is pretty content, living life as it happens. Her engagement to Greg is more than she ever expected. Certainly the other news is an even bigger surprise. "Ann, you make me sound like a gold digger."

"I'm sorry Julie, but you know what I mean."

"Your lucky, too. Mark is a great guy." Julie often wonders if Ann wishes *she* was the one marrying Greg Halloran.

"I suppose so." Mark Bradley is the laborer who wandered into Faraway Hill just before Christmas and found work at the Gale farm. The two of them hit it off right away. "Mark is a nice guy and all, but . . . he just doesn't have much ambition."

"Then why are you marrying him?"

"Well, like you said: he *is* a nice guy. There aren't too many of them around these days. And we have lots of fun together." She leans in to whisper, "and he's great in bed." Julie smiles but says nothing as Ann continues. "But, you know, mostly it's about the farm. At some point soon Munroe is going to keel over, probably after one of his drunken binges. Then Mark and I can take over --- even though I hate the place."

Julie rather likes the simple quiet of the Gale farm --- except when Munroe is around --- but it never seems to satisfy Ann. Of course, the house needs some work. "It could be nice if it were fixed up."

"That's not what I mean. I'd rather live here, in Manchester, than some hick farm. I'd sell the place and use the money to do something else."

"Like what?"

"I don't know; maybe start a business of my own like you and your mom did. But I sure has hell would not do it in *Nowhere Hill*." Julie frowns at Ann's reoccurring nickname for the town. She's been doing that since high school. Faraway Hill has always seemed like a comfortable and safe place to her.

The door opens and the new girl, Mary Armstrong, rushes in. "I'm sorry Miss King, finals and all." Mary is a petite thing, sweet and a little shy. Of course, she's only 19.

"That's okay; just don't make a habit of it. My mother isn't as understanding."

"Thanks." Mary ties on her apron. "Oh, Miss Gale, I see your fiancé is waiting outside."

"He is?" Ann turns to look out the window and sees Mark sitting in the worn, old Ford pick-up reading today's paper. "Well, I guess I should get going. I'll see you later Julie."

"Bye."

Mary watches Ann as she leaves to greet Mark. "He is such a hunk," the girl giggles. Julie just smiles.

****

Ann walks to the truck. The things Mark got at the feed store late yesterday are piled up in the back. "Thanks for letting me spend time with Julie," she says getting into the cab. A quick kiss. "No problem, babe. Ready?" Ann nods, even though she hates going back to the farm. At least she can be with Mark. They might even find time for a little play, like the other day when they made love in a back room of the barn. She slides over and lays her head on his strong shoulder as Mark puts the truck in gear and heads towards the freeway. She loves the feel of his hard muscles. Soon they are outside the city heading towards Faraway Hill, where the truck takes the off-ramp that leads right into town. For Ann, Manchester and Faraway Hill seem like night and day. As they speed through the little downtown, Ann looks up to see a familiar car parked outside the Halloran mansion. "That's Julie's dad's car."

****

Up the street, Benjamin King can see Ann and Mark ride through the town in his truck. They move too fast for him to wave, so he simply walks up to the house. It is a handsome old Georgian, a little out of place in New England, but very fashionable when John Adams was president. It was built to resemble the original White House but has gone through considerable changes since then. There have been renovations and additions and modernizations. Its still is a grand old manor, even though he notices that some of the paint is starting to peel.

The door opens and Frederick, the family butler greets him. Frederick is as much a part of the house as its portico. The first time Ben ever saw him was when his sister-in-law and Ann's mother worked as maids for the Hallorans. Back then Frederick was a spry middle aged man with a wry glint in his eye. His gate is slower now and his back a bit stiff, but he has never lost his sense of grace or charm.

The butler lets him into the Grand Vestibule just in time for Ben to hear "hey, Frederick, where's my blue suit?" Stepping through a pair of French doors, Ben looks up to see his daughter's fiancé. The young man is standing at the landing of the marble Grand Staircase wearing nothing but a robe. "Oh, hi Ben; what are you doing here so early?"

"Good morning. Your father asked to see me."

Greg looks surprised. "Why?"

"I'm not sure," Ben responds carefully and diplomatically, "but it sounds like something routine that he just wants to get out of the way."

"Oh," Greg is not quite convinced. "Frederick: my suit?"

"It came back from the cleaners yesterday, sir. I'll bring it up shortly."

"Thanks," Greg heads back to his bedroom. "See you later, Ben."

"Goodbye." Ben has mixed feelings about his daughter marrying Greg Halloran. On the one hand, he seems like a nice young man and the son of his most important client. There are a lot of obvious benefits by the match. He has every reason to believe that Greg will treat Julie well. She certainly seems happy with him. But Ben has always sensed something odd, something unspoken about Lewis Halloran's son.

****

Back in his two-room suite, Greg finds himself with nothing to do until his suit arrives. So, he plops on his bed to try and relax. But thoughts of Julie --- who has been so busy with wedding preparations that they haven't had any private time together --- soon brings him back to the problem at hand: his best man.

The first time Greg met Jack Campbell was the summer before senior year at NYU. Greg's dating history until then had been spotty. Having gone to a private, all-boys school, he had little contact with girls. Sex back then was limited to furtive play among horny teenage boys, the kind of thing everyone occasionally did at night, but never talked about in the day. College was a different matter. Then it was mostly about girls, starting with the sexy teacher's assistant who finally took his cherry. He became a player of sorts after that, changing girlfriends every few weeks with the occasional closeted frat boy breaking up the pattern. It was a time of freedom that Greg had never felt before or since.

During the spring semester, Greg was dating a very cute Biology major named Lauren. She was a red headed charmer with a lot of qualities Greg liked. She was smart, had a terrific sense of humor, a sexy body and gave great blow jobs. They had a lot of fun together in bed and out. He started to get the feeling that she might just be the one for him, and even told his dad about her. But the day the semester ended, he was shocked when she dumped him. She didn't want anything serious, Lauren explained, and she could tell that's where things were heading.

A few hours after the break-up, he was drowning his loss at a bar in SoHo when Jack walked in. Greg had noticed him on campus and was always impressed with his good looks and air of confidence. Greg was never much for sports, but Jack was different: he could and often did play almost any sport, was always the center of attention at a party and was known for dating the hottest girls on campus.

Jack sat on the stool right next to him without any hesitation. "Hey, dude," he greeted Greg with a charming smile and strong handshake. That was the start of a night spent talking about anything and everything: school, families, women, careers, politics and so much more. Jack knew something about any topic. Through those first hours together, there were times when he seemed to flirt with Greg, and other times he acted like they were just two guys hanging out. Greg couldn't tell then if they were destined to simply be buddies or something more. They ended the night with a friendly bear hug, an exchange of phone numbers and parted ways.

A knock on the bedroom door brings Greg back to the present. Frederick enters with his suit, wrapped in plastic by the cleaners, and leaves it in the suite's parlor. Greg dresses quickly, putting aside thoughts of Jack and Julie --- at least for now.

Downstairs, Greg arrives in the Grand Hall near his dad's study. "I can't believe this," he can hear Ben say through the closed door. "How the hell can you keep something like this a secret all these years?"

"I'm sure you can guess why." *What are they talking about?* Whatever it is, the lawyer sounds more than surprised. He seems upset --- and personally offended. "You need to tell them, Lewis."

"I will --- in time --- but I want to make sure these changes are made first."

Their voices grow quiet and Greg can no longer make out what they are saying. He politely knocks on the door. "Come in," Lewis calls out. Greg opens the door to find the two men standing there trying --- but failing --- to look at ease.

"Hey dad, want to go into the office with me today?" It seems odd to Greg to refer to his father so casually. He's sure it came out sounding forced. The two of them have spent so little time together over the years that Lewis seems less like a dad and more like a familiar stranger.

"No, son, you go ahead." He seems as uncomfortable with Greg as Greg is with him.

"Are you sure?" Every time Lewis and Ben are in the same room together, Greg can see how striking their differences are. Although they are about the same age, Lewis seems of a different generation with his graying hair and ragged face. The family's features that are so clear in the statue of old John in the town square are barely visible in Greg's father.

"No, Lewis, don't worry," Ben says with a resigned sigh. "I can take care of everything."

Ben shakes Lewis' hand and gives Greg a small smile before leaving father and son. Now it is time for more awkwardness, something that often happens when they are alone together. "Dad," Greg says, again sounding forced. "Is there a problem I should be aware of?"

Lewis looks embarrassed at being uncomfortable with his own son. "No, not a problem as such, just . . . something that needs correcting." It's obvious that he doesn't want to discuss it anymore, so Greg decides not to push matters. But Lewis surprises him by putting his hands on Greg's shoulders and says gently, "I've made many mistakes in my life. They include not being a good father ---"

"Dad, you don't need to do this."

"Listen to me, please," the old man's eyes looking sad. "You and your new wife will be moving in here soon." Greg starts to protest but Lewis stops him. "I know you've looking at places of your own, but I want us to be a father and son, even if its 20 years too late. Besides, this *is* the family home." His intensity is disturbing.

"Dad, what are you talking about?" Greg adds half joking, "It sounds like your dying or something." Lewis smiles; he can't quite read what the smile means. "No, son, I'm not dying. It's just that . . . over the past year, since your mother passed away, I've been thinking more and more about family . . ."

Greg almost expects a hug, but one doesn't happen. It would be even more out of character for Lewis, or at least what he knows about Lewis. Instead he escorts Greg to the door. Outside his father's study, Greg remains confused and concerned.

✸✸✸✸

The Gale farm is located at the northern edge of Faraway Hill. All of the buildings --- from the main house to the barn --- are typical of New England: simple, practical and unassuming. Ann's mother has tried to fix up the house over the years, but little money and Munroe's unwillingness to spend any haven't changed it much. The place still looks like the house that her grandfather built during the Depression.

Just a few steps away at the barn, Ann and Mark are unloading the supplies. When she looks up at the house she grew up in, the word "depression" *does* seem apt. Munroe has battled alcoholism since high school. It's like her father is two completely different men. When sober, he is kind, thoughtful and gentle. She remembers as a child hearing him read stories at bed time, and taking her to see movies together. He even used to sing to her. Some of her favorite childhood memories are summers at Hampton Beach, where they'd tour the Fuller Gardens, frolic along the beach or plays games together at the arcades. That is the man Ann loves. But whenever something happens, a problem that he can't handle, Munroe turns to the bottle. That man Ann hates. That man is bitter and mean and cruel. It is that Munroe that Ann and her mother have been living with the last several months. Before that, he had been the good man for nearly five years, the longest stretch anyone can remember. She even felt like they were getting close. But that changed one day and no one seems to know why. It has been hard living with that Munroe. This, more than any other single reason, is why Ann jumped at Mark Bradley's marriage proposal.

"Okay babe, I need to get out to the back field, there's a lot of work to do," Mark tells her as they finish unloading the truck. "Will I see you at my place tonight?" Ann has been spending more and more time with Mark. Maybe they're not in love, but she really likes him, enough to see living with him and taking over the farm with him. But she's been hesitant to spend an entire night with Mark. Fortunately, he seems cool with that. "No, I promised Julie and her mom that we'd get together for dinner --- they are throwing a sort of unofficial bridal shower for me." That's the tactful way of putting it. The truth is that Ann hasn't enough friends for a real shower. "We'll probably be late, so I'll just go home after."

Mark pulls her just inside for a passionate kiss. That is another benefit. The few boys Ann had sex with in high school and college were always timid, unskilled. Sex with them was okay, but with Mark it is so much more: here is a man who knows what he is doing. Ann almost has to force herself to break off the kiss. "Okay, okay," he chuckles. "I know: time for work." She smiles watching him get into his battered old truck and head off. But that smile disappears when she looks back to the house and sees Munroe. He is slowly walking toward his own truck, broad shoulders slouched over and a pained expression on his face. The alcohol seems to age him. It is odd to think that just a year ago he was smiling and joking with friends and family. Now Munroe climbs into his truck and drives away. It's anyone's guess where he is headed, but Ann suspects it's to find a bar that opens early.

Going into the house, she finds her mother at the kitchen table doing a little sewing on the wedding dress. Lorene Gale is a plump woman, a former beauty who has eaten too much cheap food during her marriage. Ann remembers when her mom was a young woman, thin and pretty. She is a farmer's daughter who has lived her whole life in New Hampshire. Lorene skipped college to work as a domestic --- ironically at the Halloran mansion --- before marrying. Ann has never heard her mother wish for a better life or voice a word of regret. But she has to wonder: what would her mother have done with her life if the opportunities were there, or if she married someone else? "So, where is Munroe off to now?" When he is sober, she calls him Dad, but when he drinks she refuses to call him anything but Munroe.

"He didn't say --- and please don't call him that."

Ann doesn't respond. All that would do is start an argument. Instead, she pours herself some coffee and sits quietly at the table. Lorene is very protective of her kitchen. A couple of years ago Munroe had agreed to some modest improvements: the old cabinets were repainted, and gingham wallpaper with matching curtains hung. It looks almost cheery now. Pity the old appliances haven't been replaced. "So dear, what are your plans today?" Lorene asks, not looking up from her task.

"Well, I am meeting with the minister and the caterer then I have to do some shopping. We still need some more decorations for the reception. That'll take up most of the day."

Lorene finishes her last stitches. She puts the dress on the hanger, stands up and proudly shows the completed work to her daughter. "What do you think?"

Ann smiles: she likes seeing her mother happy. And, to be fair, the dress *does* look good in a simple, elegant way --- even if it is from a clearance rack. "Its looks great Mom. Thanks."

"You are going to be a beautiful bride," Lorene beams.

****

As the day progresses, Greg sees little of his father. They pass each other in the hallway where they exchange friendly but meaningless greetings and nothing else. This is pretty typical of Lewis' usual distance and it surprises Greg a little after what happened this morning. It also adds to Greg's stress. He is still learning about the family's business interests and he really can use his father's help. The core remains textiles, with a factory in New Hampshire and another in Georgia. But the company has branched out into other areas, including property development. The family even transformed an old Halloran mill in Manchester into the mixed use building that Greg and Lewis work in. There are so many investments in so many fields now that two years ago Lewis changed the company name from the original, Halloran Quality Textiles, to the simpler Halloran Enterprises.

Complicating matters even more, there is serious talk of expanding the textile business overseas, where the Hallorans can follow other companies in exploiting cheap labor.

Greg still isn't sure what to make of his father's early morning meeting. *Why is he seeing his lawyer at home? If it really is a routine matter, why not meet at Lewis' office? And what could make Ben so upset?* It's disturbing to see Greg's father suddenly become so emotional. Lewis is always calm and controlled.

Another big concern is his fiancé. Julie has been so preoccupied with the two weddings --- theirs and Ann's --- they haven't spent any private time together for more than a week. He finds it hard going so long with out sex. He misses her soft touch and being inside her. A lot of women have trouble letting loose in bed, but Julie is like Lauren in this way: she likes to have fun. But thinking about sex --- even sex with Julie --- keeps bringing Greg back to Jack: missing him, wanting him and worrying about what will happen when he arrives.

His day is filled with one meeting after another. There are no breaks. He even skips lunch. The frustrations get to be too much and he isn't too pleasant to be around. At one point he snaps at his secretary so bad he apologizes. Finally Greg has a free moment toward the end of the day. He sends Julie a text message: "get 2gether 2night?" He really needs her.

A few minutes later, a message back: "can't meeting ann." *Shit!* Why can't she find time for him? He needs to get laid --- desperately. "We *are* getting married after all," he mumbles to himself. Greg considers his options for a moment, then sends the same text message --- "get 2gether 2night?" --- to someone else and waits. Only a minute later, he gets the response he wants: "sure."

****

Even on a weeknight, there are people still walking around the Mall of New Hampshire. Most malls are deserted after dark; but not the one on Willow Street. Pairs of elderly ladies, bags in hand, emerge from Sears. Expectant moms and their best friends delight at BabyGap. Giggling teenage girls are checking out the fashions at Aeropostale --- fully aware of the wary teenage boys checking *them* out.

But a few shop alone. They have no choice. Ann Gale is one of them. She is used to it, used to not having many friends, used to doing things alone. At this moment she is in the parking lot dropping off some purchases at her beaten up old Ford. She has to do nearly everything for the wedding by herself. Julie has occasionally helped, but even though she does have a professional planner, her wedding to Greg is so big and fancy that it takes up too much time.

With everything locked safely in the car, she walks over to the Long Horn Steakhouse. This is where her "bridal shower" is taking place. The party won't be much. Even her bridesmaids won't be here. It will just be Ann, Julie and Julie's mom. Eve King is very different from Ann's mother. She is well educated, thin and graceful. A vice president at a Manchester bank, Eve is one of the classiest women Ann has ever met. She greets them at the door with a polite "good evening, Mrs. King." The three of them head inside. There is some small talk, and the offering of silly little gifts. It goes well, but a little weird. All through dinner Eve looks at her daughter suspiciously. She is very obvious about it. "Mom please stop that."

"Stop what?"

"Looking at me that way."

"Fine," Eve sets down her wine and gives her daughter a serious look. "So how far along are you?"

Both younger women are stunned. *Is she saying what I think she's saying?* "Uh . . . what are you talking about?"

"You know what I mean. I know what pregnancy looks like and you are at least two months along." Julie, embarrassed, replies, "Actually it's almost three months." *Holy shit, how can she tell? She doesn't look pregnant to me.*

"Three months!" Eve pauses a moment to calm down. "You've known for three months!"

"Give me a break, Mom. I just found out a few days ago. You know how weird my cycle gets when I'm stressed. It really surprised me."

"What does Greg say about this?"

"He doesn't know yet. Don't get upset. Between his schedule and mine we haven't been alone together in forever. I don't want to tell him over the phone. We're having dinner tomorrow and that's when I'll tell him."

Ann smiles. "I think it's great. I really do. Maybe I'll get pregnant soon. I'd love our kids to grow up together."

"Same here, but I thought you wanted to wait awhile, save a little money."

"I'm not too worried. Mark always finds a way to earn some extra bucks".

****

Mark Bradley's little clapboard house is located down the highway on a distant part of the Gale farm. It's an old, rundown place that has seen better days. The house sat vacant for about 10 years, until Munroe allowed Mark to fix-up the first floor at his own expense. He basically lives out of a few rooms. Hardly anyone ever comes this far out, so it is easy for Greg to drive up and hide his car around the back. He gets out and quietly walks up to the door. No knocking is required, Greg just walks in.

"So how is life engaged to the farmer's daughter?" he says without any greeting.

Mark is sitting on his used sofa --- almost all of the furniture is second-hand --- wearing nothing but jeans, reading a *Sports Illustrated*. He barely looks up. "Is that supposed to be funny, dude?"

Greg marvels at Mark's hard body, built not in a gym but through hard work on the farm. He has wonderful biceps and a nice chest with little hair. Too bad he is also developing a beer gut. Fortunately, that's a small defect. "I thought so. But, really, why are you doing it? She's not much." Greg can barely stand Ann Gale. He puts up with her for Julie's sake. She seems too insecure one moment and pushy the next. He knew a lot of women like that in college and avoided them as much as possible.

"Isn't it obvious? I marry her and I get the farm when the old man dies," Mark tosses the magazine to the floor. "Especially," he says with a smart ass grin, "since you don't pay me enough." Greg is Mark's favorite client. Unlike all the old men who normally come through his door, the two of them are so close in age that they can act almost like buddies.

Greg smiles a little and takes out his wallet. "Aww, poor boy . . . then let me help you out . . . let's see, how about an extra hundred tonight, for the bride." Mark grabs the bills and stuffs them into his pocket. "I'm sure she'll appreciate it." He steps over to Greg, bringing his face right up to the other man's. "Ready?"

"Always."

The session doesn't last long. This is unusual for them. Typically the two men take their time and savor each other. On those nights Mark almost feels as if they were truly lovers --- or at least friends with benefits --- rather than a hustler and his john. But tonight Mark is just a receptacle.

Without even pulling out, Greg collapses onto Mark's chest, panting. "That was fun," Mark says sarcastically.

"Sorry, dude, it's all this shit I'm dealing with. Next time will be better. I promise."

Mark caresses Greg's back. "Next time I'll be married." That's true: they probably won't be able to get together again until after their respective honeymoons. "Well, I guess I'll be married too," Greg says catching his breath.

"I'll have to raise my rates."

Greg looks at him in surprise. Mark just smiles back and says "married men cost more."

They both laugh.

****

Lewis Halloran anxiously taps the top of his desk. He is sitting in mahogany lined study, waiting for the phone call, surrounded by mementoes reflecting generations of his family. Among them is a portrait of his stern father, looking down at Lewis much in the same way as he did while still alive. The old man always kept a distance from his son, something Lewis knows he is also guilty of. *But I'll fix that, I'm going to make sure it's all corrected.*

He picks up the phone on the first ring. "You got the papers?" the gruff voice on the other end asks bruskly.

"Of course, I have them here in my study."

"Shit, won't someone find them?"

"I have them hidden behind a painting."

"Good; I've got somebody coming to the wedding who'll get them for me."

"Your not coming to my son's wedding?"

"Shit, no; I'll be long gone by then. But don't worry: I'll be taking your money and your secrets with me."

EPISODE TWO

Wearing his best Prada suit, Greg Halloran is sitting in the little Faraway Hill Unitarian Church. It was originally built as an Episcopal church a century ago and it still has many of its original elements like beamed ceilings, carved woodwork and stain glass windows. Mark Bradley is standing at the altar wearing a second-hand tuxedo. *He still manages to look hot,* Greg thinks. Standing next to him is some young man Greg has never met. The man has to be in his early twenties, handsome, but has an odd look about him that Greg can't quite discern. He has to wonder how they know each other, considering how Mark earns his extra money.

There are not many people in the pews. Mark insists that he has no family and everyone knows that Ann has few friends. Julie's parents are sitting next to Greg. Ann's mother is in the first row. There are actually more wedding flowers than wedding guests.

The organist starts to play the wedding march. The matronly Pastor Elizabeth (Greg never did catch her last name) moves into position. The small group of guests turns their attention to the back of the church. Julie King first appears, looking gorgeous in a pale blue bridesmaid dress and carrying a bouquet. He can't help but smile. The news of her pregnancy thrilled Lewis. Greg feels especially good about it. He has always liked kids and is looking forward to being a dad. But more importantly: a pregnant wife will make it easier to deal with any temptation Jack might offer. At least, Greg hopes so.

Following Julie are two more young ladies in matching blue dresses. These are girls Ann and Julie have known since high school. Greg only just met them the other day. They are young and pretty and worth a second look. Had he known them in his wild college days, they would certainly be on his list, and probably in his bed. Of course, Mark's best man would have been, too.

The music picks up a little. Ann emerges on her father's arm. Her wedding dress is simple and elegant and looks surprisingly good on her. Even more surprising is that her father seems sober. Greg can't remember a time when he wasn't drunk. Julie told him that Munroe had been clean for years until, one day, for no apparent reason, he hit the bottle again. Having Munroe as a father helps explain why Ann is so screwed up.

As everyone takes their position before her, Pastor Elizabeth asks, "Who presents this bride?" Munroe is actually beaming. "Her mother and I lovingly present our daughter." He gives Ann an affectionate kiss on the cheek and then takes his seat next to Lorene.

"Dearly beloved, we are gathered here today to join this man, Mark, and this woman, Ann . . ." As the pastor goes through the usually rite, Julie discretely looks over to Greg. They exchange smiles. This has been difficult year for Greg. But Julie and the baby mean a fresh start. Greg is determined to make their life together work and he realizes at this moment that he is really happy to be marrying her. *And so what if I need to pay Mark for a little fun on the side? There are worse things in this world.*

"I now pronounce you husband and wife. You may kiss the bride." The newlyweds give each other a warm but passionless kiss (at least to Greg's eyes). "Ladies and gentlemen," Pastor Elizabeth announces, "I present to you Mark and Ann Bradley."

Shortly after the ceremony, the small wedding party gathers in the church's basement reception hall. The space is so tiny it makes the two dozen guests feel crowded. There is no band, just a DJ, and barely a dance floor. Dinner is a buffet of the kind of food you might find at a Saturday cookout rather than a formal event. The cake is a modest three-tier. It is very different from the big and elaborate wedding being planned for Greg and Julie. The reception lasts little more than an hour. Greg and Mark keep up the pretense of barely knowing each other and Greg manages to be civil to Ann, who seems to be treating the wedding as some sort of coronation. Even Julie is a little annoyed with her. Mark's best man pretty much keeps to himself. Eventually the newlyweds drive off on their honeymoon as the party breaks up. He and Julie offer to help clean up the room, but Eve and Lorene refuse, so the two of them emerge from the little church to stroll through the square.

It is early Saturday evening and there are quite a few locals and even some tourists ambling through town. Julie takes Greg's hand in hers and they walk over to a bench near the fountain. As they sit, he puts an arm around her and pulls her close. "That was a nice wedding, don't you think?" Julie asks with her head on his shoulder. "Small and intimate and just a few people." The pregnancy seems to tire her.

"Are you saying that our wedding is getting too big?"

She sighs. "Oh, I don't know. Sometimes it seems that way."

"It can't be helped, you know."

"I know."

Greg kisses Julie on her forehead. It is these moments with her, more than any other that Greg enjoys. "Actually, I'm surprised more people didn't show up. I mean, Ann is a local girl: doesn't she have *any* friends?"

"Well, to be fair, things have always been hard for her. Munroe's alcoholism has been especially tough. That's why she's never been good at trusting people enough to make many friends." That last part he can understand. Greg doesn't know exactly why, but he has always had the same problem. "Greg, I'm sorry, but I'm really tired. Would you take me home, please?"

****

It only takes an hour or so for the newlyweds to arrive. Rye is a popular tourist spot along New Hampshire's coastline; a wonderful, historic little place first settled in the 1620s. It hasn't changed all that much since, thanks in part to the Odiorne Point State Park protecting hundreds of acres of land. Best of all, it isn't far from Hampton Beach and Ann's few truly happy childhood memories.

Mark pulls his truck up to a white gambrel-roofed inn called Rock Ledge Manor. Featuring a wrap-around porch, gardens and view of the harbor, staying at the Rock Ledge has been a dream of Ann's since she was a little girl. The owners greet them warmly and lead them up to the second floor. Here the Bradleys find a cozy suite with a sitting room, private bath and, in the bedroom, a beautiful queen-size brass bed covered by a handmade quilt. From nearly every window there is a breathtaking view of the Atlantic.

"Oh, God," Ann almost shrieks, twirling like a ballerina, "this is so fucking great!" Mark pulls her to him. "You know, Mrs. Bradley," he says playfully, "I don't usually sleep with married women . . ."

"Well, Mr. Bradley," she giggles, "I expect you to make an exception in my case." She gives him a quick kiss. "Give me a minute." Ann grabs a suitcase and ducks into the bathroom. Smiling, Mark slips off his tuxedo blazer and walks over to a window to admire the sun setting into the vast Atlantic. It amazes him how much his life has changed. Last summer, he was broke and alone and cut off from everything he knew. But now it seems like the whole world is right there for him, just sitting there like the ocean.

Mark turns back to the room and continues to undress. Walking up to the dresser, he watches himself in the mirror taking off his cufflinks, shirt and pants. Mark likes what he sees: a strong, well-defined body that --- combined with his charm --- played such an important role in his turnaround. First, he found clients in Manchester much faster than he thought. It's a pity so many of them are old men; he'd prefer younger guys like Greg Halloran. But few young men can afford Mark.

And, right when he needed a good cover, Mark landed the job on the Gales' farm. Not only does it keep him invisible when he needs to be, but it gives him the freedom to manage his clients. Plus, the hard work is better than any gym for keeping him in shape.

He can hear Ann giggling behind the closed bathroom door. She's the icing on the cake. When Mark learned that the old man had a young daughter and needed a son-in-law to eventually take over, he knew that the stars were finally aligned right. It didn't take much to seduce her, and while she's not a great lay, he has always liked fucking women as much as men. Unfortunately, women seldom pay you for it.

The subject of women brings Mark's thoughts around to one of his former clients. Although she was old enough to be his mother, she was still amazingly sexy and really hot in bed. But keeping everything a secret from her husband was tough, especially as she grew more and more possessive. Soon she got so weird that she drove away his other clients and then all hell broke loose when her wealthy husband found out. Eventually Mark lost everything and had to start from scratch far away, ending up in New Hampshire.

His cell rings. It's a text message from Ed, Munroe's aging feed supplier and one of Mark's regular clients. It simply says "call me when back." He grimaces a bit. Ed is not one of his favorite people. The man is in his late sixties, balding with a wrinkled old body. When Mark is with Ed, he must close his eyes and pretend he's fucking someone else --- almost anyone else --- just to get a hard-on. But Ed has a little crush on him, and Ed pays, so Ed gets serviced. But if things go well with his next plan, renting himself to old men is something Mark will be able to give up.

"Good evening, Mr. Bradley."

Mark smiles as he sees his new wife standing outside the bathroom looking sexy in a white lace teddy. "Damn, you look hot, Mrs. Bradley." She smiles back. "You look pretty good, too, but aren't you a little overdressed?" He slides his briefs off. "That's much better." They meet halfway through the room for a deep kiss. Mark slides one strap then another off Ann's shoulders. She lets the teddy drop to the floor. He picks her up and places her naked on the bed. Mark loves foreplay and begins to really enjoy her body, spending an eternity causing her to writhe and moan. When he enters her, he savors the warmth hugging his cock. "Do it," she whispers into his ear. After he cums, they lay there with him still inside her, caressing each other and sharing little kisses.

Yes, thinks Mark, *things are definitely going my way.*

✳✳✳✳

Greg Halloran is so swamped he can barely think about the one thing he shouldn't think about: Jack. His days are consumed with the wedding planner, business meetings and trying to figure out just what is going on with his father. While the wedding details make it possible for him to spend more time with Julie, none of it is alone. The pregnancy isn't easy on her. Julie gets so nauseous that she calls her condition "perpetual stomach flu." Her mom insists that it won't last much longer, but Greg finds the situation frustrating --- especially since he has no discrete outlet, not even Mark.

The Bradleys' honeymoon only lasts a week. Mark is needed on the farm and Ann has been busy planning Julie's bridal shower. Greg isn't bothering with a bachelor party. Julie wasn't too thrilled with the idea, and he doesn't like the risks of getting drunk with Jack --- and where that could lead. Besides, he doesn't know enough guys his own age in New Hampshire. And a bachelor's party with just his father and father-in-law doesn't sound all that enticing.

Lewis remains as enigmatic as ever. After that one outburst of emotion, Greg's father has said little and seems to be avoiding him. Lewis hasn't even brought up the issue of Greg and Julie moving into the mansion. Greg didn't tell his fiancé about it, anyway: he knows that she wants them to enjoy the privacy of her condo in Manchester rather than live in the big house with the old man.

Julie has been particularly excited about seeing her Aunt Karen. Greg met her briefly while he lived in New York. She seemed like Old Money, an extension of her husband's wealth and connections and as much a part of Manhattan's elite as Lincoln Center. They met when he and Lauren attended a fundraiser for one of those new museums in Brooklyn and were both surprised at their mutual connection. The elegant and sophisticated Karen St. John told him that she started out in life as Karen Scott, little sister to Eve Scott, living a modest middle class life in Faraway Hill. She helped pay for college through a variety of jobs --- including, ironically, working as a maid at the Halloran mansion. The other maid was another young lady named Lorene Graves. Eventually, Karen married stockbroker Martin St. John, Eve married lawyer Ben King and Lorene married farmer Munroe Gale. "What a wonderfully small world," she said with a sly laugh. Greg was genuinely interested, but Lauren couldn't care less and just politely laughed with her.

Karen St. John knew more about Faraway Hill and the Halloran mansion than he did. She told him obscure stories about what is supposed to be his home town and some of the mansion's history. All the while Greg kept thinking how beautiful she is. Although well into middle age, Karen has this eternal beauty, like one of those classic movie stars, whose looks remain interesting and alluring through the years without any plastic surgeon's scalpel. He was in deep with Lauren at the time, but could see himself attracted to Karen, despite the fact that Greg has never really been attracted to older women --- or married ones.

Her husband, Martin St. John, had to be at least twenty years older than she. He was part of one of New York's leading families who made his own fortune in the stock market. He had been married twice before, had kids by one of his previous wives, and walked around the museum as if his large donation made him the owner. Greg never saw Martin or Karen St. John after that night, but he has heard a lot about her from Julie. It still surprises Greg that Julie worships her aunt, and loves talking about Karen's glamorous New York life. In every other respect Julie seems to be the contented small town girl.

Karen's husband died about the same time as Greg's mother. Julie has been trying to lure her for a visit ever since, and Karen always begged off. But the wedding of her only niece can't be ignored. She is coming in style: flying first class and taking a limo for the short trip from Manchester-Boston Regional Airport. Dinner will be a formal affair at the Halloran mansion. When Greg arrives home, he finds his fiancé already there conferring with Frederick. "Mom called," she says giddily. "Aunt Karen just checked into her hotel, so everything is running right on schedule." She shows him how the Grand Vestibule, the oval Blue Room and Formal Dining Room have been decorated with the same white roses and matching linen. She has candles everywhere, including the Grand Hall, and they really bring out the beauty in the house's antique Victorian furniture. There are even printed menus at each place setting. "Aunt Karen *loves* white roses," Julie says beaming like he has never seen before.

"It looks terrific." He kisses her cheek. "So, where's Dad? Is he home yet?"

"He came home, said hi, and then locked himself in his study." That bothers him. Lewis has been doing that more and more in recent days. "Greg, is there something wrong with him?" She seems as concerned as he.

"I don't know." He has trouble understanding if Lewis' mysterious behavior is normal or not, but he doesn't like it. "I wish I did." Frederick excuses himself to go into the kitchen and talk to the cook. There is one thing that will take his mind off his dad. "You know," Greg takes her into his arms, "I have to take a shower before she gets here . . . want to join me?"

Julie smiles. "I wish, but I still have things to do," she looks into his eyes as if nothing else in the world exists. "I really love you."

"I really love you, too." *I do love you*, Greg suddenly realizes, *in my own way*. Their kiss is soft and sweet and sexy. It would have gone on longer had Frederick not returned. "Well, I'd better take that shower." He reluctantly lets her go and starts to exit the dining room when Julie calls out to him. "By the way, your friend called." *Friend? I have no friends in Faraway Hill.* "What friend?"

"Jack."

Greg stops. *Jack called the house? That's a shock.* He didn't even think Jack had the number. They have mostly been texting. Trying to act casual, he walks back to her. "When did he call?"

"Not too long ago," she picks up a slip of paper from a beautifully carved table and hands it to him. "He sounds really nice."

"You spoke to him?"

"Of course; what's wrong with that?"

Again, Greg tries to act casual. "Only that Frederick normally answers the phone."

"Of course he did," Julie looks confused. "But I wanted to say hi. I mean, he will be the best man at my wedding after all." She hands him the note, which just innocently says "looking forward to seeing you" and includes his flight information. Obviously Jack wants to be picked up. Greg doesn't like that idea. It will be very hard sitting next to Jack even for the short trip from the airport. "That *is* okay, isn't it?"

Greg gives her a reassuring smile, "of course." He gives her another little kiss starts to leave when an idea comes to him: "would you like to meet him?"

"Who?"

"Jack."

"Of course I do."

"Then come with me when I pick him up." *This will be perfect. If Julie comes along then I won't have to be alone with Jack in the car.* All temptation will be kept at bay, at least during that initial ride.

"Greg, I'd love to, but, there is so much to do . . ."

"Please. He's my best friend and you're the love of my life." That is a bit of an overstatement. Greg *does* love Julie and looks forward to being married to her, but if anyone is the love of his life that is probably Jack. There is no reason she has to know that. "I want you two to get to know each other. There won't be any time for that otherwise."

"Well . . ." she obviously feels conflicted. After all, every girl dreams about her wedding and Julie has been working hard to make theirs perfect. But she can see that this is important to him. "Okay, if you really want me to come."

"I really do." After one more kiss, Greg winks at her and leaves her smiling and feeling wanted.

Up in his suite, Greg sets the note on his dresser. He is again starting to regret asking Jack to the wedding. *How the fuck am I going to do this?* The trip from the airport is one hurdle he has now managed. But the underling feelings remain. He strips off his clothes and starts the shower. Once under the hot water, he tries to wash away all the worries. It doesn't work. As much as he loves Julie, he keeps thinking about Jack: about their dinners together, the long walks, the discussions about everything under the sun. Greg misses the lack of pretense he had with Jack, the feeling of freedom. He especially misses feeling Jack inside him. Greg has never let anyone else do that, only Jack. But thinking about Jack brings him back to the same thing: it was *Jack* who ended everything, not Greg. Unfortunately that doesn't help very much. And Greg worries about what will happen if they are ever alone together. That could ruin everything, so he will just have to keep coming up with plausible reasons for someone to always be around.

❋❋❋❋

Ben King is in trouble. He is running late again, something that always upsets his wife, but it can't be helped: the last couple of weeks have been too demanding on his time. Lewis Halloran has been revisiting his will over and over, making repeated changes. That combined with his regular work load and the two weddings have eaten up the hours. Fortunately Lewis signed a new, hopefully final, version of the will today. But a crucial change he made still bothers Ben.

He pulls up to their home, a handsome Colonial Revival in Faraway Hill that they bought as newlyweds. It had been vacant for years and needed a lot of work, but Eve fell in love with the place at first sight. For nearly 25 years this is where they raised their daughter and built their life, often amid the sawdust and chaos of frequent renovations. But it was all worth it. The house today fits the successful lawyer he has become, with its carved details, front portico and side porch. Friends have remarked that it could be something out of an old movie.

No one is downstairs when he comes in, so he heads up to the master bedroom.

"Where have you been?" Eve is sitting at her make-up table, still in her slip, but nearly ready. "You're running late." She's obviously not happy.

Ben places his briefcase on the floor next to the dresser. She hates it when he brings it into their bedroom. It should be in the den. "I know. I'm sorry." He slides off his jacket and removes his tie. "I won't be long, just let me jump in the shower."

"You know Karen needs to have her audience in place for the grand entrance." Eve and her sister have always had a complicated relationship. There are times when Ben isn't sure if Eve is jealous of her or embarrassed by her. Maybe a little bit of both. Certainly the secret the three of them share always makes her nervous. It worries Ben too. This is why they've always discouraged Karen from visiting. But now they can only hope that Karen keeps to their deal.

He steps up behind her and wraps his arms around her. "Ben, please . . ." she complains halfheartedly. Ben smiles at her reflection in the mirror. "You know, we haven't had much time alone together lately." After all these years he can still see the young woman in her face. She has changed so little. "I'm sorry about that, honey; I know most of it is my fault."

She gives him a reassuring smile. "It *is* a crazy time, what with the weddings and all," Eve locks her eyes with his. "What's wrong?"

"Nothing."

"Bull shit. Something's been going on." He lets her go and takes off his shirt. "Ben, don't walk away from me. I can tell your upset about something. It's been distracting you for weeks. What is it?"

"I can't tell you, it's about a client." He tosses his pants onto an overstuffed chair.

"Don't hand me that --- and don't throw your clothes on the furniture --- I've seen you upset about a client before. But this is different. Something really bad has happened, hasn't it? Is there a problem at the firm, some problem with that new partner?"

Ben picks up his pants and folds them neatly before setting them back on the chair. "He hasn't made partner yet --- although he seems to think he has. But, no, no . . . it's nothing like that . . ." *How can I explain this?* He still has trouble with what Lewis told him.

"Does it have anything to do with Julie?"

Instead of answering her, Ben simply walks into the bathroom and closes the door behind him, leaving his wife to sit there, angry and worried. Eve's determined to find out the truth, but Ben is right: they are running late. She steps over to the closet and pulls out a black cocktail dress, something new Eve bought just for tonight. As she slides it on she can hear the shower starting to run --- and spies Ben's briefcase on the floor. She quietly picks it up and sets it on the dresser. It's locked, but Eve easily guesses the combination as Julie's birthday. And then she pauses. *Should I?* There are big things going on at Eve's office that she doesn't want Ben to find out, at least not yet. *Shouldn't I give him the same respect?* But the possibility that what he's been hiding could hurt their daughter makes the difference. Eve opens the case. Inside she finds some surprising documents, all related to Lewis Halloran's will. Paperclipped to the outside of one file folder is a note Ben seems to have written to himself. It is so shocking that Eve needs to read it twice.

"What the hell are you doing?"

Eve turns to find Ben, in his robe, toweling off his hair and furious. "Dammit, Eve, you know better than to go through my files!"

"Don't you pull that shit with me," She waves the note at him. "Is this true?"

He tries to reach out and grab it from her, but she pulls back. "This is what's been bothering you, isn't it?" Ben gives up. "Yes," he says with a sigh. Apparently it's true."

"How long have you known?"

"Not quite two weeks."

"Holy shit; and Lewis has been keeping this a secret all these years?"

"Yes, but he plans to tell everyone the truth after the wedding. So, please, Eve, don't say anything to Greg and Julie."

She angrily dumps the papers back into the briefcase and slams it closed with a bang. "But they should have been told long ago . . ." Ben pulls his wife into his arms. "Damn him, Ben. You know that Julie will get put right in the middle." He starts to rock her gently. "I know, sweetie, I know." And that is what has been bothering him so much.

****

Less than an hour later, the Kings are having cocktails with their daughter and her fiancé in the Hallorans' elegant Blue Room. The addition of white roses and flickering candles seem, at least to Eve, to lend the room a regal aura that her sister will appreciate. The wedding's schedule has been, in part, built around Karen: even the combined bridal/baby shower will be held tomorrow night, just days before the big event, so that she can attend both. On the table is a tray with lead crystal glasses along with a bottle of Champaign and a crystal decanter of sparkling water for Julie. The conversation is light and friendly. Greg seems genuinely trilled at the prospect of being a father. The only thing marring the night so far is the absence of <u>Greg's</u> own father --- who has been in his study since before she and Ben arrived.

"I can't understand what is taking him so long," the young man says, "but he's been really busy with different projects." It's obvious to Eve that Greg is trying to cover his own confusion about Lewis. She and Ben exchange a quick, knowing glance. "He <u>does</u> work too hard," Ben casually replies. "Let me go check on him." Eve watches her husband go out into Grand Hall toward Lewis' study. She remains very concerned about him. What Lewis has kept secret all these years is bad enough, but to put Ben in the middle of it us just too much for her. Eve needs to focus more on keeping an eye on her sister. "Mom . . . Mom!"

"Yes, Julie?"

"It's like you're a million miles away. What's wrong?"

Is she <u>that</u> distracted? Eve needs to be more cautious, especially around Lewis and Karen. "Nothing, Julie. Everything's fine." Thankfully the door bell rings before Julie can ask her more. All three of them peer anxiously toward the Grand Hall and watch Frederick disappear through the French doors into the vestibule. The moment seems so dramatic and filled with so much anticipation that there may as well be a drum roll. But Frederick simply greets the guest just as he always does. The woman who emerges into Grand Hall is an elegant, sophisticated lady on the early side of middle age. It has been years since they were last together and it suddenly occurs to Eve that her sister has grown to look a lot like Lana Turner --- which probably shouldn't surprise her considering how much Karen always idolized the actress. She collected everything about her, watched all of her movies and talked about her often growing up. Everything from the designer shoes on Karen's feet to the diamond brooch hanging from her neck looks like something MGM's wardrobe department put together. Eve's little sister has become everything she ever wanted. A little girl's dream has come true.

"Hello everyone," Karen says with a soft, feminine voice as she enters the Blue Room with a studied flourish. "I'm so sorry to be late." She gives her excited niece a warm, tight hug. Eve has always been uncomfortable with Julie's worshipful attitude toward Karen. She has only known the glamorous occasional visitor, not the tempestuous kid sister Eve grew up with. She grants Greg a quick peck on the cheek. "I am so happy for both of you." Only when her admirers are satisfied does Karen turn to her sister.

"Hello Karen." Eve's sister doesn't hug her or kiss, but takes a hand with hers and says "my dear sister, how wonderful it is to see you again after all these years." The words sound to Eve like movie dialog. *Did Lana ever say it*, she wonders. "It has been a long time."

Karen picks up a glass for Frederick to fill with Champaign. "So, where is everyone?"

"Ben and Dad are in the study," Greg explains as he pours Julie some more sparkling water. Karen takes a seat on an overstuffed chair. "I just realized Greg, that I don't think I've seen your father in over twenty years. He was always so handsome, wasn't he Eve? I can't wait to see him again. Has he changed much?" Eve's internal antenna goes up. *Is there some special meaning to that?* "We've all changed, Karen. I remember when you had pimples, a cheap haircut and cleaned bathrooms in this house." But Karen deflects the comment with a gentle laugh. "I'm sure my stepchildren wish that were still the case."

"Are they still giving you problems, Aunt Karen?"

"Oh, it's alright Julie. I shouldn't expect anything else from them. It's hard enough to be the second wife, but when you add being the widow --- well, never mind all that. So, just what are the plans?"

"Tomorrow is the bridal shower, the rehearsal dinner is Friday and the wedding is Saturday."

"My, what a busy week; and your mother tells me that you are pregnant."

Julie blushes. "Yes, we are," Greg says proudly. "We're really excited."

"We all are."

The four of them look up to see Ben escort Lewis into the room. Greg's father looks strangely ill at ease with their newest guest. "Well, Karen Scott, you have grown into a remarkably beautiful woman." Uncomfortable or not, Lewis can still turn on the charm.

"Thank you Mr. Halloran. I was just telling your son what I handsome man you were --- and I can see that has not changed."

"You are too kind."

"By the way, the name is St. John now. But you are welcome to call me Karen."

"Of course, and please call me Lewis."

Frederick announces dinner and the party moves into the Formal Dining Room where Karen St. John takes center stage. Over perfectly prepared lobster, she regales the group with tales of Manhattan socialites, Parisian designers and Hollywood scandals. The star is in her element, Eve thinks, hearing her baby sister drop names as easily as rain drops from the sky. She manages to survive the evening by repeating one simple message to herself: *just a few more days, just a few more days . . .*

****

Ann cannot find her father anywhere. It is early the next morning and he should be getting ready to work the farm with Mark. But Mark says that he hasn't seen him. It would be just like Munroe to go off and get drunk somewhere. Stopping by the main house, she finds her mother cleaning up after breakfast, looking very worried. "Good morning dear."

"Morning Mom; what's wrong?"

Lorene says nothing. She just keeps washing dishes. "Mom, where is Munroe?"

"I'm sure your father is out working with Mark."

"No, he's not. I was just out there. Please don't tell me that he's at that damned bar again."

"We both know nothing is open this early. And don't think the worst. Give him some credit. He was sober during your wedding, wasn't he?" True enough. She even saw brief glimpses of the man who raised her that day. But everything changed after she and Mark came home. "I know Mom, and your right. But it didn't last. It never does. And with Julie's wedding coming up, I don't have the time to keep track of him. Shit, her aunt is in town and I am trying to get everything in place for the shower tonight. Mark can't do all the farm work himself. Where is he?"

Lorene says nothing more, leaving Ann too frustrated to go on. She leaves the house slamming the door behind her and goes stomping off passed the barn, missing the discreet little door to the discreet little room in the rear. Inside sits Munroe, all alone at a beaten up old desk, his only friend a half bottle of Jack Daniels. This is the one and only place in the world where he can be truly alone. On the walls surrounding him are memories both good and bad: old school pictures, his parents' wedding portrait, 4H ribbons he won as a teen, newspaper clippings of obituaries of friends and family lost. But the one thing that keeps closest to him is the one thing that hurts the most: a photo of his daughter. It is her high school graduation picture. She looks adorable and almost grown up, in her cap and gown. He keeps it on the desk. Ann may think he hates her, but he doesn't. In fact, his love for her is so deep and complex that it pains him. This is why Munroe avoids her. This is why Munroe drinks. This is why Munroe needs to escape.

****

All day long Eve and Julie entertain Karen, taking her shopping along Elm Street, showing off the many changes that Manchester has had over the years.

Karen calls their little store "charming," a back handed compliment which annoys Eve but Julie completely misses. They meet Greg for lunch at a café near City Hall Plaza where again Karen takes her place as the star. Eve continues to remind herself: *just a few more days, just a few more days . . .* Karen just has to keep their secret and Eve just has to keep her calm. By mid afternoon she is able to excuse herself and return home to help Ann prepare the house for tonight's shower. Let Karen have her audience.

By nightfall, Eve has everything set and Ann goes home to rendezvous with the bride and brings her back to the party --- and another evening with Karen and Eve reminding herself: *just a few more days . . .*

✷✷✷✷

From a discrete distance, Greg keeps a close eye on Mark's house. Julie drove in a few minutes ago. Even though it is dark, he is close enough to see into the windows as she talks to Ann and Mark. Soon the women emerge laughing and get into Julie's car. The two of them speed off. Once they seem far enough away, Greg pulls his car around back to the usual spot.

Entering without knocking, he can hear Mark in the shower and smiles. Greg looks around and can see some womanly changes since his last visit: a few pieces of furniture have been replaced with nicer, but cheap ones from discount stores like Wal-Mart and Target. There are more pictures on the walls and various ferns and flowers are scattered around. It is no longer a guy's place and is evolving into a couple's home. He walks into the bedroom, and begins to strip. There are more ferns in here, on top of tables and the dresser. Laying casually on a chair --- another new addition --- Greg can see Ann's bra and extra jeans, and finds that the idea of fucking Mark in the same bed that he fucks his wife is a serious turn on. He throws his clothes on top of hers and waits in just his white briefs.

"I was wondering how fast you'd show up." Greg smiles at the sight of Mark, nude and rubbing his hard flesh with a towel. *His body is incredible.*

"I didn't want to waste any time. They won't be gone forever."

Mark steps up to him and brushes a hand across Greg's bare chest. "When the wives are away, the husbands will play, huh?"

"Something like that. The usual amount?"

"Sure."

Mark smiles at Greg's tight rear as he bends over to retrieve cash from his wallet. Mark takes the money and sets it on top of the dresser next to one of the many ferns in the room. He turns back to take the other man in his arms. "What's with all the damned greenery?" Greg asks as he enjoys feeling Mark's hands slide his briefs to the floor.

"The wife thinks the place is ugly, so she bought all kinds of shit like plants." Mark leans in to give Greg a slow, sexy kiss. "We've got at least a couple of hours this time, dude, so why not take things slow and get your money's worth?" Greg likes that idea, and kisses him again, pressing their chests together. They fall to the bed and make out for what seems like an eternity, with Greg caressing Mark's broad chest and biceps. Mark begins licking his client all over, from lips to nipples to stomach. He takes Greg into his mouth to get him all slick, hard and ready. Then Mark straddles his client, sitting down on him, taking him deep inside. Greg moans, "Damn your ass is great. I love being inside you."

"Better than your wife's pussy?"

Greg doesn't answer. He just enjoys the feeling. Mark begins to slide himself up and down, slowly at first, then a little faster and then even more until he can feel Greg squirt inside him. Mark starts to pull him out when Greg stops him. "Don't you want to cum? I can suck you or jerk you off."

"Can't dude, got to save it for the misses. She expects me when she comes back from partying with your wife." Mark rolls himself Greg to lie next to him. "So, can I count on you after the wedding? You're my favorite client, you know."

"Sure," Greg smiles. "Julie hasn't had much interest in sex since the pregnancy."

"And every guy's gotta get off. Congrats, by the way. I didn't get a chance to tell you earlier."

"Thanks." One of the things Greg likes about sex with guys is the lack of pretense. They can be just friends who fuck. Women generally confuse sex with something more. "So, what's it like married to the farm girl?"

Mark shrugs. "It's okay. She can be a real pain sometimes. I think she's convinced that she can do better."

"What, better than you?"

"Better than me, better than her old man, better than this whole fucking town."

"I don't envy you, dude. I haven't spent much time with her but she really gets on my nerves. I have to put up with her for Julie's sake, but I can't really stand her otherwise." Greg looks at the clock on the nightstand. "Well, I should get going." He gets out of bed and starts to dress.

"Why so soon?"

"Sorry, but Ben and my old man want to have drinks while the girls have their little party."

"Too bad." Mark watches Greg get dressed. His hair is a little mussed, but otherwise he looks pretty damn good. "Be sure to call me after the honeymoon."

Greg smiles back and says with a wink, "count on it," and leaves the house. As soon as Mark can hear the car drive off, he rises nude from the bed and walks over to one of the many ferns decorating the room. Nestled underneath a leaf is a little web cam. He unplugs it and steps into the front room where the laptop sits humming discretely. With a point and a click a little video starts to play. It begins with Mark entering the shower. Less than a minute later, Greg comes in and starts to undress. Everything is here, clear and visible: every word, every look and every kiss. Greg's face is unmistakable from start to finish and when he says "damn your ass is great. I love being inside you," Mark can't help but laugh.

Everything is in place now. Mark has his insurance policy.

EPISODE THREE

Julie starts the morning like she has many other recent mornings: in the bathroom, nauseous. She has trouble believing that her "perpetual stomach flu" (which she calls it) is normal during a pregnancy, but both her doctor and her mother insist that it will go away in time. All of the tests show that she and the baby are healthy.

Actually, the last few days have been better and taking things slow each morning seems to help. Soon she is able to shower and dress. Julie is glad that Greg asked her to go with him to pick up Jack. He hasn't many friends in the area and he could certainly benefit from having his closest college buddy around. But something nags at her a little: it sometimes seems like he doesn't want to be alone with Jack. *That's crazy,* Julie says to herself, *he's probably just nervous after not seeing him for a year.* Ready for the day, she steps into the living room to start another morning ritual: trying to remember where she put her keys.

For the past several months, she has been staying in a simple two bedroom condo. Her father bought the place years ago as an investment. It took some cajoling from her mother to convince him to let her move in, but once Julie agreed to pay the monthly condo fee as rent, he relented. He said money was the issue, but that was a poor disguise for the real reason: he didn't like his little girl growing up. The place is nice and the only thing she really dislikes is the closet-like space that passes for a kitchen. But there is a pool, the neighbors are friendly and it has easy access to the highways that can get her just about anywhere. Even the address is an easy one: "I'm on English Village Road" is pretty much all she needs to tell people.

Right now, the normally tidy living room is filled with remnants of last's night's combined bridal and baby shower. There are piles of boxes and ribbons and papers on the sofa, tables and even the floor. It was Ann's idea to merge the two and the result was an odd but fun night. The gifts were certainly a strange mixture, ranging from teddy bears to black lace teddies. Julie was surrounded by friends and laughter. Even her mother and Aunt Karen seemed to have a good time. She feels bad that Greg was all alone last night.

Julie suspects that Lewis Halloran wants the newlyweds to move into the big house, but she has made it clear to Greg that she wants them to be on their own for awhile first. Julie understands that the mansion is a family homestead and that they will have to move in at some point, but there is no rush. Let them be a little family before becoming a big one.

The keys are sitting on the counter next to the refrigerator. *Why are they always in the last place I look?* Julie grabs them and her purse and heads out. It is only a short drive to the Halloran mansion, where Greg is waiting outside under the portico. "You seem nervous," she says after he gets into the car. "Well, it *has* been a year," he answers just before they kiss. There is something unconvincing in his answer. It makes her wonder if he and Jack had some sort of falling out. It could be over a girl. She figured out long ago that Greg was a real player in college. That would make sense. But if Jack agreed to be his best man, then he must have forgiven Greg for whatever --- or whomever --- it was. Later tonight they should have plenty of time to be alone together to sort things out. And, if she can, Julie will try to give them some one-on-one time even sooner. That should help.

The airport is only about an hour from Manchester, and Greg remains quiet for the entire ride. Even after they park and head into the waiting area, he doesn't say much, just a few casual things about the weather and the traffic. He keeps checking the monitors which continually report that Jack's plane is on schedule. Julie isn't quite sure what to say or do, so she simply sits down on one of those hard, fixed plastic chairs. She misses the days before 9/11, when you could wait right at the terminal and wave at your loved ones as they came off the plane. One of her more exciting memories is traveling as a child to New York to visit her Aunt Karen. Flying was such an adventure then. It is nothing more than a chore these days.

She looks over at Greg. He is normally so steady and confident. He has been incredible handling the pressures of his new job, the wedding and her pregnancy. He takes a deep breath when the screen changes to "arrived" and turns to back to her. "I guess that means he'll be here in a little while."

Julie gives him a reassuring smile. "I'm sure."

"How are you holding up?" Most guys would be shocked and scared at an unplanned pregnancy. But not Greg.

"I'm actually doing a lot better today. The doctor keeps telling me to be patient, and I guess he's right." He seems relieved and goes back to staring at the monitors. In some ways, their relationship seems odd to her. There is a warmth and comfort in Greg's presence. Julie looks forward to seeing him everyday. And she gets the impression that he feels the same way. But there is none of the giddiness that she has seen in her other friends when they fall in love and marry. Maybe that's a sign of maturity. It is certainly not for a lack of passion: Greg is without question the best lover Julie has ever had. He is more skilled, experienced and confident in bed than any of the boys she knew growing up. It's too bad that her "perpetual stomach flu" has been getting in the way lately. She knows he's frustrated by it, but hopefully things will be better by the honeymoon.

Julie rises and walks over to Greg. Wrapping her arms around him, she whispers into his ear, "I love you." His smile reflects a depth of feeling that she has never seen in anyone else. Maybe their relationship really *is* that mature. "I love you, too," he whispers back, "more than you can know." This is one of those moments that make Julie realize that she has found the right man for her.

"Hey, dude."

The two of them turn around. Standing before them is the most strikingly handsome man Julie has ever seen. No, make that the most *beautiful* man she has ever seen. He is tall --- just under six feet Julie estimates --- with an athletic physique that looks very cool under a black leather jacket. Greg reaches out for a handshake, but Jack pulls him in to an awkward bear hug. "I really missed you Greg."

"Yeah . . . me too." *Why is he so uncomfortable?* Jack gracefully releases Greg so that he can do the introductions. "Julie, this is Jack Campbell. Jack, this is Julie King, my fiancé." Without any hesitation Jack embraces her.

"Congratulations."

The hug is more intense and intimate than expected. She can feel his muscles and hear his heartbeat. "Thank you." Julie gently pulls away from him. What follows should be an awkward moment, but isn't: Jack is also the most confident man she has ever seen. "How about we go get my bags?" Without saying another word the three of them take the escalator down to the baggage claim. Here floor-to-ceiling windows allow the sunshine to brighten the end point for any weary traveler. It doesn't take long for Jack's luggage to come tumbling down the chute.

Julie and Greg are in the front seat, Jack in the back. They say little during the short drive, just a few comments about sites along the way. They soon enter Manchester where Greg announces sarcastically "welcome to the big city" causing Julie to frown and Jack to chuckle. Julie knows that the place seems quaint to outsiders, but she is proud of it. The largest city in the state with some 100,000 people, Manchester has an active downtown and some good cultural institutions. Jack seems genuinely interested as they tell him about the Currier Museum of Art's collection of Picassos, Harpers and O'Keefes. Julie knows more about Manchester than Greg, so she describes places like the Massabesic Audubon Center, the SEE Science Center and the Palace Theatre as well as the city's short train ride to everything in Boston. "Pity the place insists on closing every night at five," Greg nervously adds, as if he is trying to sound cynical and cool. Jack just politely smiles.

They drive through the city's Millyard District, where former factories have been converted into apartments, offices and shops. "That building on the left used to be one of our factories," Greg points out. Like the other buildings, it is now a mixed use space but is still called the Halloran Building.

"Wow, that's pretty cool. Do you still own it?"

"Yeah; after Dad moved the factory down south he promised to reinvest locally. It's become a pretty good money maker for us. We even have our offices there now."

"Cool."

They cross the river into downtown. Turning left off Elm Street, Julie pulls the car into a small parking garage. They step out onto the warm summer air. "Actually, it's kind of nice here," Jack says looking around. "I could see spending weekends up this way." Three of them start walking to a restaurant just a few doors down when Julie's cell rings. It's a text message from Mary at the store. "I'm sorry guys, but I have to walk over to the café for a few minutes. The lunch rush is about to start and there is some little problem." This gives Julie a handy and unplanned excuse to leave the two of them alone for a few minutes. But Greg seems to panic. "Hey, that's okay; we'll go with you . . ."

"No, no, no," she kisses him on the cheek. "I'll just be a few minutes." With Julie gone, Greg isn't sure what to say or do. Being alone with Jack is something he really wanted to avoid, and now its here. Without saying a word Jack just follows him down the walk, smiling. Greg mind reaches for a subject and manages to land on one: "It's a shame you couldn't get a room at one of the B&B's in Faraway Hill." For the first time, Jack looks confused. "But they fill up fast during the summer. Tourists, you know. Plus a lot of the family has booked rooms for the wedding."

"Faraway Hill; that really is a weird name for a town, dude."

"I suppose so. It really is on a hill. The story goes that during colonial times it was the farthest hill from Manchester." Oddly enough, he never knew this is until Karen St. John told him at that party in New York. Greg Halloran is still very much a stranger in his own hometown. "That's how it got its name."

"I guess it makes sense, then."

They have arrived at Maxwell's, one Greg's favorite places in town. Rich mahogany lines its walls, which are decorated with photos of historic Manchester --- including a huge one near the entrance of the grand, old Amoskeag Bank building.

"Hey there handsome; nice to see you again so soon," smiles Debbie. Another thing Greg likes about Maxwell's is the costume Max makes his waitresses wear: a strange but appealing cross between the garb of a museum's re-enactor and that of a Hooter's girl. For Debbie that means pushing her breasts up to make them look bigger than they really are --- and Greg knows their true size from personal experience.

"Hey Deb, this is Jack. He's in town for the wedding."

"Wow, another good looker."

Jack just smiles back.

"Deb, Julie will be joining us. Can we get a booth?"

"Sure, follow me." She leads them past a row of booths. Each has high mahogany seats and walls that effectively create little alcoves. They arrive at the last one. Each man sits across from the other and Debbie hands them their menus, leaving a third for Julie. "The special today is traditional meatloaf. Anything to drink? How about you Greg: the usual rum and coke?"

"Sure."

"I'll have the same."

Debbie winks at Jack and leaves. "She's cute," Jack comments. "Know her well?"

"We sort of dated for awhile. Last year. Before Julie."

"Sort of dated?"

"Well . . ." the conversation reminds Greg a little of the ones they used to have and the comfortable way they could talk about almost any subject, including ormer lovers. "Let's say we stayed in more often then we went out."

Jack chuckles. "Still a dog, eh?"

"Hey, man, I'm getting married. No more of that for me."

"Sure."

Greg looks up from his menu to see Jack staring right at him, almost into him. It unnerves him. "What about you, dude?"

"Oh. I've been a real dog." Jack leans in with a wicked grin to whisper, "at one point, I was fucking the receptionist while I was also secretly fucking this cute college boy in the mail room."

Greg shakes his head smiling. It shouldn't surprise him. "Sucks to be you, huh?"

"Hey being single in New York is pretty cool."

Good; this gives him a segue toward a safer subject. Talking about sex with Jack makes Greg think too much about *having* sex with Jack. "Speaking of New York, Julie's aunt flew in the other day. Her husband died last year. Is the name St. John familiar?"

"St. John --- as in Martin St. John? Yeah, actually it is. He was one of my dad's colleagues. His office was even in our building, a few floors up. Big player on the Street; made a ton of money. Don't know him otherwise," which leaves Greg without anyway of continuing that particular subject.

They both fall silent, reading their menus, feeling awkward again. The quiet seems eternal until Jack says, "I've really missed you."

"I've missed you too. There's no one else I'd want for my best man."

"That's not what I mean."

Greg looks up to see Jack stare into him again. This is not the conversation he wants. "You're the one who ended things."

"Because I was a coward, afraid of my old man," Jack shakes his head. "That was the biggest fucking mistake of my life."

Before Greg can say anything more, Julie suddenly appears. "Sorry about that, it's the life of a small business owner." She slides into the booth next to her fiancé and opens up her menu. "Anyway, I hope you like it here, the food is pretty good. Greg loves it." She is too preoccupied to notice the tension between the two men. "If he loves it, I'll love it," Jack answer, sending a message that only Greg can understand.

They can hear loud voices coming from the front of the restaurant: the lunch rush is starting and whole groups of people are coming in. It forces them to raise their own voices.

"Of course, the food is even better at the house --- and Frederick has fixed up one of the nicer bedroom suites for you." This news takes Greg by surprise. "What are you talking about, Julie?" He thinks he knows, and it scares him. *She didn't invite him to stay at the house, did she?*

"Didn't I tell you? It seems silly for Jack to stay in a hotel so Frederick and I arranged for him to say the Halloran place. We gave him the suite next to yours."

Greg panics. "You did *what*?" His reaction shocks Julie, who is now worried and asks, "That is okay, isn't it?

"Don't worry dude," Jack says, with a slightly wicked smile and his voice rising above the growing crowd. "It'll be just like the old days."

What does that mean? Greg hadn't planned on any of this and now he's trapped. Julie looks almost scared and clearly needs reassuring, so he kisses her on the cheek. "Sure, it's fine. I was just having trouble hearing you over the noise." What else can he say? She seems relieved, but Jack's cocky grin concerns him. Her cell rings again. "Damn, it's the store. That girl needs to learn to handle things herself. I am going to try to find a quiet corner. Excuse me, guys." Julie slides out and walks a few steps away to take the call.

Angry, Greg leans in to Jack. "What the hell is going on?"

"What do you think?" Jack laughs. *He's really enjoying this.*

"I knew asking you to be my best man was a fucking mistake."

"No, way, it's perfect."

"Like shit! I am getting married."

"So?"

"She's pregnant!"

"I know that. You told me. Congratulations." He gives Greg another penetrating look. "Do you love her?"

The question surprises him. "Well, I mean . . . what kind of a question is that? Yes, I love her."

"But not like you love me."

"Dammit Jack, you can't just do this to me. Not after what happened."

"Hey, don't worry. I am not here to fuck anything up. I'll keep pretending that we're just best buds. I'll stand there smiling as the two of you exchange vows. No one has to know the truth about us. I'm the one who fucked us up, so I am the one who's going to pay the price." Jack discreetly reaches out and touches Greg's hand. "But listen to me like you've never listened to anyone before. This past year has been hell for me. I've tried everything I could to get over you: working long hours, fucking anything that walks, booze, you name it. None of it worked. I love you Greg and I need you in my life. I'll do whatever it takes. And if that means standing by while you play husband and father, then I'll do it." His intensity, his passion is unmistakable. "I'll do it for however long it takes, but I need you." Greg is left speechless as Jack pulls his hand back.

Julie returns, annoyed, but smiling. "Well, I think that's the last fire I need to put out. So, guys, what are we doing for lunch?" The rest of the meal goes off smoothly. The conversation sticks with benign matters like the wedding plans and everyone's jobs. The packed restaurant sometimes makes it hard for them to hear each other. Jack acts as if he and Greg are just good friends from college. Julie seems to like him. Greg plays along, but worries continue to float in the back of his mind.

✳✳✳✳

Ann is becoming more and more disgusted with her father. She and Mark have been working hard on the farm since they got back, but the old man disappears for hours on end. When he does show up, he is morose and drunk. Munroe hasn't been this bad in a long time, and it makes her wonder what is happening. She starts grilling her mother, but Lorene won't talk. "Is it money, has he fucked up the farm?" she demanded this morning. Her mother insists that they are not having any money problems, but Ann is still suspicious. Adding to the confusion is Lorene. Every time Ann visits the house, her mother is in the middle of some secret telephone conversation. She never tells Ann who is on the other end and always whispers into the receiver "I have to go now" before hanging up.

She has noticed something else odd: Mark seems to be getting a lot text messages. He insists they are for "odd jobs" on other farms. He'll disappear for a couple of hours and come back without a speck of dirt anywhere on him. *Who ever heard of farm work that doesn't leave you sweaty and dirty?* Ann has tried to peek at his cell phone, but Mark deletes his messages as they come in. And he always comes back with a wad of cash. When she tries to ask him more about his extra work, Mark becomes evasive. The whole situation seems very suspicious to her.

Frustrated, she decides to take a drive, alone, into Manchester. Hopefully a good talk with Julie will help. It usually does. But when she arrives at the store, all she finds is a couple of harried kids trying to please a crowd of customers. The girl, Mary, reminds her that Julie is spending the day with Greg and his college friend. That means Ann is on her own.

She is about to leave when Julie's mother, Eve, enters with her sister. Karen St. John is about Eve's age --- maybe a little younger --- but whose elegant dress and mannerisms suggest someone older, classier and more worldly. "Hello Ann," Eve says with a smile. "I didn't expect to see you here."

"Well," she grasps for a credible explanation. "I got my work done already and wanted to see if Julie needed anything for tonight's rehearsal dinner." That seems as good an excuse as any.

"She and Greg went to pick his friend at the airport today."

"I forgot."

"I really do think this place is charming," Karen says in a sweetly condescending way. "Just the right thing for a small town. No wonder the place is crowded." Ann notices Eve's frozen smile. Karen sure tries her sister's patience.

"Ann, I know you sort of met last night, but I don't think you two were introduced: this is my sister Karen St. John. She flew in yesterday for the wedding. Karen, this is Ann Gale --- oh, I'm sorry, Ann Bradley." Eve chuckles. "It'll take me a little while to get used to that. Ann is Julie's matron of honor."

"Of course, Julie mentioned it at the shower," Karen says as they shake hands. "You're a local girl? I probably know your parents."

"Probably: Munroe and Lorene Gale."

Karen hesitates for a moment. *Why is that?* "Is that Lorene Graves?"

"That's her maiden name".

"I knew your mother well. When we were young we both worked out at the Halloran mansion together." That surprises Ann. "Really? I knew she worked there for a time but I didn't know that she worked there with Eve's sister."

"Well, it was a lifetime ago."

"Julie and I hang out a lot. She often talks about you, but I'm surprised we\haven't met before."

Eve notices some merchandise piled wrong and straightens it out. "That's because Karen lives in New York and doesn't visit us very often."

"Really? Oh, I bet New York is a great place to live --- much better than\Nowhere Hill."

"Nowhere Hill," Karen asks amused, "what is that?" Eve, on the other hand, always resents such comments and gives her a disapproving look.

"I'm sorry. That's my little 'pet name' for Faraway Hill," Ann explains. "I'm a small town farm girl who hates small towns and farms. I come into Manchester as often as I can."

Karen smiles at her. "I understand. That's the way I felt growing up here. But if you really want to get out, then why don't you? I did."

"Well . . . there are a lot of issues." Or, more simply, Ann has never had the chance. But if she did, she'd probably take it.

"Of course."

Eve's patience has run out. "Well, Karen and I have some shopping to do. We'll see you tonight, Ann." Karen gives her a knowing wink as they two women leave with Ann following behind them, watching them check out the windows of different stores --- and seeing in Karen St. John the kind of woman Ann Bradley has always wanted to be.

✷✷✷✷

"What are you doing in here?" Barry is snooping again, and Ben just caught him. The kid gives him one of his cocky smiles that broadcast false sincerity. "Nothing Ben, I was just hoping he'd be here."

Ben can barely tolerate Barry Studer --- yes that *is* his name --- but his partner, Melvin Waite, insisted on bringing the young man into their firm. Ever since that day in January, the very ambitious Barry has acted more like a used car salesman that a lawyer. But Mel has put up with him, even defended him to Ben, and now the kid is sniffing around Mel's office. "Why do you need to seem him this time?"

"I've got leads on a couple of potential clients." One of the few good things Barry has done is bring in more money. But Ben has always suspected that there was more to his being here than building business. "You keep forgetting, Barry. I'm the other partner in this firm. You can always come to me."

"Oh, sure, of course dude," Ben hates to be called dude, "but since one of them is a friend of his I thought Mel would be especially interested."

"You are going after our friends now?"

"No, no, not exactly: I ran into him at the club." *Could he be any more pretentious?* But Ben tries to be accommodating. "Fine, tell me about it after the wedding."

"But, dude, we really need to move fast on this."

"Listen, 'dude,' this is New Hampshire. Nothing moves fast here." Barry practically pouts at that remark and insists "I'm sure Mel will be interested."

"I'm sure he will."

"Have you seen him at all lately?" Actually, Ben hasn't seen much of him for days and it is starting to worry him. Mel's behavior has been particularly strange for the last few weeks and makes him wonder if an old problem has risen up. If it has, it could be a disaster. "Go back to your own office, Barry." Without saying another word, Barry leaves. Ben looks around Mel's office and starts noticing little things: framed photos that used to sit on his desk are now gone. Mementoes on the shelves by the TV have disappeared.

Striding past his secretary, Ben slams the door closed on his own office and reaches for the phone. A quick dial to Mel's home results in a recorded message: "that number is no longer in service." Panicked, Ben pulls out his cell but even Mel's voicemail doesn't pick up. Now, he calls the bank. Eve isn't there, but her boss is. "Dave, I need you to check on the firm's account for me, please."

The answer is just what Ben was afraid of.

✳✳✳✳

Jack behaves himself for the rest of the day. Greg and Julie take him to King's Korner, which he calls "a great little shop" and show him a few more of Manchester's sights. The tour of Faraway Hill includes the town square and the famous Halloran statue. "He looks a lot like you, Greg," Jack says in a friendly, neutral way. Everything in his speech and body language says that they are just buds. Greg tries to follow his lead, but isn't sure if it's working. Julie acts like she doesn't notice, and maybe she doesn't, but she's pretty smart: Greg worries she'll figure it out at any minute.

When they arrive home, the place is buzzing with late afternoon activity. The household staff is gearing up for tonight's wedding rehearsal. They are also preparing for the influx of Halloran family members who will be descending on Faraway Hill starting tomorrow. The first equipment has arrived for the wedding, which will be in the garden at the house's rear. The wedding planner, a high-strung middle aged woman who seems everywhere at once, is directing every little detail. Her most important accessory is a clipboard that appears to be attached at the point where her left hand should be. "Don't worry, don't worry," she says without any greeting or introduction. "Everything is running smoothly." The chaos around her says otherwise.

"Thanks, Harriet," Julie says with a smile. Greg has found it easier to let Julie take the lead in the wedding plans. "By the way, this is our best man, Jack\Campbell." Jack gives the woman his best, sexiest smile. She actually blushes. "Well, hello there, Mr. Best Man."

"It's just an honorary title," he answers with a wink. Harriet blushes again. Julie chuckles, and Greg's stomach churns.

"Greg," Julie asks in her sweetest voice, "why don't you show Jack to his suite? You both need to get ready for tonight." He doesn't like the idea of them being alone again. Especially not after what Jack said to him at lunch. "Please? I need to go over a million things with Harriet and Frederick." Defeated Greg smiles and gives her a kiss on the cheek. He then leads a grinning Jack up the stairs, each of them carrying a suitcase.

The second floor is devoid of any staff; they are all busy downstairs. Greg can feel Jack's strong hand gently touch the small of his back. "I meant what I said earlier."

"I know." That's the problem. They stop outside the door. "This is it, Jack," Greg says as he escorts them inside. "Everything you need is in this suite: a parlor, bedroom, private bath, private phone, satellite TV."

Wrapping his arms around Greg, Jack adds "and a nice big bed."

"Jack, please, I love Julie. Don't do this to me." Greg knows he doesn't sound convincing. It feels too good to be enveloped by him. Jack leans in for a kiss but Greg manages to tilt his head away. "I know you've got a commitment with her," Jack says with a sigh. "But I also know you."

"What the hell does that mean?"

"We've both fucked a lot people in our lives --- women, men --- but we only really clicked with each other. You are going to come back to me sometime, I know it."

"Julie's different and besides," Greg says pulling away from him, "I'm still pissed at you."

"Then why did you ask me to be your best man?"

Greg hesitates. The reason is embarrassing. "Because I didn't have anyone else, that's why. I barely know anybody here and all the other guys from school ---"

"All the other guys from school," Jack laughs, "you pissed off by either fucking their girlfriends --- or by fucking them."

"You're a real ass, sometimes."

"I've heard that before, especially from you."

Greg is defiant. "I really love Julie."

"Does that mean you've been faithful to her?"

"Of course," hookers and hustlers don't count.

"Really; I know how hard that is for you." That comment really stings Greg. "Nothing happened that night." *Why is he bringing that up again?* "Jack, I told you a hundred times before: she was a former girlfriend who needed someone to talk to. That's all." The girl was someone he dated for about a month. He remained friendly with her after they broke up, even after he was living with Jack. When her mother died, she kept him up all night consoling her. Jack never liked that.

"My point is that I am the only person you were ever really committed to."

Jack's confidence sometimes morphs into pure ego. That was something Greg had forgotten. "You are such a pompous ass. I almost married Lauren and I was faithful to her."

"You two only dated a few months until she dumped you."

"It was six months and that was her choice, not mine."

"Whatever. You haven't been fucking around? Not even with that waitress with cute tits?"

"I already told you about her."

"No fuck buddies?"

"Well . . . not exactly." Jack's pushing makes it harder for Greg to compartmentalize his time with Mark.

"What does that mean?"

"Never mind. Look, we are not discussing this any more. You dumped me, so we are just buds right now --- and even *that* might change, dude, if you keep acting like this." Angry, Greg leaves slamming the door behind him.

Jack smiles: as mad as he is, Greg will come around. Before doing anything else, he pulls out his cell and dials. "I'm in," he tells the person on the other end.

****

A few miles away, another door slams shut. An exhausted Eve King comes home to find her husband sitting alone in the living room. The lights are out and the shades are drawn. He is silently nursing a scotch and soda, staring straight ahead. She has rarely seen Ben like this, but knows it well. Worried, she drops in the chair across from his and looks directly into his eyes.

"Ben, what's wrong?"

"Mel is gone."

"What do you mean Mel is gone?"

"Just what I said: Mel is gone, his phone is disconnected, his stuff is gone from the condo, he's not picking up his cell and," a scared look crosses his face. "Most of the firm's money is missing."

"Oh, my God!" Ben has spent most of his life building that firm. It pains Eve to see him go through this.

"I called Sheriff Reynolds and he's contacted the FBI."

"Is he gambling again?" In college, Melvin Waite became a compulsive gambler. But he has been straight for nearly twenty years. Eve can't even remember his ever buying a lottery ticket, much less place a bet.

"That was my first guess, but the sheriff made some quick calls and so far all of the bookies in the area say they haven't been doing business with him."

He seems so stiff and unemotional, like a dead man who has been given the final okay to stop breathing. Eve gently puts his glass on the table and takes his hands in hers. "Ben, darling, we will get through this."

"He's been acting strange for the last few weeks, as if he were
hiding something."

"That's the way addicts are, sweetheart, they try to hide their sickness."

"No, no, it's different somehow. I remember what it was like years ago. He was never very good at hiding his gambling. I'm sure if that was it I would have fig-ured it out."

"What else could it have been?"

"I don't know. I called Rebecca and told her. I know their divorced, but she and the kids shouldn't hear about it from the police."

"That was the right thing to do."

"Why?" Ben asks as if hoping the universe will provide him an answer. "Why did he do it?"

"What's going to happen now?"

He has been thinking about that. "Well, our clients don't know anything yet. But I can see losing a lot of them once they do. Getting new ones will be tough."

"I'm sure Lewis Halloran will stick by you, especially after the kids are married."

"I suppose, but that's no guarantee about anyone else. Payroll will be a bitch. I'll probably have to forgo a salary for awhile, so I can pay everyone else."

"That's okay; we have my salary and our savings. We can get through this, Ben. We can."

"You know what might be the worst part of it?"

"What?" What could be worse than being cheated by his friend and partner?

"I'll need that punk Barry even more now to drum up business," he says with a rueful smile. Eve leans in and kisses him. Everything will work out. She's sure of it.

✳✳✳✳

Ann sneaks another peek at Mark's cell phone. She thinks she's being discreet, but Mark can see her out of the corner of his eye. *This is getting annoying.* He didn't think he was marrying a nosy kid, but that seems to be the case. Mark manages to stay a few steps ahead of her --- deleting text messages, emails and password-protecting files. But she keeps asking about them and he is starting to run out of excuses. He may soon run out of patience. *What is it about women that make them so damned territorial?*

The two of them are nearly ready for the rehearsal dinner. It is the first time either of them will be in the Halloran mansion and Ann is really excited about it. She has always dreamed of living the high life. She even splurged on a new dress.

"I'm ready babe," Mark says finishing his tie. He is wearing one of his better suits, a remnant of *his* once living the high life. Ann is wearing a beautiful white strapless that shapes her body very nicely. It seems a little odd to be this well dressed and driving a beat-up old pick-up, but that truck is their only chariot. At least until Mark can fully engage his "insurance policies". They arrive at the Halloran place in just a few minutes. Ann gets a real thrill over the butler, who escorts them through the Grand Vestibule, passed gold leaf picture frames and antique furniture into the impressive oval parlor called the Blue Room. But no one is here.

"Where is everyone?"

"I'm afraid they are all running a little late, Mrs. Bradley," the butler answers. "May I get either of you some wine?"

"That would be nice."

The elderly man pours them each a glass of white and leaves them alone. Mark has been in these kinds of surroundings before, but not Ann. While he sits to wait for the others, she starts to explore the room, taking an intense look at one expensive item after another.

"Ann, don't be so nosy."

"I'm just curious. Everyone talks about this place but hardly anyone I know has ever been in here."

"Julie has and so has your mom." The wine is damned good, the best he's had in a long time. Of course, it has been awhile. Passing himself off as a common farm hand means drinking mostly beer. Mark never cared much for beer.

Ann frowns. "Julie doesn't count and my mom hasn't been inside for years."

"You'd think she'd want to again. Weren't they invited to the wedding?"

"Yeah, but Munroe is being Munroe." She takes a few tentative steps back into the Grand Hall. "Ann, don't." But she just waves him quiet and disappears. *The girl is too damn nosy, all right.* He shakes his head and enjoys the wine alone. A couple of minutes later he can hear a woman's footsteps behind him.

"Well, Ann, does the place meet with your approval?"

"It always has." The voice is familiar, but it isn't Ann's. Mark turns to see the one person he never expected to see again, especially in rural New Hampshire.

"Hello Mark, my pet. What a wonderful surprise to see you."

There she is, the woman, once one of Mark's favorite clients, who instigated the events that forced him to leave New York a year ago. "I wish I could say the same, Karen."

EPISODE FOUR

Mark glances around to make sure no one can hear them. "What the hell are you doing here?" This is like some bizarre nightmare come true. Standing before him is the last person he expected to see here --- or wanted.

"I was going to ask you the same thing," Karen replies with a devious smile.

"I live here now. I've created a whole new life, one that doesn't involve sickos like you."

Karen laughs. The classy lady suddenly morphs into something very different. Mark has seen her do this before. It always scares him.

"It's true. I'm even here with my wife."

"Your wife --- and how much does *she* pay you for your services?" The old woman practically cackles like a witch. "That's not how it is," he says trying to keep his voice low. Someone could walk in any minute. "Now why the fuck are you here?"

"It's very simple, lover. Faraway Hill is my home town."

"Holy shit . . ." How could he have known? Karen never talked about her past with him, and he pretty much chose Faraway Hill with a dart and a map. "Here I thought I was rid you of you. Where's your old man? Is he going to run me out again?"

Feeling hurt, Karen pulls back. "Martin died last year, about the time you left." She has become human again. The classy lady has suddenly returned. "It really pained me to lose you both at the same time."

"I'm sorry," Mark says trying to mask his anger and failing. The best he can do is appear unemotional. When Martin St. John found out about what his wife was paying for, the old man launched a vendetta. Mark couldn't keep up with his other clients and found himself on the run, spending nearly every cent he made.

"No, your not," Karen replies just as coldly, "you're not sorry at all, lover."

He hates it when she uses that word. "Please don't call me that."

"What?"

"You know what, calling me your lover."

"That's what you were."

"No, I was your *escort*." This was the big issue between them. Mark wanted to keep everything on a professional level: he fucks her, she pays him. But Karen began treating their relationship as something more. That was what, more than anything else that angered Martin. Then she became . . . weird.

"But 'lover' sounds much nicer."

Mark gives up. He knows she won't budge. "Why are you here tonight? Are you friends with the Hallorans?"

Karen laughs again. He hates it when she laughs at him. It usually means she knows something he doesn't. "Darling, they are almost family --- you see, my niece is marrying Lewis' boy."

Has the entire world gone insane? Mark has to pour himself another drink at that news. Karen stares at him with a wickedly curious look on his face. "Why are you here, lover?"

"My wife is matron of honor," he downs some wine in one swallow. Karen's smile turns devious again. "Kismet, that's what it is lover. Good old fashioned kismet."

Laughter from the Grand Hall distracts them as Ann leads Julie, Greg and another young man into the room. "That is so cool," Ann says practically giggling. "I've never met a famous artist before." Julie looks up and smiles. "There you are, Aunt Karen."

"Hello dear. I was just having a charming conversation with this nice young man --- what was your name again?"

"Bradley. Mark Bradley."

Ann walks up and takes his arm in hers. "My husband; we just got married ourselves."

"Congratulations."

"Thank you."

"I remember those days, when Martin and I were newlyweds. They are so special." Karen turns to admire Jack. "And another handsome young man; things have certainly changed in New Hampshire since I was a girl. I don't remember the boys being quite so good looking."

"Actually, I'm from New York," Jack explains. "My name is Jack Campbell. I'm Greg's best friend."

"And his best man, I am sure."

"My dad was a business associate your husband; my condolences."

"Thank you."

And that is how the evening proceeds, with innocuous conversations that hide what everyone is almost saying. Soon the party grows to include Lewis Halloran, several of Ann and Julie's friends, Harriet the wedding planner and an Episcopal priest that Greg has only met a few times before. Ben and Eve are not far behind. There are odd moments all night long, from dinner to the rehearsal to drinks after. One of the strangest for Greg comes when he, Julie, Mark and Jack are all at a buffet table together. He has had sex with all three of them but not all of them know that.

Ann occasionally makes a fool out of herself, trying to appear more sophisticated than she really is. Lewis stays clear of her and the Kings just humor her. The farm girl even flirts a little with Jack. Mark doesn't seem to mind --- or maybe doesn't care enough --- but it really bothers Greg. Her pretense eventually gets the best of her. At one point, she misidentifies the artist of a painting in the Green Room until Karen St. John corrects her in a way that makes Ann blush with embarrassment and Greg smile with joy.

But every so often Jack makes eye contact with him, and the meaning is very clear. But he also notices Jack glancing into Center Hall towards the direction of his dad's study. This is much stranger. *Why does he do that?*

The parents act the strangest of all. Lewis seems to be avoiding everyone without actually leaving the party. Ben and Eve act a little too casual, almost forcing themselves to have a good time. It's so obvious that Julie takes her mother aside for a quick, hushed conversation that leaves her unsatisfied.

Eventually, the evening ends with guests leaving one by one. Ben and Eve are the first to go, followed by Karen. Lewis calls it a night shortly after. Others soon follow. Mark and Ann are the last to go, and it takes some less than subtle hints for Ann to realize --- finally --- that the night is over. By that time, Greg is asleep in a wing chair and the servants are starting to clean up. Only Julie and Jack remain. The two of them sit together in the Blue Room, him sipping wine and she sparkling water. They are both a little tired and are enjoying this moment of peace. It is the first chance they've had to be alone. "So, how long have you known Greg?"

"We met the summer before senior year. I'd see him around campus but we really didn't hook-up for some time. He had broken up with this girl --- I don't remember her name --- about the same time I had, so we drowned our sorrows together." This is true, Jack realizes, if incomplete.

Julie smiles and says "He doesn't talk much about college --- I went locally --- but I always get the impression that he loved it."

"I'll bet Greg sees it as the freest time of his life."

"Freest?"

"Well," Jack chooses his words carefully. "He spent most of his life in boarding schools. Being young, single and rich in New York is pretty liberating by comparison."

"I guess so."

Julie sips some water and then says something that surprises Jack. "I'm glad you're here for him."

"Why is that?"

"Well, I know Faraway Hill is supposed to be Greg's home town and all, but he really didn't spend much time growing up here. He's a sweet, smart guy without many close friends. He deserves better." It is at this moment that Jack starts to understand Greg's feelings for Julie. They are more than just trying to please his dad or being responsible for the baby. Her physical beauty is part of it, but mostly it is an inherent intelligence, insight and compassion that is very apparent. If circumstances were different *he* might have fallen for her. Jack looks over at Greg, looking peaceful and even lovable curled up snoring in a chair. She's right, he deserves better than to be alone. But despite Julie's many wonderful qualities, Jack knows that Greg will be happier in the long run with him. They fit too well together --- something Jack didn't fully realize until he lost him. He won't make that mistake again. But first, there is another matter Jack needs to deal with, a certain dangerous person he needs to exorcise from his life. "I guess I should get him upstairs."

"Let's both do it."

The two of them walk over to the chair and nudge Greg awake. "What . . . what is it?" The little nap seems to have done him some good. He looks rested and refreshed, the first time all day.

"Time for bed, dear," Julie says in an almost motherly way. She and Jack help him to his feet. Greg yawns awake. He appears reenergized. "I'm sorry I dozed off."

"Don't be dude, we understand."

The three of them go upstairs arm in arm as if they have been close friends for years. It is strangely warm and comfortable for Greg until they reach his door. When he and Julie wish Jack a good night, Jack returns it --- with a wink that seems to have more than one meaning.

Inside his suite and alone together for the first time in quite a while, Greg gives his fiancé a deep, sensual kiss. Cupping her ass, he puts his whole body into the act until she can break free, gasping for breath and say, "I thought you were worn out."

"I've got my second wind." Greg takes her hand and guides her from the suite's parlor to its bedroom. He kisses her again, tongue on tongue, until Julie gently pulls away again. Only this time, it is to stand back and slide off her dress, dropping it to the floor. He follows suit, taking off his tie and blazer in what becomes a giggling race to see who can strip faster. Wearing less, Julie wins and pushed Greg onto the bed and pulls off his pants. She then licks her way down his body, from cheeks to nipples to stomach and finally to his cock. Taking it into her mouth, Julie's tongue plays with it just the way Greg likes. Just before he cums, she stops and climbs on top of him, sliding her pussy down. He loves that feeling, of having his cock enveloped by her warmth. She slides up and down and just before he cums he looks her straight into her eyes and say, "I love you so damned much."

"I love you too," Julie replies as she feels his cum shoot into her depths.

✼✼✼✼

The next day, the Halloran mansion becomes New Hampshire's equivalent of Grand Central Station. Halloran relatives and other people from all over arrive for the wedding, with guests coming through the door starting in the early morning and continuing all afternoon. It is an eclectic bunch. Jack finds watching them to be very interesting. He is barely introduced to each family member but he can soon deduce who ranks where by the little things --- like the quality of their luggage --- even though most of them have that upper crust attitude he knows so well. It's fun.

The servants don't even bother serving actual meals, but leave a regularly refreshed buffet in the Formal Dining Room for whoever is hungry whenever.

Harriet, the harried wedding planner, is back and even more harried than yesterday. She confers with Julie and Frederick and then spends her day putting out one fire after another. Decorations are hung in the Grand Hall, parlors and ballroom as new guests walk up the stairs. Julie plays hostess all day and Jack helps her as much as he can.

At the back of his mind are two connected issues: getting a certain something from Lewis Halloran's study to get rid of his problem person, and getting Greg to realize the truth about them. Unfortunately, the busy day makes it impossible for Jack to discretely search the den. People will see him and ask questions he can't answer. As for the other: "Where is Greg?" he finally gets to ask.

"He's with his father at the office," Julie explains.

"The office today," Jack is surprised. "That seems strange." Greg and Lewis were gone when he woke up this morning. He was hoping to spend more time alone with him. *Is Greg avoiding me?*

"Believe me I was *not* happy about it but Lewis insisted." Harriet distracts her again. Like everyone else, Jack munches on the little tidbits at the buffet. It is amazing how quickly hors d'oeuvres can fill you up. He is gracious to the strangers who fill the many parlors; but knowing so little about them makes it difficult. Finally, in the large Blue Room where most of the guests are congregating, he finds Julie resting in a Queen Anne chair. He sits on a matching chair next to her. "Are you alright?" The room has blue everywhere --- from the silk wallpaper to the drapes and even the furniture.

"Sure, I'm just getting really tired. You know, I read somewhere that the Queen of England does a couple of dozen events a month with hundreds of guests at each. That lady is now my hero."

Jack chuckles. Yes, he can definitely understand what Greg sees in her. "I've been saying hi to complete strangers all day. Do you know any of them? I see the players but don't have a scorecard." Julie smiles and says, "I do know most of them. The Hallorans have been Dad's clients for years. In fact, I probably know these people better than Greg does."

"Okay let's hear it." He almost said "dish" but managed to stop himself. Julie smiles again; she seems happy to have someone to gossip with. "Well, you see that middle aged man standing alone by whatever that plant is called? That's Robert Halloran. He's Lewis' cousin. You'd never know it to look at him, but he is a genius at real estate and owns 10% of the family business. Very quiet; no one talks about him much except about how no one talks about him much." Jack has to suppress a laugh at that. Julie starts pointing out a few other cousins all of different ages but none of whom own a piece of the company, although they benefit one way or another from a family trust that owns much of the stock. They are mostly elderly and middle age folks, but there are a couple of really hot women. He was about to ask Julie about one of them when another couple catches his eye. "Who are they?" Jack asks, pointing to the hot young guy with his arms around a woman old enough to be his mother. He noticed the dude earlier and had to fight hard from staring at him.

"That's Greg's 'Uncle' Paul," she says with a smirk.

The guy looks more like Greg's frat buddy. Or his fuck buddy. "Say again?"

Julie laughs. "That very nice looking former Calvin Klein model is married to Lewis' sister."

He's more than nice looking. The guy can easily compete with those two hot women for Jack's attention. "The lady; she's Lewis' sister?"

"Right; Paul is husband --- oh, which is it now --- number four, I think. Yes, that's it: number four. She owns 10% of the company too. What is her full name? God, it's like . . . oh, yes, its Joan Halloran Newberry . . . wait, I can do this . . . Joan Halloran Newberry Hamilton Logan Lansing."

"You remember all that?"

"I know, even I'm surprised. I wonder where Matthew is."

"Matthew?"

"Joan's son; rumor has it he and step-daddy don't get along."

"Wow, you really *do* know what's going on. Who else do you recognize?" Jack sees a handsome man in his 50s or 60s walk over to Joan and her hunky husband. "He looks familiar."

"That is Senator Richard Davis --- *United States* Senator Richard Davis --- very important in Washington. He's been Lewis' best friend since God knows when. Prep school, I think." Julie gives him a sly look, as if she has something forbidden or special for him. "Do you want to meet someone famous --- really famous --- and interesting?"

"Always," Jack replies with the same look. Julie leads them out and down the hall to the Green Room --- and, yes, it has green walls, drapes and furniture. Greg told him the house had been patterned after the original White House but he didn't fully believe it until today.

Sitting in a corner, as if she were a monarch holding court, is a small, frail old lady surrounded by fawning admirers of all ages. The woman is dressed simply but elegantly and could pass for anyone's grandmother --- except for the people staring in rapture around her. The sole exception is a middle aged woman sitting behind her, looking a bemused and a little bored. Apparently she has heard the old lady's stories over and over, including the one she is just finishing.

"So, I finally said to her, 'screw McCarthy, if you're going to be called a pinko dyke then damn it <u>be a pinko dyke</u>. This half-assed shit isn't working."

The crowd roars with laughter while the woman standing behind her smiles politely. Jack whispers to Julie, "who is that?"

"You really don't know?" He shakes his head. "That is none other than Agnes Gabler." Jack is impressed. "You know her?"

"Well, I've *met* her. The Hallorans *know* her." The crowd applauds one of New England's most famous people, whose paintings hang in museums and private collections all over the world. "She looks . . . well, even older than I imagined."

"Cut her some slack, she's turning 95 this year."

"You know, with all of the celebrities the Hallorans know, I'm surprised Gene Robinson isn't performing your wedding ceremony." Jack isn't sure why he brought up the openly gay bishop, but it seems appropriate.

"We did ask him, but he's got some thing over in England."

"I'm impressed." He can feel Julie's hand rest on his shoulder. "You know, something tells me I will *always* be impressed," she whispers in his ear, "even long after I become Mrs. Halloran."

****

"I'm sorry to take you away from the festivities, son, but it can't be helped." Greg is standing in Lewis' office at the Millyard District, in the former Halloran mill and now corporate headquarters. The room is spacious and modern like the rest of the refurbished structure. But the furniture is considerably older. Much of it is antique, having seen use in the company's original offices by Lewis' own father. The result is an odd disconnect.

"That's okay, Dad. Business is business." Actually, Greg is grateful for the break. It means one less day worrying how to face Jack Campbell --- or that Greg may slip and reveal something to Julie. He can only hope that Jack keeps his promise to be discreet.

"This mill in Thailand will double our capacity and open up new markets. But it means a major recapitalization. With nearly all the family stockholders gathering for the wedding, this is the best time to discuss it with them."

Greg nods; most men would be upset at having their wedding turned into a business meeting. But it's almost like breathing fresh air compared with the wedding hubbub and the accompanying stress. Besides, Lewis is right: the new mill will position them to better compete with other cloth makers in emerging markets. It will mean taking on some debt, but that should be manageable.

The secretary buzzes Lewis who takes a call. Greg is about to leave when his father motions him back to a chair. He sits there, marveling at the old man's ability to be decisive and get someone to do what he wants. The phone conversation is short, specific, and leaves the other person no room to maneuver. He is not rude but very determined. When he hangs up, Lewis sits and looks at his son thoughtfully --- almost too thoughtfully.

"Is everything okay, Dad?"

"Greg," his father sighs and says gently, "tomorrow is your day. I want you to enjoy it . . . But when you come back from your honeymoon, we will need to have a talk." *A talk, what does that mean?* "Dad, what's wrong?"

Lewis pauses, trying to find just the right words. "It's not so much that something is *wrong* --- but it is something important, something that I should have done years ago."

"I don't understand ---" *what is he talking about?* Whatever it is, it's big and sounds bad.

The old man raises a hand as if to calm him. "I am not telling you this to worry you. You have done nothing wrong and I'm fine. I just want you prepared, that's all. Actually, I think that you'll find it a good thing." Greg isn't sure. He doesn't know his father well enough to be able to read him. He can only take Lewis at his word.

"Great Dad, I look forward to hearing about it." Greg rises and shakes his father's hand. "I really am proud of you, son." He says that with such genuine emotion that Greg can't help but be moved. They stand there hand in hand. The moment is so odd, so out of character. It reminds him of that strange morning in Lewis' study. And it is just as disconcerting. "I don't know what to say."

"Just know that your wedding --- your marriage --- is a new start for both of us; for all of us. We will have an all new family."

"Of course, you'll be a grandfather."

"Yes . . . and it is a chance to make certain things right." Greg isn't sure what to say. But the smile on his father's face is so gentle, so . . . indescribable. Yet it touches him. It is the first time since he was a little boy that he truly feels like Lewis loves him. Another call breaks the moment, but its one that buoys Greg for the rest of the day and night. It makes him more confident about the marriage and the baby. At home, he becomes outgoing and charming to all of the guests, including the many relatives he barely knows. Even Jack seems impressed. Before leaving to spend the night at her parents, Julie takes him aside and says, "You are so terrific."

But at the end of the night, with the various guests retiring to their rooms, Jack catches Greg in the second floor hall. They say nothing. Jack just smiles at him before going into his room. It leaves him wondering again.

✳✳✳✳

When Julie arrives at home, she finds her mother and father sitting alone in the living room sharing some wine and memories. It's sweet to see them paging through the family photo album. And they are not alone: Ann emerges from the kitchen wearing an oversize t-shirt with her hair in pony tails. Julie laughs: she looks like an adult playing teenager.

"I figured that this will be our last real girl's night together."

"Oh, Ann that's so sweet, but my parents ---"

"That's okay," her dad says with a warm smile. "We'll have plenty of time together tomorrow." Her mother nods in agreement. So, like giddy school girls Ann and Julie bound up the stairs to Julie's old bedroom. Ann has already gathered the necessary items for the night: soda, chips, raw cookie dough and other goodies. It is just like the nights in high school when they would stay up late talking about boys and school and parents and boys again. The room hasn't changed much since then with movie star posters on the walls and lots of stuffed animals piled around the room. Julie changes into her own shirt and the sits with Ann cross legged on the bed.

"Oh my God," Julie says as she bites into a chunk of dough. "This so reminds me of the night we stayed up talking about the way Peter Brandt was giving you they eye in gym class."

Ann giggles. "Right, like he was so subtle about it."

"It worked; you went out with him for --- what --- six months or so?"

"What can I say" Ann sips some Diet Coke. "He was a real hunk."

"Still is, especially in that deputy's uniform. Wow."

"Speaking of hunks, what's the story with this Jack guy? How does Greg know him? Is he seeing anyone?"

"Ann, you're married now: remember *Mrs. Bradley*?"

"I'm just curious! Married women are allowed to look, you know." Ann breaks open a bag sending chips flying into the air, making them laugh. "I'll try to remember that," Julie says catching her breath amid raining snacks. "Anyway, they met in college and they were best friends."

"Were?"

"Still are, I guess. I just get the feeling that something went down between the two of them. Probably a girl; supposedly Greg was a real player back then. But enough about Jack, what's going on with you and Mark? How is married life after less than a month?"

"Well . . ." Ann breaks off a huge chunk of dough and sticks it in her mouth.

"Well what? Is something wrong?"

She tries to chew as fast as she can. "Not so much wrong as . . . weird."

"Guys are naturally weird. I'm sure it takes some getting used to living with one."

"That's not what I mean."

"What then?"

"Well . . . Mark gets these strange text messages a lot. I never know what their about; he always deletes them. Then he'll disappear for a couple of hours. I never really know where."

"Did you ask him?"

"Every fucking chance I get. All he does is give me some bullshit about odd jobs."

"Maybe that's what it is."

"Maybe . . ."

"Oh, come on; what else could it be?" That's what worries her. But Ann decides to change the subject. "So what all happened today?"

"They came from nowhere --- wow, that sounds the title of a 50s horror movie."

"It can't be that bad."

"No, it was actually pretty cool. I just mean Hallorans from everywhere showed up. And now I hear that there will be a mini stockholders meeting tonight."

"What does that mean? It's your wedding."

"That's what *I* said," Julie frowns. "But apparently there is some big deal that needs the family's approval."

"That must suck."

Julie shrugs and takes a swig of soda. "It is what it is, I guess."

"You are so damned lucky."

"What do you mean?"

"Hell, you are about to live the life I've always wanted. After tomorrow you will be rich, related to important people and hang with the famous."

It's that same old thing with Ann, the thing that always annoys people --- even Julie sometimes. Ann wishing she were more than she is and trying to prove that she can be. Like the embarrassing moment last night when she tried using a painting to brag about her art knowledge --- and Aunt Karen elegantly put her in her place.

"Greg doesn't like me, does he?"

"Well . . . I wouldn't go that far." Actually, Greg can barely stand being in the same room with her.

"Don't worry about it," Ann says, offering to change the subject. "So, did you see any famous people today?"

"Agnes Gabler is staying at the house."

Ann's eye lit up. "Cool: America's most famous lesbian artist." Julie laughs, adding "I think that's her marketing slogan. She was holding court in the Green Room. It was so weird: a bunch of wealthy, connected people treating this 94-year-old woman like she's a rock star. All that were missing were the roadies setting up equipment!" The two of them scream, and they continue to laugh and reminisce and tell stories well into the night.

✳✳✳✳

The next morning, Greg is alone in his suite. He has just showered and shaved and is now starting to dress for the big event. Standing before a full-length mirror, he adjusts the tuxedo pants and snaps cuff links through his sleeves. Now comes the tricky part: the bow tie. Greg has never quite gotten the hang of bow ties. As a child in private school he and most of the other boys wore clip-ons. At prep school the uniforms called for regular ties. The last time Greg wore a bow was when he and Lauren went to some fancy party on the Upper East Side. She had to tie it for him that night.

He tries the mirror in his parlor with no better luck. Someone knocks on the door. "Come in." Jack, looking unbelievably handsome in his tux, strides confidently inside. "Hey dude, I figured you'd be having trouble with that." Before Greg can say anything he steps over and takes control. "Stand in front of the mirror so I can see what I'm doing." Jack puts his arms around Greg and, using the reflection as a guide, ties the bow perfectly. Greg suddenly remembers: it wasn't Lauren who last did this, but Jack. When he is finished, Jack takes Greg into a full from-behind hug, smiling at him through the mirror. "You know, if I hadn't fucked up last year, <u>we</u> might be getting married --- or whatever it would be called --- today."

"Jack, please don't . . ." *I don't need to hear that*. Just being this close with him is churning up all sorts of feelings. He had managed to put them aside again last night, but this intimacy has brought them forward. It is almost scary.

"Don't what?"

"I . . . I love you Jack," Greg says fighting the urge to kiss him.

"I love you."

"But I love her too."

"I know that."

"What am I suppose to do?" Part of him just wants to grab Jack's hand and run off together. Part of him wants to punch than man for his leaving last year. And part of him wants to go down Center Hall where his bride is dressing and sweep Julie off her feet and make love to her right there in front of her astonished bridesmaids.

"You are going to suck it up and get married. That's what men do: we suck it up and do what needs to be done. It is the right thing, Greg. You love her and she's carrying your child. So we suck it up."

"Suck it up?" The pain of their last time together returns in his mind, as fresh a memory as if it happened yesterday. "Like you did last year?"

"I know, I know," for the first time since his return Jack no longer seems sure of himself. Now he is embarrassed and ashamed. "I was a real pussy, so afraid of my old man."

"And where does that leave us?"

"We'll figure out something," Jack almost pleads. "Let's just take it one step at a time." As much as Greg wants to be with him, he knows it's probably just a fantasy. "It could be years, you know, before we can ever really be together again; maybe never."

"No, not 'never,' Greg; don't ever say that."

Their eyes meet in the glass. "Yes, it could be never. It probably will be never. Its probably better if it's never."

Another knock at the door takes the two men out of themselves. They take deep breaths and separate so Greg can call out, "come in." Lewis, in his own slightly rumpled tux and with his own slightly rumpled smile, enters. "Giving the nervous groom some last minute support?"

"Just fulfilling my best man duties, Mr. Halloran," Jack's natural confidence has returned --- or at least his ability to create the image of confidence has. Greg wishes he could do that. Instead, he just stays quiet.

"That's fine; Jack, could I have a moment with my son?"

"Yes sir," Jack puts a hand on Greg's shoulder. "I'll see you downstairs, dude." Greg nods and watches the man he loves walk out the door, to help him marry the woman he loves. Lewis motions to a couple of chairs and they, father and son, sit down.

"I know what you're going through," Lewis says. "I had the same feelings you do. I remember having an identical conversation with Richard Davis. He was my best man, you know."

Greg is confused and begins to wonder: were Davis and his dad . . . "you did?"

"Of course; nervousness at your wedding is normal. All grooms go through it. And it seems that our best men help us overcome it." Obviously Lewis means something different, a more platonic best man scenario. Greg just nods and lets his father continue. "Well, I know it's customary for the father to give his son some advice on his wedding day, but I really don't what to say."

"You don't have to say anything Dad."

Lewis smiles again. "Fine, let's go down and get you married." The father escorts his son downstairs, where all the formal rooms have been decorated. Most of the guests are already seated in the garden, waiting for the big event. Greg takes his place besides Jack at the temporary altar and shakes the priest's hand. He watches Lewis sit next to Aunt Joan and her very young, hunky husband. The sight makes Greg think about his mother. It is odd how rarely she comes to mind. Lewis doesn't even like to talk about her. She wasn't a pleasant woman, but a man has only one mother. It's rather sad.

The organist starts playing. Ann --- looking rather good in her dress --- leads the other bridesmaids in their rehearsed walk down the aisle. Seeing her makes Greg think about Mark. Quickly scanning the audience he finds him sitting next to Julie's mother. He just smiles innocently. The man is really good at faking it.

The music swells with the appearance of Julie and Ben. She looks amazing in her beaded, white gown and simple veil. Even Jack is impressed, saying a "wow" under his breath. The actual ceremony doesn't take very long. The priest goes through the customary ritual and when he declares "ladies and gentlemen, I now present you Greg and Julie Halloran," the guests applaud. A few even cheer.

Soon the party is underway with most of the activities in Grand Ballroom. Agnes Gabler again takes up residence in one of the parlors where she relates tales from her rich past. Julie's Aunt Karen and Greg's Aunt Joan spend their time talking about this and that. Jack continues to play the best bud and even seems to be hitting on one of the bridesmaids --- which, much to his surprise, bothers Greg. When he takes Jack aside about it, the other man jokes "isn't it tradition for the best man to score with one of the bridesmaids?" Then Jack whispers more gently, "I may chase pussy for awhile --- but you are the only man for me." Before they can go any farther, Julie pulls them apart so that the bride and groom can mingle together.

Throughout the day, Lewis, Eve and Ben all act like proud parents ---and, in a strange way, so does Karen. Greg also notices that Eve seems to be keeping a cautious eye on her sister.

Ann spends her time dragging a bored Mark through the house. They also take part in one of the tours the Faraway Hill Historical Society is running as part of the wedding festivities. Even some of the Hallorans take part. A middle aged and slightly prissy man leads groups through different rooms.

Dinner, dancing, laughter; all fill up the day and night until it is time for the happy couple to leave on their honeymoon. The single women all gather under the portico for the tossing of the bouquet --- which, ironically is caught by Greg's teenage cousin Matthew, who happened to be walking past at just the right (or wrong?) moment.

Finally, in the limo on the way to the airport, Greg and Julie are finally able to relax. "I shouldn't have stayed up so late last night," she says resting her head on his shoulder.

"Don't worry; we've got two whole weeks to decompress," and for Greg to worry about what to do about Jack. Everything goes smoothly at the airport. There are no delays and their flight to the Bahamas has just one layover, in Sarasota. It takes a few hours in total. Fortunately they had changed into more comfortable clothes before leaving New Hampshire. Julie also insisted that they leave their cell phones behind. Greg happily complied with that request.

They are totally worn out when they arrive at the resort. There will be no love making tonight, they agree: sleep is better. It is evening and the beautiful scenery the brochure promised is veiled in darkness. A pleasant, uniformed man stands behind the counter. "May I help you, sir?"

"Yes, you should have reservations for Mr. and Mrs. Halloran. We have a suite." *Yes,* Greg thinks, *I'll fall asleep the minute my head hits the pillow.*

The clerk begins clicking away on his keyboard when suddenly stops to read something. "Oh, sir . . . there is an important message here for Mrs. Halloran."

Julie, barely keeping her eyes open, is surprised to hear her new name. "What was that?"

"Your father, Benjamin King, called 20 minutes ago. Apparently it's urgent. You are requested to phone him immediately upon arrival." Julie is worried: *what could it be?* A bellhop takes their luggage and escorts them to their suite. Before doing anything else, Julie reaches for the phone and dials. Greg tips the bellhop and sits on a chair beside the bed. "It can't be that important," he whines. "I really need some sleep."

"I don't know . . . Dad, Dad? It's me we just got in, what's going on?" Julie listens to her father intently. A shocked look crosses her face as she turns to look directly at her new husband. "Oh, my God . . . I can't believe it . . . when . . . no

Dad let me tell him. You just hang on because I am sure he'll have some questions." She sets the receiver on the bed and gently steps over to him.

"Julie, what's wrong?"

"Sweetheart, I'm sorry to tell you, but . . . your father is dead."

EPISODE FIVE

Murder: that's what Ben King told him. "I'm sorry son, but your father was shot to death." The police were going to call, but Ben thought it would be better if he did it. And now, just half a day later, a wracked Greg Halloran and his bride are flying back to New Hampshire.

Right after Ben called with the news, Greg called Sheriff Reynolds. Apparently it happened an hour after the newlyweds left and the guests were settling down for the night. Lewis had been shot right in the head while sitting in his study. A silencer was used, so no one heard anything. A little over an hour after that Greg's cousin Matthew Newberry found the body. The poor kid was just looking for a book to help him sleep.

Everyone connected with the wedding --- except the governor and Senator Davis --- have been instructed not to leave the county while the Faraway Hill police investigate. So far, there are no leads.

Greg got almost no sleep last night, first angry and then tearful until finally he collapsed exhausted. After he fell asleep, Jack called to say he'd meet them at the airport in Manchester. "Reporters are all ready calling," he told Julie. "You guys better be ready for that." On the layover in Sarasota, they could see some of CNN's coverage on TVs in the airport's lounge area. The reporter, some woman neither of them could recognize, stood in Faraway Hill's main square:

"Police are still interviewing everyone at the wedding --- guests, household staff, caterers and others --- and so far are not reporting any leads. All we know for sure is that Lewis Halloran was shot in the forehead and was later found by his nephew. They've got the family mansion cordoned off from the public and the media. The town square here in Faraway Hill is the closest we can get." The anchor asks her about the Hallorans. "As you know, the Hallorans are old money New Englanders. They date back to colonial times as owners of one of the region's first and largest textile mills. John Halloran --- the man depicted in the statue behind me --- was an aid to New Hampshire's representative at the Continental Congress where he witnessed the vote for independence. It is said that John Halloran and his son were such supporters of the new nation that, years later when they built the family mansion, they patterned it after the original White House. It was in that mansion that Lewis Halloran was murdered."

The food court was airing Fox News, which is being especially aggressive, repeating the few available, gory details over and over. They are also referring to the Halloran family as "liberal stalwarts" as if being liberal is an insult. "Those fucking bastards," Greg muttered angrily.

At this moment, they are sitting in First Class on the last leg of the trip. Greg is very quiet. It worries Julie. "I wish you would talk to me."

"What is there to talk about?" *How can I explain this to her?* The man was actually reaching out to him just hours ago. Greg was starting to feel like he has a father, really have a father, for the first time in his life. And now someone has stolen that from him. What makes it worse is that Greg has no memories to reflect on. There are no images in his mind of Dad throwing him a baseball or yelling at him for not doing his chores or telling him about girls. All he has are vague recollections of formal Christmas dinners, brief chats in the old man's study and expensive presents mailed to him on birthdays. Of his mother, Greg has even fewer memories.

Julie places a comforting hand on his. "Maybe I should call home and see what's happening." Greg just nods. She swipes a credit card in the Airphone and dials. Frederick picks up on the second ring but he has no new news. "I'm sure Mr. Campbell will have more information for you, Mrs. Halloran." Jack gets on the phone and tells her the police have set up a perimeter around the mansion to keep the press at a distance. There is a lot of gossip among the guests. "The kid --- Matthew --- is really taking it hard. And his mom hasn't been much help."

"Why is that?"

"It's asinine. She goes from babying him one minute to ignoring him the next. I think the young husband easily distracts her. The kid really hates that. I'm trying to be a friend to him but seeing Lewis like that really shook him up."

"I'm sure."

"How is our favorite guy doing? Can I talk to him?" Julie hands Greg the hone. "Hey dude, how are you holding up?"

"I don't know," he says so quietly his voice is barely audible.

"Don't do this. I know you. Don't go into that shell. You're not alone in this Greg: you've got Julie there and me here. I'll be meeting you both at the airport. We'll get you through this. Got it?"

Greg remains silent. It is hard for him to say anything at all right now.

"Got *it*?" Jack asks more emphatically.

"Yes, I got it." Greg gives the phone back to Julie, who asks him, "Jack can you do something for us?"

"Anything; what do you need?"

"During the layover we saw Lewis all over the news channels. I bet the Manchester airport will be really bad."

"The police tell me that there are reporters camping out all over Faraway Hill."

"I'm sure. Can you speak to Sheriff Reynolds about helping us out when we get there? I'd like avoid any problems at the airport."

"I'm already on it. I'll be there in some special area with a police escort. You guys will be allowed off the plane before anyone else. Actually, they should have radioed the crew by now. Someone onboard is supposed to brief you."

"Really? You're doing all that?"

"Anything for him, Julie: Anything."

"You are the best. Thanks, Jack."

****

Ann and Mark arrive at the Faraway Hill sheriff's office. Ever since the news came of Lewis Halloran's death everyone in her family has been acting strange. Her mother is in tears. Her father is more sullen than ever. And Mark is acting so nervous --- skittish, really --- that it makes her suspicious. As usual he won't give direct answers to her questions. But the authorities insist on interviewing everyone from the wedding. No exceptions. They have no choice. This really annoys Ann: she'd rather be getting ready for Julie's return so that she can support her best friend during this crisis.

They identify themselves to a clerk, who soon escorts Mark to a back room. Once he is gone, a handsome young man in a deputy sheriff's uniform appears. Apparently he was waiting until she is alone. "Hello Ann." She smiles at him. Ann and Peter Brandt used to date in high school. But at the time he didn't seem to have much direction, just a jock who liked hanging out with the other jocks. That made him a cool boyfriend for a teenage girl, but not much else. The breakup didn't go well and she has managed to avoid him in the years since.

"Hi Peter. I see you got promoted. Congratulations." *Who knew he'd turn into someone with real ambitions?* But by the time she saw that in him, too much time had past and besides, Ann had met Mark. Now part of her wishes she had waited. Peter is no longer a cocky, arrogant kid but a young man with a mixture of confidence and humility who has apparently put what happened between them in the past.

"Thanks," he says in warm, friendly way. "I need to talk to you, in private." Ann nods and follows him to his small office. It has only one window, a computer and some metal furniture. There are a couple half-empty boxes on the floor. "Sorry, I'm still getting settled." She smiles. There are pictures on the walls of his glory days in high school, where he played on the football and softball teams.

They each take a seat, Peter across from her with his hands folded on the desk. He hesitates, leading Ann to worry about what he wants to talk about. "There is something you need to know. Actually, I'm not even supposed to tell you about all of it, but I think it's important."

Now she is worried; very worried. "Okay, about what?"

"It's about Mark . . . just what do you know about him?"

What a weird question. "Well, he lost his parents as a kid and he has drifted around a bit." Ann starts to guess where this is leading. "Look, he told me that he had some problems with the law as a teenager but that was long ago and strictly kid stuff."

"Is that all he told you?"

"What are you getting at?"

Peter takes a deep breath and opens a file folder on his desk. He skims a computer printout. "I'm afraid there is more to Mark than what you know."

"What do you mean?"

"He really hasn't told you anything else?"

"Well, come on Peter!" Now Ann feels defensive. This *is* her husband after all. "It's not like people do background checks on farmhands --- or fiancés for that matter. What could it possibly be?" It is with that question that a possibility comes into her head: *could it be drugs? Could that explain the strange text messages and his mysterious disappearances?*

"Mark has been arrested numerous times over the past few years in Baltimore, New York and Boston. All of the incidents involved . . ." she braces to hear the word "drugs" but instead Peter says, "prostitution."

That comes as a shock. She has never seen him with other women. There has to be a mistake. "That's ludicrous. Are you saying my husband's a *pimp*?"

Peter suppresses a smile. *Why should that be funny?* "No, Ann --- he's not a pimp, he's a hooker. Actually, I think 'escort' is the correct term. Most of his clients are elderly men. Granted there have been a few women, but . . ."

"Oh, my God . . . you can't be serious!" Could her husband --- the hunky, masculine, confident very straight acting Mark Bradley --- be a *gay hooker*? It seems too bizarre. But Peter is certain. He refers to the file in front of him. "None of the cases ever got very far because his clients were too well-connected. They didn't want the scandal."

None of this makes any sense to her. But there has to be a reason. "Well, I suppose with Mark's horrible childhood it makes sense. I'm sure he stopped when we got engaged . . ."

"He's still doing it Ann, and has been since he moved to New Hampshire last year. He's been pretty discreet. We only find out a week ago. One of his clients is a doctor Mark was blackmailing who decided to skip town."

Nothing in her life could prepare Ann for the news. "He's fucking men for money? Even after we've been married . . ." The thought frightens her and she still has trouble believing it. Peter looks at another page in his file. "That feed supplier from Faraway Hill --- Ed Connor --- I think your father does business with him." Ann nods still too stunned to say anything. "Well, Mark does business with him too. They were together the other night. Connor claims Mark stole money from him."

"The other night, you mean the night before Julie's wedding?" Peter nods and hands her a one-sheet report. Its true, everything Peter is telling her: on the very night she and Julie were talking about marriage, Ann's own husband was having sex with another man for money. She has known Mr. Connor since she was a little girl, but here is a report with him confessing to hiring Mark over and over for months. All Ann can think of to say is, "but Mr. Connor is so old."

"Mark is being questioned in connection with the murder --- and we are booking him right now for solicitation and theft." Peter gently lays his hand on hers. "I'm really sorry Ann. If we knew all of this sooner, I could have told you before your wedding." A tear running down her cheek, she simply nods. For a time there it seemed as if her life were finally coming together. But it was all a lie. "Actually, Peter, the more I think about it the more it makes sense."

"How so?"

"Mark always gets these text messages. He never tells me what they are about and he always deletes them. He'll disappear for a couple of hours at a time. I never know where. When I ask him he gets annoyed and defensive." Another horrible thought comes into her mind. "Oh, my God . . . what about AIDS, if he's fucking all of these men, does that mean . . ."

"It could mean that he's infected."

"And me too."

Peter nods. "You'll want to get tested."

Ann leans back in her chair, crying a little, and tries to get her bearings. "I am such a fool, a big fool . . . Now I don't know how I'm going to face him or anybody else now. Julie and Greg will be back today. And my parents . . ."

"Don't be so hard on yourself; he was really good at hiding it. As for Mark, you've got at least a day; maybe longer. He's definitely being booked for the prostitution charge. A judge won't be available until tomorrow at the earliest. Plus we have questions for him about the murder."

"Why? We had left the house by that time."

"Well, that brings me to the official reason for talking to you. It's possible that Lewis Halloran was one of his clients and that something went wrong."

"Like what?"

Peter shrugs. "Could be anything; maybe they had a 'session' and Lewis refused to pay. Maybe it was something else. Do you know where your husband was between ten and four?"

It seems that this is one of the few things she *does* know about her husband. "Actually, I do: at home with me."

"You can verify that?"

"He fell asleep before I did. I was too wound up from the day. I think that I finally nodded off around two."

"Well, that probably clears Mark of having anything to do with Lewis' murder."

Maybe, but doesn't clear up anything else for Ann. "Peter, what am I going to do now?" He smiles at her, a surprising and welcome source of strength. "What do you want to do?"

Ann looks at the files again. They are detailed and shocking. The pain and humiliation is too much --- not to mention the fear that Mark gave her HIV. She knows what her mother goes through being married to a man who hurts her over

and over. Ann vowed years ago never to let herself be put in that kind of
ituation. She wipes away her tears, looks Peter straight in the eye and says with a
determined voice: "I want to be rid of the bastard."

✳✳✳✳

The Manchester airport's VIP lounge is a simple but comfortable little room.
There are sofas and waiters and a cash bar among the amenities. But none of
them make the circumstances any easier for Jack Campbell. There are too many
people here as far as he is concerned. Eve and Ben's presence makes sense to
him: they are Julie's parents and Ben the family lawyer. But he wishes Greg's
aunt, Joan Lansing, had stayed away. Greg barely knows the woman and,
besides, her son Matthew is still in shock over finding Lewis' body. She should
be comforting the kid. At least she had the good sense of not bringing her
boy-toy husband along. Karen St. John's presence makes no sense at all. Plus,
having the two of them in the same small space is a little ridiculous: they are both
middle aged rich woman accustomed to dominating a room so much that neither
can do it here. Instead they almost circle each other like two panthers in the wild,
waiting for the other one to make the first move.

Above all, Jack wishes he could be here alone so that he can take Greg in his
arms and tell him everything will be all right.

His cell vibrates. Jack turned the ringer off an hour ago, after another phone
conversation with the one man he hates dealing with the most. "I couldn't get
into the den," Jack told him this morning. "The kid got there before me and
found the body. Then it was chaos." The other man simply got angry, which
made Jack angry: after all *he* is the one being forced to steal something from the
man he loves --- but the opportunity to do it may be gone forever. The man is
calling again. But Jack lets it go to voicemail.

Someone from the airline enters to tell them that the plane has landed and is now
taxing up the runway. The tension level rises with the news. People practically
jump when Ben's cell phone rings. "Couldn't you have turned that thing off?"
Eve says, annoyed.

"No, the sheriff's office needs to be able to reach me," he replies, his exhaustion
obvious. Ben opens the clam shell and steps over to a corner for discretion. "He's
just trying to be a good father, Eve," Karen chastises her.

"I am well aware of that."

Since this morning Jack has been sensing a weird vibe between the two sisters.
He is not sure what it is about and doesn't really care: he just wishes they'd focus
on what is important right now. Ben claps his phone shut and turns back to the
group. "Well, that was the sheriff's office again. They are still interviewing

everyone and searching the house. It could take a long time, so the kids may need to stay in a hotel or Julie's condo."

"This whole situation is preposterous," Joan huffs. "They grill us over and over again and then kick us out of the house. My brother is murdered and we're being evicted from the family homestead." Jack feels like strangling her over that statement --- and from the looks of things other people in the room feel the same way. Joan recognizes this. "I'm sorry. I'm just upset about everything." Eve takes Joan's hand in hers, as if to offer forgiveness for the entire group. Jack doesn't care about forgiving Joan or anyone else. He just cares about Greg.

"In any event," Ben explains, "we've been asked to wait here with the kids. The sheriff himself is coming to brief them. That should give us a better idea of what happens next."

The lounge's door opens as the airline representative escorts Greg and Julie inside. Jack's fears are confirmed: Greg looks distant and morose. Julie is keeping a close watch on him. Before anyone else can do it, Jack pulls his former lover into a bear hug. No one else understands the significance. They just smile warmly as if the two men are something like brothers. Jack reluctantly lets him go, so that everyone else can finally approach them. Joan is the first, taking her nephew briefly into her arms. Everyone else follows, one by one, giving each newlywed a hug or a kiss or a hand shake. Soon they all sit. "Sheriff Reynolds will be here any minute," Ben explains. "He'll have an update on the . . . situation." It is interesting the words people chose to be polite or diplomatic. A murder is now a "situation."

"And don't you worry about the funeral arrangement Greg," Joan says, "I took care of everything --- well, almost everything --- when your Uncle David died. I'm prepared to handle everything for your father." She is determined to act like the Halloran family matriarch. The woman has buried one brother and about to bury another and acts as if this is a source of familial pride. *Ease up,* Jack says to himself. *You are being too hard on her, on everyone.* After all, with her parents and brothers dead Joan *is* the Halloran family matriarch now.

Greg remains quiet. He simply nods. It's a little scary. Jack wishes he could kick everyone else out, even Julie, just to talk to him. But he can't; he must keeping playing the "best bud" role, at least for now.

The door opens again. This time the airline people are letting in Faraway Hill's sheriff and a couple of his officers. Jack met Sheriff Reynolds earlier in the day, when he was being questioned, and he wasn't too impressed. This is a man who has had too many Big Macs in his life and still wants more. He likes his privileges. Fat with graying hair, George Reynolds carries himself off with a kind of overconfidence that borders on arrogant. It comes from holding the same small town job for years, always running for reelection with no challengers, and few checks on his power. He kept referring to Jack as "boy" and "son" in such a condescending way that Jack nearly proved his manhood by punching the old man in his face. "Hello my boy," the sheriff says; only this time he's addressing Greg. "I am very sorry." Greg simply nods. Joan decides to take charge. "Have you found out who killed my brother?"

"This is an ongoing investigation, Mrs. Lansing. There is very little I can tell you yet." Joan is about to say something more when Ben stops her with a warning look. "All right Sheriff," he says in his best lawyer voice. "What *can* you tell us?"

Reynolds puts a hand on Greg's shoulder. It looks a bit ridiculous to Jack: the two never met before and yet the sheriff acts like a surrogate father. "Are you sure that you can handle this, son?" Greg, his cheeks damp from tears, directs his bloodshot eyes to him and simple says in a week voice, "tell me."

"Your father's autopsy is scheduled for later today. It will take a few days for the coroner to provide any helpful information. I can tell you he was shot with a single bullet in the forehead at close range. It was obviously by someone who knows the house well and knew that he could get in and out without detection. It could have been a guest or a member of the staff --- or just anyone with an issue with your father, like a business associate. Does anyone come to mind?"

Greg shakes his head. "I've never known my father to have any enemies." Of course, that's not saying much as Greg knows so little about his father.

"What was your father's relationship with Mark Bradley?" It is a surprising question, one that comes from far left field. Greg swallows hard: *what does he know?* He looks around to see everyone else is also confused. For some strange reason Karen St. John seems to be suppressing a smile. "I . . . I don't understand the question."

Reynolds pauses, obviously trying to find a gentle way to say what he needs to. He can't so he just says it straight out. "Earlier today Mark Bradley was arrested for solicitation."

"Solicitation," Julie asks. "What are you talking about? Soliciting what?"

"Prostitution: he is an escort. It seems that Bradley has been selling his sexual services for years --- mostly to older men --- including men in the area since he moved here. We have a statement by one of his clients and a search of his criminal record reveals a history." Greg stays cautiously quiet while everyone else in the room tries to absorb the shocking news. Mark has been pretty good at hiding his side career, at least until now. Will the police trace him to Mark? Did Mark keep any records? Greg never considered this before. It scares him. "Poor Ann," is all Julie can say. "Does she know?"

"One of my deputies told her this morning. You may want to call her later. I hear she is taking the news hard."

"You think my father was one if his . . . clients?" Greg asks. He hopes not: that would be too weird.

"We have no evidence. It is only a theory. One I may soon discard: Bradley has an alibi that checks out so far." Good, Greg thinks: maybe they will not connect him with Mark. That would be a disaster. "So, what happens now?"

"We are searching the house for any clue, but I suspect that the killer slipped in and out without leaving anything behind, much less the murder weapon. We should know more after the autopsy." Reynolds pauses again, obviously faced with another sensitive matter. "A clue may be in your father's will."

"His will?" Greg looks up at Ben, who is as surprised as he. "If you are thinking that someone killed him to get his money, that doesn't make any sense. I'm his only child. Aunt Joan and a few other relatives may get something, but none of them need to kill for it. They have their own money"

"I understand. We just have to rule out everything. When was the last time he changed his will? Does anyone know?"

"It was just a few weeks ago," explains Ben, avoiding his wife's worried gaze. "But the will is sealed. I can't release it to you until its read --- or judge orders it." The sheriff nods and says that is just what he'll do. In the meantime, either a Faraway Hill officer or a Manchester officer will escort everyone to wherever they need to go until the mansion is all clear. "They can stay with us," Eve offers. The sheriff says his goodbye just as the airline staff arrives with the luggage. But before they leave, Greg takes Ben aside. "Why did Dad change his will? What's in it?"

"I can't tell you Greg, I'm sorry," Ben says looking a little guilty. "You'll just have to wait until the reading." His father's murder, Mark's arrest, Jack and Julie --- this is yet one more thing for Greg to worry about.

✱✱✱✱

Ann spends the day at home, alone. She ignores her mother's calls on both the land line and cell. Julie called twice but Ann isn't ready to talk to her. Mark also called the cell. It was probably the only call the police allowed him to make. She let it go to voicemail.

The first thing Ann did after coming home was throw herself on the bed, pound the mattress with all her might and then cry. These were not tears of sadness but of anger. She had long vowed never to suffer at the hands of a man the way her mother does with Munroe. But that is just what happened: Mark doesn't love her.

He never did. He married Ann for a cover. That became clear from the information Peter showed her. The fact that he --- through Ann --- would eventually inherit the Gale family farm was probably another incentive.

The next thing she did was call a locksmith. One will be at the house first thing in the morning.

Now Ann is packing up all of her husband's belongings: clothes, books, even his sheets. She managed to find plenty of empty boxes in the little house's vacant second floor. She packs up his laptop; including the webcam and the various DVDs he has burned. She doesn't know what is on them and doesn't care. Even the furniture will go: she'll donate it to Goodwill. Most of them are used anyway. They can be replaced.

Ann keeps the wedding album and her dress. She puts her ring back into its box. They can be lifelong reminders never to let something like this happen again.

It is late in the day when Ann finishes. She puts everything into the back of Mark's truck. He can keep that. It was his to begin with and Ann has her own car. A tarp can protect everything until Mark picks it up.

There is only one last thing to decide: her name. Ann always hated the name Gale; it sounds a little too "Wizard of Oz" for her. Besides, it has always been a minute-by-minute reminder that she is Munroe's child. Maybe she'll stay Ann Bradley. That will be the one good thing Mark gives her in the divorce.

****

Down the road inside the farm's main house, her mother isn't thinking about any good things. Lorene is worried. Peter Brandt called earlier in the day to tell her about Mark. She's glad he did --- he has always been a good boy --- because Ann wouldn't on her own. She tries several times to reach her, but Ann won't pick up the phone. If her car wasn't in the shop, Lorene would drive to Ann's house. But she is stuck at the farm with her worries.

All the TV news channels spend the day reporting Lewis Halloran's murder. Every hour they run variations of the same report: that he was killed last night and the police are "moving fast" to solve the crime. The stories always mention the family's business and their history from Colonial times to today. But by late afternoon there is something new: MSNBC begins reporting that "one of the wedding guests has been arrested" but no one is being named. Lorene hopes that doesn't mean Mark. That would be far too humiliating for Ann. Besides, the sooner the murder is solved and put behind everyone the better.

It certainly would be better for Lorene's husband. Munroe has locked himself in that little room at the back of the barn. He thinks she doesn't know about it, but he has never been good at hiding things from her. Every so often she sneaks out to spy on him through the dirty window. While Ann worries her, it's Munroe who scares her. They both know what is coming up and he can't handle it. He managed to sober up for their daughter's wedding, but has been slipping every day since. When word of the murder came, he retreated into the little room and into the bottle. This time he may never emerge. But she needs him and so does Ann. Especially when everyone hears the really big news.

It will change everything.

****

Greg slowly opens his eyes to see Brad Pitt staring back at him.

It takes him a moment to get his bearings. Brad is actually a poster, one of many, covering the rose wallpaper in Julie's childhood bedroom. He also sees a menagerie of stuffed animals from giraffes to monkeys. These strange creatures with their strange smiles are propped on the mock Queen Anne dresser and the mock Queen Anne desk. This is a girl's room with all the silly things girls collect. One of Greg's college girlfriends decorated her dorm this way. Sex with her felt like polyester bestiality --- with an audience of celebrities watching.

The window is open and a slight summer breeze floats in. The sky is dark. Greg has been asleep for hours. Julie insisted that he take a sleeping pill. He had been that stressed ever since getting the news about his father, which was made worse by his worries over Mark. She was right; he feels much better now. Good enough to go downstairs.

"So, are you feeling better?" Eve smiles at him. She is in the living room with Ben and Jack where the three of them are relaxing with some iced tea. Julie stands in the corner, cell phone in hand, deep in a serious conversation.

"Yeah, much better, thanks." He sits in an overstuffed chair and pours himself some tea. "I'm really sorry about being so much trouble."

"It's no trouble," Ben assures him. "We're family now." That makes Greg feel good, really good, for the first time in nearly a day. But Julie, trying to end her conversation, has a worried look on her face. "What's going on?" he asks the others.

Ben and Eve are hesitant to answer, which seems strange to Greg. "She's talking to what's-her-name's mother --- the matron of honor, Ann," explains Jack, "apparently Ann has been out of contact all day ever since learning about her husband."

"Is he still in jail?"

"Yes," says Ben. "He'll be there at least until tomorrow." Greg wonders what Mark is telling the police; hopefully not much. The prospect of yet another scandal ties a knot in his stomach --- especially a scandal that would cost him the support of every person in this room. "I hope you all haven't been just sitting around worried about me." Eve gives him one of her warm smiles. "Of course we are worried about you."

Jack refills his glass. "Sure we are dude, but actually I just got back. All of us staying at the house had to move to hotels while the police investigate. It's been an all-day thing. Apparently the folks around here are deep into the tourist season, so it's been hard."

"So where is everyone?"

"Well, I'm not sure. I know your aunt took some rooms at a B&B in Faraway Hill. I had to get a room at the airport. I really can't speak for anyone else."

Julie claps her phone shut. "I'm sorry," she gives her husband a quick kiss on the cheek before taking a seat. "Mrs. Gale is so worried."

"Has she heard *anything* from Ann?"

"No Mom, nothing at all. I've tried calling her too but she just won't pick up. Who knows how she's reacting to the news about Mark. I'm worried for her. Her whole world has been turned upside down." It's hard for Greg to sympathize. Finding out your husband fucks men for money can hardly be compared to your father being murdered. Besides, considering how much she annoys people Ann Gale --- or Bradley, if you prefer --- could do with a little heartache. As long as Mark keeps his mouth shut, that is.

"Are you feeling any better Greg?"

"I am Julie, thanks." He has to make sure that whatever Mark says or does, it won't cost Greg any more than he already has. Besides, he has a bigger worry: "I still don't understand why anyone would kill Dad."

Ben shrugs. "Neither can I; I've never known him to have enemies like that. Sure, he could play hardball with the best of them, but . . . I just can't think of anyone."

"I'm surprised the sheriff didn't ask for a list of suspects," Jack points out. "I mean, isn't that what they are suppose to do? I always see that in movies and on TV." Ben offers a rueful smile. "Sheriff Reynolds has never dealt with a murder case before. He seems to be guessing his way through this. Personally, I'd prefer he turn it over to the State Police."

"Great, my dad is murdered and we've got Officer Incompetent running the show!" No one knows how to respond to Greg's outburst. He takes a deep breadth to calm down. Maybe there is more going on than he realizes. Maybe answers will be coming soon.

✶✶✶✶

Munroe has been drinking all day, wallowing in his misery, waiting for everyone to learn the truth. Every so often he starts a letter to his daughter, each time trying to explain what happened in hopes that she'll forgive him. But he only gets so far and the tears begin to flow. He crumples up each attempt and tosses it to the floor --- and pours himself more vodka.

A gentle but firm knock at the door startles him. No one knows about Munroe's little hideaway. But someone is there. He tries to ignore them. It doesn't work: the person knocks again. "Munroe, I know you're in there." The woman's voice is familiar, but he isn't completely sure who it is. "Munroe, open the door. I need to speak to you. I want to help you." Hesitantly, he rises and stumbles to the locked door. Opening it, a ghost from his past stands there smiling. It's Karen St. John, looking elegant in a long black dress, black veil on her head and even black gloves. "Hello Munroe. It has been much too long."

It has been a long time. They haven't really spoken in twenty years, not since small town girl Karen Scott left Faraway Hill and eventually married the older and very rich Martin St. John. "Why are you here, now?" Karen just smiles and gently pushes him aside to let herself in. The room surprises her a little. It is like a little memorial to his life with Lorene and Ann: photos all along the walls from birthdays, school events and family trips. A battered old metal file cabinet has the faded drawings of a little girl to her father; all hung with promotional magnets from feed suppliers and hardware stores. And on the desk and floor are wads of crumpled paper.

Munro is not happy to see her. He plops back into his chair and pours himself another drink. "How sad you are, my friend," she says, "just sitting there all alone."

"We ain't friends. We was never friends. Hell, you and Lorene were just maids together at the big house. That's all."

"No, that's not all. Lewis Halloran hurt us both." Munroe frowns but says nothing. Karen knows too much about him and his life as it is. "It's true, Munroe. I had to leave town because of him, and you have had to raise Ann under a cloud all these years because of him."

"It don't matter no more. The man's dead."

"Yes, yes he is," Karen looks closely at one photo. "This one is nice. Where was this taken, at Applecrest?" Munroe just nods. Applecrest Farms over in Hampton Falls has been around for nearly a century. It is a popular spot for area families. The picture must have been taken during one of the farm's fall weekend festivals. Ann looks to be about seven or eight as she stands next to a smiling Munroe. "You two look so happy there."

Munroe says nothing but Karen can see a tear slide down his cheek. "Let me help you, please." She opens up her purse and offers him a little brown bottle. "You'll love this." He looks it over. The label has been torn off. "What is it?"

"A flavor enhancer; some of the better nightclubs in New York are using it these days."

He shrugs, unscrews the cap and pours a little of the clear brew into his vodka. But before he can try it, Karen pulls something else out of her purse, something unexpected. "What the hell are you doing with *that*, woman?"

"You're right; I shouldn't have it. Please take it." Munroe grasps the gun firmly by its handle. He hates guns. Despite being a rural man he loathes hunting. "Why the devil do you have a gun?"

"Why, it's the gun I used to kill Lewis Halloran."

Shocked, Munroe throws it across the room, letting bang hard to the floor. "Are you *insane*, woman?" Her calm is even scarier than her statement. Karen treats murder like ordering dinner. "Of course, not; I am quite sane. Everything I am doing has been carefully considered. It will be best for all of us, including you."

"Get the fuck out!" Instead, Karen pulls up a battered old wood chair and takes a seat. She picks up one of the crumpled papers from the desk and unfolds it. "A letter to Ann; how sweet." Munroe tries to grab it from her and fails. "That ain't none of your business." Karen starts to read it out loud: "Let's see, 'my darling Ann, you have always been a better daughter than I deserve . . .'"

"Stop it and get the hell out --- and take the damned gun with you!" But Karen doesn't move. She just sits there smiling. Frustrated, Munroe reaches for his glass. The vodka tastes odd, something he can't quite identify. He looks up at Karen. "What the fuck is this?" She says nothing and joins the world in becoming blurrier and blurrier, darker and darker until there is nothing at all.

Once she is satisfied that it is over, Karen starts to read each of Munroe's at-tempted letters. Some will work better than others. These she will leave behind; the rest will come with her. A careful examination of the room reveals nothing that can be traced to her. When Karen leaves, slamming the door behind her, it automatically relocks from the inside.

The police will find what they need to find. The whole moment is very satisfying. There is nothing like a plan working as intended. Expect, maybe, one woman's personal justice.

Her daddy would be pleased.

EPISODE SIX

As jail cells go, this one isn't bad. Compared to the one he stayed in just outside Baltimore, this cell is a 4-star hotel room. The upper bunk is fairly comfortable and the space not too cramped. There are no sick urine smells. And he doesn't have to contend with a cellmate. Still, Mark Bradley would rather not be here, lying on his back staring at the ceiling.

The cops kept asking him questions about Ed Connor and his other clients --- at least, the clients they know about, which aren't many --- and even about Lewis Halloran's murder. But Mark has been around the block enough to know that the best response is no response. He simply declined to answer any of their questions; they in turn declined to let him go home. He spent the night.

One thing that really angers him is Ann, who still has not returned his call. *What the hell good is it to have a wife if she won't bail you out?*

A loud bang gets Mark's attention. He sits up to see the young deputy sheriff standing on the other side of the bars. He does not look happy.

"We're letting you go," Peter Brandt tells him.

"I guess the wife finally came through for me."

"Not exactly," he tells Mark. "Old man Connor is dropping the charges. Without them, everything else we suspect you for . . . well, let's just say the rest just can't hold."

Mark laughs, "bummer, dude; better luck next time." Peter isn't sharing the joke. He seems to have one of his own. "Actually, it all kind of sucks for you more than it does for me."

"I don't get it."

"The reason Mr. Connor is dropping the charges is because his wife doesn't want to deal with the scandal any more. Considering the fact that the word is out about your little . . . well, your little side business, I think it's safe to say that your other clients won't have anything to do with you, either."

"Shit." That means everything is collapsing for him. Again.

"Oh, it gets even worse." Peter finally laughs. "Your wife --- the one you were counting on to bail you out --- also knows about your clients. She's kicked you out. All of your stuff is in the back of your truck which is parked right outside. You've been fired from the Gale farm. Ann has even changed the locks on your --- her --- house. So now your jobless and homeless, *dude.*"

Furious, Mark pounds his fist against the wall.

"The only good thing is that we've cleared you of Lewis Halloran's murder." That's *not the only good thing*, Mark thinks, but he lets the junior cop enjoy his moment. The guy stands there with a cocky grin for a moment and then opens the cell door. After about an hour of processing, Mark is back on the street. Sure enough: his pick-up is parked right outside the sheriff's station with boxes under a tarp in the back. He digs around, opening boxes until he finds his laptop. With everything else lost, it's time for Mark's insurance policies to kick in. He takes out his cell and texts Greg Halloran: "Meet me today ASAP or else."

When Greg gets the message, he's alone in Julie's room. She's down the hall in the shower and he is nearly dressed for the day. The message from Mark stokes his worries: *what did he tell the police?* Something must have happened to get him out so fast. They definitely *do* need to meet ASAP.

Unfortunately it seems, so does everyone else. He has several voicemail and text messages. Some are from business associates expressing condolence. But most are from family members asking for details on the crime and especially on funeral plans. The funeral: Greg hadn't even thought about it until this morning. He has no idea what his father would want. They never discussed it; but then, they hardly discussed anything important until very recently.

He had already decided to go into the office today to start distancing himself from all the drama. Julie isn't happy about it, but maybe she will be willing to handle the funeral arrangements. He'll ask when she returns from the shower.

Staying in the King household has been a little odd for him. Greg has lived in dorms and mansions, penthouses and hotel suites. Aside from his New York apartment, he has never really spent time in a "normal" home. The King house is so perfectly upper middle class --- something close to a 1950s sitcom --- that it feels a little surreal.

Greg sends a text to Mark instructing him to meet in a vacant part of the Millyard. There are parts of the huge former mill still being developed. It will be the easiest, quickest and most discreet place they can meet.

And hopefully it will be the last time.

****

It seems a little strange to wake up alone. Ann has only been married a few weeks, but she quickly became comfortable sharing her bed with a man.

Unfortunately, so did her husband.

The whole house, small as it is, seems empty with Mark's things gone. As good as it felt taking charge of the situation, Ann still feels like a failure. Getting married was the first truly adult thing she has done in her life, and it exploded in her face in the most shocking, painful and humiliating way possible.

But she must face the world again. There is no other choice.

The TV news channels are still running stories about Lewis Halloran's death, which also made the front page of this morning's *Union Leader* for the second day in a row. Yesterday's edition had only the basics because the death was reported so close their print time. Today's paper has extensive coverage on the man's life and his legendary family. You'd think royalty had been assassinated; then again, the Hallorans probably *are* the closest to royalty that New Hampshire has.

Ann showers, dresses and takes drives up the highway to the main farmhouse to deal with her parents. It is definitely not something she looks forward to. Lorene will probably cry and act like it's her fault somehow. Munroe will gripe about how the world is against him and then retreat to wherever he retreats to drink away the day. And Ann will leave them feeling guilty.

But nothing could prepare her for what she *does* see driving through the gate: police cars parked around the barn. Worried, she pulls up to one of the officers. He looks familiar but Ann can't think of his name. "I'm the Gales' daughter. What's going on?"

"Sorry miss, I'm not allowed to say," he gives her a second look. "Oh, yeah I recognize you. Your husband was brought in yesterday. Aren't you Peter Brandt's friend?"

"Yes, what's happened? Are my parents okay?" A scary thought comes to her mind: *would Mark get even with me by hurting them?*

"I think you'd better talk to him." He directs her to park next to the house. Peter meets her at the door. The look on his face telegraphs something awful. "Oh, my God, Peter, what's going on?" Peter ushers her into the living room and puts his arms around her. His warmth and caring are comforting, but she still needs to know. "Peter, is my mother all right? Did Mark do something to them?"

"Your mother is fine and Mark isn't involved." He gently sits them both on the sofa. "Mom is okay," she asks "but not Dad?" *Did Munroe finally do it? Did he finally drink himself into oblivion?*

"I'm sorry Ann, but your dad died last night, a suicide. It looks like he deliberately took some poison."

"Oh, God," as disgusted as she gets with Munroe, she wasn't expecting this. "He killed himself . . ."

"I'm afraid so."

Ann starts to cry. Unlike last night, these tears are ones of sadness and regret rather than anger. The sober Munroe, the good Munroe, is the man she misses. That Munroe took her to carnivals and read her stories. She wanted him to come back. She was hoping he'd come back. But the drunk Munroe stole him forever. She surrenders herself to her grief, drenching Peter's shoulder with her tears. "Where is my mother," she asks, finally composed enough to wiping away her cheeks.

"Upstairs. She found the body and it really freaked her. The paramedics had to sedate her. We were about to call you when you came."

She gets up. "I should check on her." But Peter stops her. "Ann, wait, there's more." She sits again, but he hesitates. Whatever it is, the news is pretty bad, even worse than the news of Munroe's suicide. "Peter, after everything I've been through in the last 24 hours, I just wish you'd come right out and say it."

"Okay . . . we found a gun." Ann finds that very strange. "That doesn't make sense. Dad hated guns. Always did."

"It's the same make and model as the one that killed Lewis Halloran. It even has a silencer." Ann looks him straight in the eye. The thought is incredible: "Are you saying that my father killed Mr. Halloran?"

"No, no . . . I mean we don't know for sure. It could be just a strange coincidence."

"Peter, its more than that: it's crazy. They didn't know each other. They had no connection."

He nods. "I understand. Like I said, it could be a coincidence. We'll know more after we dust for prints and run a ballistics test."

"He couldn't have Peter," she explains. "Dad was too much of a coward. That's why he drank. He probably bought the gun and was too afraid to use it."

"You might be right."

"Of course I am." Ann rises, takes a deep breath and walks over to the stairs. She needs to check on her mother. But before going up, she stops and turns back to him. "Peter, did Dad leave a note?"

"Sort of . . . it looks like he had started to write one, even went through a couple of drafts, but for whatever reason didn't or couldn't finish it." He adds gently, "but it was addressed to you." She doesn't know what make of that. The two of them barely got along since he began hitting the bottle again last year. Instead, she goes up to her mother's room where she finds Lorene in a deep sleep. Ann lies gently on the bed next to her. With her father dead and husband gone, the only family she has left in this world is the lonely woman who gave birth to her.

Outside, Peter meets up with Sheriff Reynolds. The old man, as fat as ever, even finds simple walking taxes his stamina. He looks around for a placed to sit but finds nothing. "Is that the daughter who came by?"

"Yes, sir; she's up with Mrs. Gale right now." Reynolds takes a moment to catch his breath then looks intently at his deputy. "You know what I'm thinking boy."

"Ann says Mr. Gale barely knew Mr. Halloran, and that they have no connection."

"Nope, they have a connection: we just haven't found it yet."

"But sheriff, how could he have gotten into the house without anyone seeing him or knowing about it --- and what about the lack of fingerprints?"

"Boy, sometimes the easiest explanations are the right ones. You forget: Mrs. Gale used to work in that house. Sure it was years ago, but the place hasn't changed much. He's been there before, knows the layout. Add all of the people coming and going --- caterers, temp workers for the wedding and such --- he could have easily blended in. As for fingerprints: anything is possible. He owns a farm, and farmers have plenty of gloves."

Peter nods. That makes sense, but "what's the motive?"

"Damned if I know, but we'll find out. It's probably staring at us in the face."

✳✳✳✳

Julie knows little about Joan Halloran's other husbands, but her current one probably should be studied in a laboratory somewhere. Almost young enough to be her son, he has the wide-eyed wonder of someone even less sophisticated. Paul Lansing has been treating their trip to the funeral home as an adventure, and Joan seems just fine with that. Every so often Matthew has to urge him "not to touch that".

To be fair, even Julie is impressed with the Goodwin Funeral Home. She has heard about the place, but has never been inside before. Housed in a handsome Victorian mansion, the Goodwin has been providing funeral services to

Manchester's elite and near-elite since the 1870s. Only two families have owned it in all that time. Joan called them the minute the sheriff's office said they could take Lewis' body. Julie has been especially grateful for their speed and discretion during the last few dizzying hours. They are making things so much easier.

Still, there are decisions that need to be made and Julie and Joan have been designated to make them. Part of her likes being useful, but Julie admits to herself that she does feel a bit cheated: this is supposed to be her honeymoon, after all.

Matthew has reluctantly agreed to take Paul on a walk through the well-manicured grounds so they can meet with the staff. A big issue will be security. Julie's first impulse was to hold the service in a church. But both the Faraway Hill Police and the Manchester Police strongly advised against that. The Goodwin's grounds --- there very ones Matthew and Paul are exploring --- can provide a buffer from the media and other unwanted people.

But just as that was getting started, Julie's cell rings. It is the deputy sheriff, so she politely excuses herself to the hall. "Hello, Peter? What is it? Any news?"

"Sort of; I know you're close to the Gales so I thought I should call you."

"Oh, my God, don't tell me Mark is causing them trouble. I know Ann kicked him out; did he try something?"

"No, no, it has nothing to do with Mark."

"Then what is it?"

"Munroe Gale is dead."

"Oh, my God . . . what happened?"

"It looks like suicide. I'm sorry, I can't tell you anymore. But since your Ann's friend I thought you'd like to call her."

She thanks him and quickly dials Ann's home phone. The machine picks up. Instead of leaving a message, she calls the cell. Voice mail. This time Julie leaves a message and wonders what is going on with the world these days.

✶✶✶✶

The Merrimack River starts in the middle of the state, where the Pemigewasset and Winnipesaukee rivers meet. It flows southward, traveling 110 miles past Concord, Manchester and Nashua before dipping into Massachusetts and flowing east to the Atlantic. It is a beautiful river, historic and impressive. Navy ships have been named in its honor, and Henry David Thoreau wrote about it. It is one of the first and best things one sees when entering Manchester. The second thing is what lies adjacent to it: the city's historic Millyard District. It is here where the fabric was created that made little New Hampshire a big deal for generations. Dominating the district is the old Amoskeag mill, a sprawling multi-building complex that powered the region for almost a century. There were other mills of course, including the Halloran mill. But they were all --- are all --- dwarfed by the Amoskeag.

While the architecture of the Amoskeag is fairly simple, the former Halloran mill is very much high Victorian. Completed around 1900, it was the family's attempt to be impressive on a smaller scale. It has towers, detailed overhangs and beautifully carved doors. Newspapers across the country wrote about it as "a grand palace for New Hampshire's working class." Today production has moved elsewhere --- a smaller factory a few miles away and giant one in "right to work" Georgia --- neither of which can be called a palace.

Most of the Halloran mill has been remodeled, but there is still a section not far from the river where work is still in its early stages. The interior has been gutted, but only a minimal amount of construction has begun. There are plenty of crates and equipment everywhere, but there are no workers today. They are busy on other projects in other parts of the building. It is a perfect place for Greg Halloran to meet discretely with Mark Bradley --- hopefully for the last time. Unfortunately, Mark is late and Greg is getting impatient. He begins pacing when he hears, "sorry for being so late, dude."

Mark is standing at the entrance, confidently smiling, with a laptop hanging from a shoulder strap. "It couldn't be helped. I had to prepare."

Greg just wants to get this over with. He needs to go back and deal with business --- and especially to find out what the police are doing. "How did you get out of jail?"

"Same way I always do. Upstanding men like you hate it when the world finds out they've been fucking a guy. You should know that."

"In other words, the charges --- whatever they were --- were dropped." Mark shrugs, walks over to a crate and sets-up his laptop. Greg is still worried, though, and wonders just what he is up to. "What did you tell the police?"

"Nothing, dude; I've dealt with cops before. The best thing to say to them is nothing. By the way, my sympathies about your dad --- have they caught the bastard yet?" Greg doubts that Mark really cares. He points at the laptop, suspicious. "Why is that here?" Mark enters his password and clicks open a file. "Don't get pissed and don't bother trying to wreck my computer. I've got copies of this."

"Copies of what?" Mark clicks an icon and Windows Media Player opens with a picture of his bedroom. The shower can be heard in the video's background. On the screen, Greg enters the room and quickly strips down to his briefs when a naked Mark appears at the bathroom door to ask "I was wondering how fast you'd show up."

"You fucking bastard!" Greg rushes to the laptop but Mark grabs it and raises his hand to stop him. "Don't try it dude. You know full well that I can beat the shit out of you --- and I really don't think you want to explain how *that* happened to your bride." Mark has him and Greg knows it. "You are an ass," is all he can think to say.

"Nope, just a businessman; and like all good businessmen I like to be ready for a changing marketplace." *In other words,* Greg realizes, *Mark wants money.* "So what do you want?" He has no idea what to expect. He's never been blackmailed before.

"Well, it seems my own marriage has hit the shitter, so I'm skipping town."

"Good; don't let the door hit you on your way out."

"Wow, man that was almost funny. But I'm leaving in style." He pulls a thick manila envelope from his pocket and tosses it to Greg. Inside is the lease to an apartment in Greenwich Village and bank account information. "You are my new patron, dude. The rent includes utilities and you are sending me two grand a month on top of that." Greg forces himself to remain steady. He has never been this angry before. "That's a hell of a price. How long do you expect me to keep supporting you?'

"As long as I've got you on tape, that's how long."

"Like hell; if I'm giving you money, you're giving me that recording --- and all the copies."

"You think I'm a fool? This is my insurance. All you need to do is pay."

"So this is eternal blackmail."

"Think of it as a long-term investment --- unless you want this thing posted all over the web. Personally I think it'll be a hit. The show is pretty cool --- you even arch your back when shoot into me. People will love it."

"You fucking little . . ."

Mark laughs, takes his laptop and leaves Greg all alone, knowing that he has no other choice.

****

Greg is so furious when he returns to the office that he ignores his secretary and slams the door closed behind him. He is about ready to smash something when she timidly knocks on the door. "What!" It opens and the diminutive young lady with auburn hair cautiously steps inside. "Sir, your wife has been calling. She says it's important." He takes a deep breath and nods. "Fine, I'll call her shortly."

"Are you alright sir?" She is still a little shaken by Lewis' death.

"No, I'm not, but then the whole world is fucked up these days." She just stands there quietly, not sure what to say or do. He's feeling a little calmer now. "You know, maybe coming in was a mistake. Why don't you take the day off? I'll be leaving soon myself."

Grateful, she smiles, thanks him and quickly leaves after turning off her computer and grabbing her purse. After she is gone, Greg looks at the crumpled folder in his hand and decides to get it all over with. With one phone call and a fax, all of Mark's arrangements are made. Everything about the process makes him cringe, from calling his banker to signing the lease and pressing "send" on the fax machine. Hopefully Greg will never see the bastard again. But he doubts it.

It suddenly occurs to him how quiet the place is. Most of the executives chose not to come, presumably out of respect for his dad. There is hardly anyone at all in the company's suite. This is the first moment of true peace Greg has had since before the wedding and he is determined to enjoy it. He takes off his blazer, loosens his tie, and lies across the sofa. It's not very comfortable, but it will do.

The view from the window creates something of a disconnect: he can see, but not hear, people coming and going from the many redbrick buildings of the Millyard District. The effect leaves Greg feeling like he is separate from the world in a nice, safe bubble. He drifts off into a comfortable slumber.

Sometime later Greg hears another knock on the door. "Who is it?" he growls.

"It's me."

Greg opens his eyes to see Jack standing at the doorway. He looks concerned. "Quiet around here today, huh?" Greg isn't sure how he feels about their being along together. He sits up. "More than I thought." He feels a little disoriented. Outside the window, large groups of people are walking to their cars to go home.

"Everybody's been trying to get hold of you."

"Sorry, I had a meeting I couldn't get out of. What time is it?"

"About 4:30."

"Shit," he can't believe how long he's been asleep. That seems to be all he's been doing the last two days. "Sorry about that. I lost track of time; any news?"

"Well, the police released your dad's body today. Julie and your Aunt Joan are working on the funeral arrangements. They want to do it tomorrow night, while the rest of the family is still in town." That makes sense. Everyone will need to go back to their lives as soon as the cops give the green light. "I'm sure whatever they decide will be fine with me."

"They want to know if you feel up to speaking at the service." Greg thinks about that for a minute. He realizes that he'd have nothing to say. Lewis was such a peripheral part of his life for so long that the local obituary editor probably knows more about his father than he does. "No, let other people do it."

Jack sits down next to him and puts his arm around Greg. It feels more brotherly than the act of a former lover. "I wish you'd talk to me. I love you, man, and I want to help."

"I know, but everything is so . . . confusing right now."

"I believe that."

"Dad and I, we weren't very close. But the last few weeks he was really trying to change that."

"Cool; how?"

"Well, like the other day --- right down the hall in his office --- he referred to the wedding as a 'new start' and a chance for him to correct some things."

"He sounds like a great guy." *Yes, he does.* So, Greg remembers, is Jack. "I love you too, Jack, but I can't leave Julie."

"I know," Jack says, "and I owe you an apology. A lot of apologies: for breaking up with you last year because I was too cowardly to tell my dad about us; for the last few days, playing these little games with you." It feels good to hear him say that. Greg wishes Jack had come through like that long ago.

"You know, I have told my mom and brother."

That is a surprise. Jack was always circumspect where is family is concerned. "You told them about me?"

"Not exactly; I told them I'm bi."

Greg is impressed. He has never had the guts to tell his family, although he was willing to for Jack's sake. "How did they take it?"

"Mom freaked a little, but seems okay with it. Nick didn't seem all that surprised. I'm not sure what to make of that."

"What about your dad?"

Jack shrugs. "Mom says to wait. She really insisted. But I will tell him when the time is right."

"It's not that big of a deal anymore. You might fall in love with a girl. I did."

Jack smiles. "Let's get you home."

****

Sheriff George Reynolds has come to the conclusion that he is too old, too tired and too important to deal mundane matters like driving. So he returns to the Gale farm with Deputy Sheriff Peter Brandt at the wheel. The last few days have been very stressful for the aging sheriff, whose crimes rarely go beyond traffic tickets and the odd domestic disturbance. A high-profile murder is not par for the course.

The initial result of their investigation has convinced Reynolds of what happened in the deaths of Lewis Halloran and Munroe Gale. He is certain of the what, when and where of the cases --- he just wants to confirm the why. Young Brandt has been encouraging him to wait and do a more thorough investigation. But Reynolds is determined that his sleepy little town go back to being a sleepy little town as soon as possible.

Besides, he has a pretty good idea Munroe's connection to Lewis. It is so obvious, the sheriff thinks to himself, that it is a wonder no one thought of it before.

Ann Bradley greets them at the door. She seems relieved to see Peter, who asks her "have you seen or heard from Mark?" She shakes her head. "Well, I doubt if you will. We had to let him go, but it looks like he skipped town this afternoon. One of our people spotted him at the airport."

"Good, I hope I never see the bastard again."

It is a bad sign of the times, Reynolds thinks, that a good farm girl like her should get mixed up with a gay prostitute. Those damned fags will ruin this state.

"Have you spoken to Julie at all?"

"Yes, a little while ago. She offered to come over but I didn't want to put her out. She's up to here in rushed funeral plans." That is something Ann will also need to deal with soon.

She escorts the two officers into the living room where a nervous Lorene Gale is sitting quietly on the sofa. Ann joins her, taking her mother's hand in her own. She looks to Peter for support and he offers a comforting smile.

"Ladies," the sheriff begins a bit too ceremonially. "We have been able to answer a few questions, but we need your help to answer the rest."

"Of course," Ann says. Both women have been crying on and off all day. It has obviously been an emotional rollercoaster for them. "We'll help however we can." Lorene stays silent. The older woman looks like a little girl whose has been caught in a lie. Reynolds suspects that is very much the case.

"It seems young lady that your father was attempting to write you a suicide note. But for whatever reason he couldn't finish it before taking his own life." Lorene starts looking scared. Reynolds expected this. Ann doesn't like his approach, which he also expected. "Must you be so blunt?" she asks. "Peter, please ask him . . ."

"I'm sorry, Ann. The sheriff needs to do this his way."

"Thank you, son . . . now the gun we found in the barn *has* proven to be the one used to kill Lewis Halloran. The only fingerprints on it are Munroe's." Ann is shocked at this news --- and her mother's reaction: it is as if Lorene knows what is coming and is more frightened by it than anything else in her life. All of this is happening as Reynolds predicted. "The bottle of poison contained a fertilizer derivative, something a farmer can easily have on hand. His were the only fingerprints on it. There is no evidence of anyone else involved."

"But none of this makes any sense," Ann protests. "My dad hardly knew Lewis Halloran."

Reynolds stares directly into Lorene's eyes, as if piercing into her. "That isn't quite true, is it Mrs. Gale?" Lorene starts to cry. "Please don't . . ." *Bingo*, thinks Reynolds: he is right. He just needs the woman to say it.

"Mom, what is he talking about?"

"I think that we should let your mother tell the story. How about it Mrs. Gale? I'm sure you have been expecting this moment for a long time. You've probably rehearsed it in your head over and over."

Lorene takes a deep breath to regain some self control. The moment she has feared for 23 years has finally happened. "Ann, dear, I want you to know that what I did, I did because I love you. So did your father."

"Mom, you are really starting to scare me."

"Mrs. Gale, please start at the beginning, which I suspect was years ago." Lorene nods, her eyes slowly tearing. "More years that I care to admit . . . it all started back when Karen Scott and I were working as maids at the Halloran mansion. It was the night of Lewis' bachelor party. They were having it in Faraway Hill while Lilly --- his fiancé --- was having her bridal shower in Manchester. Lewis' brother David was there and some of their college friends. A small group." Lorene pauses a moment to gather her thoughts and try to control her emotions. A worried Ann glances at Peter who says nothing because the sheriff made it clear earlier that he shouldn't.

"Anyway," Lorene continues, "Frederick the butler had to have some last minute surgery so everything about the party fell to Karen and me . . . we were young, so young and the only women among these rich, handsome young men . . . soon we felt more like party guests than servants . . . it was a wonderful time." She smiles at that part of the memory and reaches for a tissue to dab at her eyes. "Well, at one point Karen went off with one of David's frat buddies. I never really knew what happened except that she quit a few days later. Eventually I was alone with Lewis. It was so nice. We talked, really talked. No one ever had a serious talk with me before. Not even Munroe --- and we were engaged." More tears roll down her cheeks.

Ann is confused and worried. "I don't understand where any of this is leading, but it's obviously upsetting her, Sheriff. Peter, please . . ." But Reynolds interrupts her to say, "You got pregnant that night didn't you Mrs. Gale?"

"Yes, Sheriff, I got pregnant with my daughter that night." Embarrassed, she avoids Ann shocked expression. Her daughter has never heard this story before, and it contradicts everything Ann has ever known or assumed about her parents. "I had to keep it a secret --- Lilly Halloran demanded that --- and Munroe agreed to marry me despite it all."

"Are . . . are you saying that *Lewis Halloran was my father*?" The news shocks Ann as nothing else can, not even learning truth about her own husband just 24 hours ago. *Can it be true?* There were times growing up when she fantasized that someone other than Munroe was her father, usually a celebrity or a TV character. When she was ten, she used to pretend Mike Brady. It was a silly, little girl thing to do. Now it seems a childish fantasy might actually be real.

"Munroe raised you. He loved you so much. You were his daughter in every other way."

Hurt and angry, Ann pulls her hand from her mother. How could she lie to her like this all her life? "Oh, my God . . ." The act of distancing herself seems to pain Lorene more than any knife. "Lewis cared about you too. There were so many times when he wanted to claim you. But Mrs. Halloran --- Lilly --- wouldn't have it . . . and every time poor Munroe would start drinking."

"Is that why he started up again last year, when she died?"

Lorene nods. "He was so afraid to lose you. He always was. He'd hide in a bottle when that happened. A week ago, Lewis told us he was changing his will to make sure you would be included. He planned to tell the world after Greg's wedding."

"Which is why Munroe killed Lewis," Reynolds says concluding the story, "and since he couldn't live with the guilt, Munroe committed suicide."

Through her tears, Lorene can barely say, "I suppose so."

Ann falls quiet, too furious with her mother to even speak. Lorene reaches her hand out but her daughter refuses to take it. Instead she rises, turns her back on Lorene and asks the sheriff coldly, "now what happens?"

Reynolds wasn't sure how Ann would handle the news, but he didn't expect this. "Well, young lady, I am meeting with the Hallorans in the morning to tell them the truth. Then I am holding a press conference to inform the media. We'll formally wrap up the case in about a week."

"Fine."

"The coroner will release your father's body in a few days," explains Peter. "I'll be glad to help with the arrangements if you like." Ann still won't look at Lorene. Instead she simply says, "Talk to Mrs. Gale about that; it doesn't involve me." And then, without saying another word, she walks out the door slamming it shut behind her.

EPISODE SEVEN

Brady-Sullivan Plaza rises 20 stories over Manchester's busy Elm Street. Arguably the most prestigious office building in the city, the Brady-Sullivan is a handsome, modern glass and steel structure built in the early 70s, encompassing an entire city block with its tower and shopping mall. It was quite a victory when, ten years ago, Ben King and Melvin Waite moved their small law offices to the 17th floor. It said to all of New England that these two men had Arrived.

Unfortunately, what will arrive this morning is a federal investigator.

It really annoys Eve, as they enter the lobby, that the FBI chose today of all days to meet with her husband. Lewis Halloran will be buried this afternoon, and she still hasn't had a chance to call Lorene Gale about Munroe's death. But the feds insist on moving full speed with their investigation, so now they must confront head-on Mel's embezzlement.

Just before they get to the elevators, she picks up a copy of this morning's *Union Leader*. The front page has another large story on Lewis' death. This time, there is a lot more about the sheriff. "For a man who says he hates dealing with the press," she complains during the ride up, "George Reynolds sure likes the attention." In about two hours he'll be briefing the Hallorans on what the investigation has uncovered. The Kings will be there, lending their support. Then, in an oddly theatrical style, the sheriff will hold a press conference in Faraway Hill's town square with the famous statue of John Halloran behind him. It will be a good backdrop on TV news.

"You mean, good 'ol Sheriff Taylor?" Ben says in a wonderfully mocking tone that makes his wife smile. Neither of them has ever liked Reynolds. They certainly didn't vote for him.

A few pages in is a small article on Munroe Gale's suicide. "Poor Lorene," Eve sighs. "I keep meaning to call her." But mostly she worries about Julie and Greg and the coming news --- no one but Ben and Eve knows what's in Lewis' will --- and it will shock everyone. Eve also worries about her husband. Ben has been strong, almost stoic, since learning that his partner ran off with most of the firm's money. Maybe just a little too strong. She wouldn't mind it if he shed a tear or two. But that is not his style.

Today's meeting is supposed to be mostly a briefing. The federal investigator assigned to the case will update them and then request whatever materials he needs. "What is this man's name again?" she asks as they enter the firm's suite of offices. "King & Waite: Attorneys at Law" is emblazed in gold letters on the glass door.

"Agent Pembroke; that's all I know."

The suite is filled with empty chairs. Barry Studer and the secretaries were given the day off in honor of Lewis' death. They might even be at the funeral today. The two of them go directly into Ben's private office. "This shouldn't take too long. We can be at the Halloran place in time to be there for the kids."

Eve sits on the leather sofa on the far side of the room. She helped him pick out all of the office's furniture, and she loves this sofa. It is warm and comfortable. "Well, I can't believe that the sheriff has news so fast, do you?" Ben checks messages on his desk, but there is nothing important. He sits next to Eve, placing his arm around her. "I don't know," Ben says with a sigh. "The problem with small town police --- like in Faraway Hill --- is that they are used to small town crime. I wish he'd asked the State Police --- or even the Manchester Police --- for help."

"He's so damned arrogant. I think he's held that job for 17 years too long."

"Eve, he's only had it for 16."

"My point exactly." Ben smiles at that and is about to say something more when they hear a noise in the outer office. He rises, walks over to the door and sees a handsome middle age woman standing there. Her face is as severe as her navy suit, and just as formal. "Are Benjamin King?"

"Yes, and you are ---"

"Agent Carol Pembroke, FBI."

They shake hands. She barely smiles: this woman is definitely all business. Ben escorts her into his office where he introduces her to Eve. "Good morning," the agent says perfunctorily. "I'll get right to the point: Melvin Waite left the country five days ago. We've tracked him to the Caribbean and then to Belize, where the trail as gone cold."

That was fast, Ben thinks, and asks "What about the money? Does he have it with him?"

"Before leaving, he wired most of it to Luxembourg. Unfortunately Mr. King, they have some of the most secretive banking laws in the world. We can't even be sure the level of cooperation to expect from the authorities there." Ben nods with a frown. He has heard of that before. It's possible that the money is gone forever. A lifetime of work disappears through a few clicks on a computer keyboard.

"Why did he do it?" Eve wonders out loud. "Does anyone know? Was he gambling again?"

"Not that we can tell, Mrs. King. It seems like something he planned very quickly. That's why I thought it might be a good idea if we met here, personally. What were his activities in the last few weeks?"

"Wow, that's tough to say," explains Ben. "Mel and I have separate schedules and separate clients. Plus, my daughter just got married . . . and there is her father-in-law's death . . ."

"Yes, I know sir --- and my condolences on Mr. Halloran's murder --- but surely there was something unusual."

Ben thinks about it a moment. "Well, he had been pretty secretive and I guess he *was* avoiding me. I was so swamped that it wasn't until I discovered he was gone that I was aware of anything wrong."

"What about the other staff members?"

"We are a small, specialized office. It is just me, Mel and our junior attorney, Barry Studer. And we each have our own secretary, plus a receptionist."

"I'd like to speak with them." Ben isn't happy with that prospect. "Is there a problem Mr. King?"

"No, just that . . . I haven't told them anything yet."

"I don't think that can be avoided any more, sir." Ben nods. That doesn't mean he's looking forward to it. It also means the media will find out, along with all of the firm's clients. If it isn't all handled well, the firm could fold.

They get down to work. Agent Pembroke insists on going through key files to try to learn more about Mel's intentions and activities. There is a lot, and it takes awhile. For much of the time Eve can only sit patiently. Eventually she turns on the news to see a reporter in Faraway Hill's town square with a brief update. But Ben and Pembroke aren't done yet, so Eve goes into the outer office to call her daughter. "I'm sorry dear, but your father and I might be delayed."

"Oh, I hope not Mom." Julie says, back at the Halloran mansion with Greg and the family. She can hear the worry in her daughter's voice. "Everyone here is so anxious and stressed. They think the sheriff knows who killed Lewis and they are worried that someone else may be next."

"Well, considering the circumstances I suppose a little paranoia is understandable."

"And the press is out there again today. The Manchester Police had to come and help manage them."

"Faraway Hill was never meant for this kind of attention." Eve peers out the floor -to-ceiling window. The view always impresses her. You can see most of the city from up here. Even the bank where she is a vice president and the little shop she owns with her daughter. "How is Greg?"

"Not good. He's sitting in one of the parlors with Jack. I'm so grateful he's here to help." *The poor young man,* Eve thinks; *and things won't get better at the will reading tonight.* "That's good to know; how is the funeral coming along?"

"Pretty good; at first I was bothered that Joan was taking over or whatever, but she really knows what she's doing." Julie goes on to detail the funeral arrangements, which sound simple and appropriate to Eve. "Greg doesn't want to say anything at the service. I guess it's too emotional for him."

"Well, there are other people, your dad for one." Ben motions for her. "I'm sorry, Julie, but I have to go."

****

A few miles away, in a discreet corner of the Halloran's carefully manicured garden, Julie is talking to Eve on her cell. "Please get here soon." It makes no sense to Julie that her parents are so late for such an important event.

"We'll do our best," her mother says through the earpiece and not sounding too confident. Julie ends the call and wonders back into the enormous house. It goes without saying that she and her new husband are moving in right away. Someone has to. Julie is not sure she is ready to be the mistress of such a house. Their plans for being a "small family" before being a big one ended with Lewis' sudden death. And there are so many responsibilities with the place that she really wanted to grow into them slowly.

As she strolls through the ballroom, Julie can see the fear and grief in the eyes of the servants. They, like the family and guests, had all been somewhere in the house when the murder happened. Apparently the crowd made it easier for the killer to get in and get out. Of course, one of *them* could be the killer --- an idea that must be going through their minds. It certainly goes through hers --- and it frightens Julie more than she lets on. Still, they all continue to do their job, which now involves mostly removing wedding decorations. It is a sad sight. Only two days ago they reflected joy and promise. But now each floral arrangement is just a reminder that a murder has forever scarred the most important day of her life.

With most of the guests gone, the big house seems even bigger than usual. Julie smiles at maids she barely knows and searches through the house for her husband. In Grand Hall she meets up with Patrick Halloran. A junior at Columbia whose late father was Lewis' baby brother, he seems to have been looking for her. "I'm sorry, but I have to leave tomorrow," he explains. "After I see Mom, of course; school just can't wait." Patrick's widowed mother, Katherine, is confined to a special care facility in Concord.

"I understand Patrick, and I am sure Greg will too."

"He told me, but I still feel bad about leaving." Patrick is a sweet young man. He seems to be well equipped to handle all the baggage that comes with being a Halloran. "We all have to live our lives," she says with a sympathetic smile. "By the way, where is Greg?"

"Everyone's in the Green Room. Aunt Joan thinks that's the best place for the meeting with the sheriff." Julie nods and, arm in arm, they walk into the parlor. Like the rest of the house, the room in an extraordinary space. Green silk damask clings to walls trimmed in white paint, with elegant, antique Victorian furniture filling the parlor. Joan has a point: this room has plenty of seats for everyone. Julie sees her sitting on a settee next to her young son with her nearly as-young husband in a wing chair nearby. "I don't know what she sees in him," Patrick whispers to her with distaste. But Julie chuckles, "never underestimate the value of a washboard stomach and a tight butt." Patrick laughs a little too loudly, causing heads to turn.

At a corner, around a heavy oak table, sit Greg and Jack with Robert Halloran and Julie's Aunt Karen. She is so glad Karen is here. It makes Julie feel like someone is on her side. After all, she is a new Halloran and it will take awhile to be fully accepted. She and Patrick stride up to the table, their arms still locked. Greg, much more calm and relaxed now, looks at them and says, "Isn't a little soon for my wife to be taking up with another man?" It's a lame joke, but good enough to make her smile. "Don't worry sweetheart," Julie replies, giving him a kiss on the cheek. "It's just a meaningless fling."

"Have you spoken to the Gales?" Karen asks Julie, who shakes her head. "No, Mrs. Gale seems too emotional to talk and Ann won't pick up when I call --- not her home line, not her cell. It worries me."

"Well, it's sad for them, of course, but Munroe has never very happy with his life. Maybe now he has found some peace."

"I hope so."

Frederick appears at the door and announces the arrival of Sheriff Reynolds and his deputy, Peter Brandt, and escorts them in. They are early. Julie's parents won't be here for at least half an hour. The man is so big he almost waddles across the room. She has seen the sheriff around Faraway Hill all her life, and the man just seems to get wider with every year. With each new inch, he also seems to grow just a little more insufferable. It amazes Julie that such a man could be re-elected so often. Peter offers her a quick, friendly smile.

"Good morning," Reynolds announces. Everyone turns to look directly at the old man, anxious for whatever news is available. He really does relish all this attention from the town's rich and powerful. Peter moves a heavy wing chair over for the sheriff's convenience. As he sits on the antique, Julie has the mad idea that it will collapse under him. It doesn't. Peter hands him a file folder. "As we all know this has been a terrible, terrible crime. But the investigation has revealed that it is the result of one man's great pain and sadness. There are only victims in this story." It sounds to Julie like he's rehearsing for the press conference. "Last night, a local farmer named Munroe Gale committed suicide. We found among his possessions a letter he had been trying to write to his daughter. We also found . . . the gun that killed Lewis Halloran." He stops, allowing everyone in the room to absorb the news. For Julie, the whole thing is a shock. *Munroe, a murderer?* It makes no sense to her. He seemed too timid, too unsure of himself to do such a thing. *And poor Ann . . .*

Julie turns to look at the others. Greg seems to have had all the emotion drained from his face. Joan is seething, trying to contain her anger. Everyone else appears too shocked to grasp his meaning --- everyone that is, except Karen. She is surprisingly calm. "Are you saying that Munroe Gale murdered Lewis Halloran?"

"Yes, Mrs. St. John that is exactly what I am saying."

"Who the hell is Munroe Gale," Joan fumes, "and why would that bastard want to kill my brother?"

"Because of his daughter, Mrs. Lansing, that's why." That is a bizarre statement for the sheriff to make, one that causes Julie to finally speak up: "That makes no sense. What does Ann have to do with this?"

The old man pauses again --- for dramatic effect it seems, something else he rehearsed --- and explains, "Because Ann Gale was Lewis Halloran's illegitimate daughter. Mrs. Gale confirmed this last night. Mr. Halloran was planning on embracing his daughter after young Greg's wedding. But Mr. Gale would not have that. Afterward, he could not deal with his guilt over the crime and killed himself."

All eyes turn to Greg, whose expression has changed from quiet shock to outright fury. "That bitch's old man killed my father."

"That 'bitch,' young man, is your half-sister."

"Like hell she is." Greg pushes his chair back so hard it tips over and hits the floor with a loud bang. "Like hell," he says once more and storms out of the room.

✳✳✳✳

It's hard to hide in a small town, especially one as small as Faraway Hill. Ann spent more than an hour last night driving around. She had no clue what to do or where to go. Within a mere 48 hours her entire life has been irrevocably changed. She no longer knows whether to cry or throw something. She has no clue, none at all, what to do.

She definitely did not want to return to the little house she shared with Mark. Despite packing up all of his belongings, every corner reminds Ann of his humiliation. The entire town must know by now that her husband was fucking old men for money. People always spoke badly about her before. In school, she was subject to one rumor after another. It was a surprise when a jock like Peter Brandt agreed to date her. But Ann always dreamed of a life better than he could provide. But she eventually realized that it was a childish fantasy. Settling down with Mark seemed like the grown-up thing to do. But now they must be *really* laughing at her. And it will only get worse when everyone finds out --- on live, national TV no less --- that her father murdered one of the richest men in New England.

Her father. Ann is still angry at her mother's lifetime of lies.

Eventually, she settled on a simple motel on the highway. It is small and cheap, but the rooms are clean and relatively comfortable. It took awhile, but she managed to get some sleep. Now, as the morning light streams through the plate glass window, Ann is sitting up in bed wondering what to do next. Sheriff Reynolds has probably told the Halloran family already. There is no way to know about how they feel about Ann being one of them, but it's a good guess they are furious with Munroe.

Turning on the TV, she starts mindlessly flipping the channels. On one station, a mid-80s Michael J. Fox is trying to convince Helen Slater that they can save some company from a silly hostile takeover. On another, Granny is trying to convince Mr. Drysdale to take her tonic. And on a different station, a college age reality show contestant is trying to win a date with a slutty girl before she can say "next." *No wonder people are turning to the internet.*

One more click on the remote and, staring directly into a crowd of reporters, is Sheriff Reynolds. They are in Faraway Hill's town square. The statute of John Halloran is clearly visible in the background. "Munroe Gale, who committed suicide about 30 hours ago, is confirmed as Lewis Halloran's killer . . ." he goes on to explain Munroe's motive, and Ann true paternity.

Her humiliation is now complete. Now, the big question before Ann is: *what do I do?*

****

Greg feels pathetic. Just like a little boy, he got mad, ran up to his room and slammed the door behind him. It made a great scene in the Green Room, but just makes him feel childish and a bit ridiculous. And it leaves him wondering what to do next.

He angrily paces his suite's parlor. Their luggage is still scattered about because Julie declined Frederick's offer to have the staff unpack for them. She isn't accustomed to having servants, but that will have to change. They will be living here now.

The entire situation is too incredible, too intolerable for words. That annoying hick *cannot* possibly be his sister. Greg will never accept that. It might not even be true: what proof is there? No one has provided him with any. It's just a claim made by a farmer's wife that some lazy, small town sheriff has bought into. Besides, even if Lewis is her biological father, Munroe raised her. Munroe was her dad. And Munroe murdered Greg's father, the father who finally started treating him like a son. The father he never really knew and never will.

Greg wants to throw something, scream something or punch someone out. Or maybe cry. Instead, he kicks a suitcase across the floor letting it crash into a table.

Even if Ann *is* his half-sister, how can he ever look her in the face knowing what Munroe did? Every day will be a reminder that her old man killed Dad. *Every fucking day*. How can he live with that? How could anyone?

Greg can hear muffled voices out in the hall. Two people are arguing about something, and he can guess who they are. Finally, a soft knock and Julie cautiously opens the door. Greg can see Jack standing behind her. Both look very worried. "Greg, sweetheart," she asks tentatively and nervously. "Are you okay?"

"How the fuck do you think I am?"

The two of them cautiously enter. Julie's head turns to see the suitcase Greg kicked. "Take it easy, dude," Jack says diplomatically. Greg can tell that they each want to be alone with him, but the other won't allow it. "She's just worried about you. We all are."

"Some shithole alcoholic farmer shoots my dad in the forehead *and* I've just learned his daughter might be my bastard half-sister. How the hell am I supposed to be?"

Julie sits on the settee, right next to a pile of his shirts. She still seems a bit jet lagged from the quick, round-trip flights. "Greg, it's not Ann's fault. None of it is." But Jack points out, "What does that have to do with anything? She's a walking, breathing reminder of his dad's murder."

"That's not fair! I've known Ann all my life. She's the closest thing to a sister I have. She shouldn't be blamed for what Munroe did."

"Maybe not," Greg says trying to control his anger. "But he's right. And don't you defend her."

Now Julie gets angry. "Excuse me? Are you giving me orders?" Greg tries to come up with an apology when a frightening thought comes to his mind: "No, of course not, but . . . Oh, God, what if Dad changed his will?" It's possible. "Julie, he met with your father before Ann's wedding, did you know that?"

"Greg, Dad was Lewis' lawyer. They met all the time."

"No, I mean here at the house. It was weird. After that, Dad started talking about family and making things right and shit like that. I thought he meant between us, but . . ." instinctively he looks straight at Jack for understanding, who finishes Greg sentence with "he could have meant Ann."

Greg picks up the clothes from the settee, dumps them on the floor, and sits next to his wife. *She has to know something.* "Has you dad said anything about the will?"

"No, honey, and he wouldn't. Dad is very . . . well, anal, about client confidentiality. If Lewis promised him not to say anything until the reading, then he won't. Not even to me. Maybe not even to Mom."

This news worries Greg. *What could he have left the bitch? Is it something token, a trust maybe --- or a piece of the company?* That would be the worst. And what if she's not really his sister? "Oh, shit," is all he can say.

****

Agent Pembroke seems satisfied, at least for the time being. Ben King has spent all morning with her going through every conceivable document. Unfortunately, they could not find any one piece of paper that solves the mystery of why Mel stole the money. "There seldom is," she explains. "A solution usually comes in pieces, which make little sense until they all fit together." Ben makes arrangements for her to come back in a few days to speak with the staff and escorts her out. When he returns, he finds his wife turning off the small TV in the office kitchen. "I'm sorry Eve, but it couldn't be helped. I guess we'll just have to go straight to the funeral home." She doesn't say anything. "What's wrong?"

Eve, looking shaken, hesitates before finally says, "Reynolds just told the world that Munroe killed Lewis."

"What! That makes no sense." They have known the Gales for years and there are inviolable certainties with them: that Lorene will always ignore Munroe's drinking, and that Munroe drank, in part, because he was a coward.

"He says it's because of Ann. Apparently Lewis told him he was going to claim Ann and Munroe couldn't handle it."

"Come on, Eve, we both know Munroe didn't have the balls to shoot someone."

"The sheriff says that there's a suicide note," she shrugs, "and the gun they found has Munroe's fingerprints on it."

"And this is the gun that killed Lewis?"

Eve nods. "They confirmed it."

"Holy shit . . ." It is a mind blowing revelation, and maybe, just maybe, Munroe did do it. But it still seems strange to Ben.

"Poor Lorene."

"Poor Lorene? Can you imagine what Greg is going through?"

"I know, I know," the situation is horrible for everyone, especially the kids. "Anyway, we really need to get going Ben." The funeral will be starting soon. But Ben has another concern. "We still have to get through to Lorene and Ann about the reading."

"I've tried them both all day. No one is answering their phone. You are going to have to do it without them." They could drive out to the farm, but then they'd miss the funeral. The kids won't like that. "We'll just have to keep trying."

****

The Goodwin's staff has really come through for the family. The tapered and votive candles provide a warm, comforting glow. Photos of Lewis Halloran at different stages in his life --- from infancy to his son's wedding --- are scattered about the room. The beautifully carved casket, lid open, makes an impressive centerpiece. All of this combined with the historic mansion's natural elegance makes a nearly perfect scene.

Unless, of course, you count the reporters roped off outside.

Ben and Eve King arrive just as the afternoon's service is about to begin. They sit next to Karen St. John. All the Hallorans who came for the wedding and stayed for the investigation are here. The governor and Senator Davis have returned. Faraway Hill's aging mayor, who was too ill for the nuptial is here. So are the mayors of Manchester and Concord and other cities. There are various business leaders. All of them crowd the Goodwin's largest room.

On one table sits cards and flowers from dignitaries across the country and even from a few overseas.

A mixture of tension, anger and grief bind everyone together. No one says much, but Ben can actually feel it when people turn to look at him. *They want to know what is in the will,* he thinks. *And I really can't blame them.*

The service lasts about an hour. The Episcopal priest --- the same one who officiated at Greg and Julie's wedding --- does most of the talking. Joan, in her brief remarks, becomes a little too emotional, like she's trying to prove to the world how grieved she is. Ben's remarks are also brief, commenting on Lewis' business and community accomplishments. It is odd, to Greg, as he studies his father's peaceful face in the casket. All these people were his dad's family and friends and associates. Yet they seem to know almost as little about the man as his son.

The ride to the cemetery is a quiet one. Julie sits next to Greg, holding his hand, in one of the limos rented for the day. So many cars are needed that some were brought in from Boston. Jack is in another, with his weeping Aunt Joan and her family.

This is the second time in little over a year that Greg has been to Valley Cemetery. People are rarely buried here anymore. The cemetery was founded in 1840 but became so full so fast that most burials ended by the 1860s. Some of New Hampshire's most famous and historic citizens --- including two governors --- slumber eternally at Valley. These days most people are buried in Manchester's much larger Pine Grove Cemetery. Greg's mother, who died last year ago, was the first person interred at Valley in nearly a decade. The Hallorans are afforded this honor simply because the family mausoleum, the cemetery's largest, still has room.

Unfortunately, the Valley is in poor shape. It was designed as a "garden" cemetery with paths, streams and bridges. But many of them need serious repair. The place is still impressive, though. From the handsome Pine Street Gate to the

Frederick Smyth Tomb, it is hard not to be in awe. "When we were kids," Julie says to Greg as they approach the Halloran Mausoleum, "we used to tell stories about the Valley during slumber parties." Greg smiles a little. He can actually picture Julie, a pre-teen with her friends in their pajamas, trying to scare each other with tall tales and a flashlight.

The internment is brief and solemn. The priest says a few more words and Joan cries a few more unnecessarily loud tears. She is starting to embarrass herself. The casket is gently slid into the wall, right above the slot holding Greg's mother. "Do you want a few minutes alone with them?" Julie asks him. But Greg shakes his head. "Maybe I'll come back sometime." Hopefully a time when his head will be clear and he'll know what to say about the strangers he barely knew but called mom and dad.

When everyone returns to the mansion, all of the wedding decorations have finally been removed. The tables and chairs in the garden are gone. The household staff now has the Blue Room all set up for mourning. It is interesting how the place functions so smoothly. The first thing everyone does when they come in is scope out the buffet table. Apparently there is nothing like free food to lift people's spirits, even rich people. Karen St. John seems almost happy. But Greg is more interested in speaking to his father-in-law and takes Ben aside. "I'm sure you know what's going on."

"If you mean Munroe and Ann, yes son I do." Ben sympathizes with him. Nothing about this situation is good for him. "And I'm sorry we couldn't be here this morning. The meeting was too important."

"Ben, I can't imagine anything more important than my dad's murder."

"I know son, and when we have some more privacy I'll explain everything to you and Julie."

"What's in my dad's will? Is that bitch in it?"

Ben tries to contain his anger. "I'd prefer it if you didn't use that kind of language. I've known that girl her whole life. She doesn't deserve that." Greg doesn't care. "Maybe not, but I deserve an answer."

"And you'll get it . . . later, when it's just the family left."

Greg knows better than to push him, so he waits out the rest of the day in frustration. His Aunt Joan seems to be feeling the same way; Greg sees her having a tense conversation with Ben who convinces her to back off too.

The only person who appears free of any stress or worry is Karen St. John. Even her family is surprised by it. But she explains philosophically, "what's done is done, I'm afraid. All we can do is deal with everything one step at a time." Ben and Eve practically roll their eyes at that statement. But nearly everyone else, especially Julie, takes it as a piece of deep, meaningful advice.

Eventually the party breaks up as one by one guests leave, but not before expressing their condolences to Greg, Julie and Joan. By early evening, only a handful of family members are left: Greg, Julie, her parents; Joan with her husband and son; Robert Halloran and Patrick. Karen and Jack round out the group, and Ben graciously asks them to step into another room. It is time read Lewis' will. Looking nervously at his audience, Ben clears his throat and begins to read:

"I, Lewis John Halloran, being of sound mind and body do hereby declare this to be my last will and testament, forswearing all previous wills and codicils . . . To my sister, Joan Halloran Newberry Hamilton Logan Lansing, I leave our mother's personal papers and her beloved collection of imported china . . . to my sister-in-law Katherine Anders Halloran and her son Patrick, I leave joint title to the cabin in the White Mountains that was so very special to me and my brother David growing up . . . to my nephew Matthew I leave my personal collection of first edition novels, including the two by Mark Twain . . ." Ben pauses a moment to take a sip of water. This is the important part. Everyone in the room can see it. "As to the matter of my stock in the family company, Halloran Enterprises: This firm, in one form or another, dates back to our family's earliest days as textile manufactures in colonial America. The family trust, which owns and manages the house, also owns 40% of the stock or 400 shares. 300 shares are currently owned by Katherine Halloran, Robert Halloran and Joan Lansing. This leaves the 300 bequeathed to me by my father . . ." Ben looks embarrassed and worried, which signals to Greg that the worst has happened. "After much consideration and regret, I have decided to embrace my daughter Ann Gale and am leaving her 100 of these shares, or 10% of the company as well as an equal place among all the Hallorans in the family trust . . ." there is a gasp by everyone in the room. 'In addition, I extend my heartfelt apologizes to my daughter's mother, Lorene Graves Gale along with the sum of five million dollars." Joan is about to say something when he son gives her a warning look. *It seems the boy has some balls after all,* thinks Greg. "The balance of my estate, including my remaining 200 shares I bequeath to my son, Gregory Halloran along with my love and wishes for a long and happy life." Ben pauses for a moment and then reads the last important line of the will, "I ask and expect my entire family to embrace the daughter I have wanted to claim all these years but for various reasons could not. She is one of us. She should be treated as one of us."

"Like hell," Greg mutters so quietly that only Julie can hear him.

✱✱✱✱

No one says much for the remainder of the evening. They don't even have dinner together. The events have been too overwhelming. Instead, everyone goes back to their room or hotel or house. The mood is excruciating, with family members too depressed or grieved or angry or worried to do much else.

Everyone, that is, except Karen St. John.

People whispered how calm she was, how graceful. Nothing phased her. Not a frown on her face, or wrinkle in her dress or even a strand of hair out of place. She was seen as a steady force, a rock for her niece. Only Eve sensed something odd in her sister but said nothing.

Right now Karen is soaking in the Jacuzzi in her comfortable suite at the Hilton Garden Inn. The hot, bubbling water feels good. Like a little reward for a job well done. Everyone else is coming to terms with their grief or their anger. But Karen is different. Karen has always been different. She is not in tears, she is not pacing the floor in frustration. She is simply satisfied. She very logically crafted her plan and put it in place. And it worked.

Just before climbing into the tub, Karen logged on to the *Union Leader's* web site. It amused her to read about what George Reynolds uncovered and what he didn't. There is nothing like a lazy small town sheriff to miss what is really important. The story, for tomorrow's edition, tells about that party so many years ago, when Lewis Halloran and his friends celebrated his wedding. It has enough facts there to fill Reynolds' need to end the case: Lewis and Lorene sneaking off, getting pregnant. Lewis prohibited from claiming his daughter, and Lorene marrying her fiancé Munroe Gale. Years later, when Lewis finally could call Ann his own, Munroe flipped out, killed the millionaire and then himself. A neat circle. Perfect. The kind of logic Karen's daddy taught her.

But there is so much more.

Karen closes her eyes to let the hot water take her back in time to that night. Lewis and his friends were so handsome, so charming. It was a magical evening for two small town girls. Lorene Graves and Karen Scott were fresh out of high school and working part time at the Halloran mansion. They were saving money for college. Karen's "uncle" --- actually, a friend of her mother --- was the Halloran family lawyer, and he helped them get the jobs. The pay was good, but just as important was walking through that fascinating, historic building with its many rooms and many stories. Karen soaked them all up. The two girls jumped at the chance to plan the groom's party. It was no secret in the house that Lewis Halloran was unhappy about marrying Lilly Stephens. A product of all the best schools, she was beautiful, refined and the ultimate bitch. She was also three months pregnant. Lilly tried to control everything and everyone around her. Karen suspected that her unplanned pregnancy wasn't all that unplanned. Apparently Lewis suspected that too, and saw the little party as break from his stressful fiancé.

But for Lorene and Karen it would mean much more.

What few on the staff --- and no one else --- knew at the time was that Karen had a crush on one of Lewis and David Halloran's frat buddies, a smooth handsome charmer named Alexander Mundy. He was athletic and confident and damned sexy. Alex was a social climber, determined to please his ambitious parents through his friendship with the Halloran brothers.

He figured out how Karen felt and soon they were having a secret affair. Alex was the brothers' closest friend and he'd visit often. Whenever he stayed at the house, they'd find a way to sneak off together. He was her first lover and did the most incredible things to her. Karen learned a lot about her body and what it can do, thanks to Alex. He made her feel beautiful and sexy and special. It was empowering. No one had ever made her feel that way before.

Lewis' gathering was to be an all-male affair, a bachelor party without the tackier elements like strippers. Lorene and Karen were the only servants involved and the only women there. Being so close in age with the guys combined with Karen's relationship with Alex soon had them feeling more like guests than maids. They laughed and flirted and drank. It was the best night the two girls ever had. Lewis was taken with Lorene and her natural sweetness, her small town simplicity. Eventually the group started breaking up. A couple of the guys passed out, a few others left. David and a buddy went upstairs to his suite. Karen and Alex made love on the floor of the Green Room. That left Lewis and Lorene alone in the Blue Room; alone for the first time.

Karen smiles at the memories of that night, the youthful energy and the magical feeling that the world was theirs for the taking. But it was all fleeting, all of it.

Two days later Karen learned she was about three weeks pregnant. Alex was stunned and angry. That shocked her. She expected him to be thrilled. But it wasn't part of Alex's life plan to have knocked-up the maid. His family was dead set against their marrying. He tried pressuring Karen into an abortion but it frightened her too much. Alex refused to have anything more to do with her and denied being the father. Lewis backed him up. When Karen's mother found out she was livid. Mom's anger was directed at her, not the Hallorans. Her father, a philosophy professor, was a big fan of the use of logic and Karen failed to use any. It was a relief to the family that he didn't live to see one of his daughters being so foolish. Her mother was ashamed.

About a month later Lorene got her own news. By this time, Lewis and Lilly were already married. He was willing to take responsibility. But Lilly would have none of it. Munroe came to her rescue. He loved her enough to be the father of another man's baby. Ann became a source of joy and pain for Munroe. He thought of her as his own, but the threat of losing her always hung over him. Munroe was a weak man and anything he feared drove him to the bottle. Money, health, his family, whatever the crisis Munroe hid with alcohol. Every few years Lewis would make an effort to reach his daughter, but Lilly always blocked him and Munroe binged.

The water has gotten too hot now. Karen steps out of the tub, picks up the towel and begins to drive off. But she cannot step out of her mood, her mind now focused on the past. For her solution was very different from Lorene's. Karen was forced to give up her baby and move away. And she vowed revenge.

Ironically, the lessons she learned from Alex were incredibly helpful. He gave her the self confidence she needed in and out of bed to climb up first Boston's and then New York's social world. The pinnacle came with marrying the much older and very wealthy Martin St. John. But every day she looked for the right opportunity to pay back the two men who had hurt her.

Alex has proven the most frustrating: after college, he disappeared. No one can say what happened to him after his parents and sisters died. So she has had to focus on the other man, on Lewis. The stars starting lining up when Daddy's logic helped her get rid of Lilly Halloran from a safe distance. Karen knew her death would free Lewis to claim his daughter. But she needed an excuse to visit Faraway Hill, a reason that everyone could believe. That came when Julie announced she was engaged to Lewis' son.

Now dry, Karen slips on her robe and lies down on the bed. The mattress is surprisingly comfortable. She is used to fancier accommodations but the Hilton Garden Inn has turned out to be a good choice.

It was so easy. Like with many things, it took some careful thought and planning. She applied Daddy's logic. The chaos of the wedding made it simple for her to slip into the mansion, fire the silencer, and slip out again. Karen knew Munroe would provide the perfect cover. All she had to do was wait until he was drunk enough to be pliable. Within a matter of days, she got her revenge against Lewis Halloran while releasing an old friend of a lifetime of pain. To Karen, it was a poetic plan --- and the logic would have impressed her father.

But the greatest, most poetic irony of all is Julie. The child Karen was forced to give up --- the daughter raised by her sister Eve --- is now married to Lewis' son. Karen's grandchild will inherit part of the Halloran empire.

And this is the thought that puts a smile on her face as she drifts off to a peaceful, satisfied sleep.

EPISODE EIGHT

It's early morning. The sun is climbing into the sky. The air is fresh and dew is on the grass. Summer is over and the town of Faraway Hill, New Hampshire is slowly waking to what will be a cool but pleasant day.

Greg Halloran is jogging around the town square this morning, with the famous statute of John Halloran dominating the center. So much has happened over the last few months, leaving him frustrated and angry.

Despite Lewis' will, the Halloran family --- especially Greg and Joan --- have not embraced Ann. Even after returning home to Boston, Joan has supported Greg's efforts to keep Ann from her inheritance for as long as possible. They have been doing this by insisting on multiple DNA tests. Since each test can take at least four to six weeks, they have been able to delay implementation of her inheritance for months. Ann is now living rent free in Julie's old condo, her savings nearly depleted. The whole situation has put Ben --- and especially Julie --- in the middle of a virtual war. Greg has made it clear he wants nothing to do with Ann while Julie keeps defending her childhood friend. This has seriously strained their young marriage.

He turns and crosses the street, passing a couple of antique shops, a restaurant and a dollar store. No one is inside any of them; it's still too early in the day. This is a lull period for them anyway. The summer tourist season is over and the fall season is about to begin. Julie tells him that a different group of visitors come this time of the year, mostly elderly people and single couples. Many of New Hampshire's farms have embraced these people with fairs, hay rides, Halloween attractions and even wine tasting.

Jack Campbell returned to New York shortly after the will reading. But the two of them keep in touch through text, chat and email. He has become more important to Greg as his relationship with Julie deteriorates over the Ann Issue. The newlyweds have tried to concentrate on the coming baby --- Lamaze classes, redecorating the nursery, buying clothes --- but Ann keeps asserting herself. He wishes the bitch would go the hell away.

Greg makes another turn to cross another street. He still isn't sure how many times around the square constitute a mile and doesn't really care. Just pumping out the tension every morning helps him get through the day.

Greg is starting to understand why he saw so little of his father growing up. More and more of his days are taken up with business. He visits the family's huge textile mill in Georgia at least once a month and the smaller New Hampshire facility about every other week. The new mill in Thailand is more complicated. There are so many things to handle. Greg really should fly over there, but is hesitant to make such a long trip while Julie is pregnant. If something goes wrong, it's much easier to get to Faraway Hill from Atlanta than it is from the other side of the world. So, every issue must be dealt remotely through contracted people there.

Another turn and he is on another street. Here are more mundane stores, less for the tourists and more for the locals: a family-owned grocer, video store, florist and a consignment shop.

Greg is also doing all he can to help his father-in-law. Melvin Waite's embezzlement could have ruined Ben King's law practice and career if the Hallorans weren't standing behind him. Julie appreciates this, but Greg's reasons aren't entirely altruistic: he needs Ben's help to keep Ann at bay. Unfortunately, they have just about run out of options. Greg may have no other choice but to accept Ann Halloran --- yes, the annoying bitch dared to change her name --- as his half-sister. This means letting her into the family trust and everything that goes along with it. It also means giving her 10% of the company.

What frustrates the situation more than anything else is that Greg has no one to talk to about Ann. Despite her support, Aunt Joan has resumed her life of cocktail parties and fundraisers in Boston. The other family members also hate having to embrace Ann but they have gradually come to accept it as inevitable. And then there is Julie. Every time the subject comes up, they get into a fight. Each fight has gotten progressively worse. It seems that just by breathing Ann is ruining their marriage before it has started.

They rarely make love any more. Greg really misses it. He has always had a hard time with celibacy, ever since discovering the joys of sex with the other boys at boarding school. Adding girls to the mix in college just made sex even more fun. But the Mark fiasco has left him wary of any sort of extracurricular sex, be it with a man or a woman. He can't handle another scandal, or the risk of AIDS. After learning from the sheriff that Mark had at least a dozen clients, Greg secretly got tested. Fortunately he is negative. But the lack of intimacy just adds to his frustration.

That leaves Jack, far off in New York, but still accessible through the web. They chat and text almost every day. Sometimes he just lets Greg vent, other times they tell each other off-color jokes. Occasionally they talk about business. Sometimes, when their respective offices have closed at they are the last ones behind, the chat turns dirty. It's a good thing Yahoo doesn't monitor their messages. The last one was so hot, Greg jerked off right at his desk.

Greg makes another turn, but is too exhausted to go on. He collapses onto a bench. This happens every day now. He has no idea if he'll be able to do morning jogs when winter comes along. But until then, this is his only release. This . . . and Jack.

****

There is something wonderfully, simply and intrinsically beautiful about New Hampshire in autumn. It lacks all complication: the entire world is getting ready for its annual winter slumber, just as it has for thousands of years.

It is later in the morning and Eve King is driving north on the highway past Faraway Hill. She is going to visit the famous Agnes Gabler. The artist has had her accounts at Atlantic-New Hampshire Bank for years. But her account manager has retired and Eve is taking over. It's quite an honor. It means she'll be meeting with the elderly woman and her daughter regularly.

Gabler's home is a renovated sugar house which has been in her family since the late 1800s. Sugar houses still exist in much of New Hampshire. They are key part of the state's rural tradition. It is in these cabins where sap collected from maple trees is turned into syrup. Their numbers have dwindled in the last fifty years. But they are popular places for residents and tourists alike. Many have expanded into gift shops and even restaurants. Whenever they can, Eve and Ben drive out to Mason to treat themselves for a hearty pancake breakfast at Parkers Maple Barn. The restaurant is like a small, encapsulated piece of New Hampshire farm life. It really is a renovated barn, with former cow stations used to create the unique tables and all kinds of antique farm equipment decorating the walls. Julie used to love going there as a little girl. Every visit is topped off by a trip to the gift shop.

But the Gabler place hasn't been used as a sugar house since the 1940s. It was at that point when Agnes formally converted it to a studio and living space. She had started painting there as a little girl, back when her "primitive art" style was still seen by many of the locals as nothing more than nice pictures. Little did they know how the sophisticated art world would praise these paintings. Today, it is the center for her art. She has hosted everything from children's groups to presidents here. And now it is Eve King's turn.

As she pulls up, Eve is struck by how the house itself is a work of art. Agnes' own murals --- painted long ago and fading now, but still beautiful --- cover most of the façade. Set against the browns and greens of autumn, the whole building is a dramatic statement of bright living colors.

Agnes' daughter Scarlet greets Eve at the door, Bluetooth clasped to her ear. "That's not the deal we discussed," she says to the person at the other end. To Eve, she whispers, "sorry, but this is one of those little crisis that come up from time to time." Eve smiles and nods. Even in rural New Hampshire, there is no escape from the wired world. Scarlet gestures her inside while wrapping up her conversation. The main parlor is an interesting hodgepodge. Along with comfortable, well-worn furniture are items and memorabilia collected from a long, rich life. Native carvings from Africa and Asia share space with autographed photos of notables like the King of Spain and various U.S. presidents, starting with Truman.

"I'm sorry about that," Scarlet says with a polite smile. She takes off the Bluetooth and sets it on an antique table. "This gallery in Milan is doing a special showing but they keep trying to make last minute changes that they aren't supposed to."

"I'm sure that's frustrating."

"Yes, and normally I'd go over there myself, but I just can't right now."

"Well, I'll try not to take up too much time. Where is your mother?"

"She's in her studio, but there's something I wanted to talk to you about first." Scarlet gestures to some chairs and they sit. "I suppose you read in the papers about that hotel fire last week in Concord."

"Everybody did." It made news across the state. One of Concord's most historic inns suffered from a wiring problem. "Apparently the damage is extensive."

"It is. In fact, it'll take up to a year for them to fix it all. That's the problem. We were going to use it for Mom's 95th birthday celebration. But now we are having trouble finding someplace big enough. I've called around Concord, Manchester and even Portsmouth, but no one has a ballroom large enough that is available for the right dates."

"Have you tried Boston, or even New York?" They would certainly have hotels big enough, not to mention more prestigious ones. But Scarlet shakes her head. "We can't. Travel is starting to be a problem for her. That's why we're doing the Milan show by long distance. Besides, Mom really wants to keep it in New Hampshire. This is her home."

"I understand. Is there something I can do to help?"

"Well, I don't want to impose, but . . . the Hallorans have that large ballroom. It was so beautiful for your daughter's wedding. And, of course, it's an historic house. Lewis and Lilly Halloran were some of Mom's biggest supporters. Do you think your son-in-law would let us use it?"

Eve hesitates. Things haven't been too good between the kids lately. Adding hosting duties for such a big event could be more than they can handle right now. But it's hard for her to say no. "I can ask him." That's the best Eve can do. Scarlet smiles, relieved that one problem may be solved. "But I can't promise anything." Scarlet nods, "I understand."

The two of them rise and Scarlet escorts her to a smaller room just a few steps into the rear. There she sees Agnes, sitting in a wheelchair wearing an old splattered smock, working at a canvas.

✳✳✳✳

Ann Halloran is standing at the corner of Merrimack and Elm Streets, right in the heart of downtown Manchester. The streets and sidewalks are bustling with traffic. Across Elm she can see people strolling through Veterans' Park admiring the leaves changing color. Just a few blocks away the Verizon Wireless Arena is gearing up for the Manchester Monarch's first game of the season. The world around her is crowded and busy and getting things done. But Ann has never felt more alone.

She has never been very popular or outgoing. But hardly anyone talks to her anymore. Mostly, people avert their eyes or stare or whisper to each other whenever they see Ann. It doesn't matter if she is on the street or at the mall or even wandering through the Currier Museum. Everyone knows. All the dirty details about Ann, Munroe and Mark have been in the papers and on the TV news. They are still telling jokes on talk radio. Munroe is dead and Mark has disappeared, and Ann must live with their humiliation every day.

Her cell rings. It is a text message from her new lawyer. Ann had hired someone right out of the phone book to handle the divorce, which happened faster than she anticipated. But the woman declined to help her fight the Hallorans. So she needed another one to help with the estate issues. Julie's dad helped her find this lawyer; another woman whose small office is located above one of the shops on Stark Street. Usually it is a message about yet another delay. This time she asks her to call. Hopefully it's good news, but Ann suspects that it is about the bill. Money has grown increasingly tight the last few months. It is odd: the will leaves her millions of dollars that she can not touch. Ann Halloran is a rich woman with no money.

She turns left and walks a few blocks toward Julie's café. As usual, people pretend to ignore her.

Ann could ask her mother for money. Lorene got her bequest; apparently the Hallorans had no way of delaying that. But the two of them have barely spoken since that night when the sheriff got the truth out of her. Ann just can't bring herself to face the woman who had lied repeatedly her whole life, and forced her to accept Munroe Gale as a father.

When she arrives at King's Korner, decorated for Halloween, customers turn to look at her, their loud conversations dropping to whispers. Ann pretends not to notice. She walks up to the counter where Mary Armstrong finishes up a sale. The girl looks up with a smile, "Good morning Mrs. Bradley." Mary's smile disappears. "Oops, I mean, Miss Halloran," she says embarrassed. "Sorry, I don't know why I keep doing that."

Neither does Ann. The girl has known about the name change for more than a month. "That's okay. Is Julie in?"

"Yes, but she's in back on the phone."

Ann nods and orders an iced coffee, picks up this morning's *Union Leader*, and selects a table toward the back. As she speed dials her lawyer, Ann can see Mary walk back to the office, leaving her to think that the girl shouldn't leave the counter unattended. What she doesn't know is that Mary is again checking on Julie, because she can hear her boss' sobs through the door. Worried, she gently taps on the door. A pause and Julie answers, "what is it?" Mary slowly opens the door to see her wipe her face. "I'm sorry, Mrs. Halloran, but Miss Halloran is out front."

Julie nods. Ann comes by the store every day, and every day things become a little worse for her. The months-long fight between Greg and Ann has really taken its toll. "Just give me a minute okay?" Mary nods and closes the door behind her. The girl has been a life saver. She has been taking on more and more responsibilities over the summer. Unfortunately, school starts soon and Julie wonders how she'll make it with Mary's reduced work schedule.

Slowly, carefully, Julie rises from her chair. Now in her third trimester, the pregnancy's added weight puts pressure on her back. The pain can hit suddenly. But she has learned that the slower she takes even the simplest things, the better. Julie is learning this and other tips from her doctor and her Lamaze instructor. Oddly enough, her mother has been less help. Every time Julie asks her for pregnancy advice, Eve's responses are pretty vague and of little help.

Julie carefully walks over to the small mirror on the wall by the office door. One of the few things that have gone right in her short marriage is the pregnancy. Whenever Julie and Greg focus on the baby, their problems shift to the background. Some times it can even be fun, like when they go shopping for baby clothes or meet with the decorators about the nursery. But all it takes is the mention of Ann to change the mood of any situation.

Ann. It seems like Julie has spent her whole life defending her. But she's really been the only true friend Ann has ever had. Kids picked on her in grade school, teased or ignored her in high school. College wasn't much better. But the situation with Lewis, Munroe and especially Mark has made her a laughing stock across the state. How can Julie abandon her now? "Because I'm your husband," Greg always answers when that question is raised. *Maybe he's right.* Julie's parents have hinted at as much, even as they claim to be neutral. "This is something the two of you will have to solve," her mother repeatedly advises. "But I think Greg has a point."

Julie takes a deep breath, fixes her make-up, and opens the door. The store is buzzing with activity, but Mary seems to be doing just fine by herself. The girl's efficiency is really impressive. Ann clasps her cell shut, a smile on her face, and waves Julie over. "I have great news." Julie takes a seat across from her. "Good, I'm sure you can use it."

"My lawyer says that the Hallorans have run out of options. They have no choice now but to give me my inheritance."

"I'm glad," Julie sighs in relief. "Now you can get on with your life and do all those things you've wanted to do: get your own place, travel, shop eternally." Ann laughs at the last one. "My God, I don't think there is enough money in the world for that."

"And hopefully this means we can all put the last few months behind us."

Ann takes Julie's hand in hers. "I can't thank you enough for everything. Letting me stay in your condo, defending me to Greg --- all of it; even the free coffee here every morning." Julie smiles, "well, I guess we've always been like sisters --- and now we kind of are."

"I know."

"So, have you decided where you want to live? Maybe buy a place here in Manchester?"

Ann shakes her head. "I don't think so."

"Oh, come on Ann. You can't avoid your mother forever. At least buy something local and try to make up with her. She only did what she thought was right."

"Well, maybe, but that's not what I mean."

"What, Boston? That's still pretty close. And you've always wanted to live in a big city." Boston might be the best place for her.

"Yeah, that's true, but its something my lawyer told me." That statement sparks worry in Julie, who asks suspiciously, "what did she say?"

"Well," she answers carefully, obviously worried how Julie will react. "I *am* included in the Halloran family trust now and everyone in the trust has certain rights and privileges."

She's not thinking . . . she had better not be. "Ann, are you talking about the house?" Ann gives her a slightly wicked smile. "I have the legal right to live there if I wish."

Julie's heart sinks. That would be the worst thing Ann can do. "Oh, my God Ann, please don't do it. Promise me you won't do it."

"I'm not giving up my rights, Julie. Not after all the shit I've gone through."

"You can keep your right to live in the house and not actually *live* in it." Having Ann there every day wouldn't mean ending the war between Ann and the Hallorans --- it would escalate it. There is no way Julie and Greg can survive that.

Ann is defiant. She's getting her birthright now and be will damned to give it up. "But it's my home now, just as much as it is Greg's or Joan's or any of them."

"God no," Julie begs. The very thought scares her. "Ann, listen to me: I have risked a lot for you. So please, *please*, do not move into that house."

"But . . ."

"Don't you get it? You move into that house and my marriage is over. It's *over*." Ann can see the fear in her friend's eyes. "It . . . it can't be that bad."

"Yes, it is. You are the only thing Greg and I fight about and the fights have been getting worse. There are times when we can barely talk. You move into the mansion and . . ." Ann realizes that she can't do that to Julie. She has come through for her over and over again. "Okay, okay," she reassures, "I guess I can be a Halloran and live in Manchester."

"Thank you," Julie says with a relieved smile. She looks genuinely happy at the news. Until this moment, Ann hadn't fully realized how tough it has been for Julie, the only real friend she has. These days, that is something more precious that a big, fancy house.

✶✶✶✶

Greg Halloran is not having a good day. All morning he's had to field calls about ludicrous problems at the Georgia mill while watching online streaming from the BBC about a possible coup in Thailand --- which could affect the newly acquired Halloran mill there. He tried keeping a chat open with Jack, but meetings kept the man away from his computer. Greg was left alone.

In the midst of all that, he got a call from his father-in-law. The battle with Ann is essentially over, and she's won. There is nothing more that the family can do to keep her from her inheritance. Greg threw his coffee mug hard against the wall after getting the news. It loudly broke in two. The noise scared his secretary; she even screamed. Greg had to spend twenty minutes calming her down.

He had lunch alone at Maxwell's. For months he and Julie often had lunch together. But the Ann Issue changed that. These days when he eats at his favorite restaurant, Greg sits by himself amid the Mahogany walls and historic photos. He just reads the newspaper or some report while eating his meal. He has also begun flirting with Debbie, the sexy waitress he occasionally hooked up with before the engagement. She is starting to make it clear that she's open to a little fun on the side. Greg is starting to consider it.

Now he is standing on the sidewalk outside Brady Sullivan Plaza, staring up at the twenty stories. The moment is at hand. Greg Halloran now has to accept that asinine farm girl, the daughter of his father's murderer, as his half-sister. He wishes he had another coffee mug to throw.

Instead, he takes the elevator up to Ben King's office. There, he immediately encounters Barry Studer. The annoying young lawyer acts a little too much like a used car salesman. He's been especially bothersome since Melvin Waite disappeared. Studer goes from networking event to networking event trying to drum up new business. People laugh about it all over southern New Hampshire. It's a wonder Ben doesn't let him go.

Although, the kid *does* have a nice ass --- as Greg observes while Barry escorts him to Ben's office.

"Hello son," Ben says when they are alone. "I know how hard this is for you."

"Let's just get it over with."

Ben nods and produces a document. As co-executors of Lewis' estate, all major paperwork requires both their signatures. It is a simple, one-sheet that formally releases Ann's inheritance. Within a few seconds, it is done. The assets, including a sizable amount of cash, will be transferred within a couple of days.

They say little, except when Ben puts a hand on Greg's shoulder. "I know this is a private matter, but I have to tell you, that I'm worried about my daughter."

"I know she's been caught in the middle." Greg has felt guilty about it as often as he's been angry. He assures his father-in-law that with the Ann Issue put to rest; things are bound to get better. Ben seems relieved. Maybe it's because Greg really does mean it, or at least hopes for it. Whether it will happen remains to be seen. It still angers him when Julie defends the farm girl.

Back at the office, Greg Messengers Jack. "It seems my whole life is fucked up," he types. "My dad's been murdered, I'm over my head at work, my wife and I barely get along and now I have to deal with that bitch as my sister." Keying that last word is like a painful stab in the gut. Jack types back, "It'll get better. You'll be a dad soon and a real cool one at that." Then he adds, "I love you. Always remember that. Things will work out." Another call comes in with another stupid problem in Georgia. Greg tells his secretary to book a flight to Atlanta in the morning and arrange for a luxury suite at his favorite hotel, the Four Seasons. He then types to Jack, "I've got to replace those idiots in Atlanta. I have to fly there again tomorrow." A few seconds later, and Jack writes back, "That's a hassle, but think of it as a two-day break from everything. Who knows, dude, you might enjoy it! LOL" Maybe, but Greg doubts it.

Arriving at home that night, Frederick tells him that Julie has arranged for his favorite foods and set out the good china. Obviously she knows the news about Ann. She probably found out about it before he did. The bitch has been staying in Julie's condo and stopping almost daily at Julie's shop. "When did you hear?" he asks her after a brief kiss outside the formal dining room.

"This morning."

Greg decides not to respond right away. It's better to think about something diplomatic to say. Julie fidgets nervously. "Greg, this means it's over."

Again, he doesn't say anything for a moment. Finally, with a pained sigh, he says, "actually sweetheart it's just starting."

"Greg --- "

"It's true. Every time there is a family event or a board meeting, I have to sit across from her. I have to deal with her being your best friend. I have to deal with people calling her my sister. I have to deal with the fact that the man who raised her murdered my father --- and he did it for her. And I have to deal with all of that for the rest of my life."

Without a word, Julie takes her husband into his arms and holds him tight. Greg loves sharing their warmth, and of feeling their baby boy inside her. It makes them laugh. "See, even your son says it'll all work out," she whispers to him. "He's already kicking your ass." It is moments like these that remind him why he fell in love with her and why he married her, despite his lingering feelings for Jack. She releases him and takes his hand in hers to guide him to the formal dining room. Just before they sit, her cell rings. "I'm sorry; I thought I turned it off." Julie looks at the number and by her expression Greg knows that its Ann calling. "Just go ahead," he tells her. It is part of what he will have to deal with from now on. Julie flips open the phone.

"Hi, can I call you back? We're just sitting down to dinner . . . what are you talking about . . . Ann, you can't mean that." Julie glances up at him with a mixture of worry and fear. Something awful is about to happen. "You promised me Ann . . . I don't care what your lawyer says; you don't have to do it . . . please, please talk to her again. Explain everything to her. I mean it, Ann, you can't do it . . . talk to her again and call me tomorrow. Bye." She looks up at Greg. This time it is just fear in her eyes.

"What's the bitch done now?"

"I've asked you not to call her that."

He doesn't want another fight. "I'm sorry, what does she want now, the family silver?"

"No, it's . . . it's probably not going to happen so let's not worry about it."

"What's not going to happen?"

"Well . . . Ann promised me this morning that she wouldn't do it."

"Do *what*?" Now Greg is getting angry. The bitch now has everything she wants and is *still* causing them problems. Julie looks at him and gently says, "Move in with us."

"Your damn right she's not moving in here!"

"Greg, please don't yell . . . you know what the family trust says. Anyone included in the trust can live in the mansion. That now includes Ann."

"But you just said that she promised not to move in."

"Yes, she did, but . . ."

"But what?"

"Considering all that's happened over the last few months, her lawyer thinks it's important that she exercise her right to live here. It'll end any questions about her being a Halloran."

Greg rises from his chair, having not touched any of the food. "I'm not hungry."

"Oh, God, Greg, please understand . . ."

"I have to fly to Atlanta in the morning; more problems at the mill there. I'll only be gone a couple of days."

Without saying another word, he leaves her sitting alone at dinner, just as he sat alone at lunch. But while Greg had a newspaper keeping him company, Julie just has her tears.

****

"You're really pissed at me, aren't you?"

It is the next morning and Ann Halloran is feeling embarrassed, anxious and even a little scared. She and Julie are in the family dining room of the Halloran Mansion, right across the hall from the formal dining room where Julie's hopes for a happy meal last night crumbled. This time she isn't crying. She isn't saying anything. She just sits there, eating her breakfast. Ann isn't eating, but standing just inside the door, as if she is barely aloud in the room. "Julie, please understand . . ."

Greg is gone. He left for Atlanta this morning, after a night so tense that he and Julie never said a word to each other. That has left Julie angrier and more hurt than any fight could. "I understand just fine."

"My lawyer, she thinks . . ."

"That's bull shit, Ann, complete bull shit. You lied to me yesterday."

"No, I swear, I meant what I said."

Julie sets down her juice glass to look directly and firmly at her sister-in-law. "Ann, how do you expect this to work?"

"What do you mean?"

"Living here; this house isn't *that* big. So, do you plan on eating meals with Greg and me? Celebrating Christmas with us? We'll be raising our son here. Are you going to do that, too --- get married and live here with your family? How will that work?"

Ann doesn't know what to say. These are things she hasn't really considered.

"Think about it Ann. Greg never liked you; never. Not when you were just his fiancé's best friend. Now you're the half-sister whose step-dad murdered his father --- *in this house*. My God, he can't even walk into the study; it's been locked for months. He hates to say your name. He and my dad have spent all summer blocking your inheritance."

"I have a right to live here."

"That's not the reason. You want to live here because it fulfills some childhood fantasy of yours --- and, I think, to get a little revenge."

"Revenge on whom?"

"Greg, Lewis, Munroe, take your pick." Julie has a point, but Ann insists, "I'm not changing my mind."

"Oh, I know that. I've known you too long. I even told Frederick to give you that two-room suite on the northeast corner. But this is going to be a daily hell for me, Ann. And I think I have the right to be pissed at you for a long, long time." Julie says nothing more and resume eating, a signal to Ann that she needs to leave. Ann still feels the need to justify herself, but isn't quite sure how to do that.

"I really wish you could understand Greg's point of view," Julie says wistfully. "Every time he sees you he can't help but think the same thing: that Munroe killed his father." That is a statement Ann cannot let pass. "All these months and the ridicule and all the fighting and no one seems to understand that that's something Greg and I have in common: *Munroe killed my father too*. The father I never got know." Now feeling justified, Ann leaves Julie to sit there alone with the remnants of her breakfast. Unable to eat any longer, she glances up at the beautiful antique brass clock on the wall. Greg left very early this morning; he's probably on the way to his hotel now. She picks up her cell and dials. Two rings and her husband answers.

"Hi there, how was the flight?"

Greg is miles away, speeding down the highway in a cab. "It's okay," he says. "Look, I'm really sorry about last night. None of this is your fault."

"I know, but there isn't much we can do about it."

Julie's right. Looking out the cab's window, watching the strip malls and big box retailers in suburban Atlanta pass by, Greg begins to realize how powerless he really is, at least as far as his home life is concerned. Four months ago everything seemed to be coming together: the business, his wedding, the pregnancy. But everything collapsed overnight. "She's moving in, isn't she?"

"I'm afraid so. Frederick is preparing that suite down the hall, in the corner. It's about as far from us as possible."

"Aunt Joan will love that," Greg says sarcastically. "That was her suite growing up."

"Well, I'm sorry, but it's the best I can do."

"I know." Greg feels sorry for Julie. She is trying to be fair to everyone, but the only result is her being fair to no one and nothing --- especially their marriage. He needs an anchor, a lifeline, but so far he has nothing. The closest are his chats with Jack. They are not quite doing the trick.

Greg reassures his wife that everything will work out. A lie, he knows, because Ann's presence will just make their lives a nightmare every day. He knows that she isn't responsible for Munroe, but that doesn't matter. Just the mention of her name reminds him of the murder. It is something that can't be helped.

Julie suggests that he stay in Atlanta for a few more days. This will give her time to arrange things at home while giving him a much needed break. Her offer reminds him of the fact that they still have not had a honeymoon. It makes him feel a little guilty. Anyway, he agrees. A vacation from Manchester and Faraway Hill could be just what he needs.

After dropping off his luggage at the Four Seasons, the cab takes Greg back out of the city toward the huge Halloran mill there. For the next several hours he meets with different key people and takes yet another tour of the loud, busy facility. None of this is fun, but Greg has found it easier put out fires in person in a single day that trying to put them out over the phone.

At mid afternoon, his secretary calls him. Both CNN and MSNBC are reporting calmer conditions in Thailand as rumors grow that the king will negotiate a compromise between the parties. This is good news; it means the new mill there won't be affected any time soon.

The sky begins to darken when one of the mill's managers, anxious to please the boss, drives him back to the hotel. Greg just lets the man prattle on. He's too tired to care and is looking forward to crashing. Atlanta's Four Seasons is an elegant, European-style hotel with a neoclassical look housed in one of the city's premier office towers. He always takes a luxury suite: with two rooms and one and a half baths it feels less like a hotel than a small, well appointed apartment.

Arriving, Greg manages to convince the man to just drop him off rather than escort him inside. Greg needs a break from everything, including business. But stepping through the hotel's handsome glass doors, he finds a surprise: looking comfortable in an overstuffed chair is a smiling Jack Campbell.

Faraway Hill

The Cast of Characters

Karen Scott St. John

After growing up as the youngest child of a popular university professor, Karen Scott left New Hampshire for the glamour of Boston and New York City where she married a wealthy stockbroker. But beneath her polished façade is a woman with a dark side that twists and turns in shockingly evil ways.

Greg Halloran

A member of New Hampshire's leading family, Greg has always felt apart. Now he feels divided: torn between the woman he loves (and is marrying) and the other great love of his life —- college lover Jack Campbell.

Julie King Halloran

Beautiful, smart and confident, Julie King's life seems to be coming together nicely: a wonderful fiancé, a baby on the way and a successful little business.

She has no idea what's in store for her.

John (Jack) Campbell

All of his life, handsome and athletic Jack Campbell has been the most popular guy in the room. He grew up with wealth, has enjoyed lovers of both genders and generally a cool, cushy life.

But a former lover re-enters his world with a revelation that that risks everything.

Ann Gale Bradley

The only child of a struggling, alcoholic father, Ann Gale has always dreamed of something better. Instead, she's settling for life married to a hunky farmhand with a secret career that will help make her New Hampshire's most scandalous woman.

Eve Scott King

Karen St. John's older sister (and Julie's mother) has a great career at a Manchester bank and a happy marriage with successful attorney Ben King.

Unfortunately, Karen has the ability to upend Eve's entire world.

Benjamin (Ben) King

One of New Hampshire's most successful lawyers, Ben King is about to go on an emotional and professional rollercoaster that will leave his head spinning —- and maybe dead.

Lorene Graves Gale

The sweet, quiet wife of troubled farmer has a past no one, not even her daughter Ann Gale, could possibly imagine.

Lewis Halloran

The patriarch of New Hampshire's leading family, Lewis has a skeleton in his closet that he plans to reveal on his own timetable and in his own way.

Too bad that someone else has a different plan.

Mark Bradley

Handsome, hunky and arrogant farmhand Mark Bradley knows how pleasing others can be profitable —- very profitable.

But he has recently learned that blackmail is an even better moneymaker.

Vivian Guthrie Stevens Bickel

Vivian Bickel found love with her first husband and friendship with a Faraway Hill family. Sadly, a double tragedy would send her out of town and into the world of a cruel man with a bloody career.

Agnes Gabler

New Hampshire's greatest living (and most colorful) artist is hailed throughout the world for her remarkable paintings.

About to turn 95, Agnes offers her friends wonderful tales and valuable advice.

Joseph (Joe) Westbrook

Joe is a charming, young single dad whose life began very differently —- and that unusual origin may cost him and his little boy their lives.

Richard Davis

Senator Richard Davis comes from one of New Hampshire's great families and has reached an impressive level of success.

Soon that success will be at risk thanks to a sexy young woman with a scandalous past.

Joan Halloran

Four husbands, one son and a big bank account make it possible for Joan Halloran to lead a luxurious life in a spotlight of her own creation —- a spotlight that rival Karen St. John would love to steal away.

Robert Halloran

Within the family, he's known as the "Quiet Halloran" who is a life-long bachelor focused on his business interests.

If only they knew the truth.

Mel Waite

Recovering compulsive gambler Mel has built a successful law firm with friend and partner Ben King. But Mel is reverting to old habits with a gamble that will either leave him very rich —- or dead.

Peter Brandt

Handsome and idealistic, Peter Brandt loves his family and his hometown, Faraway Hill.

Unfortunately, he's also drawn to women he shouldn't have.

Patrick Halloran

College student Patrick is about to join the most powerful, secret society in America —- but worries about paying the high price of membership.

Matthew Newberry

The only child of Joan Halloran and her first husband, Matthew is about to embark on a new phase in his life that requires the ultimate commitment.

Denise Sullivan

A party girl and college pal (in bed and out) of both Greg Halloran and Jack Campbell, beautiful Denise is starting a new job filled with equal amounts of glamour and horror.

Michael (Mike) Bickel

Mike has had a tough life and it has made him a tough man. These days he's working for a man even tougher than himself, and people die because of it.

Barry Studer

Young, up-and-coming attorney Barry Studer is passionate about his career but its another passion that may end in tragedy.

Munroe Gale

Everyone in Faraway Hill knows about Munroe Gale's alcoholism and struggling farm.

What they don't know will cost him his life.

EPISODE NINE

Every time Greg Halloran visits the Four Seasons, he is struck by the beautiful way the lobby melds a classical style with modernity. From the marble floors to the Grand Staircase, this 21st century hotel in Atlanta would not look out of place in 1900 Paris. He has been using it on each trip to the Georgia mill. For Greg, stepping through the door has become like stepping through a portal to some distant, special place far from the many problems back home. Here he can set aside his troubled marriage, heavy workload and scandalous half-sister. Every visit starts with a smile. These smiles always come naturally, easily. But he has never smiled as he has today, a smile of pure joy. All because Jack Campbell is here.

"Aren't you going to say something, dude?" Jack is sitting on a chair in one of the lobby's elegant conversation areas. His briefcase is on the floor and some papers are stacked on the table next to him. He's obviously been here for awhile, killing time with some work. "I made a special trip just to see you."

"You did, why?"

"Because you need me," Jack says with a warm, caring smile of his own, just as natural as Greg's. "And chatting online isn't doing it anymore. Not for me and sure as hell not for you."

"How did you find me?"

"Your secretary; she remembered me from the wedding. All I had to do was sweet talk her to get what I need." Greg knows very well how skilled Jack is at sweet talk.

Jack smiles at him again, this time waiting for an answer. Greg knows he's vulnerable right now and Jack knows it too. Maybe that's a good thing. His marriage is floundering and he is having trouble seeing how to survive the onslaught of Ann living with them day in and day out. Jack has made it clear for months that he regrets the break-up. Maybe Greg needs to look beyond the hell he is trapped in if he wants to find happiness, or some peace; even if it's something temporary in this special oasis. "I'm glad you're here Jack."

Hungry, Greg suggest the hotel's elegant eatery, the Park 75. It's still early in the evening and there are not many people yet. They are alone in the restaurant, or at least alone enough to really talk. Once the waiter has taken their order, Jack leans in and asks simply, "so how are you doing, really?"

"Not great," he says with a sigh. "The farm girl won."

"You pretty much expected that."

"I know." Ben repeatedly warned him that it was inevitable.

"So, what all does she get again? You said she took the family name."

Greg rolls his eyes. Calling herself Halloran stills annoys him. "Yeah, that's bad enough. Well, for starters she gets 10% of the business and the funds to help pay the tax."

"Is that going to make it hard for you to run things?"

"Doubtful; I get 20% and the family trust still owns 40%. My aunts and Dad's cousin own the rest. But the worst of it all is that she's *in* the trust."

The waiter returns to pour them each a glass of wine, a nice red the server recommended, and then leaves. Jack takes a sip. "The family trust; I'm not sure what that all means."

"It means she gets money from it, has a say in it and, worst of all," Greg pauses to take his own sip of wine to fortify himself, "she has the right to live in the house with us."

"Holy shit! She's not going to it, is she?"

"Oh, yeah: yesterday morning she told Julie that she wouldn't but last night the bitch calls to say that she *will*. I was so damned pissed off when I heard that . . . well, Julie suggested that I stay in Atlanta for a few more days while she tries to 'work things out' --- more like so I can cool off."

"I'm sorry dude."

Greg wistfully stares at a watercolor on the wall. Something with flowers he can't identify. "It's going to end my marriage."

"You don't know that," Jack answers. Greg can hear the hope in his voice even as he tries to mask it. "The two of you have only been together a few months."

"I really love her, I do," Greg tells him, a simple statement of fact. "I love talking to her and making love to her and just spending time with her. I've been faithful to her since our wedding. But . . . I am beginning to think our marriage is cursed . . . all because of that fucking farm girl and her old man." The waiter comes by with their order: pasta for Greg, a chef salad for Jack. It occurs to Greg that he should go with salad too. He's put on a few pounds over the summer despite almost daily jogs. "I guess that seems strange to you, all the lovers you've had," he says to Jack after the waiter leaves.

"What does that mean jackass?" Jack sounds insulted. "I fell in love with *you*."

"I mean with a *woman*. You love chasing them and you love fucking them, but you never really loved one. Not like how I loved Lauren or Julie."

Jack sets his fork down. He seems compelled to set the record straight. "Believe it or not, dude, I *was* in love with a woman once."

"You were? That's news to me."

"I never told you about it because, well, it was really painful for a long time."

"You don't have to, you know."

"That's okay; it's not too bad now. I was 18 and it was the summer before college. She was a sophisticated older woman at the ripe old age of 25." Greg laughs so hard at that he nearly chokes on his pasta. Even Jack chuckles; it was a good line.

"Her name was Jacqueline. Everyone called her Jackie and we had a lot of fun with that: Jack and Jackie." Jack smiles at the memory. "She was sexy and smart and kind of a tomboy --- she knew more about football than any man. There was always something . . . different . . . about her. I could never really figure out what it was, but it was a hell of a turn on. I was just a kid and I fell for her. I fell hard. I offered to give up school, everything, just for her. But that's when Jackie dumped me. She didn't want anything that serious. It hurt, dude, it hurt for a long, long time."

Greg obviously understands. "Just like what Lauren did to me."

"After that, I just fucked around with whatever was available. Girls, guys, it didn't matter . . . until I met you."

'Then you dumped me too."

"The dumbest thing I ever did."

Their meal finished, Greg and Jack just sit there and stare at each other. Not caring who might be watching, Jack reaches his hand across the table. Greg takes it into his and asks, "Did you get your own room?"

"No," Jack replies. "I was hoping I wouldn't need to."

The waiter comes by; there will be no dessert, just the check, which Jack offers to pay. After that, nothing more is said. Jack simply follows Greg to the elevators and up to the 19th floor. Greg's suite has a sitting room, bedroom and 1 ½ baths.

But just as they close the door behind them and before he can offer anything like a tour, Jack takes Greg into his arms for a deep, sensuous and probing kiss. That's all Greg needs. Jack has him. They alternately kiss and strip, stumbling and laughing their way from the sitting room to the bed, plopping naked together on top of the pillows. They make out for what seem like an eternity, their hard cocks rubbing against each other, until Jack breaks away. "I've so missed being inside you. I *need* to be inside you, lover."

"Then do it."

Jack grins and pulls Greg's legs apart to lick his ass, making him squirm, lubricating with his tongue. And then, without saying a word, Jack mounts him and pushes his hard cock inch by glorious inch into him. There is some pain; Greg has never bottomed for anyone but Jack, the man who took his cherry. And the last time they fucked was a year and a half ago. But once Jack is completely merged with him, the pain subsides, and Greg wraps his legs around his lover. They kiss again, even more urgently than before. Finally Jack feels the urge to start pumping, saying over and over again to Greg's delight, "I've missed your ass so much . . . it's so perfect for my cock . . . so perfect . . ." until Greg can feel Jack cum inside him, filling his ass with warm liquid. They rest for a moment for Jack to catch his breath. Then, keeping his cock inside Greg, Jack starts to jack off his lover. "Do it for me, dude." It doesn't take long, and Greg's own cock complies, coating his stomach and chest. Jack, still inside him, collapses on Greg's sticky body. "I love you so much, Greg."

"I love you too, Jack"

****

The next morning, Ann pulls her used Toyota Camry up to the portico of the Halloran mansion. She was so proud when she bought the car, using money she earned at various jobs. But one drunken night Munroe bumped it with his truck, putting a serious dent in the passenger door. Mark often talked about fixing it, but he never did. None of that matters any more. Now that her inheritance is finally coming through, she plans on buying something new; something to make the girls who teased her in school jealous.

But there is one person she doesn't want to hurt, so she just sits in the Camry for a moment, looking at the house. Ann feels guilty about what she is doing to her best friend. It is true that her attorney is pushing for this, but Julie was right last night: Ann *wants* to live here. She didn't lie in the café; Ann meant what she said. But after thinking it over, she realizes that she has to do this. It isn't about some childhood fantasy or revenge --- at least as she sees it --- but about justice. This is where she should have been all along.

Emerging from her car Ann walks up to the door and rings the bell. The butler, Frederick, called late yesterday to arrange this orientation. The elderly man opens the door with a polite, "welcome madam." Stepping into the Grand Vestibule, she is again impressed by its size. This entry is more than twice as big as her parents' living room --- and this is just where guests are greeted. "So, where is Julie?"

"Mrs. Halloran is upstairs with the decorator and has asked me to guide you." That is a surprise. After last night Ann was certain Julie was too angry to do anything to welcome her. "She doesn't need to hire a decorator for my room."

"She didn't," the butler replies with a slight, ironic smile. "The decorator is for the nursery."

Too embarrassed, she doesn't respond.

"Shall we begin, madam?" Ann nods and follows Frederick into the aptly named Grand Hall. It seems everything in this house is designed to impress. He begins to explain everything in a very business like manner. He describes the vestibule's purpose and even a little of its history, repeating and augmenting many of the things the tour guide told wedding guests months ago. They walk east toward the ballroom. The door on the left, he explains, leads to the servants' quarters in the lower level. There is a button on a wall in each room that can be used to summon him.

They come into the ballroom. Ann remembers it well from the wedding, but it looks even bigger now that she sees it empty. Turning around and heading west, Frederick reintroduces her to the handsome Green Room and the huge oval Blue Room. He points out the study where Munroe shot and killed Lewis Halloran, but does not take her inside. The door is locked and has been for months. Next to the study is the Formal Dining Room.

Across the hall is the family parlor. This was one of the many spaces that were off limits during the wedding tour. It is one of two true informal rooms on the entire ground floor. It has casual, comfortable furniture of the kind you'd find in anyone's home. A plasma TV dominates one wall. It is much smaller than the formal rooms. Next to the parlor is the family dining room --- just as informal as the family parlor --- and the mansion's kitchen.

The Grand Staircase, at the western end of the Grand Hall, is a beautiful marble structure with brass railings. She has not been above the first floor before. As Frederick leads her up, Ann is again reminded of the wedding tour. "There are key differences between the Halloran Mansion and the White House," the guide explained. "For example, where Lewis Halloran's den is currently located is where the Red Room was in the original Executive Mansion. The upper floor, which we are not allowed to tour for privacy sake, are all bedrooms. But in the first White House, it was upstairs that the president had his office and where the cabinet met. There is no Oval Office in the Halloran home --- because there was none in the original White House."

Arriving on the second floor, Ann is amazed at her first sight of Center Hall: it runs, non-stop from one end to the other culminating in an elegant arched window. "During the reconstruction in the 1960s," Frederick tells her, "the second floor was redesigned to reduce the total number of bedrooms and create a collection of suites." Each suite has a parlor, bedroom and full bath. Except for the master suite; this is on the south side of the house, right above the Green Room, Blue Room and study. The suite's rooms are the same dimensions as its counterparts on the first floor, with the suite's parlor an oval shape just like the Blue Room.

Across from the master suite is the nursery. Ann can see Julie through the open door, where she is conferring with the decorator as wall paper is being hung. Ann smiles at her best friend, hoping things are better today. They are not. Julie says nothing to her and closes the door between them.

Disappointed, Ann follows the butler to a door at the very end of the hall, the furthest place on the floor. The location is another clear message to Ann that she really isn't welcome here.

The suite is decorated with rose wallpaper and faux French Provencal furniture that it looks oddly tacky and out of place in so historic a home. Frederick explains that it was Joan Halloran's suite growing up and that if she wants to make any changes, it should be fast. "Mr. Halloran will be back in a few days," the butler cautions her. 'You are expected to be settled by then." It is at this moment that Ann realizes that Frederick must feel the same way about her as do the Hallorans. His good manners and helpful demeanor are simply part of the job. But Ann decides not to let any of it get her down and says with a smile, "then I'll have to get started right away."

Frederick steps back into Center Hall, giving Ann a moment to better assess the space. Yes, the furniture has to go. It seems unlikely that she'll be able to repaint or repaper the walls in only a few days, so she'll have to live with it for now. Ann is about to go out and talk to Frederick about the plans when her cell rings. "Hello, Mr. King."

"Good morning, Ann. We have the papers ready for you to sign. With that, you'll have full access to your inheritance." The timing couldn't be more perfect. But Ann is surprised by the speed. "That soon?"

"Well, I thought it would be good to get it out of the way." He sounds a little testy. Ann is unpopular with everyone these days. "I can be there in a little while." She claps the cell shut and informs Frederick of her plans. He escorts her past the nursery's closed door and back down stairs. Within minutes, she's speeding along the highway away from Faraway Hill and toward Manchester. There isn't much traffic at mid morning, but finding a parking place at busy Brady Sullivan Plaza proves to be a bit challenging. Fortunately the garage on Amherst Street has space.

Ann arrives at the offices of Waite, King & Associates thinking about how tough things have been for Ben and Eve since learning about the embezzlement. The battle over her inheritance has probably made things worse. But there isn't anything she could or would do to change it. Ann is finally going to have the life she always wanted.

Ben's secretary buzzes her in right away and she is surprised to find Eve there with her husband. Neither of them looks happy. "Good morning Ann," Eve says. There is no smile her face. *No,* Ann thinks to herself, *they are not happy.*

"Good morning, Mrs. King." Ben motions her over to his desk. "Here are the papers you need to sign." He points out what each document does --- one is from Atlantic-New Hampshire, the bank Eve works for; the rest are about transferring stock title and relate to the family trust. Ann signs them quickly, and asks "when can I access the funds? I need to buy some furniture today."

Ben and Eve exchange hopefully glances. "Does this mean you are getting your own place?" Eve asks her.

"No, I need to prepare my suite at the mansion." The look the Kings exchange now is very different. "I was really hoping that you wouldn't do that," Ben says.

"I'm sorry, Mr. King, I know what I told Julie yesterday, but my lawyer is really insisting that I take up residence. Besides, it's my ancestral home just as much as it is Greg's."

"No one is disputing that, but we are very worried about our daughter."

"I love Julie. She's like a sister to me. I plan to make every effort to get along with everyone. Now, is there anything else I need?"

Disappointed, Ben shakes his head.

"You'll be able to access funds today," Eve says handing her a letter. It tells anyone interested in doing business with Ann how to confirm the funds are available along with a temporary debit card. Ann thanks them and leaves. Just outside the door, he can hear Ben pound his desk and yell, "damn!"

****

Some people might find confinement in a hotel room claustrophobic. But for Greg and Jack, it feels more like cocooning. Except when Greg needs to slip on a robe to accept orders from room service, they remain naked all day. With the sex over, their nudity is all about intimacy rather than orgasms. It doesn't matter what they are doing. They can be in the shower together, necking under the hot water. Or they can just be lying on the sofa, watching an old movie on TV as Jack curls Greg's pubic hair around his finger.

And, of course, they talk.

The two of them talk about anything and everything. Something on the news, a business deal --- and especially family. "I have to admit," Greg tells him. "The Lamaze classes are actually pretty great. It's the only time Julie and I feel like a couple again. But then something with the Farm Girl gets in the way and we end up fighting again or worse, not speaking to each other." Jack discusses his family, including how supportive his kid brother has become. "He's
Even curious," Jack chuckles, "and asks me the craziest --- sometimes dirtiest --- questions."

"Maybe he's bi, too --- or even gay."

"He might be. Of course, I think mostly he's trying to embarrass me. Nick likes yanking my chain." But Jack's father still doesn't know. "His health isn't good, you know, and he's so damned Catholic. I want to tell him; I think I'm over the fear now that Mom and Nick know. But Mom is worried about how he'll take it. I *will* tell him, when it's right. I owe you --- all of us --- that much."

Greg has always enjoyed lying around naked with a lover. He did it often with Lauren and every Sunday with Jack was essentially Nudity Day. But the last time he did anything like this was a year ago, with Debbie the waitress in her tiny studio apartment in Manchester. Both women had terrific bodies that he liked to explore, but Jack's is nearly perfect in its proportions and definition. He has always been such a jock, a confident often cocky jock. That was what attracted Greg to him in the first place. But now the best moments are these, just lying together, nude and doing nothing but enjoying it.

Julie has never really got into just being naked. She always insists on wearing a robe in what are supposed to be relaxed, intimate moments. It's gotten worse with the pregnancy as she is even more sensitive about her growing body. He loves the changes and feeling the baby move inside her. But for some reason she feels differently. Thoughts about his wife bring Greg back to the big question, the one they've been ignoring: "what do I do now?"

"There isn't much choice, dude," Jack answers, holding him tight. "You've got a kid on the way."

Greg loves feeling Jack's warmth envelope him. "I know, but how do I face her after this?" Going back home, Greg will have to pretend nothing has changed. And sharing a bed with her again might be awkward even though Julie isn't into sex these days.

"Don't worry about that. You can hide us from Julie, at least for now. I spent a lot of time with her at the wedding. She's smart, but there is no reason for her to be suspicious. As far as anybody in Faraway Hill knows, we're just best buds."

"I suppose so. But there's the Farm Girl to consider. Having her around every day will just make everything more stressful."

****

Even the blackest of black sheep will find doors open to them, if they are members of the right family. Ann is learning that quickly. Immediately after leaving Ben's office she drives northeast to the corner of Valley and Wilson streets. There she stops at one of the stores she always dreamed of shopping: the impressive, elegant, 130-year old C. A. Hoitt Furniture Company. All she needs to do is present Eve's letter and the debit card and the staff is all too happy to serve a Halloran, even if this Halloran is New Hampshire's dirtiest joke.

The associate most helpful is a middle age woman named Maureen who reminds Ann of her mother. They have the same build, the same smile, a similar hair color and names that rhyme. She even walks a lot like Lorene. They are so alike in so many ways that it is a little disturbing.

Maureen admits that local history is a hobby of hers and has read everything published about the Halloran mansion. She tells her little things about the house, including the big renovation that happened long before Ann was born. People generally avoid talking to her about anything, and especially about the Hallorans. But the woman ignores the scandals of the past four months and treats Ann as someone special. She helps pick out the furniture --- including a handsome sleigh bed --- and makes the necessary calls to expedite delivery. Ann especially enjoys hearing someone call her "Miss Halloran" without a trace of irony or contempt. It's nice for a change. But the reality lurks in the back of her mind: the first person to treat her as a true Halloran isn't a Halloran.

It gets Ann thinking about her own loneliness. Soon she will be living in a big house among a big family with a big bank account and still be alone. No one: not a husband or a father or maybe even a best friend. No one, that is, except her mother. The mother who built Ann's life on lies, raised her amid rural poverty and gave her an alcoholic for a father. The mother she hasn't seen or spoken to since that night months ago when the truth finally came out.

The only mother Ann has, the mother this kind sales lady reminds her
so much of.

"Are you alright Miss Halloran?" Maureen asks. Ann realizes that she has =
started to cry. "Yes, I'm fine." She wipes a tear from her cheek. "Let's wrap this
up, okay?"

****

Eve King almost forgot about Halloween. Tonight is Faraway Hill's scheduled
trick-or-treat, and she has volunteered to be a safe stop. The decorations have
been up for a few days, but she bought the candy only this afternoon.

Dinner at the King home is normally a quiet affair, but not with the doorbell
ringing every few minutes. "This won't go on for much longer," Eve assures her
husband. Most of the kids' costumes are of the drug store variety. They are
generally polite and their smiles are sweet. Normally she finds it endearing to see
little boys and girls all dressed up, but tonight the distraction is a little annoying.

"Its fine," Ben replies getting up from the table. He hasn't been eating well
lately. It concerns her. Between their daughter's troubled marriage and trying to
save his law firm, Eve has seen the strain grow over the last few months.

Ben steps back into the living room. Exhausted, he plops on the sofa and again
opens the folder provided by Agent Pembroke. He's been looking at the papers
over and over all day. *I wish he'd leave it alone, at least for a little while.* The
agent has been providing them with updates on the case. They found Melvin
Waite in Belize. Someone there sent photos back. The problem is that there is no
extradition treaty, so he can live comfortably there with little harassment. The
pictures show Mel laughing, dining and shopping. All with money he stole from
the firm he and Ben created. "I still don't understand," Ben says to his wife. "I
mean, it's not like he stole millions. He can't live on this forever. What does he
expect will happen?"

Eve wants to sit next to him and comfort her husband, but the doorbell keeps
pulling her away. Eventually, fewer and fewer kids come by and the official trick
-or-treat time ends. "What do you think he'll do," she asks him, "when the
money runs out?" Ben shrugs. "I have no idea. He's usually a good planner,
almost anal retentive about details. It all seems so strange." Eve has no idea what
to say, and the phone rings before she can think of something.

"Hi Mom."

"Hello dear, how are you feeling today?"

"Not too bad, but that back ache has returned; any ideas what to do about it?"

"Oh . . . well, you may want to go back to that spa in Manchester." Eve hates that fact that she cannot provide her daughter with real pregnancy advice. She knew this might happen some day, but that doesn't make it any easier. "A good massage always helps."

"Is that what you did when you were pregnant?"

"Your father was very good about that," Eve lies. She also hates to lie. But after doing it for 25 years, she can certainly disassemble with the best of them --- like Karen. "Doesn't Greg rub your back?"

"Of course, but he's still in Atlanta."

"I thought he was due back today."

"He was, but considering everything I suggested he stay there a little longer." *In other words,* Eve realizes, *to let Ann move in while hopefully avoiding a scene.* It makes sense, but she can't help but think Julie is delaying the inevitable. But rather than push it, Eve changes the subject. "How is the decorating coming along?"

"Pretty good; the nursery will look so adorable when it's done. Would you like to go shopping with me tomorrow, to pick up a few things?" Mother and daughter agree to a rendezvous at the Mall of New Hampshire the next morning.

After hanging up, Eve turns to look at her troubled husband and thinks about her troubled daughter, and how people like Karen and Mel can screw up so many lives.

****

Jack borrows Greg's robe just long enough for a room service attendant to remove the dishes from dinner. The entire day has been wonderful, reconnecting with the man he loves more than anyone in the world. Shedding the robe, he peers into the bedroom. Greg looks so sexy, lying there naked and asleep. It reminds him of the good days, back in college. He wants to climb into bed and wrap his nude body around Greg's and drift off with him. But there is something else Jack has to do first. So he gently closes the bedroom door and rummages around the parlor's floor for his cell phone. It rolled off during their mad strip last night and found its way under the sofa. He dials. The other person picks up on the second ring. "So, what's the news?" the man asks brusquely.

"Hello to you, too," Jack says, thinking what an asshole the old man is.

"Don't give me that shit. Did everything go as planned?"

"Of course it did. Was there any doubt?"

"Considering how badly you fucked up over the summer, yeah, I'd say there was plenty of doubt."

"Shit, his father was murdered," Jack tries to keep his voice down. The last thing he wants right now is for Greg to wake up and learn what's happening. "There was no way I could get to it then. All the cops and reporters and family around the house. You know we had to wait for another opening."

"Whatever. So, you two love birds are together again," the man sniggers. "Should I send you a card?" If he wasn't thousands of miles away right now Jack would be kicking his fat ass. "Look, the point is that I can now arrange for another visit to Faraway Hill. I can get it then --- and you can get the hell out of my life --- forever."

"That's fine by me."

"But even after I get it, you'll see nothing until I get those photos. How do you plan on doing that? I'm sure the Feds are watching all the airports."

"You let me worry about that. Just call me when you get the stuff. Hell, don't worry: this will finally be over. Then you two faggots can live together in same-sex wedded bliss."

"You really are an asshole, Melvin Waite."

****

Ann finishes up her little Lean Cuisine dinner, eaten alone in Julie's condo without anyone or anything --- even the TV --- to keep her company.

It is interesting what loneliness will do. Often it will encourage someone to shut out the rest of the world even more. Ann realizes that's what she has been doing for weeks. *I can't go on like this.*

Scattered around the room are the suitcases and boxes she has been packing. This will be the third time in less than a year that Ann has moved into a new home. And this is the one she is least welcome to.

Its time to reconnect with her mother: throughout this busy, stressful day she has been thinking about it. Too much has happened. She needs someone on her side.

Since downtown Manchester shuts down by six, she drives her Camry to the Mall of New Hampshire. After checking out a few of the specialty shops, she picks out a pair of expensive but tasteful diamond earrings at Macy's. A

Hallmark store just a few steps away have elegant little gift bags. Properly prepared, Ann drives out to the Gale farm.

But things are not the same.

Ann hasn't been back to the farm since that night when Lorene admitted that Lewis Halloran is her father. The farm she left hadn't changed much since she was a little girl. The buildings were old and dirty. Junked tractors and other equipment lay about covered in rust and weeds. As a child and especially a teenager, Ann hated bringing friends home. So almost never did. The farm was too embarrassing, Munroe too shameful.

But a lot can happen in four months.

She knew Lorene had accepted Lewis' bequest. But since mother and daughter had stopped speaking, Ann had no idea what she did with the money. Now she can see it: all the junk is gone. The yard around the house is nice and tidy. The house, barn and even silo have fresh coats of white paint with pale blue trim. The gravel drive has been paved. The entire farm has received a makeover so impressive and surprising that Ann sits in her car just staring at it.

Finally, she picks up the little gift bag and steps up to the door. Her first instinct is to just walk right in. But Ann doesn't live here anymore. She is about to knock when she notices a doorbell button --- never there before --- and presses it. A warm, welcoming chime can be heard from inside, followed by some footsteps. Ann takes a deep breath as the door opens with a surprise so unexpected that all she can say is, "who the hell are you?"

EPISODE TEN

Ann Gale used to love poetry. She read some almost every day. It was the perfect escape growing up, especially since she had no TV in her bedroom. As a small child it was the rhymes of Dr. Seuss. As a pre-teen she fell in love with classic romance poetry. The stories of King Arthur and his Guinevere enthralled her. Reading *Don Quixote* in high school opened her eyes, with a hero that in many ways resembled Munroe. Her father always seemed to be fighting against something, but until her mother's revelation this year, Ann had no idea what.

Like all kids in New Hampshire schools, she read the works of Robert Frost, who lived and wrote at a little farm in the town of Derry. Many of his most famous poems were created amid the cold and the snow. His use of everyday speech to express to express complex emotions grabs a teenage girl's soul.

But it is unlikely that Frost any of those other poets could explain the shock Ann Halloran feels seeing a stranger standing at her mother's door.

"Who the hell are you?" Just as she says the words, Ann realizes how rude it was. "I'm sorry," she quickly adds, "I didn't mean it that way."

The woman, a handsome if not beautiful middle age African American with graying hair and oversized glasses, looks at her warily. "Can I help you?" she asks Ann, caution underlying every word in a way no poet could do justice.

"I don't know," she says confused. *Is it possible mom moved without telling me?* "I'm looking for Mrs. Gale. Does she still live here?"

The woman looks at her more intently know until her face suddenly brightens with recognition. "Are you Annie?"

"Wow, no one's called me that since I was little."

"That's probably because that's the last time I saw you," the woman says with a warm, welcoming smile. "Come in, dear."

Ann steps into the house feeling more like Alice stepping through the looking glass than a prodigal daughter returning home. It is the same living room she remembers growing up, but also very different. Gone is the old furniture and fading drapes. Aging wallpaper has been removed. The entire room has been redone in comforting browns, tans and greens with a matching sofa and loveseat set. The only things left over from her childhood are the photos: old images of Ann and Lorene and, yes, even Munroe including the framed family portrait ---- taken when she was just ten --- and still hanging over the fireplace.

Your mother is in the barn taking care of something. I've just made some tea, would you care for any?"

"I suppose so . . . but, if you don't mind my asking: just who are you?"

"Oh, I'm sorry," the woman laughs gently. "I'm Vivian."

"Hello Vivian."

"Your mother and I are, well, good friends."

"You are?"

"We knew each other many years ago, when I lived here in Faraway Hill. We still wrote each other often, more so when you were in school. Anyway, when your father passed I offered to come and be with her."

Ann has no recollection of Vivian, no memory of her mother mentioning the woman. Yet, she seems to know Ann well. "You still have that lovely hair. Such an adorable little girl you were. I remember seeing you take your first steps --- it was from the fireplace to . . . there, yes right there. You had a little trouble with balance, but you did it. It was so cute." This is a story Ann has never heard before. It just adds to the strange feeling of this strange moment.

Vivian leaves to get the tea. Ann looks around the room a bit more closely. The place looks so nice now. Growing up she was too ashamed to have anyone from school come to the house. It was a big reason she had so few friends. *Too bad it wasn't like this back then.*

"Ann?"

She turns to see her mother standing just inside the door. Lorene has also changed: she's lost weight, changed her hairstyle and no longer wearing second hand clothes. Its like ten years have been erased from her. She looks wonderful. "Hello mom," Ann says, feeling a tear on her cheek. "I'm really sorry."

Lorene says nothing. Instead she walks over to Ann and takes her daughter in her arms for a long overdue hug. Vivian, standing nearby carrying a tray, looks on with a smile.

✳✳✳✳

Greg and Jack finally get out of the hotel and spend the next few days being tourists. Greg has never taken the opportunity before and this is Jack's first visit to Atlanta. They check out the Georgia Aquarium and its huge tunnel that makes visitors feel as if they are underwater with the fish and animals surrounding them. A tour of the High Museum of Art reminds them of New York and, to a lesser extent, the Currier in Manchester with its collection of old masters like Monet as well as regional artists that neither man has ever heard of before.

The necessary evil of cell phones often intrudes. Greg gets calls from the office updating him on the Thai situation and from Julie keeping him informed on Ann's move. Jack makes calls to his office, to check in enough to keep out of trouble.

They consider a tour of the restored home of Margaret Mitchell, author of *Gone with the Wind*, which seems like a good idea --- until both men admit with a laugh that neither read the novel nor watched the entire film.

In one of her calls, Julie tells Greg about hosting Agnes Gabler's birthday party. It will be a big affair, with lots of media attention. He'd prefer not to do it. But Greg agrees. She needs something take her mind off Ann. Besides, it's hard to say no to you wife while your lover is standing next to you. He still loves Julie and looks forward to being a father. But what will come next, he is not sure.

The men continue exploring Atlanta. They even check out the World of Coca Cola, a museum to the soft drink, where they enjoy a good laugh at the mockumentary about Coke in the theater.

Eventually, on what is their last night together, Julie calls to tell Greg that Ann has moved into the mansion. It is a somber moment. It seems to call for something to lift his spirits. But the options seem limited: None of the city's teams are in town, so a game is out. Clubbing holds little appeal; both feel they are too old for that.

Instead, they return to Greg's suite to make love again. This time, it is slower and sexier as they caress each other's bodies and whisper hot things to each other. Jack allows Greg to top him, relishing the feel of his lover's cock. But even with that pleasure inside him, Jack can't stop his mind from wandering to Melvin Waite and the task he can no longer avoid.

****

Julie Halloran is starting to wish they had elevators in the early 1800s. The mansion's grand staircase may be one of the house's more beautiful elements, but the marble steps are not fun --- at least not for a very pregnant woman just weeks away from her due date. She uses them as little as possible, but use them she must. Frederick is gently helping her slowly climb the stairs. They stop at the landing to let Julie catch her breath. "Are you alright, madam?" the butler asks.

"Yes, just give me a moment." The stairs aren't the only thing Julie has been avoiding. There is also Ann. Her sister-in-law moved in yesterday and they haven't spoken yet. Julie is still angry --- and worried. Greg comes home today, and the tension in her body is almost unbearable. There is certain to be a confrontation if precautions are not taken.

Julie nods to Frederick and they continue up the stairs. Now she has to deal with that long hall running the entire length of the building. About half way they take another break, as she sits on an antique chair. There are a lot of antiques in this house. It sometimes makes Julie think she's living in a museum rather than a home.

Finally they reach Ann's door and Frederick knocks for her. Ann, wearing jeans and sweaty t-shirt, opens it. "We need to talk," Julie tells her without any greeting and before Ann can say anything. Frederick agrees to wait in the hall. Inside, there are still boxes scattered around and a maid is helping Ann get settled. Her new furniture arrived yesterday morning. It's impressive how fast Hoitt could fill the order.

Julie asks the maid to leave them for a moment. Once they are alone, Ann tries to reach out with "I know this is all tough for you, but . . ." Julie motions her to be quiet. "I just came to tell you that Greg is coming home today and I don't want any problems --- and I especially don't want a scene."

"You won't get one, not from me."

"Good. I have too much on my plate right now to play referee. The Gabler party, the baby, the holidays and the store all take up my energy." Not too mention the back pain. Ann sees it and guides her to the parlor's new settee. "Are you okay?"

Julie nods, sitting with a groan. "I just need to pace myself better." Ann places a pillow behind Julie's back. "Thanks."

"I hope now that I'm here I can help. No --- I mean that. It's not like I have a job and I *do* want to be part of this family. I even made up with Mom."

"You did?"

"I saw her the other day; the first time in months. She has a friend living with her now, and she's fixed up the farm really nice."

"You're not angry with her anymore?"

"No. I understand she was in a no-win situation. So was Lewis Halloran."

"And Munroe?"

Ann has trouble answering that question. The bad things he had done are still strong in her memory. Julie can see this and takes her hand. "He was a good man, Ann, at least when he was sober."

"He murdered Lewis. He killed my father."

"*Munroe* was your father. Besides, that's why I still think --- no, why I *know* it's a mistake moving in here."

"I know how you feel. How everyone feels. But Munroe is responsible for what Munroe did, not me." Ann squeezes Julie's hand. "I am willing to be part of this family, to be a sister to Greg. I just need a chance."

"We've been all through this. I agree with you about Munroe, but you are a reminder to everyone what happened."

"Are you saying that I should leave the house --- or leave Faraway Hill? Or maybe even New Hampshire?"

"That's not fair. I'm already in the middle more than I'd like."

"Then let me talk to Greg."

"Oh, God no," Julie says, shuddering at that prospect.

"I am a Halloran. I live in the Halloran house. I am going to be here for Thanksgiving and Christmas and your baby's first birthday. At the very least he and I should call some sort of truce."

Julie thinks about this for a moment. Ann has a point. Maybe she can bring him around enough to at least tolerate her and be civil. "I'll see what I can do, but I can't promise anything." Ann helps her stand up, which is becoming a bit of a struggle lately. "In the meantime, keep out of sight as much as possible. Okay?"

"Okay".

✳✳✳✳

Normally, sitting down with a client is simply a job to do. It's typically tedious, sometimes frustrating, often boring. But Eve King really enjoys her time with Agnes Gabler. The elderly lady is smart and funny and a delight. Because the Gabler account is so important --- and so prestigious --- Eve's boss is giving her a lot of leeway in servicing it. This means she can travel to the frail artist's renovated sugar house for their meetings rather than bring her to the office.

Managing the account is relatively easy. Although the amounts involved are large, Miss Gabler prefers conservative investments to protect her legacy. Upon her death, the sugar house and the land around it will become a center for young artists.

Conservative may describe her investment strategy, but certainly not her life. Eve's favorite part of each meeting, held every two weeks, is hearing the woman's stories while they sip herbal tea. She ran off to explore the world as a young woman, dabbling in everything from the dying days of Vaudeville to the hedonism of post-war Paris. Along the way were lovers (male and female), an out-of-wedlock daughter, a smattering of famous people and lots of art. Yet, Agnes Gabler always found her way back to this place. "No matter where I go," she explains simply, "New Hampshire is always my home. I love it here. My favorite places in the entire world are in the White Mountains: swimming near The Basin, hiking through the Presidential Traverse, climbing Profile Mountain." Eve can see that young girl in Agnes' face and picture her running through the woods leaping and laughing with joy. But the image doesn't last long. The old woman falls quiet for a moment, a soft smile of realization on her face. "I'm sorry; I sometimes forget I can't do those things anymore." Eve reaches out to take Agnes' hand in hers. The reassurance, the connection, feels so good.

Like everyone in New Hampshire, Eve has her own memories of the White Mountains. "You know, I cried so hard when the Old Man collapsed." The Old Man of the Mountain was a series of granite cliffs on Canon Mountain that, when viewed at the right angle, looked like a human profile. It had been there for as long as anyone can remember --- no one is certain exactly how long --- until it collapsed early one morning. The Man was so revered that it became the symbol of New Hampshire. Its unexpected demise felt like the sudden death of a family member to everyone across the state. "We all did," Agnes says understanding.

The melancholy mood, which so quickly replaced the joy of Agnes' wonderful stories, just doesn't want to leave them. "Yes, Eve, the suddenness of life can be overwhelming. Things don't always last forever or go as you plan."

"I know that very well."

Agnes pours them some more tea. Her daughter Scarlet is off running errands and the nurse companion --- whose name Eve still has trouble remembering --- is puttering about in another room. "This isn't really about the Old Man, is it? Your sadness, I mean."

"It's nothing for you to worry about, Agnes."

"Nonsense; we are friends now. Besides, you realize we old dykes are known the world over to be the wisest people."

"You are?" Eve answers with a smile. It would be nice to have someone to talk to, really talk to, about what is going on in her life. Most of her friends seem more interest in gossip than anything else.

"Of course: why, the Dali Lama consults with one of us all the time." They both laugh. It's a relief to have someone unselfishly reach out to her like this.

"There is so much going on. My husband and his practice, my daughter and her marriage; it's all just a bit much sometimes."

"I hear rumors about that girl, Ann, are all over --- what is it called?
The blogosphere."

Eve is surprised. "You know about things like blogging?"

"Darling, I'm only 94. It's the centenarians who are *completely* out of touch, "the old lady says with a giggle. "Actually, my grandson keeps me up on these things. Of course, it's mostly rumor and hearsay. Why, what is happening? Tell me some *real* news."

"Ann has decided to move into the big house."

"The family can't possibly be pleased about that."

"No," she says quietly, "they're not." What the kids are going through really worries her. She must be telegraphing these fears, as Agnes asks, "May I give you some advice, dear?"

"Please."

"We fret about our children. We do that a great deal; mostly because we like to. Fretting about them makes us feel important and wanted and needed. But it also makes us feel frustrated when the fretting leads to nothing."

"I certainly feel frustrated."

"But ultimately, there is something very important to know about fretting."

"And that is?"

"It doesn't mean much. In the end, no matter how much we worry about whatever it is we are worrying about, the universe will still do what the universe wants to do."

"And where did you pick up that piece of wisdom?"

"Why," Agnes answers with a naughty grin, "from the wise old dyke who advises the Dali Lama, of course."

****

Jack Campbell returns to New York with a briefcase full of papers, a stuffed overnight bag and a cell phone with several unreturned messages. He has been keeping the real world at bay and now he must return to it.

Jack lives in one of SoHo's many interesting, cast iron buildings that date back a hundred years. The loft is a big cavernous space divided into something like rooms by handsome industrial columns and brightened by curved windows looking out onto Wooster Street. He bought it while in college. This is the place he brought his girlfriends, the guys he hooked up with online and where he and Greg spent their happiest, most intimate moments.

It is also the place where his kid brother, Nick, sits on the leather sofa aggressively steering a car through an imaginary street on Jack's Xbox. "Hey dude, where have you been?"

"Away on business," Jack says tossing his briefcase and bag onto the bed. "Why are you here?"

"You said I could stay over." That's true; Jack forgot about it. He agreed to hang with the kid when he learned Greg would be in Atlanta. "Sorry, it just came up."

Nick steers a fake corner. "The old man's been asking about you."

"He's awake?" Their father, battling cancer, has been slowly growing sicker for months. A tough often unfeeling man with his family, he is proving equally tough with the grim reaper.

"Sometimes; it gets really depressing what with all those nurses hanging around the house. I hate going there; it feels too much like a hospital or a nursing home."

"That's what Mom wants." She seems to enjoy playing the martyr. This is odd considering how often she fought ---and nearly walked out on --- the old man.

"Yeah, I know. But he *does* want to know where you've been. He is such a fucking control freak. The man is about to die and he's still demanding reports on everything and everyone. Are you going to see him?"

It's probably something Jack should get out of the way before heading out to New Hampshire. "I guess I can see him tomorrow night." He should be able to handle a couple of hours with the family.

"You were with that guy, weren't you? That guy from college." Nick asks without taking his eyes from the TV. Jack told him about Greg months ago, when he came out to his mother and brother.

"I love him."

"But you fucked it up, Bro. Now he's married with a kid on the way."

Jack loosens his tie. "That won't last."

"How the hell can you know that?" Nick asks with a smart-ass smile. "Don't you think having kids changes things?"

"You've become wise in your old age. Be careful, soon you'll be twenty and senility will kick in."

"Hey, it's the truth and you know it. Besides, you've got a bigger problem. Dad may be sleeping a lot but he's still Dad."

"I know." The last thing Jack needs is to be reminded of the very obvious.

"If he finds out his son's a fudge packer you can kiss your inheritance goodbye."

"Nick, go out and chase some tail or sneak into a bar or something."

"Okay, I'll cool it --- for now. Want to order something from that Greek place down the street?" In other words, Nick is staying and the topic will come up again. *The damned kid is getting too smart for his own good.*

"By the way, this guy showed up this morning."

"Guy, what guy?" Could it be one of his past hook-ups? That would be embarrassing.

"Dunno; maybe somebody you dated. Anyway, he said his name is Westbrook and you knew his sister."

What an odd coincidence, Jack thinks, this after telling Greg about Jackie. "Actually, I dated *her* --- the sister --- years ago. But I don't remember a brother."

Nick drops the player. "Really --- wait --- I think I remember: is she the one? The older girl you were so serious about the summer before college?" Jack nods.

"Weird; Anyway, he left a note. It's by the 'fridge." Jack walks over to the counter and picks it up. The note reads *I really need to see you. It's about Jackie and it's important. Call me ASAP.* There is a number. "He seemed really stressed or scared or whatever, bro." *Could she be sick? Is she dead?* Jack hasn't heard from her since their painful breakup almost six years ago. But the thought she may be in trouble . . . he picks up his cell and dials. It answers on the first ring. Whoever this guy is, he's desperate to talk. "Is this Joe Westbrook?"

"Jack, Jack is that you?" His voice sounds familiar --- very familiar. Maybe they did meet when he was dating Jackie. But Nick is right; he also sounds desperate. "Yes, this is Jack Campbell.

"Thank God." Yes, there is a familiarity that is almost eerie. *Did we more than just meet --- did we hook-up, too?* It occurs to him that's he's fucked so many people over the years that he can no longer remember names. "I need to see you Jack. Right away; it's important."

"Your note says something's happened to Jackie. Is she alright?"

"No, she's not. She needs you. How soon can we meet?"

This all sounds a little weird. "Well, I just got back into town --- "

"Please, dude, tonight. We can meet anywhere." The guy sounds more than panicked; he actually sounds afraid. It makes Jack cautious and hesitant. "What's wrong with Jackie?"

"I can't tell you over the phone. It has to be in person." Jack hesitates again, but concern over the woman he almost gave up everything for can't be ignored. But he has no interest meeting a complete stranger in his loft. It needs to be someplace public. "Okay, there is a Starbucks down the street from me."

"Yeah, I know it. I'm there now." *Has the guy just been hanging out for hours?* "Okay, I'll be right there." Jack claps his phone shut at the same time Nick gives up on the game.

"I guess that means your going. Are you sure that's smart?"

"It's just down the street," Jack shrugs. "If he gets weird or anything, I'll just walk out." *Of course, it's already pretty weird: what could be wrong with Jackie and why is her brother acting so mysterious about it?* Jack tightens his tie and grabs his blazer. Just as he closes the door he hears Nick call out, "get something for dinner!"

****

"I told you she'd come around, eventually."

Vivian has been such a comfort for Lorene these last few months. Left all alone with her husband dead and daughter estranged, the woman had little in her life besides a crumbling farm and a big bank account. Vivian's sudden call --- needing help herself --- was a blessing .

"I know," Lorene responds, happier than she can ever remember. The two of them are in the kitchen, making dinner. Like the rest of the house it has been completely remodeled with new cabinets, wallpaper and appliances.

Vivian and Lorene have a natural comfort around each other. Eachh seems to understand the other in ways that cannot be easily explained. It surprises some people, even themselves at times, considering their differences in race and background and their years apart.

Their relationship began more than 20 years ago when both of them were young and newly married yet feeling very alone. Back then, Munroe and Vivian's first husband worked the Gale farm together while they labored to, quite literally, build homes. From plastering to plumbing, the women turned the farm house and little satellite house (the one Ann and Mark would later call home) into tolerable, if not fashionable, places to live.

It was a challenging time. Lorene was a new mother dealing with an alcoholic husband. Munroe could be so sweet at times, but whenever there was a problem he'd become depressed and withdrawn and turn to the bottle. Only Don, Vivian's husband, seemed able to draw him out. Don and Vivian Stevens had moved to Faraway Hill to get away from the racism and financial limitations of rural Georgia. Although New Hampshire was --- and still is --- primarily white, there were opportunities for them here they could not find back home. Lorene Graves first met them when Don hired on to do maintenance at the Halloran mansion. His friendliness and inherent goodness endeared him to her immediately. Munroe also took to him right off. After the scandalous night that left Lorene pregnant, the Stevens' became her biggest supporters and eventually came to work the Munroe's family farm.

Don's sudden death changed everything. Munroe began one of his worst periods, disappearing for weeks. The police were even contacted at one point. The two women, having no one else, grew closer; much closer. It began as two friends seeking solace in each other. Eventually they became lovers.

Their first night together was so incredible, so emotional, that the memory is seared into their minds and hearts. Each woman had the right touch and soft breath and knew just how the other's body works and what she needs to feel and hear. Even now, two decades later, those feelings and images still hover between them as they do something as mundane as cook dinner.

Munroe returned nearly three months later, feeling guilty and begging his wife to take him back. Lorene was torn. This man was her husband. He loved her and agreed to be a father to her little girl. But there was Vivian. Lorene did not want to let her go. But Munroe was so sincere, that Vivian graciously stepped aside and moved to California.

They cried in each other's arms when Vivian left and cried again when she returned.

The women kept in touch through the years, writing countless letters. Lorene kept her correspondence hidden, knowing how her husband would feel. Vivian married again, this time to a man who seemed as sweet and charming as Don. But she would soon learn differently. Her new husband earned his money in terrible, scary ways. Whenever Vivian would challenge him, Mike Bickel responded with cruel words and painful fists. When she learned of Munroe's death and Ann's estrangement, Vivian decided the time had come to escape. Lorene secretly sent her the money needed to come back to her.

Now, they are happily preparing a small chicken dinner in Lorene's beautifully remodeled home. Tonight they will share the same bed, making love, remembering that first time and knowing now what they knew then: they are truly each other's best friend.

✱✱✱✱

Starbucks, as always, is overflowing with people. There is a long line at the counter waiting for lattes and frappachinos. Normally Jack gets annoyed with crowds. This time, though, he is glad: it makes meeting the mysterious stranger much safer. The man can't get dangerous or too weird with so many people around them.

This being SoHo, the coffee shop has an interesting mix of customers. There are young artists with strange things sticking out of their faces and middle age professionals in overpriced suits. Most of them are clamoring on a cell phone or to a barista and even a few to each other.

"Jack," a voice pierces the din, "over here!"

He looks toward the back of the café to see a handsome man about 30, sitting next to a cute little boy of maybe five or six years old. The man waves Jack over. He is definitely related to Jackie Westbrook: the similarities are too obvious. The man, Joe, has her family's natural beauty. Jack remembers seeing it in Jackie's mother. Joe is well built with nice angles to his face and wavy hair. Definitely the type he used to hook-up with in school. *He must be Jackie's brother or maybe a cousin,* Jack thinks; *that's the only explanation.* But he wonders why Jackie never mentioned him before.

"Son," Joe says to the little boy, "please sit at that table while the gentleman and I talk. But stay where I can see you." The little boy picks up his juice and coloring book and moves to the empty little table beside them. Most people come to this Starbucks to order carryout. Several of the tables are empty.

"Cute kid," Jack says with a smile trying to be polite. "I take it you're Joe Westbrook?"

With a relieved look on his face Joe reaches out and shakes Jack's hand. He has a firm grip. "It's good to see you again."

Jack sits next to him. "Thanks, but, I'm sorry, I don't remember you. I mean, you seem familiar but . . ."

"You're not sure we've ever met before."

"Right."

"Actually, we *have* met; we were really close at one time." Jack has trouble believing that. Maybe they did hook-up, but Jack would definitely have remembered fucking such a handsome dude more than once.

"Poppa," the boy says cautiously, obviously shy around the stranger. "Can I have more juice?"

"Maybe; what's the magic word?"

The kid sighs with the same frustration every kid has with his parents. "Can I *please* have some more juice?"

"Okay, Jack," Joe reaches for his wallet and gives the boy some money. "But stay where ---"

"I know, I know, stay where you can see me." Annoyed, Little Jack takes the bill and walks over to the line. "You named him Jack?" Big Jack asks in surprise.

"Yes."

"Did you name him after Jackie?" That would make some sense. After all, Jacqueline was her given name; everyone just called her Jackie. But Joe fidgets a little, unsure how to explain. "Yes, sort of." He keeps a worried eye on his son. Fortunately, the line is moving at a decent pace right now. Joe motions Jack to lean in and whispers, "Jackie is in danger. She needs your help."

Danger; how could she be in any danger? "Fine," Jack whispers back. "But where the hell is she? I haven't seen her in years, not since before I went to college. Why isn't she asking me herself?"

Little Jack returns to his table next to them, happy to have more orange juice, and starts coloring again. Joe seems relieved to have the boy close again. *This whole scene is too fucking weird.* "Are you Jackie's brother, cousin, what?"

Joe pauses for a moment. He looks afraid to say something. After glancing back to the boy once more to make sure he's okay, Joe again whispers, "not exactly." Jack, on the other hand, is getting annoyed. "I don't get it," he says with a rising voice. "Just tell me what the hell is going on."

"I'm not Jackie's brother. She's never had any brothers or sisters." With a deep breath, the man takes Jack's hand in his. It seems odd at first to have a stranger do this. But it makes the sense of familiarity stronger. Jack can feel it in his grasp and see it in his eyes. "You have to understand something Jack, and I don't know how to tell you except to tell you straight out . . . shit, this is so hard, I wish I didn't have to do this . . ."

"Fuck it all," Jack nearly yells. "Tell me or I'm getting out of here. WHERE IS JACKIE?"

"Oh hell . . . Jack, *I am Jacqueline Westbrook* --- and your son and I need you."

EPISODE ELEVEN

Jack doesn't quite hear the news.

The noise in the coffee shop has gotten louder. Some guy with a Jersey accent is complaining about his espresso, upsetting the other customers. He is making such an ass of himself that everyone else in line rolls their eyes. The boy Jack actually finds it amusing. He sets aside his coloring book to giggle at the silly adults.

"Jack, dude, did you hear me?"

The Jersey man starts screaming at the barista, an overwhelmed girl in her twenties trying frantically to get his order right. One of the other customers tries to get Jersey Guy to calm down, but it doesn't work. Little Jack goes from giggles to outright laughter.

Joe says something again, this time completely lost amid the noise. He tries once more and Jack still misses it. Finally, he yells at the top of his lungs: "I HAD A SEX CHANGE OPERATION".

And the entire coffee shop grinds to a halt. The crowd just stops and stares at them. "Only in New York," Jersey Guy grumbles as he takes his remade espresso and stomps out the door. With a few chuckles and shaking of heads, the staff and customers return to their routine as if nothing happened. But Little Jack still finds it all funny and keeps laughing. Big Jack, however, is shocked.

"It's true Jack," Joe says embarrassed, but in a quieter tone. "I am --- was --- Jackie Westbrook."

Jack has no idea what to say. *Is this guy serious*?

"It's me; really. I'm Jackie. I had my last operation two years ago. Look, I still have that mole on my left shoulder, remember? You always said it looks like a little rose. I can show it to you again if you want."

He is serious. Jack suddenly understands those strange feelings of familiarity. *Holy shit: the man sitting across from me used to be the woman I loved!* "Oh, my God . . ." Suddenly another realization hits and Jack looks over at the little boy who has gone back to his coloring sweetly oblivious to everything else.

"Yes, Jack, he's your son --- *our* son. And it's a real long story."

****

Greg is acting strange. Not bad or negative, just . . . strange. Julie notices it immediately when she meets him at the airport. In one sense, he seems at ease, as if the last few days away have done him good. He walks up to her with a smile in a relaxed, confident manner. He gives her a warm hug and a loving kiss. He gently rubs her stomach and asks about the baby. None of this is surprising or unusual. It happens every time Greg returns from a business trip.

Yet, he also seems distant, reserved. It's very subtle. Greg says all the right things and does all the right things. Nevertheless, Julie can sense a change in her husband. She can't quite figure it out, but it is there.

On the ride home Julie updates him on the news. She has agreed to host Agnes Gabler's big birthday party. It is a huge deal and coming up very soon. "Fortunately, the event planner and Frederick have been able to work everything out," she explains. "I've just had too much on my plate with the pregnancy and the café and all." The "and all" is, of course, the unspoken subject of Ann. "I pretty much just have to buy a dress --- or at least a sequined tent," she says patting her large stomach. Greg smiles, "you look great in anything." Again it is the right thing for him to say and the type of thing he would say. But something still seems off to Julie.

"So, what did you do those extra days?"

"Not much," he shrugs. "Went to the mill a lot, did a couple of museums; pretty boring stuff actually."

They arrive home, pulling up under the portico. Frederick is there to greet them and to take Greg's luggage. Again, nothing in this is unusual. Except for the feeling that nags Julie, the feeling that is now taking the form of the thought that *something happened in Atlanta; something big.* But it will take a few more hours, while they are in bed, before another thought creeps into her mind: *he met someone in Atlanta.* The idea will leave her crying softly, quietly, next to her sleeping husband.

****

Joe is reluctant to leave the boy. But Jack convinces him to let Little Jack spend time with Nick in his loft. They can play Xbox together or whatever they like, but the boy will be safe there and, more importantly, Jack needs some answers. Let the kids have their fun while the grown ups have a very grown up conversation.

They are now in a discrete little corner booth in a discrete little restaurant just a few blocks away. Joe looks even more nervous now than he did in the coffee shop. It is as if talking about his secret is even harder than revealing it. But Jack needs those answers. Looking more closely at Joe he can see the woman he once loved, the woman he slept with. He can see it in the man's eyes and his smile and in many other little ways. There are no words to describe how strange the sensation is. "Tell me *everything*," he insists.

Joe frowns. "Everything is a lot."

"I don't care. What the hell happened?"

The waitress comes up to take their order. It surprises Jack a little to hear Joe order a scotch & soda. Jackie always preferred white wine. Of course, in those days Jack wasn't even old enough to buy liquor so she would share a bottle with him. She'd sneak it to him for picnics or discrete trysts in his bedroom.

"It's a long story."

"I'm not going anywhere."

Joe smiles again, the smile Jackie used to make. "I've always liked guys," he shrugs. "Girls made no sense to me. I never really felt like one of them."

"You could have fooled me. You were the hottest chick in the world. Hell, I was fucking in love with you!"

Joe starts to reach out to take Jack's hand in his but thinks better of it and pulls it back. "You were a kid --- a sweet, sexy, wonderful kid just out of high school."

"That's what you said when you dumped me." Jack remembers well the pain of that day.

"I know, I'm sorry but it was true." A tear trickles down his cheek. He tries to fight it. "Damn it, Jack, I'm seven years older than you! Hell, you weren't even old enough to go into a bar or get a decent job or anything. We were at two completely different stages in life. I knew we wouldn't work . . . Especially considering how I felt about myself."

"How about how *I* felt? What about how I feel *now*? God, you never told me you were pregnant. You dump me and disappear from my life. Now you show up years later with my son and, well, and *this*!" Joe looks so hurt that Jack takes a moment to calm down. The last thing he needs is have Joe start crying. "Okay," he says more calmly, "let's take with one thing at a time. Start at the beginning."

"You mean my surgery?"

"Yeah, let's start with that."

The waitress returns with their drinks, giving Joe a wink. She obviously thinks he's cute. *If only she knew*, Jack says to himself.

"I've always liked guys," Joe says after she leaves. "Ever since I was little, I just *relate* better to them. Girls are nuts. They really are. You wouldn't believe the dumb conversations my girl friends used to have. They'd talk silly things about hair styles and boy bands and their endless, asinine gossip -- but not me. I tried; damn how I tried. But I just couldn't get it --- or them. I mean, my college roommate kept dating these assholes. I mean real shit heads, and then she used to complain about them; every fucking time. Eventually I just yelled at her 'you're the one who chooses them' and she broke down in tears. Nuts, girls are just plain nuts. But boys are different. I always seem to understand them better, like I was one of them. They like to be in control. They don't put up with a lot of bullshit. I like that. I like the confidence, the camaraderie. The ability to connect without saying a word and when you do say something, you mean it. There are no little games, no dropping hints. Eventually, with a lot of therapy, I realized that the reason I felt like one of them is because *I am* one of them."

Jack tries to process it. Part of Jackie's appeal to him was that she seemed different in someway --- but he never conceived of *this* way. "I never, I mean, when we were together . . . you seemed all woman to me. Hell, you seemed like the *ideal* woman."

"Back then, when you were just out of high school and I was just out of college, I was starting to realize that I wasn't meant to be a girl. They were alien creatures to me. I don't know how else to explain it." Joe then pauses, a reflective smile on his face. "But then you came along. You were my ideal of a true guy: athletic and strong and confident and sexy. You were even a little cocky. I really liked that. I wanted to *be* that. Every time we made love I felt like I was embracing a little bit my inner manhood. But I soon came to my senses and realized that you were so much younger than me; too young to deal with a trans boyfriend --- much less a trans boyfriend with a baby."

"That's why you broke up with me, because you were pregnant."

"I had already made up my mind about the surgery --- but the pregnancy was a big surprise. I thought about ending it, but I realized that this would be my one and only chance to have a child of my own. I can't tell you how cool it was learning it would be a boy. My dad was so proud to have a grandson. But he died before I could tell him about my other plans. I went through with them anyway. I actually rushed them. The doctors wanted me to take it all slower, go through more therapy and stuff before the surgery. But I insisted we go ahead as soon as possible. That's what having a lot of money can do for you. My mom, on the other hand, couldn't handle it. She was never very stable to begin with and last year she met and married this guy . . ."

"What guy?"

"The ultimate asshole," Joe almost growls. "His name is Vincent Bologna."

"Italian."

"More than that; he is a living breathing stereotype. I not kidding you, dude. Italian Americans all over the country should picket every time he steps out of the house. He is smooth, slick with lots of old world charm and old world ideas --- and old school mob ties."

"Shit!" There aren't many of these guys around any more, but Jack has encountered a couple. Back in the day, his dad sometimes had to do business with them.

"He actually took me aside for a little talk after the wedding," he chuckles. "Vincent wanted to bring his new stepson into the family business. It was a beautiful speech about family and the future and all --- until I explained to him that his stepson was once his step*daughter*."

Jack can imagine how that went down. "Wow, what did he say?"

"He practically shit in his pants. He thought he was marrying into this respectable LA family that could give him cover and legitimacy. Instead he found himself marrying into a freak show --- his words not mine --- and got very worried. Not about me or my mother's feelings, but how his pals in the business would react."

"I don't understand; what could he do to you?"

"First he tried intimidating my mother into cutting me off --- not financially, they can't touch my inheritance --- but from everything else. It almost worked until Mom started missing Jack. She is crazy about him and loves being a grandmother." Jack can see the fear return to Joe's face. "That's when the *really* scary shit started to happen."

"What scary shit?"

"Vincent told me up front that I had to give them Jack to raise as *their son* while I left forever. I refused --- I will *not* give up my son --- then someone broke into my house. They didn't steal anything; but it was obviously a warning from Vincent." He nervously looks around before continuing. "Then I started being followed. At a bar one night there was an incident --- something weird, I'm still not entirely sure what --- that involved a shooting. It even made it to the news. But it was getting pretty clear that I became a target."

Holy shit. "Are you saying Vincent is trying to kill you?"

Joe nods. The fear is so clear that Jack can almost feel it radiate across the table. "One of his henchmen --- a guy I hooked up with from time to time --- told me that Vincent had hired some big, ugly black guy named Michael Bickel to rub me out."

Jack leans back to take a deep breath. All of this is almost too much to take.

"Jack and I have been on the run for months. But it is getting harder and harder to do this on my own. I can't call any of my other friends or family without risking them. But Vincent and this Bickel dude don't know a damn thing about you. They don't even know your Jack's father --- they think it was some drunken frat boy --- so you are the only person I can turn to. Please Jack: *your son and I need your help.*"

What can he say? As bizarre as the situation is, he can't help but agree. He pays for the drinks and they head back to the loft. "How much does Jack know . . . about everything?"

"Not too much," Joe answers, keeping an eye on the SoHo crowds for anyone suspicious. "He was really young during my transition and calls me poppa. As to Bickel and Vincent, he just knows that some bad men are after us."

This leads Jack to a question; it may sounds selfish, but he needs to ask. "Okay, but if you're his poppa --- who am I?" Jack has thought about being a father. He likes kids. But until recently, when he reconnected with Greg, he just assumed it would be with a girl he marries. His dad would prefer that. But Jack never expected this bizarre scenario.

"We'll work that out," Joe says in a supportive voice. He seems to understand Jack's confusion and his needs. As they enter Jack's building, something else Joe said hangs in the back of Jack's mind. "You said something about this guy you were hooking up with."

"I'm a gay man, Jack." Joe looks at him curiously. "Is that okay with you?"

"I guess so; why wouldn't it be?" Actually, it *is* a little strange. *Aren't most transmen strictly into women?* That's what Jack always heard. But he tries to be cool about it.

"Well, you were always such a *guy*, what with all the girls you were scoring with."

They step into the elevator. There is one other thing floating in Jack's brain, but he is too embarrassed to ask. It seems too puerile. Fortunately, Joe senses the unasked question. "I know what you are thinking: yes, I have a penis, yes it is attached and, yes it works --- sort of."

"Uh, okay," Now Jack is even more uncomfortable. "Whatever that means."

Joe smiles at him like a sympathetic parent might to his overly inquisitive child. "It means dude that I can get hard and all but can't actually cum or get a girl pregnant. My dick doesn't matter all that much sexually anyway: I'm a total bottom. Having the dick just makes me feel more complete as a man."

"Oh." They fall silent again as they ride up until Jack finally says, "Truth be told, I don't really consider myself all that straight. I've fucked plenty of women --- and quite a few men." This surprises Joe. "I never expected that."

The elevator arrives at Jack's floor. But before they go into his loft, Jack gets an idea of how to best help Joe and their son. "There is this guy I know in New Hampshire."

"A friend," Joe says with a naughty smile that makes Jack feels like he's a teenager caught in a lie.

"Okay, he's more than that. My point is that he lives in this little town outside Manchester called Faraway Hill. It could be the best place to hide you."

"Sounds good to me," Joes says clearly relieved. Jack is not only coming through, but in a way that might work well. "I don't know anyone in New England. It's probably one of the last places Vincent or Bickel will look."

****

Eve King drops her husband off just outside Brady-Sullivan Plaza. They often ride to work together these days to save money while Ben tries to rebuild his practice. It isn't easy; Melvin Waite's embezzlement is well known now and has really hurt the firm's reputation. These days the Hallorans and a few other accounts are the only things keeping the office going. He has even allowed the annoying junior member, Barry Studer, to be more active in hustling new business.

It starts to drizzle a bit with little drops of cold water descend from the sky. Ben stops to buy a copy of today's *Union Leader*, pleased that Ann and the Hallorans are no longer big news. The front page is all about the economy and the latest political tussles in Concord. He is about to enter the building and escape November's chilly rain when he is confronted by a familiar face.

"Mr. King, it's nice to see you again." Peter Brandt is an officer in the Faraway Hill sheriff's office who went to high school with Julie and Ann. He has been gone for months as a volunteer somewhere. Ben can't quite remember the country. He has always liked Peter.

"Hello Peter, it's been so long. Are you back to stay?"

"Yes sir, I've done all I can to help with the draught and besides, my leave of absence ends next week." Peter is bundled up in civilian clothes today. Ben is accustomed to seeing him in uniform.

"We are all very proud of the work you were doing in Africa." Ben now wishes *he* were bundled up too, rather than wearing a simple raincoat. "Not too many young people volunteer for things like that these days."

"Thank you sir; how is Julie? Isn't she due soon?"

"Yes, in just a few weeks. We are all very excited about it." They exchange a few more pleasantries but the temperature keeps dropping. Ben politely excuses himself and enters the Brady-Sullivan. Seeing him again makes Peter think about Ann and Julie. He walks down the street to King's Korner, but the young girl behind the counter says that Mrs. Halloran isn't due in today. Mrs. Halloran. That is who she is now. And Ann is now *Miss* Halloran. Strange how so much has changed so soon. But even in Africa, tending to the neediest of needy people, Lewis Halloran's murder always remained in the back of Peter's mind. During the investigation he really wanted Sheriff Reynolds to call in the State Police. They have people trained for murder cases and a good record in pursing them. But Reynolds wouldn't do it, wouldn't even think of it. Faraway Hill is *his* town and no one else's. It was enough to ask the Manchester Police to help with securing at the Halloran estate. Anything more would have crossed the line as far as the old sheriff is concerned.

Its raining harder now; the freezing drops can be heard hitting the café's big windows. Peter orders a coffee and starts paging through the morning paper. There is a story about the governor's latest initiative and some follow-ups on last week's Manchester Marathon. But nothing can take his mind away from that crime so many months ago. His frustration was so great that when the volunteer request was made, Peter jumped at it. But now he is at home with friends, family and his doubts.

Munroe Gale never made much sense to Peter as Lewis Halloran's killer. Peter knew the old farmer most of his life, and saw him often while he and Ann dated. Munroe was too insecure, too scared of the world to do anything other than crawl into a bottle. He hated guns. But Munroe's suicide conveniently ended the case as far as Sheriff Reynolds and Faraway Hill are concerned. When Peter voiced his doubts to the sheriff, the old man just growled, "Fine kid, who the fuck do *you* think did it?" Peter had no answer then. He still doesn't.

But the doubts still won't go away.

****

This November morning is typical for New England: darker, colder and wetter than the rest of the year. An outsider might find it depressing. But for a true New Englander it is as if the world is simply getting ready for a winter sleep.

Julie wakes up determined to not let what happened in Atlanta --- whatever it was --- affect her marriage or her life. But she needs help. Her first thought is her mother, but in many ways Eve has been acting stranger than Greg, and has been for months. It's weird. This is her first pregnancy, so naturally Julie is looking for advice. But every time she asks her mother a question, she just gets a vague answer, as if it came from a text book or a TV talk show, rather than from the woman who gave birth to her. All of this seems amazing to Julie: after all, Eve was the first person to figure out that her daughter was pregnant.

Right now, she is sitting alone in the master suite's parlor listening to the freezing rain outside. She and Greg had breakfast up here. It was nice; Julie thinks they should do this more often. They had an easy time, talking mostly about the baby --- and staying clear of sensitive subjects like Ann or Atlanta. He seems truly happy with how the nursery is coming together. Greg is looking forward to fatherhood. But that feeling remains: the feeling that Julie's husband did something or met someone in Atlanta. Instinct keeps telling her that he was with another woman. Yet, Greg has done nothing specific to make Julie suspicious. *Could I be imagining the whole thing?*

She is about to get up and test those tricky marble stairs when her cell rings. "Hey Mom."

"Good morning. I just dropped your father off and am heading into the office. Are you going in to work today?"

"Mary is doing just fine on her own."

"Yes, but we still need to get those October receipts to the accountant."

"Mom, can you please do it? My back is really killing. Besides, the weather doesn't look too good."

"I know and I'm sorry, but I've got meetings all day."

Julie carefully rises and looks out the window. The roads will start getting slick by midday, so if she goes she'll need to go now. "Fine; I'll do it then."

"Thanks --- and be careful. It's supposed to get really bad by tonight."

"Okay; Mom, can I ask you about something?"

"Sure."

Julie isn't sure how to ask the question. After all, she might just be imagining things. "When you were pregnant, did you ever, I don't know, have strange feelings?"

"I don't understand."

"You know, little bits of, I guess, paranoia." There is a silence. Julie has had this from her mother before. It's as if she is thinking of a safe answer. "Ah . . . no. Is everything okay? Is there a problem with the baby?"

"No, no, I guess it's just a mood swing or something." Once again, she is no help. "I'll go in this morning and take care of everything. Bye." Julie closes the phone a little too fast. These conversations of theirs are damned frustrating. She is left with one option and calls her Aunt Karen in New York.

"Good morning, dear."

"Good morning, Aunt Karen. I hope this isn't too early to call."

"Oh no," she answers with a sigh. "I had to have breakfast with Madeline today." Madeline is Karen's stepdaughter. Julie has never met her. All she knows is that she is close to Karen's age but they've always been far apart where Madeline's late father is concerned. Julie assumes it's an adult child's jealousy. *And who can blame Madeline? Aunt Karen is an amazing lady.*

"Is there a problem?"

"Just the usual; nothing for you to be concerned about, although I think I should get out of the city for awhile and relax somewhere. So how are you feeling?" Aunt Karen has become the only person Julie can really talk to about the pregnancy. They've been calling each other at least once a week since Lewis' funeral. Karen understands about the nausea, mood swings, diarrhea and other problems. "I'm doing just fine; it's only my back that keeps bothering me."

"Well, all that will ease up soon. Just lie flat on something hard and it will loosen your muscles. Or have Greg massage you some more." It is amazing how good

Karen's advice is. "He does that quite a bit," Julie answers almost defensively. "He's getting good at it."

"I'm glad to hear that. Have you picked a nanny yet?" The Hallorans, especially Joan, have been asking the same thing for months. But Julie is hesitant; after all, she never had one growing up. "Sweetheart," Karen tells her with a soothing, maternal voice. "You have that big house to deal with, a husband with a demanding job and your own little business. You *will* need the help."

"No, I haven't hired anyone, but I will." Karen is probably right. But more importantly, Julie wants to ask her straight out about Greg, and the possibility that he is seeing another woman. But something holds her back. She isn't sure if its shame or embarrassment --- it could be nothing more than paranoia --- but it occurs to Julie that it might be easier for them to talk in person. So she invites her for a visit, knowing that it's unlikely she'll come to Faraway Hill. It was hard enough to get her to come for the wedding. But Karen surprises her by saying "I'd love to."

"Wow."

"Don't be so shocked." Karen chuckles. "I so enjoyed the wedding so much that I have been looking for an excuse to visit again."

"Believe me, Aunt Karen, you don't need an excuse; just come." It is nice to talk about her wedding without someone bringing up Lewis' murder. The two are permanently entwined in everyone's mind. "How soon can you get here?"

"I'll be there in a few days."

✳✳✳✳

When Ann invites her mother to go Christmas shopping at the Mall of New Hampshire, there are certain things she expects. History is a good guide. She expects her mother to dress very simply, to be shy around the crowds. She expects a little awkwardness at spending time together again after being so long apart. She expects to coax her into actually buying something rather than just window shop. She also expects an embarrassing moment or two. What Ann doesn't expect is for her mother to arrive with Vivian.

"Hi," Ann says, trying not to sound surprised --- especially after seeing the excited smile on Lorene's face. "I hope we're not late." Ann kisses her mother on the check and exchanges polite but cautious greetings with Vivian. *Why is she here?* This question remains with Ann all morning as they start at the Macy's side and move through the mall. She watches them carefully. Her mother is dressed nicely, almost stylishly, as if she has become accustomed to shopping at places other than Faraway Hill's little consignment shop. The two older women act with a comfortable familiarity. They laugh and compare tastes and look at each other in ways that confuse Ann. Lorene and Vivian seem more than friends, they seem something closer to sisters. Lorene also acts freer and happier and more confident than Ann can ever remember. She's glad that her mother --- who went for years focused on her, Munroe and the farm but little else --- finally has a friend. But the vibe Ann picks up suggests something odd between them.

While examining rolls of wrapping paper at the American Greetings store, Ann wonders aloud, "I wonder if I should buy things for my new relatives." *Of course they probably won't accept anything from me*, she keeps to herself.

"I think that's a very good idea," Vivian suggests. "After all, you want to be a family with them, right?" Lorene stands next to her, as if a supportive spouse. It occurs to Ann that is precisely what they *do* seem like: a couple. "Of course," her mother adds. "After all, someone has to make the first move; so why not you?" The sight is disorienting. *Could it be?* It takes Ann a moment to bring her mind back to the conversation. "Um . . . well, I suppose I could try."

For the rest of the morning, Ann hangs back just a little, letting her mother and Vivian take the lead in selecting gifts, while wondering what is going on and what to do.

****

The train ride from New York to Manchester takes only a few hours. Actually, Jack finds that when you factor in the drives to and from airports and those perpetual airline delays, Amtrak is almost as fast as flying. The only complaint he has is that the train will only sell seats rather than compartments for such a short trip. He'd prefer the privacy. There are still so many questions.

Seated next to him are Joe and a very excited Little Jack. The boy is thrilled with his first train trip and has been taking in every nuance of the adventure. It's sweet and funny and wonderful to see. It makes Jack want to be a father to his son: to hold him, laugh with him and simply enjoy being a dad. Unfortunately that has to wait. Joe has the boy call him Uncle Jack for the time being. But he promises that will change.

Nick had a lot of questions, too. Jack needed his help in making the arrangements, so he came clean to his little brother. "Holy shit," is what he said over and over until Jack yelled at him to stop. "Does he have a dick and everything?" Nick asked. It was the same crude question that Jack considered, but had the good sense not to ask. He replied to Nick with a simple "so he says."

Joe had cash wired to him so he'll have money to spend in New Hampshire. Jack then paid for everything else, so that Bickel can't track Joe through credit card charges any more. The whole bizarre situation is happening so fast --- too fast for Jack to fully comprehend.

Jack did manage to find time to call that bastard Mel Waite and let him know that he's going back to New Hampshire. The old man was thrilled. "Finally," he grumbled. "Get what I need fag and this will all be over." Calling him was the last thing Jack did before going to bed last night, and he nearly through the phone against a wall.

He has been trying to reach Greg since early this morning. Jack wanted to speak to him last night but too much needed to done immediately. The office says that Greg is in meetings all day, catching up on the things he missed while in Atlanta. All Jack can do is keep sending his lover text messages. So far, none of them have been returned.

Nick agreed to stay in New York and square things with the family. Jack made him promise not to tell them about Jackie and their son. "Let's face it," he told his little brother, "Dad will never understand."

Little Jack keeps peering out the window, watching people and places speed by. He is so enthralled. *My son,* Jack thinks; *this wonderful little boy is my son*. The thought gives him a warm feeling, like something he's never experienced before. He has had to repeatedly restrain himself from giving the kid a bear hug.

Jack's cell rings. It's Greg. "Hey dude, I'm sorry not to call back sooner. It's been a bitch of a day."

"That's okay, look; I'm on my way to you now and need your help."

"Why, what's going on? Has something happened with your dad?"

"No, no, nothing like that," Jack tries to stay calm but the urgency of the situation seeps into his voice. "But I'm not really able to talk now."

"That's cool. But the weather is getting shitty here, so I don't know how soon I can get to the airport."

"I'm not flying."

"Driving?"

"No, the train."

"The train," Jack can hear Greg's puzzlement. He can even imagine the look on his face. "I don't get it."

"I can't explain now. Can we meet somewhere, not in Faraway Hill, but in Manchester?"

"Sure."

Jack gives him their arrival and hotel information. Since both are downtown it'll be easier for Greg to pick them up. Jack wishes he could tell him more, but it will be better in person and in private. Clapping the phone shut he turns to Joe who looks worried. "Are we really screwing things up for you?"

"No, but . . . I have to come clean with him about . . . everything. There's no other way."

Joe nods his head in a way that again reminds Jack of Jackie. At the weird core of a weird situation is sometimes, very briefly, forgetting that Joe *is* Jackie. His transition from female to male is so complete that a casual observer would never know the truth. But every so often, the man moves in a way or speaks in a way that could only be Jackie's.

"Poppa," Little Jack exclaims, "this is so neat! Can I have a soda now?"

****

It takes Julie longer to get ready than she expected. She finds taking things slow helps her avoid any nausea or stress to her back. This is another thing that Aunt Karen taught her.

With Frederick's help, she navigates those ancient marble steps leading to the first floor. "Perhaps someone should drive you into town Mrs. Halloran," the elderly butler suggests as they reach the bottom. "This morning's television news is already talking about ice forming on the streets." Her first instinct is to decline the offer. After all, Julie grew up with New Hampshire's changeable weather. She's driven in far worse conditions than today. But a quick glace through a window convinces her that maybe the butler is right. So, she sits in the family room while Fredrick makes arrangements for a car and driver from Manchester.

While waiting, Julie switches on the big plasma TV and randomly surfs. So many channels, so many repeats and silly reality shows. No wonder fewer people watch TV anymore; there's little worth watching.

Fredrick tells her that it'll be at least an hour before the car arrives, which is fine with Julie. She decides to make a day of it: delivering the material to the accountant, having lunch in the city and maybe a little shopping. Considering all the stress with Ann and Greg and the baby, playing a little hooky from the world could be just the therapy she needs.

The surfing resumes: Judge Judy barks at some asshole who has screwed his ex-girlfriend out of some money; Oprah's fans cheer the latest unknown author; a reality show contest has just said something that needs bleeping. Hardly the type of shows Julie watches, but these are just about the only ones on. All three news channels have talking heads, yelling at or pontificating about something. Finally, she stumbles across a soap, in which a woman is confronting her husband. Clad in an unbelievably clinging, satin teddy she cries, "just where *were* you last night Steve?" The man, a fantasy creature in nothing but satin boxers and with the most defined chest Julie has ever seen responds dramatically: "I was with . . . Caitlin." The camera zooms in on the woman's shocked face and then fades to black, leaving Julie to wonder if she'll be living such a scene some day soon.

Eventually, a handsome Lincoln Town Car arrives. The air is cold and the rain freezes as it hits the ground. The front steps under the portico are so slippery that Julie would have fallen had Frederick not been there. Fortunately the back seat is warm and comfortable. This is one of those moments that Julie truly appreciates being Mrs. Halloran. The car pulls out of the driveway and down the lane into Faraway Hill's main square. The roads here are a little slick, and the driver wisely slows down. But once they are out on the highway, he speeds up. They are soon in downtown Manchester where they stop outside King's Korner as Mary runs the file out to Julie. The accountant's office is on the other side of town. Fortunately, Julie doesn't need to brave the weather here either: his secretary comes down. The business chore is done. She instructs the driver to take her back to downtown and one of her favorite boutiques. Christmas is just weeks away and Julie has barely started her shopping.

The town car pulls up to the store on Willow Street. It has some wonderful little designer items in the window including imported pieces that would make a great gift for Aunt Karen or maybe Joan. But it is raining harder now, causing the driver to ask if she would rather go to the Mall of New Hampshire. "Oh, I think that I can handle this," Julie says as she opens the door. The store's entrance is nearby up a small flight of steps. She has climbed them many times before without a problem. But today is different: Julie hears the old, rusty ornate wrought iron banister snap as she grasps it. The surprise catches her off balance and she tumbles down to the sidewalk, hitting each step on the way. The pain is sudden and so severe that she can barely speak.

"Mrs. Halloran!" the driver yells as he rushes over, nearly falling on a patch of ice. The shop's door opens and one of the clerks peers out to see what happened.

"Help me," is all Julie can say as tears mingle with the rain flowing down her cheek.

EPISODE TWELVE

In the two years that Greg Halloran has lived --- really lived --- at his family's ancestral home, he has come to truly appreciate Manchester. Not Faraway Hill, but Manchester. It is an interesting and welcoming blend of big city with small town: big enough to have some impressive cultural assets and a sophisticated population, but small enough not to be overwhelming. It is also small enough that nothing is very far from anyplace else. This is why it only takes Greg a few minutes --- even on slick, treacherous roads --- to get from his office in the Millyard to the emergency room at Elliot Hospital.

A surge of fear ran through his body when Frederick called him with the news. Despite the bad weather, Julie went shopping where she slipped and fell outside some little store. He immediately rushed out without saying much to his secretary, except to cancel everything and to call Julie's parents. All sorts of horrifying possibilities have been going through his mind as he struggles with Manchester's icy roads. He turns onto Auburn Street where he sees the Kings park their car in the hospital lot. Their offices are much closer so it makes sense that they would arrive sooner. He pulls up next to them. "What have you heard?" a panicked Eve asks.

"Not much," Greg answers as the three of them practically run to the entrance. "Only that she took a really bad fall." The cold hard drops are making it difficult to keep them from taking their own big falls. They are met inside by a chauffer. Greg has seen him before; whenever the family hires out a car and driver he is the one usually assigned. Pity he can never remember the man's name. "Mr. Halloran," he says looking scared. "I'm really sorry."

"Please, just tell me what happened."

"Well, sir," he says nervously, almost as if he expects to be blamed. "We were called this morning because Mrs. Halloran needed a car but didn't want to drive in this weather. I came and got her. After we delivered some business papers, she asked to be taken to this boutique she likes."

"Business papers?" Greg asks confused. But Eve explains: "I asked her to take some papers to the accountant. You know, about King's Korner. I just expected her to go right home after." She turns to Ben, "If she's hurt or lost the baby . . ."

"Sweetie, don't imagine the worst."

"I can't help it, Ben. It'll be my fault."

Greg supposes he should say something supportive to his mother-in-law, but he doesn't trust himself: Eve may be right and Julie and the baby might be seriously hurt. A young man in blue scrubs walks up to them. "Which of you is Mr. Halloran?"

"I am. What is happening? How is my wife?"

"Please follow me sir."

"May we come too," Ben asks. "We're her parents." Greg thanks the driver and lets him know he can leave. The three of them follow the nurse through the trauma center. Doctors and nurses rush around tending to patients in little cubicles blocked from view by flimsy hospital drapes. One unseen patient cries for help. A couple of doctors huddle in the corner conferring about something. The nurse brings them to a small room with a table surrounded by a half dozen hard plastic chairs. "Please wait here; the doctor will be with you in a moment," he nurse explains before leaving the three of them alone to worry some more. Eve, in tears, sits on one of the pieces of molded plastic as her husband whispers something comforting to her. Greg turns to find himself looking at one of those light boards doctors use to view x-rays. That must be what this room is normally used for: quick staff meetings about an emergency room patient.

The door opens and a doctor, an attractive middle age woman of Indian descent, walks in with the nurse close behind. "Hello, I am Dr. Nora Singh."

"How is my wife?"

"She took a very hard fall down a short flight of steps. She has sustained a broken leg" and then the doctor starts using medical jargon that means little to Greg except that, as a precaution, they will perform a cesarean. "Fortunately your wife is in general good health and is in her third trimester, all of which will help the fetus. I think things will go well if we move fast enough."

"Can I see her?"

"Only very quickly."

Ben gestures that he will stay with Eve, so Greg follows the doctor and the nurse back into the main part of the trauma center where they direct him to a little cubicle. There, Julie lays unconscious on a bed. Her hair is matted from the freezing rain and there are some bruises on her face, but otherwise she looks okay. Monitors beep and all sorts of wires are connected to her. Greg leans in and kisses his wife on the forehead and whispers "everything will be okay; I promise." He is about to say something more when the doctor and some nurses arrive to take her to surgery. They gently move her onto a gurney and wheel her away, leaving Greg alone and in tears.

****

The weather is getting worse. The highway is fine --- the state is pretty good at that --- but the streets in little Faraway Hill are another matter. While in town, Ann has to be especially careful and manages to arrive safely at her new home. She walks into the Grand Vestibule carrying bags of gifts for relatives she has barely met and don't want to know her. But Christmas is coming, and Vivian --- no matter whom she is or what she is to her mother --- may be right: if Ann wants the Hallorans to treat her as family, *she* needs to treat them as family.

But before she can head upstairs to her suite, Frederick stops her with some terrible news: Julie has been in an accident and is in Elliot Hospital. Her first instinct is to get back in her car and rush over. She even drops her bags on a table in the Grand Hall; but Frederick stops her from leaving. He very tactfully suggests calling ahead first. His meaning is obviously: Greg won't want her there. Frustrated, Ann pulls out her cell and dials Eve. "Mrs. King, I just heard the news. What happened? How is she?"

"Julie had a terrible fall. She's in surgery now." Ann can tell that the woman has been crying, although she seems calm now. "They think she and the baby will be okay, but we won't know for sure until it's over."

"Oh, my God," despite their recent problems, Julie has always been like a sister. She has always been there for Ann; now it's Ann's turn to be there for her. "I'm on my way."

"No, no, please don't" Eve sounds almost panicked. "That would not be a good idea." Again, the reason is clear: because Greg doesn't want her around. She almost goes anyway, but realizes that a scene with him is the last thing Julie would want. "Okay, I'll wait for the news."

She notices Frederick politely motioning to her. "Hold on a moment, Mrs. King. What is it?"

"Mr. Halloran called from the hospital a short while ago. Mr. Campbell is due to arrive by train this afternoon. I was going to hire a car to pick him up . . ." Ann is surprised. She always thought that the butler was against her, but his suggestion fits Vivian's advice: act like a member of the family, whether they want her or not, and they may come around. *This could be my first opportunity.*

"Mrs. King, please tell Greg, that I am doing him a favor: Jack Campbell is coming in today and I'll pick him up myself." Maybe this act of kindness will soften her new brother's attitude toward her.

"That's very nice of you," At least Eve understands the gesture. "I'll let him know."

"Thanks, and please keep me up to date. You know how I feel about Julie. I'll be praying for her."

"I know dear. She loves you too. We all do."

Ann claps her phone closed and turns to Frederick. "Thank you." The old man says nothing. He simply smiles, hands her a note with the information and gestures a maid to take the bags upstairs.

****

The sky over Central Park is darkening. It is the middle of the afternoon, but the same cold, rainy weather hitting New Hampshire has been moving south and east. The early loss of the sun is marring the view from Karen St. John's penthouse. Her new personal assistant, a young woman named Denise, stares through the glass. "I hate it when the weather gets like this," she explains with a sigh. "It's so depressing."

"It's hard to imagine you getting depressed about anything," Karen says with a smile. She did her homework before employing the girl and knows about some of Denise's . . . well, *adventures*, may be the right word. Her past connections were a key reason Karen hired her.

"Pardon," the girl says, not quite sure if that remark was a compliment or not.

"You always have such a sunny personality."

Denise smiles, choosing to take it as a compliment. She is young, in her mid twenties, and despite her fairly conservative dress, definitely a party girl. Actually, no matter what she wears, Denise somehow manages to look just a little slutty. Karen knows all the signs; she was a bit wild when she first came to the city too, although she likes to think with far more class. Karen never anticipated that researching Greg Halloran's past would turn up a girl like Denise Sullivan. Of course, her private investigator is the best money can buy.

In all fairness, the girl has been doing a good job so far. Denise is managing to learn everything she needs with very little direction. She even made their travel arrangements today without a fuss.

Karen had her PI do some digging when it became clear that Julie's marriage is in trouble. Greg seems like a nice young man, but so did his father and all of Lewis' friends before that night so long ago. Karen learned the hard way not to take any man's charming façade for granted.

The PI's biggest surprise was Jack Campbell. The final report was filed less than a week ago. In it, Greg's colorful college years are detailed and fascinating. Most of his dalliances were with girls like Denise. That is to be expected; most young people have brief affairs while in college. Certainly Halloran men have a history of unzipping their pants when the opportunity comes. What Karen did not expect was Greg's occasional one-niters with young men --- and what was apparently a serious, romantic relationship with Jack that lasted a full year.

And that is just the beginning.

"Did I tell you," Denise says, still idly looking out the window, "that I knew a guy in college from New Hampshire?"

"Did you?" Karen does know this. She knows this and much more. And if what she suspects has happened, she'll make sure that her little girl's problem will be solved anyway necessary.

****

Please God, please help them, Greg says to himself over and over as the hours drag on and on. The wait is almost unbearable. His mind keeps returning to all of the problems of the last few months: the murder, Ann and Jack. Of all the complications in his life, the one thing that made him happy has been the prospect of fatherhood. No matter what issue was getting in their way, Greg and Julie always came together on anything involving the pregnancy. Whether it was Lamaze classes or doctors visits or meeting with the decorator about the nursery, they were rarely out of sync. All their worries disappeared at those moments.

But now there is the fear he will lose them both, his wife and his son.

Please, oh please God, help them.

Greg and Eve are back in the cramped, little conference room. Eve is also worried, but to Greg's eye she seems strangely calm. Maybe that comes from being a mother; she knows what the risks are and is better prepared. But that isn't exactly the feeling Greg is picking up. Then again, he is not the best judge of other people's emotions --- especially now.

Please, oh please God, help them.

Ben has gone to the cafeteria to get everyone some coffee and a little food. He went even though Greg and Eve said that they don't want anything. But now Greg realizes that he is getting a little hungry. Something to eat might be a good idea after all.

Please, oh please God, help them.

Greg isn't sure how he feels about Jack's sudden visit, or about Ann volunteering to pick him up. *Is she trying to score some points?* Julie keeps reminding him that Munroe killed his father, not the farm girl. But he just can't help the way he feels.

Please, oh please God, help them.

Ben returns with a cardboard tray of paper cups and a bag. "The cafeteria just made some fresh bagels," he says, trying to be stoic. But Greg can see the fear in his eyes. "I can't speak for the coffee."

Please, oh please God, help them.

Just as Ben starts to pass the cups around, Dr. Singh enters. She has a tired smile on her face. "How is she?" Greg asks before anyone can speak.

"Everything went as planned," she says with a wonderfully reassuring voice. "Julie has a cast on her leg, but is recovering nicely from the surgery."

Oh, thank you God.

"And my son?"

"He seems to be doing very well, especially for a preemie. We have him in an incubator but he is breathing on his own and appears fully developed. As I said early, we are fortunate Julie was late in her third trimester. We want to keep them a couple of days to be sure, but everything looks promising."

Oh, than you God.

"When can I see them?"

"Julie is heading toward post-op, but you can visit the baby at any time." Ben and Eve gesture that Greg should go ahead and he follows Dr. Singh back into the bowels of the hospital to a room where he is instructed to put on scrubs and wash his hands. He even has to wear a face mask. "We have to be careful with infections when it comes to preemies," she explains, "for both mother and child." Greg is then escorted into a section of Maternity where his son, tiny and helpless and utterly beautiful lies in a small incubator. The boy is sleeping, blissful to the din that came with his birth. Other than a couple of wires attached to his chest, he looks like any healthy infant.

"He's doing very well," Dr. Singh tells him. "We are pumping oxygen to him and watching his vitals, but he is already breathing on his own and his heart rate is good."

Greg reaches out to touch the clear wall protecting his son. *Thank you, God.*

A nurse, also in scrubs, comes up to whisper something to the doctor, who turns to Greg and says that he can see Julie now. He follows them a short distance to another room, filled with patients in various cubicles for various reasons. Julie is in one of these, covered in her own protective plastic. A cast is on her left leg and all sorts of things are attached to her, but otherwise she sleeps as blissfully as their child. Greg pulls up a chair, sits, and slides his gloved hand under the plastic to hold hers. Julie is at a greater risk of infection, Dr. Singh explains, but she is already responding well to antibiotics. *Thank you, God.* The staff will know tomorrow when they can go home.

But what happens to their little family then, Greg has no idea.

****

The Manchester Transportation Center is conveniently located on Canal Street not far from the Merrimack River and the Millyard District. It's always a busy place, where people can take a train or a bus to almost any point in New England. Ann has used it before and knows it well. But it surprises her that someone with Jack Campbell's money would take the train rather than fly. A flight from New York must take half the time, and he can certainly afford to go First Class.

Just like her half brother, Ann Halloran has been repeatedly praying *God, please help her* throughout the day. She cried in relief when Eve King called her with the news that both Julie and the baby are going to be okay. *Thank you, God, thank you.* It took her nearly an hour to fully compose herself after worrying for so long.

The rain has stopped, but it is still very cold outside. Fortunately, the city crews are out. Ann had a scary encounter in Faraway Hill with a slick patch of ice, but Manchester's streets are in pretty good shape.

Ann arrives at the center and parks in the garage. As she enters the waiting area, she immediately sees Jack Campbell standing just inside the door. Next to him are another man and a cute little boy, who is looking around him in wonder. The kid has obviously never been in such a place before and it takes the other man --- apparently his father --- some effort to keep him from wandering away. The other man appears older than Jack and is handsome in a slightly different way, one that Ann can't quite figure out. There is definitely something odd about this trio.

When Jack sees her, he seems surprised and uncomfortable. This is very different from what Ann saw in the man earlier this year at Julie's wedding. He was more than confident back then; he was downright cocky. But not today; today he seems worried about something --- and that worry has increased by seeing her.

"Hi, I'm sorry that Greg can't make it," she says and tells them about Julie's accident. Jack's worried expression deepens even after she says that "fortunately, it looks like they'll be okay."

"Wow," Jack responds. She can't quite read his face. *Is he sad about the accident or about something else?* Ann decides to ignore it for the moment and turn to the other man. "Who's your friend?"

"Um . . ." Jack seems to have trouble answering such a simple question. "This is Joe Westbrook. He's . . . a friend from school."

Joe extends his hand in a shake that is firm and confident. "And this is my son, Jack."

Ann looks at Jack Campbell in surprise. *The boy is also named Jack?* Jack stumbles a bit, obviously trying to come up with an explanation. Joe saves the day by saying, "Jack and I were best buds in school. Besides, my mom liked the name."

"Oh." *I guess that makes sense.* Saying nothing more, the men pick up their luggage and follow Ann to her car. "I hope you won't think this weather is normal for November," she tells Joe. "It usually doesn't get like this until January. Normally, fall in New Hampshire is cool but very nice."

"I'm sure that's true."

"Have you been here before?"

"Nope. First time."

"Then take Little Jack to the SEE Science Center. It's a great place for kids. He'll love it."

Big Jack surprises her by saying that, rather than staying at the house, he's booked rooms at the Radisson on Elm Street in downtown Manchester. It's a nice hotel with great views of the city and the river. Still, Ann would think that Greg's best friend would stay at the mansion. There are four empty suites on the second floor.

Jack starts asking questions about Julie and the baby during the short trip. Ann tries to update him as best she can. "Apparently if things go well tonight, they'll both be home in a couple of days. It was so damned scary. I really wanted to be there but . . . well, no one wanted to overwhelm Julie." That excuse is certainly less painful than the truth. "By the way, he has a name. They decided weeks ago but wanted to wait until he was born."

"What is it?"

"John Benjamin Halloran. John for the Halloran who served Josiah Bartlett at the Constitutional Convention --- he built the family business and the mansion." Everyone who grows up in New Hampshire learns the story of the first Halloran and how he used the connection he made at the convention to start the family fortune. "Benjamin is after Julie's dad. Great name, isn't?"

She pulls up to the Radisson's entrance. "Yes," Jack says wistfully, "a great name."

****

Ben King steers his Lexus north toward Faraway Hill. It's dark now. As exhausted as he is, Ben is feeling a lot of relief --- and even pride. His daughter will recover. She is resting peacefully with her husband nearby. And his grandson, John Benjamin Halloran, has been named in his honor. Just thinking about this wonderful gift makes Ben King smile.

But he still worries. He worries how the kids are going to work things out. Ann has been an issue between them for months; and now she's living with them. Now that the baby has arrived, maybe Greg and Julie can concentrate on their own little family and put Ann off to the side. But Ben has his doubts.

He still has other worries. Replacing those lost clients hasn't been easy. Mel Waite may have dealt a death blow to a career Ben has spent his entire adult life building.

Sitting next to him, and just as tired, is his wife. Eve is on her cell, trying to reason with a pesky, needy Ann, who insists on visiting Julie first thing in the morning. "Okay, okay," Eve says giving up. "If you insist on going, please be civil to Greg . . . Good, I trust that you will . . . Fine . . . Goodnight." Frustrated, she claps her phone shut and turns to Ben. "There is no stopping her."

"Well, the girls did grow up together. It makes sense she'll want to see Julie."

"So will her other friends, but most people know better than . . . oh, never mind." She can see the happiness in Ben's face. "Look at you."

"Me?"

"You're beaming."

"*Beaming*? Did you actually use that word, Grandma?"

"Yes, Grandpa," she says with a wink. "I said beaming." Eve leans back in her seat and watches buildings along the highway speed past. "I think escorting Jack to his hotel is making Ann feel . . . useful; too useful."

"I suppose so." Ben doesn't walk to talk about Ann.

Eve continues to stare out the window, deliberately not looking at her husband as she reminds him that "there is someone else we need to call tonight."

Ben says nothing; he doesn't have to. They both know that Karen can't be put off. She'll want to know right away or there will be hell to pay.

It's another thing he has to worry about.

✻✻✻✻

Jack is sitting on the floor, leaning against the sofa, watching a college football game on ESPN. The mute is on and he is barely following the action. There is enough action in his own life these days.

The Radisson has a collection of two-room suites. Jack has taken one, and the other --- where he is right now --- is for Joe and Little Jack. The three of them had a simple dinner in J.D.'s Tavern, a restaurant in the hotel. That and the train ride was enough for the little boy who finally became too tired to continue. Joe is now emerging from the bedroom where Little Jack is softly snoring. "He conked out almost immediately," he says with a smile. "It's been quite a day for him."

Joe opens the mini-bar and pulls out a couple of bottles of beer. He hands one to Jack and sits on the floor next to him. The game on TV has hit a weather snag: snow has forced a time-out. "It's been quite a day for you, too, huh."

That is has. Jack knows Greg. With the accident and premature birth, Greg will feel obligated to stay with his wife and son. Their dream of being together again, this time for good, may be over.

"You know," Joe says, "I only had my cousin with me when I gave birth to Jack. It was the last thing I did --- really did --- as a woman."

"Did you hate it?"

"Giving birth?"

"No, being a woman." It's something Jack has been wondering about.

Joe swallows some beer. It goes down hard. The memories of that very different life are still painful. "There were a lot of nights when I'd cry myself to sleep."

"How come I never saw that?"

"I told you: you were really young and I was still so confused."

Now it's Jack's turn to swallow hard. Jackie --- Joe --- is probably right. Jack was such a kid back then, not really knowing what he wanted. The game has resumed on the TV but he's no longer thinking about it. He knows what he wants now, but it looks like it's too late. "I'm going to lose him."

"You don't know that."

"He's spending the night at the hospital."

"Dude, she's his wife. She's just had an accident and had to give birth early. He has to be there. It's the right thing to do. He must be a real stand-up guy."

"That's my point." He takes a bigger drink now. Getting drunk won't help matters, but it won't make them any worse either. "He won't leave her now."

Joe says nothing because Jack may be right. But this is one of those rare moments when he feels like Jackie again and has an urge to take Jack into her arms and tell him that everything will be alright. The feeling doesn't last long. Joe is more reserved than Jackie. He no longer cries himself to sleep at night. He is a man now; a man who just puts a supportive hand on the bud next to him as they watch the game and drink their beer.

✳✳✳✳

Ann is sitting in her parlor, alone. The two-room suite feels like an oddly decorated hotel, with her new furniture contrasting with the fading wallpaper. This was Joan Halloran's suite growing up. Little had changed until Ann moved in. She might have been given the suite across the hall, but that would have put her bed on the other side of a shared wall from Greg and Julie. That is obviously too close for her step-brother's comfort. The bastard daughter needs to be as far away as possible.

Bored, she gets steps out into Center Hall. This is the vast space that runs nonstop from one side of the second floor to the other. Midway through on her right is the redecorated nursery, looking charming with its yellow walls and oak furniture. Greg will certainly be hiring a nanny. A nanny. How different John's childhood will be from hers.

Ann walks down the Grand Staircase to the first floor. As old as the building itself, these handsome marble steps have survived every renovation and restoration the huge house has endured. There is something comforting in that.

She encounters Frederick at the bottom as he emerges from the Family Dining Room. Ann asks, since no one else will be home tonight, if she can have dinner in the Family Parlor. It'll be a nice change from being exiled to her suite again. The elderly butler smiles and says he'll make the arrangements.

Walking down Grand Hall --- nearly every part of this place seems to have a formal name --- Ann stops at the door to the study. It is still locked and has been ever since Lewis Halloran's death. She gently places a hand against the carved wood. It was on the other side of this door that Munroe fired the shots that ended her father's life and changed hers.

Next to it is the vast, oval Blue Room. Antique furniture, some of it historic and some recreations, sit elegantly surrounded by royal blue walls. Through the huge bay windows Ann can see the garden, which wraps around three sides of the house. In the summer it is lush with trees and flowers. But now, in November, the trees are bare and the walkways empty. Through some of the branches she can see something she never noticed before.

"Pardon me, Miss Halloran," Frederick politely interrupts her thoughts. "Dinner will be ready in a few minutes."

"Thank you Frederick. What is that building out there?"

The butler steps next to Ann at the window to see where she is pointing. "That, madam, was constructed for servants housing. It was built in the late 19th century."

"I thought the staff lives in the house, in the lower level."

"We do madam, the live-ins that is. No, that building was used for residences before the remodeling."

"What is it used for now?"

"Nothing; the late Mrs. Halloran had the interior gutted and roof replaced before she passed away. She had no specific plans for it, but since it like the rest of the estate is on the National Register of Historic Places, she felt an obligation to keep it in good shape."

"I see." There is still so much for Ann to learn.

✳✳✳✳

If the little old man with the wrinkled face and thick, graying hair were anyplace else, no one would notice him. But in tiny Faraway Hill, this eighty-year-old stands out: he has been the town's mayor for half his life. The man, Francis

Fitzgerald, has been reelected unopposed every two years. People say hi to him in the town square, where merchants offer small gifts or a free meal. He always thanks them with a thick Irish brogue that he copied from his beloved father. Tourists love to hear Frank talk. The locals accept him as part of Faraway Hill like the square and its famous statute. Such is life in a small rural town.

But Frank hasn't survived in politics for so long just on his charm. Maintaining good relationships with the powers that be in Concord and Manchester has been the real key to his success. And that is why his grandson is driving him to a discrete meeting at the sheriff's office. The men he knows who are in the know have told him things he can no longer ignore.

There are only a few people in the cinder block building at this time of night. Even the few criminals in Faraway Hill generally work nine to five. But the mayor insisted that Sheriff Reynolds meet with him tonight --- and made it clear that declining was not an option.

Normally a sheriff would come to the mayor's office for this kind of meeting. But, again, Frank Fitzgerald knows about relationships. Coming to the sheriff would show both respect and underscore the importance of his message.

"Francis, my friend," George Reynolds greets him with a forced smile. The two have known each other since grade school. They played ball together, double dated, went to the same classes and attended each other's wedding. But they have never truly been friends.

"George, I appreciate your meeting with me." They shake hands and the mayor asks his grandson to leave them alone. They sit across the sheriff's desk from each other. To an outsider it might look like two elderly men about to have a harmless chat. But the mayor and sheriff know better.

"How are you feeling Francis?"

"I'm as spry as any eighty-year-old with every malady discovered can be," the mayor says ruefully. He knows the real reason Reynolds asks is because he'd love to be the sole powerbroker in town. "I am afraid that an issue has been festering in the capital for the past several months that is about to come to a head." One of the few benefits to being old is that you can cut to the chase. At this stage in life, a man has little time to waste on small talk.

Reynolds just shrugs. "I don't give a tinker's damn about Concord. As long as my funding comes through, they can screw themselves."

"Yes, well, I *do* care what they think in Concord. That's part of my job."

"So, what's the problem?"

"The governor is considering an investigation into the handling of Lewis Halloran's murder."

As Frank expected, the sheriff doesn't like this news. "They got no fucking right!" Reynolds yells, pounding the desk with his fist.

"You should have just turned everything over to the State Police. Every other town in the New Hampshire would have."

"Faraway Hill isn't like every other town in New Hampshire. We're an independent corporate township. That's why we have a mayor and town council to govern us, not the county --- or Concord."

"Oh, come on, George; this can't be a surprise to you. It was a high profile case that brought the national media. You even held a fucking press conference right in front of John Halloran's statute!"

That embarrasses him. As much as George Reynolds hates the idea of anyone stepping into his territory, he *did* enjoy the spotlight those few, fleeting days. "I solved it, didn't I?"

"You did huh? Quiet, insecure Monroe Gale, an alcoholic farmer who hated guns and confrontations took a gun and murdered a man. And he did it in the fanciest mansion in the state, filled with wedding guests, who didn't see or hear a damned thing."

"His fingerprints were on the weapon. He confessed in writing. There were no other possible suspects."

"The richest man in the state, and there were no other suspects? Come on, George! The State Police never bought that."

"They're *too* smart."

"Maybe, but they got the governor's ear."

"So do you, Francis. What do I gotta do to keep this from happening?"

"That's my point, George," the mayor rises, too frustrated to continue dealing with Reynolds' arrogance. "I don't think there is anything either of us can do."

With that, he leaves the sheriff alone to fume.

****

Ben King tries another piece of chicken, but it is just as fatty as the first.

Neither Ben nor Eve felt like cooking or going out tonight, so they stopped at strip mall along the highway. The mall has a new Chinese restaurant. It seemed a safe choice for a tired couple. But now Ben is having second thoughts. Nothing tastes very good, even simple things like the egg roll.

Across the dining room table, Eve's chair remains empty and her food is getting cold. She decided to call her sister right away to get it over with. But the call is taking much longer than either of them expected. Ben considers going into the living room to see what is happening when his wife enters, frustrated and worried.

"I guess Karen didn't take the news well."

"That's only half of it," Eve takes her seat, but isn't too interested in eating. Something else is on her mind. "She's coming to Faraway Hill."

Ben drops his fork on the table with a bang. "*What!*" The very idea is scary. It was tricky just having her in town for the wedding. Karen can be so damned unpredictable; who knows what she may say or do.

"She says Julie invited her this morning."

"I don't believe that."

"Oh, I do. Karen has played the too-cool-for-words aunt all of her life, so Julie idolizes her."

"Julie is much too centered for that."

"Not where Karen is concerned," Eve says staring at her food. "Is *this* what they call General Tsoa's?"

"Apparently."

Eve doesn't even want to try and pushes the plate away. "Karen is up to something."

"Julie is *our* daughter," Ben insists angrily. *We* raised her!" He instantly regrets his outburst. Maybe Karen will stick to their deal. She did on her last visit.

Still, they worry.

****

Still, she worries.

A small, frail woman sits in her simple, stucco-faced home in a blue collar suburb of Los Angeles. The man standing by the window has assured her that she has nothing to fear. But the woman, an elderly Hispanic lady with her gray hair tied into a tight bun, nervously tugs on her floral muumuu.

"I'm not here to cause you no problems," Michael Bickel says, a big insecure smile across his dark face. "I just got to know where my wife is."

"I told you, she ain't told me. Vivian just left one day. That's all." Vivian was very careful not to tell Sofia where she was going. But Michael doesn't believe her. He can sense the old woman is hiding something; unfortunately, that something is that Vivian is supposed to call Sofia today. It could happen at any moment.

"You know, it's sad when a wife leaves her husband. It ain't natural. It ain't right. There are certain things that are supposed to stay as God meant them." In his mind, Michael starts mixing his anger with Vivian with his disgust over that freak Jacqueline Westbrook. No wonder his boss wants the girl-turned-guy whacked. Part of him wants to do the same to Vivian. The woman needs to learn her place.

The phone suddenly rings, causing Sofia to jump with fright. But she doesn't answer it. She just lets it ring again and again as Michael carefully watches. The answering machine kicks in and after Sofia's simple recorded greeting, they can hear a familiar voice. "Hello Sofia dear, its Vivian. I guess you went to bed early. I hope that means the new meds are working. Anyway, I am fine. More than fine; things are so much better for me here, so don't worry. I'll try calling you again in a few days. Bye."

After the click, Michael smiles at Sofia again. It is a different smile. It is a genuinely malevolent expression that frightens her even more. "Where is she?"

Embarrassed and scared, she looks away and says, "She ain't told me. She's says it's to protect me."

It doesn't matter. Vincent simply walks over and looks at the caller ID. The entire number is there, starting with the area code 603.

That's all he needs.

EPISODE THIRTEEN

It's interesting how much things can change in just a few hours. Yesterday it was cold and raining ice. But this morning it is bright and sunny with temperatures expected into the upper fifties. Such is the weather in New England this time of the year.

Greg Halloran has spent the entire night at Elliot Hospital, barely getting any sleep in the waiting room. Dr. Singh told him he should go home, but somehow that didn't seem right to him. He can feel clouds of guilt hanging over him just as they did in the sky the day before. This crisis has made him realize that he's made the Ann Issue much too big in his life and marriage. Then there is his affair with Jack in Atlanta. Greg has no idea what to do or where to turn; but spending the night here seemed like the right thing to do.

It isn't just the weather that can change in a few hours. One of the day nurses tells him that Julie and their son are doing so well that Julie has been moved to her own room and John into Maternity with the other newborns. He'll be able to see them soon. If things continue this way, he'll probably be able to take them home tomorrow. The news makes Greg feel justified about staying. He calls Eve King to let her know; she happily tells him they will come by the hospital after breakfast.

While waiting to see Julie, Greg checks his voicemail. There are a couple of business matters with little importance. Some relatives have called: his cousins Patrick and Robert leave nice supportive messages while Aunt Joan is a little too effusive in her sentiments. Then there is Jack.

Jack's message is a mixture of different worries. Greg can hear it in his voice. So many issues between them are intertwined: Julie, the baby, their relationship, Jack's dad, the future and whatever it is that brought him back to New Hampshire. Greg doesn't blame him for worrying; he worries too. Greg is beginning to regret starting things up with him again. His marriage is not even a year old and he effectively gave up on it while in Atlanta. It is one thing to have a mistress or a fuck buddy or even a hooker like Mark Bradley on the side. But it's another matter to be secretly in love with someone else. Everyone loses in this kind of scenario.

A cute young nurse steps over to him. "Mr. Halloran," she says with the shy smile of someone meeting a well-known person. "Would you like to see your son now?" Greg nods and follows her to Maternity, trying not to stare at her well-rounded ass. The sight reminds him of the girls he used to hook-up with in college. It brings another issue comes into his mind: *can I even commit to one person?* Maybe not --- and that just adds one more complication to his already complicated life.

✳✳✳✳

"Jack, stop playing with your food."

Joe and Little Jack are sitting in the Radisson's atrium restaurant, the Café on the Park, enjoying pancakes and muffins as the morning sun brightens the room. The boy is swirling the syrup with his fork, amazed at the way it moves about the plate.

"Jack," Joe says with a firm, one-word warning. The boy starts eating properly again.

The other Jack, the big one, slowly walks into the atrium. He isn't exactly hung over --- he didn't drink enough last night for that --- but he is definitely feeling woozy. It may take awhile for him to get up to speed again.

"'Morning, Uncle Jack."

"Jack, don't talk with your mouth full."

The boy swallows. "Yes, Poppa."

"Good morning," Joe says looking at Jack cautiously. "Are you feeling okay?"

"Yeah, just give me a few minutes." Jack orders some coffee from the waiter and scans the menu. "How are the pancakes?"

"They're really neat, Uncle Jack," the boy says enthusiastically. "You should have some."

Jack smiles at his son. It feels good, despite the odd reality of Jackie's change, for the three of them sit here together. It is almost like being a family; a feeling Jack hasn't experienced much since being a boy himself.

"Apparently," Joe explains, "they tell me the syrup is made locally. It's pretty good."

The boy starts swirling again. "I like it a whole lot."

Jack takes up the recommendation and places an order. "So, what are you guys doing today?"

"Well, I was thinking about what your friend suggested and go to that science museum. I checked out their web site last night and it looks like it'd be perfect for Jack."

"Sounds like a plan." Jack is about to excuse himself from going with them when his cell rings. It's Greg. "I'll be right back." He steps over to the window next to an empty table and flips open the phone. "Hey, Dude."

"Hey".

"How is she . . . and the baby?"

"They are doing pretty good. It looks like they'll be coming home tomorrow."

"That's great news, dude, it really is."

"Yeah, I was scared for awhile."

"I'm sure."

"Listen . . ." *here it comes*, Jack thinks, and he braces himself for it. "We need to cool it for awhile, at least until things settle down."

"Hey, Greg, I understand, okay? I love you and get what you're going through. Just give it a little time."

"Thanks, that means a lot to me."

"But, you and me, we have to talk and soon. There is some big shit going down that I have to tell you about."

"Okay, I just don't know when."

"How about tonight?" Tonight would be good; tonight Greg can let Jack into the study and get the papers that will finally rid him of Mel Waite.

"No, it can't be tonight."

"Tomorrow?"

"No, that's when Julie and John come home. Look, I'm sorry, I have to go, my in -laws are here." With that, Greg ends the conversation. *Damn.*

Upset, Jack walks back to see the waiter set his plate on the table. "Is everything okay?" Joe asks, as if he can guess what the call was about."

"Sure," Jack takes his seat. "You guys what some company at that museum today?"

****

Ann is feeling giddy as she picks up her new Prius from the lot. She loves the sleek, aerodynamic design, the fancy gizmos (some of which are voice activated) and the eco-friendliness of the engine. This car is as cool and stylish as a car gets. It is a world away from the beaten up old Camry she has been driving for years. But then, the Halloran mansion is also a world away from what she has been living for years.

A world away: that is the irony. Since she was a little girl, Ann Gale has dreamed of a better life, one more glamorous than what Munroe and his struggling farm could provide. She could have friends in that better life, people who would like her and maybe even envy her. Now that Ann *Halloran* is living that life she is feeling lonelier than ever.

Thoughts of the farm bring Ann to those of her mother, and the strange relationship she has with Vivian. The more Ann considers it, the more convinced she is that they are a couple. But there is only one way to find out, and her new car offers the best excuse. The cool electric motor whisks her north on the highway back to Faraway Hill and up that newly paved road at the Gale Farm. Ann is still impressed with the changes her mother made. Maybe Vivian had something with that, too.

"Why, what a wonderful surprise!" Lorene says with a big, beautiful smile as she opens the door. These days she looks more like she did when Ann was a teenager. It is as if something --- or someone --- has brightened her life in a way that Munroe never could, no matter how hard he tried.

Before anything else, Ann gives Lorene a tour of the new car, pointing out all of the high-tech features. "You mean, this is one of those new electric cars?"

"Yes, Mom: it has both a gas tank and an electric motor. It's so cool and I got the full package. Even the headlights are LED!"

Lorene seems genuinely happy for Ann, although she doesn't quite understand everything about the car. It doesn't matter; mother and daughter are enjoying each other too much to care. "Vivian knows much more about cars than me. We should show her when she gets back."

That's good; Ann can finally have a private moment to discuss this new woman in Lorene's life. "Oh," she tries to sound as casual as possible. "Where is she?"

"She went into Manchester to get her hair done. She doesn't like that beauty parlor in Faraway Hill that I go to."

"Oh."

"Anyway, the car is very nice."

"Thanks Mom." The two women step into the house. The remodeled kitchen still has the sunny, gingham motif that her mother had for years, but now it is freshened up with new wallpaper, paint and cabinets. The beaten up old appliances have been replaced with stainless steel. Lorene pours them some tea as Ann sits at the table and carefully asks, "Mom, can we talk about something?"

"Certainly," Lorene hands Ann a cup and sits across from her. "About what?"

"About Vivian."

Lorene says nothing, just sits there looking uncomfortable. She obviously never expected the question. Ann realizes that she needs to take the lead. "She seems like a very nice lady. I'm glad you have someone." That seems to relax her mother. "I just . . . well, I do worry about you . . . and, I just want to make sure I understand the two of you."

"It's very private, what we have."

"I figured that."

Lorene looks surprised. "You did?"

"Mom, when we went shopping the other day, the two of you acted like, well, like a married couple. That's what I want to talk about . . . is that what you are?"

"Would that be . . . so bad," Lorene asks nervously.

Ann smiles, as she tries to be understanding and supportive. "No, Mom, it wouldn't be --- if this is right for you."

"I think it is. I am sure that it is."

"Then, please, just help me to understand. Vivian says she knew us long ago, but I don't remember."

"Of course you don't; you were so young."

"Please tell me."

Lorene takes a sip of tea. She seems to need a little boost before telling her story. "Well . . . it was shortly after your father and I were married and took over the farm. Vivian and her husband needed work and we needed help. So they came here. They lived in that little house you shared with Mark. Anyway, Don --- her husband --- became your father's best friend. Odd to think about, because they were so different; I don't just mean because Don was black. Don had a sense of confidence that Munroe needed. They were good for each other. Don suddenly died one night. He had a heart condition no one knew about. Our whole world came crashing down. Your father couldn't handle it, and disappeared."

"He'd done that a lot."

"Oh, but this was the first time. And he was gone so long that it looked like he wasn't coming back. Throughout all that, it was just you and me and Vivian." Lorene's smile is an interesting mix of sadness and comfort at a distant memory. *That's it, that's the first time they became lovers.*

"So, what happened when Munroe came back, Mom?"

"Well . . . he was gone for about three months. When he came back, he felt so guilty and was so determined to make things right that . . . that Vivian decided to leave so that we could remain a family."

What an awful choice, Ann thinks: even back then having same-sex parents had to have been better for a little girl than an alcoholic father. But then, in those days no one had even heard of civil unions or anything else. The world has gotten a little better since then, especially New Hampshire.

"Her new husband isn't very nice; in fact, he is in business with some terrible man out in California. Vivian needed to get away from him, and I needed to have someone in my life."

"Oh, Mom, I am so damned sorry . . . I should never have yelled at you back then or stopped talking to you."

"Considering what I told you about Munroe and Lewis, I think it's understandable."

"Maybe; but I sure wish I handled it better. Are you and Vivian . . . happy together?"

"Oh, yes, much happier than I expected."

"That's all I care about, Mom."

✱✱✱✱

The sight is like a beautiful painting come to life, as Ben and Eve arrive in their daughter's hospital room to see her sitting up, smiling and feeding her newborn son.

"I wish I had my camera for this," Eve says. Ben steps over to the bed and gives Julie a fatherly kiss on her forehead. "How do you feel?" he asks her.

"Like a fool."

"Why?"

"Because Dad, I'm a New England girl: I should be able to handle weather like that. I grew up with it for heaven's sake." She points to her left leg, fixed in its cast.

"Don't be ridiculous," Eve reasons as she takes a seat. "It was an accident. Those steps were too slippery and the railing gave way. That's not your fault."

"That what Greg keeps telling me, but I still feel like a damned fool."

"Well, don't, young lady: that's an order."

"Yes, sir, Dad, sir" Julie answers in a mock military-style voice that has them all laughing with relief. Little John seems oblivious to it all; he stops suckling and starts his nap while still in her arms. He is such a miracle. Holding him, hearing him breath, seeing his big brown eyes: she and Greg spent much of their time this morning just admiring their son.

"Speaking of which, where is Greg?"

"Oh, Mom he spent the whole night in the lobby just to be near us. I finally insisted he go home and get some real rest. He'll be back later today." Despite all of their problems --- and her suspicions --- Greg has really risen to the moment. He loves her, Julie knows that. She could feel it again today. But . . . that vibe just won't go away. She still wonders if there is another woman.

Ben cautiously glances at Eve before delicately asking Julie, "Have you spoken to your Aunt Karen?"

"Yesterday; I invited her to the Agnes Gabler birthday party. But she may come sooner."

Again, Ben and Eve exchange concerned looks: *just how soon is soon?*

"Is there a problem?"

"Of course not," Eve responds, almost convincingly. "It will be wonderful to see her again."

✱✱✱✱

Greg may hate his new half-sister, but Jack and Joe soon learn that the farm girl is right about one thing: their son is having a ball at Manchester's SEE Science Center.

The three of them spend the day there together, feeling even more like a family. The two men watch Little Jack's joy and wonderment at the hands-on exhibits. There all sorts of things about light, sound and electricity. The boy's favorite is the Moonwalk, with his fathers watching and smiling as he bounces around.

But for the grown-ups, the most fascinating part of the museum is the Lego Millyard Project. Using about three million standard Lego bricks
--- no custom-made pieces, just the same ones you can buy in the toy store --- a replica of Manchester's famous Millyard District has been created. The installation is impressive. Even little Lego people can be seen going to and from "work" at the mills in a scene recreating the district of the early 1900s.

Little Jack stars losing steam as the day winds down. It has been a lot of fun, giving Jack a chance to forget his problems and experience a small taste of fatherhood. Joe takes their son into the men's room while Jack quietly outside watching other parents escort their kids in and out. His cell rings. He doesn't recognize the number and almost doesn't take the call, but flips it open anyway."

"Where the fuck are you?" It's Mel.

"It's nice to hear from you, too."

"Don't get sarcastic with me, faggot."

"Watch it, shit head. You're lucky I even answered. I didn't recognize the number."

"It's one of those pre-paid phones. I'm back in the country."

"Good; then you can get those damned papers yourself."

"Like hell I can, and you know it! Where are you?"

"Manchester."

"Well, it's about fucking time. Got the papers yet?"

"Nope; just got here last night."

"What are you waiting for? Faraway Hill is practically around the corner."

"I have to get a reason for going to the house."

"I already gave you that. Now get over there. I can't stick around too long, but I can be in Manchester tomorrow."

"That's not enough time."

"*Make* it enough time, boy. You fucked up too much at the wedding, and I won't let you do that again. Get it done tonight or the old man gets some unhappy news."

✱✱✱✱

Michael Bickel hates to fly. He hates the way his stomach churns at take-offs and landings. He hates the way his ears pop. But most of all, he hates having to sit in a cramped chair next to an idiot.

The elderly man to his right has been chattering about one bit of nonsense after another. If they were in a bar, Mike would have just yelled at him to shut up. But, he doubts if the stewardess in coach will be as understanding as a bartender.

Trying to ignore the man's latest topic --- some bizarre and ridiculous story involving a rude produce boy during a quick trip to the grocery --- Mike pulls out a photo. It was taken almost a decade earlier. He and Vivian are seen smiling together. Mike had started working for the Bolognas at that time and everything in his life seemed to be working out. Except that the bitch wouldn't behave, not the way he wants.

"Is that your wife, young man?"

"Yeah, she is." And she will be again. Her leaving was a humiliation. But he'll teach Vivian a hard, painful lesson, and then drag her back to LA.

"She's very pretty," and the old man goes on with another boring tale, this one about his wife.

Maybe Mike can get the stewardess to shut the geezer up.

✱✱✱✱

Unintended consequences. Her previous plans have worked so well that Karen hasn't thought too much about this concept in recent years. Her father used to go on and on about it to his students at Keane State College. Daddy fit the role of a philosophy professor even as a young man: graying hair, wrinkles in all the right places and a penchant for talking even when no one was listening. This was especially true of his daughters, as Karen and Eve learned when to tune him out.

His favorite concept was that of the unintended consequence. He could --- and often did --- go on and on for hours about it. Professor Scott loved using it in historical context, talking about how, for example, a collection of treaties crafted to prevent war actually made World War I possible. Then he would bring up smaller, more personal examples to drive the point home.

Karen is thinking about him and his favorite topic while sitting next to Julie in her hospital room. No one else knows she arrived an hour ago: Eve and Ben have come and gone and Greg is still at home freshening up; Denise is handling their luggage and hotel rooms. The nurse has brought the baby in for another feeding and Karen takes great joy in holding her unacknowledged grandson for the first time. But, hearing her little girl talk about the past few months has Karen thinking again of her father and unintended consequences.

"Greg has tried so hard, really he has," Julie explains after the nurse takes John away for his nap. "And we have great times together. Any time we can just be by ourselves, things are wonderful. But, everything about Ann . . ."

"Does he blame Ann for Lewis' murder?" Karen certainly never expected that development, and has been watching from a distance as the Hallorans fought Ann over her inheritance.

"Not exactly; he just gets reminded of it every time he sees her --- or even hears her name. And I've been no help; I've spent months defending her to him and him to her. I mean, she's like a sister to me --- we were only born three days apart --- and he's my husband. The whole mess has really been stressing me out."

"You never told me it was this bad." In his report, Karen's investigator has focused mostly on Greg's college years. She's had to rely on Julie and Eve to keep her current on happenings in Faraway Hill. Neither was this detailed before.

"I'm sorry Aunt Karen; but you have your own life in New York. Between your charity work and problems with your stepchildren . . ."

"Sweetheart, listen to me very carefully: there is no one in this world who means more to me than you."

"Thank you," Julie says with a smile; and then, with some embarrassment, she adds "there is something else."

"What?"

"I think that there may be another woman."

Karen knows better: there isn't another woman, but another *man*, in Greg's life. "But, Julie, you two haven't been married very long. How can that be?"

"To be honest, I have no proof. It's just a vibe I get --- and I could be wrong."

"How long have you had this 'vibe'?"

"Not too long; just since his last trip to Atlanta. I'm sure it's nothing."

"Of course it is, dear. He loves you. There can't possibly be another woman."

Yes, unintended consequences. Even the best laid plans can result in them. Karen will need to embrace some of Daddy's other philosophical ideas to make things better.

So, Karen thinks, who should die to make things right: Ann or Greg?

Or maybe, just maybe, there is someone else who should be eliminated.

****

The sun has set, the day is over and Greg Halloran can finally relax. He went back to the hospital this afternoon and stayed until Julie fell asleep. After that big scare, his wife and child are doing well and will be home tomorrow. He still doesn't know how to handle everything with Jack or Ann, but for the moment, all is right with the world.

Greg is reclining in his private parlor, the large oval room in the master suite flanked by matching bedrooms. He is dressed in just a t-shirt and boxers. Unlike most of the house, there are few antiques here. Just good, comfortable, upper-middle-class furniture. He can lie on the sofa with a small glass of brandy and forget all his problems. At least, he can until someone knocks at the door. "I am sorry for interrupting, sir."

"That's okay Frederick." There is probably some small issue regarding the Gabler party. The caterers will be coming tomorrow to start setting up the ballroom. Instead, the butler has some surprising news: "Mr. Campbell is downstairs. He insists on seeing you." *Why is he here? I told him we need to cool it for awhile.* It isn't easy being in love with two people, and again he wonders if maybe the real problem is that he can't commit. One of his college girlfriends made that claim when they broke up. But Greg shrugged it off; he was young at the time and enjoying life in the big city. But now he is a married man with a son. Something needs to change. He knows that; but facing Jack is the last thing he wants right now.

Greg sets down the glass, slips into his robe and follows Frederick into Center Hall. There, at the top of the stairs, they encounter Ann. She is in her own robe, carrying a tray of snacks, obviously going to her own suite. It's the first time the two siblings have been face-to-face in months. Ann has followed Julie's advice and stayed by herself, but now the inevitable has occurred. The three of them stand there in awkward silence until Greg manages to says, "Thanks for taking care of Jack for me."

"Sure," she answers equally uncomfortable. "I've also spoken with the party planner. Everything is set for the Gabler party; you and Julie don't have to do a thing. She doesn't even have to come downstairs if she's not up to it."

Greg still sees Munroe when he looks at her. He can still picture the drunken farmer pulling the trigger that killed his father.

"Um . . . okay, thanks for that too." He quickly scoots past her and down the stairs. Frederick tries to follow as best as his aging legs can carry him. "I am sorry about that sir," the butler says when the reach the main floor.

"That's okay, it was bound to happen." And it will happen again. There has to be a way to get rid of the farm girl. "Where is he?"

"The Green Room."

He waves the butler away, takes a deep breath and opens the door. Jack is standing there looking as nervous as Greg feels. This is their first meeting since they parted ways in Atlanta. Greg closes the door behind him. Before he knows what to say, Jack quickly steps over and kisses him deeply, sensually, the best and only way a lover can. Instinctively, Greg wraps his arms around him and returns the kiss. *How can I give this up? How can I choose between them?* He gently pulls away.

"I'm sorry dude," Jack says catching is breath. "I just saw you and I couldn't . . ."

"I know, I know." Greg finds himself fighting the urge to take him upstairs. "What's going on?"

"A lot; how are Julie and the baby?"

"Their doing great; I'll probably be bringing them home tomorrow."

"Cool."

"What did you need to talk about?"

"Well, a couple of things; really big things."

Greg motions for them to sit. This is one of those antique-filled rooms that make the house feel more like a museum than a home. "I guess I should start with the weirdest thing because, well, part of its weirdness is that is actually simpler." Holding his lover's hand, Jack starts telling him the tale of Jacqueline Westbrook. He begins by repeating what he told Greg in Atlanta: about his teenage affair with the sexy older woman who would abruptly dump him. "But there were a couple of things she never told me --- until now." And this is when Jack tells him.

"Wait, wait . . . a kid, a sex change *and* a hit man?" Greg finds the whole thing incredible. "Holy shit!"

"Yeah, that was my first response, too."

"You know, this whole thing sounds pretty damned . . . well, are you sure this Joe guys isn't trying to pull one over on you?"

"No, dude, he's not: I look at him and I can *see* Jackie. Plus, Jack's age is just right. That's another part of the weirdness: it all actually makes sense."

"Fuck . . ."

"And . . . and, there is one other thing. Something less weird but something that I'm more scared to tell you about."

"What is it?"

"I'm being blackmailed."

There is one thought that comes immediately to Greg's mind, and he finds himself saying out loud, "does this have anything to do with Mark Bradley?"

"Who?"

"The farm girl's husband; remember him?" That would be too much if the bastard was milking Jack for money each month along with Greg. *How many other people does the ass have on the hook?*

"Oh, yeah, that hunky guy that got arrested for hustling. Nope; I haven't seen him since the wedding. Why?"

"Never mind. Who's doing it?"

"You know him; he did business with your old man: Melvin Waite."

"Yeah, I know him: the asshole was my father-in-law's partner. He ran off with almost everything the firm had. The Feds have been trying to find him for months."

"He's certainly an asshole: he's got pics of me with his nephew, a senior at Columbia. The kid and I had hooked-up a couple of times."

"How long has this been going on?"

"You don't seem so surprised."

Greg is too embarrassed to admit being blackmailed himself. "Well, that's the risk we take, isn't it? Besides, it doesn't really compare to having your ex-girlfriend show up with a new son and a new dick."

"Yeah . . . anyway, there are some papers hidden behind a painting in your dad's study. Mel has somehow sneaked back into the country and will be town tomorrow. I am supposed to give him the papers and he'll give me the disc with pictures. What is it?"

"I don't know," Greg answers softly, painfully. "I haven't been in there since Dad was killed. No one has, except the police." He has even ordered the servants to stay out. Only Greg and Fredrick have keys.

Jack gives him a slight kiss on the lips and gently says, "I'm sorry; I wish there was another way."

"Sure there is: call the fucker's bluff."

"Oh, no, no, no . . . that means my old man finds out and cuts me off. And you can be damned sure that it will lead people to you and me." *And*, Greg realizes, *to Julie*.

"Maybe, but I need some time."

"Dude, I'm running *out* of time."

"*Mel* is running out of time. Whatever those papers are, they must be worth a lot of money. We hold more of the cards than he does."

Jack looks at him in amazement. "How the fuck did you get so smart about these things?"

Greg doesn't say anything, but answers quietly in his own mind: experience. He escorts Jack out to Center Hall, where his lover implores him: "Greg, *please*, do this. It'll get rid of him and fix everything. We can work out our own shit after that."

Greg walks Jack over to the Grand Vestibule and the front door --- unaware that Ann is standing discretely on the landing, watching the two men. "Maybe," Greg tells Jack as they step out of her view. "But I need some time."

What the hell are they talking about? Ann wonders.

EPISODE FOURTEEN

There is something about a good, long, hot shower that clears the mind. Jack stands in the stall, legs apart, letting the water pound his skin and massage his muscles, rolling down his face, his arms, his legs, his dick.

He woke up this morning to find two voice and one text message from Mel Waite. *The prick just won't give up.* It doesn't matter; things are starting to change. Jack now has an ally against Mel. Jack has Greg on his side.

Sure, Greg is hesitating about going into his dad's study. But who can blame him? It was in there that the old farmer pumped a bullet into Lewis' head. Even with all their issues, Jack might feel the same way if it were *his* father. *Now that Greg knows what is at stake, he'll come around.* And, anyway, outing him to his old man won't help Mel at all, because Jack's incentive to get the papers will be gone.

That's something else Jack has come to realize: he has a stronger hand that he first thought.

Stepping out of the shower, he can hear the cell ring again. He doesn't rush to get to it. Instead, he casually dries off and wraps the towel around his waist. The phone goes silent as the call shifts to voicemail. Jack smiles: he knows it will ring again soon. He spends the next few minutes picking out clothes. Sure enough, it rings again. This time Jack answers.

"Where the fuck are you, fag boy?"

"I'm still in Manchester, shit head."

"Don't you dare call me that, you damned little . . ."

"You know Mel, I've been thinking: it was *your* nephew taking up the ass, not me and my old might kick the bucket before you can get to him. Plus, *you* are the one the cops are after. So tell you what: give me a few more days and I'll get you want you want. So chill, dude." With that, Jack slaps shut the phone. He hasn't felt this good in months.

✱✱✱✱

"We can work out our own shit after that."

Those words, from Jack to Greg, have been bouncing around Ann's head all night. It was such a strange scene in the hall. The words could mean anything, of course, but there was something odd about their body language. If she can figure that out, Jack's words might make sense.

Greg has already left the mansion to pick up his wife and son from Elliott Hospital. His early departure allowed Ann to come downstairs and have breakfast in the family dining room rather than eat in her suite. Unfortunately, she is so distracted by last night that she has barely touched her waffle.

"We can work out our own shit after that."

Whatever the "shit" is must be pretty big. Jack looked desperate and Greg confused. But there was something else in the way the moved, the way they stood together that --- strangely enough --- makes Ann think of her mother and Vivian. *No, it can't be; that makes no sense at all.*

She hears some noise in the Grand Hall. It can't be the caterers: they aren't due to arrive until this afternoon. She steps out to see maids rush to the vestibule, a group of elderly women almost giggling like school girls. Walking down the hall, Ann can see why: Greg and Julie are home, and everyone --- even Frederick --- is excitedly looking at the cute, new Halloran heir sleeping in his mother's arms.

"He is *so* adorable, Mr. Halloran!" shrieks one of the maids. She is old enough baby John's grandmother. Greg thanks her with a smile. Frederick composes himself and gently directs the women to return to their chores. "We have hired a nanny, on a temporary basis of course, Mrs. Halloran. She will arrive this afternoon." Julie can decide later whether to keep her or replace her.

"Thank you, Frederick." Julie looks up to see Ann standing just outside the vestibule. Julie smiles, but Greg, who followed her gaze, does not. He is still uncomfortable around her. And there is something more, something behind his eyes --- or maybe Ann is just projecting, trying to figure some things out.

"It's great to have you home, Julie."

"Thank you, it feels good to be home."

Ann politely steps aside to watch the new little family climb the Grand Staircase and out of sight.

"We can work out our own shit after that."

Jack and Greg? Make it *does* make sense after all.

****

Michael Bickel let himself sleep in this morning. The long flight from Los Angeles was too exhausting, and then he had to deal with the frustration of finding a decent hotel. Apparently there is some big convention coming up and rooms were getting booked fast. Fortunately, he found space at the downtown Radisson. Mike fell asleep just as his head hit the pillow. By mid morning, he finally rouses himself enough to step out and explore Manchester. He finds it odd that his woman should choose New Hampshire; as he walks around he seldom sees another black face. Mike knew Vivian and her first husband lived out east, but she seldom spoke about those years. Of course, he was never interested. But walking about and meeting and encountering the polite residents and interesting shops it occurs to him that maybe Vivian came here because she initially *left* here: this place might have been her home.

One of these interesting little shops is on Elm Street and called King's Korner. Looking through the window, Mike can see inside to a book and gift store with a coffee counter. *They must sell maps,* he thinks, *and they might be better than the ones at the hotel. Probably some local books, too.* He had Googled Vivian's phone number before leaving LA and found it belongs to someone named Munroe Gale who lives in a little town a few miles north called Faraway Hill. There were other links about Gale, but he disregarded them; they didn't seem important.

Inside the store, he encounters a cute white girl with "Mary" on her nametag. She directs him to rack of books about the state. Mary seems friendly enough, so he asks her "what do you know about a town called Faraway Hill?"

"Faraway Hill?" Her face brightens. "Lots. Its one of the more famous little towns in New Hampshire: that's where one of the state's richest families lives. My boss --- the store's co-owner --- she is married into them and lives there."

What a lucky coincidence, Mike thinks, until he realizes that maybe Vivian hooked up with some really powerful people. Maybe he should have looked at all those other articles Google came up with; these people could be too important to mess with. "That family, are they called the Gales?"

Mary's expression suddenly changes; the friendliness draining from her face. "Ah, no . . . they are the Hallorans." She looks at him curiously. "You don't know about the Gales?"

"Should I?"

"Both families made the national news, like, earlier this year."

Mike doesn't pay too much attention to the news. He spends most of his time and energy on his own little world. Beating and killing people can be murder on your free time. "Kind of, but I really wasn't following."

"Oh, well," she looks around like a school girl about to tell a bit of gossip. This seems odd, since there are only a couple of other customers. With a whisper she explains, "The whole story is weird. Someone should write a book about it. Mr. Halloran --- my boss' father-in-law --- he was murdered by a local farmer named Gale. Then it came out that Gale's daughter was really *Mr. Halloran's* illegitimate child --- and that she had married some gay hooker!"

How fucked up are these people? "So is the Gale in prison or what?"

Mary shakes her head. "He committed suicide. His widow got money from Halloran and still lives on the Gale farm. I hear she's fixed it up real nice. But her daughter --- the illegitimate one --- she now lives in the big house with the other Hallorans." This information complicates matters. Gone is his original plan to just pick up Vivian, slap her around as punishment, and take her back to LA.

"The Hallorans are old money," Mary explains. "They are having this big party for Agnes Gabler in a couple of days. Lots of important people will be there." Mike has no clue who Agnes Gabler is and doesn't much care. He picks out a couple of travel books and thanks the girl. *Shit, I definitely need to get back online.* He needs to know as much as possible and move as carefully as possible.

Emerging from the store, Mike stops on the sidewalk to get his bearings. He'll need them to get his woman back. He starts to walk back to the hotel when he sees, just a few blocks away, something he never expected on a Manchester street corner: Joe Westbrook. *What the hell is that freak doing here?*

****

The little motel along Interstate 93 has no wifi, no business center and just basic cable. The rooms barely have beds. But the middle aged man with the balding head can't be choosey. He needs to be discreet. The big payoff is just within reach. Once that rich fag comes through for him, Melvin Waite will be able to skip the country permanently. This time, it won't be with tens of thousands of dollars. It will be with ten *million.*

Mel had found out about Ann Gale just after Lilly Halloran died. But it was only the start of Lewis Halloran's many interesting secrets. By the time Mel confronted him, the textile baron had no choice and agreed to pay for the lawyer's secrecy --- but demanded that Mel "get the fuck out of my sight" first. So Mel stole what he needed from the law firm and left the country, knowing that he could force Jack Campbell to courier documents for an offshore account. *The asshole deserves far worse for corrupting my nephew;* Mel thought then and still thinks now.

Lewis had hidden away the papers to an overseas account in his study, and was suppose to give them to Jack Campbell, who would send them on. The old man never knew who his contact would be; Jack was supposed to tell him the night of the wedding. *But that damned Munroe Gale had to kill Lewis before Jack could get the papers.* Everything got fucked up after that.

Now, Jack Campbell is the problem. *"It was* your *nephew taking up the ass, not me,"* the kid barked at him this morning. *"Plus, you are the one the cops are after. And my old man is about to kick the bucket. So tell you what: give me a few more days and I'll get you want you want. So chill, dude."* Mel is still pissed at the faggot for speaking to him that way. Jack picked the worst time to grow some balls. Now Mel sits stewing alone in a rundown little motel, feeling powerless.

But there is one more possibility. Hidden in a drawer of the nightstand is a pistol Mel bought two days ago from some farmer in Fitchburg. It was a no-questions-asked, cash deal. He could sneak into the Halloran mansion himself. And, as one last bit of familial revenge, he could also take out Jack Campbell.

"Now *that* is what the faggot deserves," Mel grumbles.

****

The mansion is in such chaos today that it's a wonder that Julie and the baby can get any rest. The party planner and catering crew have effectively taken over the ballroom and much of the first floor, getting ready for Agnes Gabler's big event. Ann offers to help, but soon realizes that the planner and Frederick have everything under control. Even Agnes' daughter, Scarlet, comes by to put out fires but finds few flames. Giving up, Ann decides to go into Manchester and do some more Christmas shopping.

She is not the only one out and about, as she finds the shops along Elms Street busier than usual. A few shoppers still give her a second glance and whisper but its nothing like it was over the summer. Of course, some of these people are visitors in New Hampshire for Gabler's party. While the really big stars are staying at hotels in Boston, there are enough famous people milling around that Manchester's one and only TV station has gone on a sort of "celebrity watch" the last couple of days. Ann hasn't seen the actual guest list --- only the party planner, Julie, Frederick and Scarlet have that --- so she is as interested as anyone about who will be there.

It feels good to spend time just exploring the city. It's surprisingly warm for a November day. Ann has shut herself away for too long. She feels like she's missed everything the last few months, from her mother's love to the Manchester Marathon. It is time to live again, now as Ann Halloran rather than as Ann Gale.

She considers her options along Elm Street, including Elizabeth's, a store that specializes in hand-made pieces created by New Hampshire artisans, when a voice behind her says: "there is so much more to Manchester these days, isn't there?" Ann turns around, surprised to see Karen St. John standing next to a young woman.

"Hello, Mrs. St. John, when did you get into town?"

"Yesterday; Julie invited me to the birthday party."

"Did she?" This is news to Ann; *it must have been a last minute thing.* "Then you know about the accident?" she asks carefully.

"Oh yes, I visited her in the hospital. So frightening; but she and the baby seem to be doing well." Karen St. John is so poised, so amazing; Ann really feels like she's in the presence of someone truly remarkable.

"They came home this morning."

"I am so glad," Karen says with a smile of relief. "I'll call her later." Ann looks curiously at her companion. "Do that --- and who is your friend?"

Karen, embarrassed, explains, "How silly of me. This is my new personal assistant."

"Hi: I'm Denise Sullivan," the young woman explains, offering Ann her hand. Ann's first impression is that she is a *Playboy* playmate dressed to please Hef: her suit jacket shows some serious cleavage and her skirt fits snugly. *This woman is Karen St. John's personal assistant?* Ann thinks. They hardly seem like a good match: Karen is dressing as she always dresses, with the impeccable elegance of an old time movie star. Denise, on the other hand, dresses like a Hooters manager. "Hello, I'm Ann Halloran."

"Really? Oh, how cool: I went to college with your brother."

"You did?" *Denise went to NYU?* Looking at her, Ann thinks that she'd better fit at a college for porn stars.

"Oh, my, I'd forgotten that," Karen says without much conviction. "You and Greg dated for awhile, didn't you Denise?"

"Mrs. St. John, I wouldn't call it *dating*; we just hooked up a few times." *Yep,* that confirms it to Ann: *Denise was the college slut.* Fucking for fun; Ann has never done that. She's likes to think that it's beneath her, but secretly she just hasn't the confidence.

"Well, whatever it was, it's just another sign of how small this world can be."

Something beeps; Denise pulls a PDA from her tiny purse. "Mrs. St. John, this is a reminder of that call you need to make to New York."

"Already," Karen says rolling her eyes. "My stepchildren give me no end of grief. Ann, dear, would you please let Denise accompany you? She has never been to Manchester before and I hate to just abandon her."

As lonely as she is, spending time with someone like Denise Sullivan would not be Ann's first choice. But she finds herself agreeing. Karen thanks her and walks in the direction of the Radisson, the same hotel Jack and his friends are staying. This prompts Ann to turn to Denise and ask, "Did you also know Jack Campbell when you were in college?"

"Oh, yes, I hooked up with him, too." Denise smiles; obviously remembering some *very* good times. "Both guys got around a lot, if you know what I mean."

"I hear they were serious ladies men."

"Not just the ladies; I know they each hooked up with guys once in awhile. *They did what!* "They hardly said anything, but everybody who was anybody knew about it. Of course, I shouldn't talk, some of the wild things I did. There was one party in particular, but, well, I guess I shouldn't say anything. Greg is married and a dad now; all of that is behind him."

She can't be serious, Ann thinks, but she is so . . . casual with the news that Ann is inclined to believe her. "So, uh, they both got around a lot?"

"Except for senior year; it was pretty clear that they were just into each other by then. It was cool. Lots of people do things like that; I was heavy into this girl from the English Department one semester. I think they broke up around graduation. Why, have you met Jack?"

"Jack was Greg's wedding; he was best man." That scene Ann witnessed last night is starting to make sense: Greg and Jack may not be a couple now, but having been one in the past would explain quite a bit.

"Holy shit," Denise laughs. "That's fucking weird; I thought they stopped speaking to each other. They must be just buds these days."

"Yes, just buds." Maybe spending time with Denise will be worth it. The girl likes to talk, and Ann wants to listen. "Let me show you some of my favorite shops."

✼✼✼✼

The view from his window high up Brady Sullivan Plaza offers Ben King a marvelous vista of downtown Manchester, including the many people and cars populating the busy city center. He is too far from the street to make out any details, but it is still impressive. His firm used to be just as busy. Sadly, that has all changed.

Ben has been forced to let go of nearly everyone. The only full-timers left are he, his long-time secretary Helen Armstrong, and that annoying but effective Barry Studer.

That leaves a lot of empty space on the seventeenth floor. The Halloran account is keeping things afloat. Barry has managed to drum up some new business, but it hasn't been enough to make up for the losses. Three important clients left this month, one that had been with him from the beginning. The stories of Mel's embezzlement make many people think that the firm is going under. At this rate, they may be right.

Ben hasn't told his wife, but lately he finds himself driving the long way to work, going past a gun store on Daniel Webster Highway. It has fueled a new fantasy, one that picked up steam this morning when Agent Pembroke called. The authorities have learned that Mel has reentered the country with a false passport. The Feds are trying to track him from a distance, and signs are he is coming back to New Hampshire. Ben has no idea why the bastard has returned. But he'd love to confront him and demand an explanation for destroying a lifetime of work.

Maybe he'll drive by the store on the way home tonight.

✳✳✳✳

Talk about coincidence: after trailing the girl-boy, Michael Bickel soon realizes that they are staying in the same downtown hotel. Of course, the rich bitch has taken one of the fancy suites upstairs; Mike just has a standard room. He had to be careful to make sure Jackie Westbrook --- or whatever she calls herself now --- wouldn't see him. Taking her out in a busy, popular hotel is too risky. Mike needs to find another way. So he put a call in to Vincent Bologna and is waiting to hear back.

In the meantime, Mike has another mission. He opens up his laptop and immediately gets a signal. He Googles "Munroe Gale New Hampshire" and waits. Within a matter of seconds the page fills with links --- a lot of links. Most of them are to newspaper stories. Mike clicks one and begins to read. The whole sordid tale --- at least what is public knowledge --- is laid out for him. *Holy shit!* Getting his woman back is going to be much more complicated then he thought.

His cell rings. It's the old man. "Yes, Mr. Bologna?"

"You got news for me, Bickel?" Bologna's impatience comes through loud and clear, even a continent away.

"Yes sir, she's in New Hampshire."

"New Hampshire? What the fuck is Jackie doing in New Hampshire?"

"I'm still working on that sir, but she brought the boy and they seem to be with some other dude. I don't know who he is yet, but I'll find out."

"How did you manage to track her there?"

"Just old fashioned hard work, sir." *Actually, it was dumb luck.* But Mike isn't about to let his boss know that.

"Well, good work; but I gotta tell you: I'm fucking sick and tired of all the problems this freak is causing me." Mike can just imagine the rumors --- not to mention the jokes --- going around Vincent Bologna's cronies. He can hear the frustration and embarrassment in the man's voice. He doesn't blame the man for feeling the way he does; Mike knows he'd feel the same way if something this sick happened in his family.

"Let's get rid of her, Bickel --- right away." That order is a surprise; Vincent is usually more cautious.

"Sir?"

"As soon as you can, whack her. Just don't hurt the kid. He needs to be brought back here to us so he can be raised normal."

The order makes Mike uncomfortable. He has killed before and he is good at it. But those were always in circumstances that could be controlled. They don't really exist here. "Sir, if I rush it, it could get sloppy." Besides, Mike still has Vivian to deal with. She will not humiliate him any more. *Vivian, Jackie: are women really worth all this fucking grief?*

"I don't give a fuck. Get rid of the freak and bring my little boy home. Pronto. Got it?"

"Yes, sir."

****

A few floors above Michael Bickel, Karen St. John is in her suite, considering which of two designer dresses to wear at tomorrow night's big event. There are so many decisions to make. What to wear, what to say, whom to kill.

New Hampshire's libertarian gun laws have come in handy: she has already acquired two guns, both carefully hidden, and neither with her fingerprints. They will be perfect, once Karen makes a decision.

She has successfully eliminated everyone who has hurt her, and done it in a methodical well-planned way. Daddy would be proud of her logic and follow-through.

Karen hears a knock on her sitting room door. Opening it, she lets an excited Denise enter. She is carrying several shopping bags and has a proud smile on her face. "It went great, Mrs. St. John."

"Did you tell her everything?"

"Not quite; but plenty. She was trying to be *real* subtle. We'll probably get together again in a few days."

"Good," what Ann does next will help Karen make her decision, and one of those guns will have a purpose. For the moment, she lets a giddy Denise show her all the tacky things she bought today. In a little while, they will meet with the real estate agent. This, too, will help Karen reach a decision.

****

Having surrendered the mansion's first floor to the party planner and army of caterers, the Hallorans have retired to their respective suites. Ann is down the hall, eating her dinner alone. Little John is asleep in the nursery, being tended by a charming nanny hired from an agency in Boston. Her name is Maggie, a grandmother herself, and with the most delightful Irish accent imaginable. Julie was taken with her immediately.

Right now, the new parents are sitting at a table enjoying the quiet and a simple meal. They don't say much. A lot has happened in the last few days. Both of them have a lot on their minds. Julie is thinking about Greg and their baby and wondering if there is another woman and how serious a threat she may be. Greg is thinking about Julie and their baby, and what to do about Jack. It is an odd moment: both realize the other is preoccupied with something important and both are close to knowing what it is. Close, but not quite there. Instead, they share feelings about their new son. They talk about his smile and who he looks most like. "Aunt Joan will be thrilled we named him John," Greg says chuckling.

"I'm sure; did you see how Dad felt about his middle name being Benjamin? He was miles high with that." Julie's leg, in its cast, is resting on a chair and itching slightly.

"Well, he deserves it: he's been great to us, despite having a tough year." *Could I really give up the woman I love,* Greg wonders; *could I give up being a full-time dad, having supportive in-laws, all of that? Could I give that up for Jack?* That was the plan. But that was in the warm, distant world of an Atlanta hotel. Now he is back in reality. And reality is so damned hard.

✳✳✳✳

With another busy and exciting day behind him, Little Jack went to sleep right after dinner. Often his papa needs to cajole or even order him to hit the sheets. But not tonight; some mac & cheese was all the kid needed.

Big Jack, on the other hand, seemed to Joe to be on some sort of emotional rollercoaster all day. He started the morning at a high point, feeling empowered after coming clean with Greg Halloran the night before. But as the day wore on, Jack's moods started changing. Every time his cell rang, he thought for sure it was be Greg. But each time it was either the office or his brother. Right now, he looks like a little boy abandoned by his best friend.

Joe can relate; he went through the same thing, only much worse, during his transition. Jackie's father had died, her friends couldn't relate and her mother is still in some denial. "Any news?"

Jack shakes his worried head. "No . . . I thought coming clean would help, but . . ."

"He just brought his wife and baby home from the hospital today."

"I know . . . I'm hoping that's all it is; but he is a little freaked about going into that room."

"Can you blame him? That's where his dad was killed. Besides, you'll see him tomorrow at the party."

Jack nods with a sigh. Looking at him now, he looks so much like the young man Joe knew and loved in a different lifetime. The sight brings up a mixture of feelings for him, too: of nostalgia and a desire to offer comfort, all underlined by a newly realized attraction. In all of the craziness of the last few days, Joe had forgotten how sexy Jack is. It has been such a long it has been since Joe was intimate with anyone; he even went on Craig's List last night to check out the options.

Checking his watch, Jack sighs again and says without any enthusiasm, "I guess I'll just go crash in my room."

Joe stops him by gently grasping one of his biceps. "You don't have to go."
Looking directly into his eyes, Jack understands what he is offering. And the
message Joe receives is just as clear: it would be too weird for Jack --- to fuck
Joe after having fucked him as Jackie.

"I'm sorry."

"That's okay." Jack says nothing else and leaves Joe alone with a sleeping child
and a bruised ego.

****

New Hampshire rarely sees a night like this one. Certainly, little Faraway Hill
seldom does. Movie stars, politicians, singers and even a couple of ambassadors
arrive at the Halloran mansion. They travel in limos, Hummers, flex-fuel cars and
even a bus (carrying the band, a famous 70s R&B group). For Ann, it's the
glamorous life she's always dreamed of coming true. Ironically, instead of
relishing it she finds it all very intimidating. So, she hangs back and watches
everyone and every thing around her. It feels safer.

It also gives Ann a chance to ponder the odd conversation she had yesterday with
Karen St. John's new assistant. Ann tried to play it cool and keep the subject of
her half-brother as casual as possible. But inside she is still shocked: *Greg and
Jack were a couple in college?* Sure, she can understand someone --- especially a
guy --- doing some same-sex experimentation. Even at the University of New
Hampshire she knew of a few people who did that. *But an actual relationship?*
Maybe: it would certainly explain what she overheard the other night.

Jack is here tonight. He and Greg act like they are just best buds. Jack even jokes
a little with Julie, who is making an appearance before retiring early. The guys'
conversation --- what she heard of it --- made it sound like Jack wants to start
things up again but Greg isn't so sure. *Should I tell Julie?* Part of her thinks so,
but another part urges caution: there is still so much she doesn't know. Maybe
Greg said no and Jack has accepted that choice. Maybe they *are* just best buds
now and nothing more. If so, telling Julie could cause her nothing but pain ---
and make Greg resent Ann all the more.

There are, of course, other Hallorans at the party. Not all of them like at the
wedding. Greg's Aunt Joan --- now, her aunt, too --- is here along with her
teenage son Matthew. Her hunky young husband is nowhere to be found.
According to the bits and pieces she picks up during the evening, the two have
split. Apparently an empty head and tight abs can only hold a marriage together
so long.

Patrick Halloran, a cousin, is here too. He is handsome and confident and friendly. But like his Aunt Joan, he keeps his distance from Ann. Such is the life of the bastard child.

Most of the guests have gathered in the ballroom where Agnes Gabler holds court, just as she did at the wedding. The old woman loves being the center of attention and regales the crowd with more tales of her colorful life. Her daughter and grandson sit nearby. She is currently in this wonderfully detailed story of her first meeting with Andy Warhol at his famous Factory. Among the crowd of well -known people, Ann's attention keeps going back to the movie star couple holding hands and laughing. They were on the cover of *People* only a week ago.

"I have a special announcement to make," the old lady says grandly. The room falls quiet. "As you know, I love New Hampshire. I adore it here." The crowd applauds and cheers until she waves them silent again. "Yes, yes, this is no secret . . . but as I travel the world I have noticed that people often don't realize how this very rural state can often be quite sophisticated. Of course," she winks, "maybe we should keep *that* a secret." The audience laughs. "I firmly believe that an important reason for that sophistication is our education. I don't just mean our colleges --- they are unquestionably an asset --- but the fact that all of our towns and cities, no matter how small they may be, have their own libraries. Reading and learning from childhood through our grey haired years --- well, I have always subscribed to that. But sadly, I learned recently that is actually one --- and only one --- town in New Hampshire that, until recently, had no library. It's true. It is located near Concord. But the good people there would not be daunted. They pooled their resources and renovated a beautiful 18th century barn which they stocked, equipped and furnished --- and then ran out of money." People in crowd shake their heads sadly. Ann has heard about this town. New Hampshire pioneered the very concept of the public library back in the 1830s. It is part of state pride. The news makes her want to open up her check book. Agnes Gabler's grandson wheels out a draped easel. The old lady then proudly announces that proceeds from the sale of, this, her newest painting, will benefit that town. The audience cheers her once again, as the drape is removed revealing a naïve work in Gabler's signature style of the renovated barn-turned-library.

"I see you like to stand back and just observe."

Ann turns to see, standing behind her, Senator Richard Davis. He is even more handsome in person than on TV. Despite his advanced years --- he could be Ann's father or maybe even her grandfather --- his chiseled face and silver hair reminds her a little of Paul Newman.

"Well, it seems safer." It feels so good to be acknowledged. "Are you sure you want to be seen talking to New Hampshire's most scandalous woman?"

"I prefer to think of you as New Hampshire's most *interesting* woman," he answers with a friendly smile.

****

Karen St. John peruses the buffet set up in the Formal Dining Room. The selection is impressive and it's hard to make a choice. The other guests marvel at the display. But standing next to her is a young actress, famous for her teen movies, looking so thin she is almost transparent. She seems to find the options a little overwhelming. *I guess the anorexia rumors are true.* It almost makes her wish she'd brought Denise to the party; she would have enjoyed all of the gossip potential. But Karen's aims are better served using the girl in small doses.

"I wish you'd let me network, dude" Barry Studer whines as Ben King drags him into the room. "This is the perfect opportunity to score some new clients" the cocky young lawyer insists.

"No, I won't let you do it." Ben looks frazzled. Eve enters the room, equally upset. "How could you, Barry?" she asks. "Making a pitch at that poor man; his wife just died!"

"How could I know that?"

"Oh, I don't know," Ben rolls his eyes. "How about that big obit in the *New York Times* --- you know the one the *Union Leader* reprinted only three days ago!"

"Fine, I'll keep my mouth shut and we'll be screwed. Happy?" With that, Barry practically stomps out of the room mumbling something about needing to get laid.

"Don't be too hard on him Ben," Karen advises. "He is young and trying hard." Not that she cares too much, of course. This is the man who effectively stole her little girl. But eliminating him would hurt Julie too much; so Ben is safe.

"Thanks, Karen; I'll keep that in mind." Neither he nor Eve is happy that she's here and has been avoiding her last couple of days. This is the first time the three of them have been together. "Are you enjoying the party?" Karen asks them with her well-practice sweetness.

"Yes, Karen," Eve tries to be civil. "It's a great night."

Eve's response is the perfect segue for Karen's revelation. She's been waiting for this moment. "It reminds me of the parties I used to have in Manhattan. I'll miss them. There won't be quiet as many at my new place."

Ben and his wife exchange worried looks. "New place?" he asks carefully. *They've taken the bait, as planned.*

"Yes," Karen says with a smile. "I'm buying a house in Faraway Hill."

****

The doctor warned Julie that she should be taking things easy for awhile. So, without saying a word to anyone --- not even Greg --- she quietly slips away from the rich, powerful and beautiful people (at least, as quietly as her crutch makes possible) to go upstairs. It seems the doctor was right: Julie felt great this morning, but the party proved too much. She'll just have to learn to pace herself.

The stairs are a little tricky, but she is getting better with the crutch. Hopefully the cast will be off by Christmas.

Julie hobbles to her suite and finds the bottle of pain pills and a pitcher of water next to the settee. Her leg has been throbbing for the last hour or so. The pills help, but they also tend to make her drowsy.

Placing the crutch firmly under her arm, she makes her way across Center Hall to the nursery. The room is dark and quiet. Maggie, the new nanny, is downstairs taking a break and having her dinner. Julie leans the crutch against a wall and hops on one leg over to the crib. She reaches in and caresses the smooth cheek of her sleeping son. He looks so beautiful, so peaceful. The doctors say he came into the world early, but the timing seems perfect to his mother.

"What about Julie?" she hears a familiar voice out in the hall ask. "I saw her in the ballroom with the others a few minutes ago," says another. Curiously, she peeks out the door to see her husband and his best friend in Center Hall. She grabs the crutch and is about to join them, when something in their body language stops her. They stand very close to each other, Jack's hand on Greg's arm. This discussion looks important for them and Julie doesn't want to interfere. "I know I've been a real shit head about everything," Jack says.

"No, not really, but damn I wish you'd quit pushing. I can't deal with all this right now. Julie, the baby, now this; it's too much."

Jack takes Greg into his arms for a bear hug. It is so warm and supportive that Julie smiles at the sight. *Yes, its good Greg has a friend here; someone to be a brother to him.* She's glad she stayed hidden in the nursery. "Please?" Jack asks him, almost pleading. Greg takes a moment to think. There is a pain in his eyes that Julie remembers from his father's murder months ago. Finally, Greg hesitantly nods and says softly "we'll do it tomorrow night."

And then it happens, something Julie never expected: Jack Campbell gives Julie's husband a deep, passionate kiss.

****

Munroe Gale always tried to be romantic. The most important goal in his life was to make his wife and daughter happy. But he had little money and less imagination, so whenever Munroe attempted to romance Lorene he would always fall short. He would then commiserate with a bottle in his secret room and try again another time.

For his widow, true romance finally blossomed when Vivian Bickel reentered her life. Now they lay, naked in each other's arms, basking in the glow of their love making --- and the three dozen candles placed around the room. It was all a wonderful surprise: Vivian arranged for the whole thing after dinner, while Lorene met with the farm's new foreman.

"This was so special, thank you," she tells Vivian before kissing her. After all these years of struggle, everything in her life is now nearly perfect. Even Ann has given their relationship her blessing. But Lorene can still sense the worry in Vivian. "Are you still thinking about Mike?"

"I can't help it. I know him: he'll try to find me." Lorene has seen the old bruises on her lover's body: dark reddish blots on her ebony skin. One thing Lorene can say about Munroe, he never once landed a hand on her or Ann.

"But he doesn't know anything about Faraway Hill, does he?"

"No, and I still haven't told Sofia where I am." Sofia is an elderly Hispanic woman whom Vivian befriended about the time she met Michael. She called her a few times in California, but has never given Sofia her number or address. "But I know him, and he will keep looking for me."

"Your safe here, I'm sure of it."

"Maybe," Vivian says, still looking scared. Lorene can see something else in her lover's eyes: something that she has been thinking about but is too nervous to bring up.

"What is it, what else are you thinking about? Please tell me."

Vivian touches Lorene's cheek and slowly, carefully asks, "Sweetheart . . . do you know where I can buy a gun?"

****

Breakfast at the mansion the following morning is a simple, relaxed affair. The caterers are packing things up in the formal rooms. The VIP guests have all returned to their hotels. Agnes and her family are back in her famous, converted sugar house. Only Hallorans stayed at the house last night: Joan, Matthew and Patrick. Greg's aunt is still upset that Julie gave her childhood suite to Ann, but they remain civil to each other. That seems mostly to do with the baby. "We haven't had a John Halloran for, I think, three or four generations," Joan told her with no small amount of approval. "It's a wonderful choice."

Thanksgiving is only a week away, but Joan tells Julie that Christmas is the really big holiday, when nearly the entire family converges on the mansion. It is a not-so-subtle hint that she is behind on issues like decorations and planning. But mistletoe is the last thing on Julie's mind right now: she is still wondering about last night. That kiss came out of the blue and seemed totally out of character. Neither man has ever given her the impression of being anything but straight. Certainly, Greg has been with plenty of women; and when they make love --- well, Julie has enough experience to understand that he really enjoys her. But that kiss was one between lovers. In any other circumstance, catching her husband cheating would make Julie confront him immediately. Infidelity is not something she was raised to tolerate. But this situation is just too bizarre and confusing. She might have spent the night ruminating about it if the meds hadn't knocked her out. When she awoke this morning, Greg acted as if nothing happened.

Breakfast is over. The servants bring down the luggage. Family members prepare to leave. Julie wonders if she should say something to him after they have gone. *But how do I ask a question like that? And do I really want to know the answer?* Then a thought hits her: maybe Greg *didn't* cheat on her with another woman; maybe he had a rendezvous with Jack in Atlanta. *Is it possible they've been having an affair since the wedding? What does this make Greg? What does this mean for our marriage?* Never in her life did Julie Halloran ever imagine dealing with these kinds of issues.

Just before everyone leaves, Patrick takes Greg into the Green Room. It doesn't last long, maybe a two or three minutes. When they emerge, both have confused expressions. After the goodbyes, Julie asks him what Patrick wanted. She's too uncertain about the other questions to dare them yet.

"It was weird; he said something to me in Latin as if he expected some kind of response."

"What was it? It's been a long time, but I took Latin in high school."

"It was, 'es vos meus frater?'"

Julie leans on her crutch, thinking about it for a moment. *Es vos meus frater*. "I think its some sort of question about brothers. Sorry; I guess I don't remember as much as I thought."

"I guess it's not important," Greg shrugs. "But it was strange."

"Do you have to go into work today? I'd like us to spend the day with John."

"That was my plan all along." He takes Julie into his arms and gives her a kiss that, again, feels contrary to what she saw last night. But as they climb the Grand Staircase, Julie getting better with her crutch, he says casually, "by the way, Jack is coming by this afternoon. I figure it's about time that I go into the study again. He's going to help me with that."

✶✶✶✶

Ann eats breakfast alone in her suite while the family has theirs together downstairs. It is part of her promise to Julie not to cause any problems. She is determined to use the holidays to help break the ice with her new relatives. But rushing it will be counterproductive. At the party last night, for example, Ann was very careful of what to say and whom to speak with. It wasn't easy, but she knows that she can't embarrass the Hallorans --- not if she wants to be considered one of them. And Ann has a history of embarrassing statements, things that often got her in trouble at a school party or just among friends.

She also tried to discretely observe her half-brother and his friend. Ann is still not entirely convinced that Denise wasn't pulling her leg. Neither man acted in any odd way during the party.

Spending time with Richard Davis was the best part. The senator is much older than Ann. But he was charming and funny and yes, in a way, sexy. This is a man who knows himself and his place in the world. They spent most of the night together. He told her stories of his career, from the Faraway Hill town council to the state house in Concord and now Washington. Richard asked Ann about her life and never pitied or belittled her when she opened up to him.

He invited her to visit him in Washington after the holidays. "Most people don't realize it," he explained. "But the city is beautiful during the winter." She said yes, amazed that someone as sophisticated and fascinating as Richard Davis would be interested in a little farm girl from Faraway Hill.

Maybe it's finally happening, Ann thinks to herself, *maybe I'm really going to have the life I've always dreamed of.*

✶✶✶✶

This is a difficult and painful afternoon for Greg Halloran. He and Jack have just unlocked the door to his father's study. No one has been inside for months. There is still crime scene tape on the floor. Papers are strewn across the desk. A bullet hole remains in the mahogany paneling. Greg can see reminders of the brutal crime everywhere.

Even nature seems to feel the loss: through the windows they can see the sky darken, as a fall storm makes its way to Faraway Hill.

"Where are they supposed to be," Greg asks hoping to get this over with soon, "in the safe, right?" Which seems odd to him: *wouldn't the police have found them while investigating the murder?* He walks over to the leather desk chair and touches it, as if doing so let him touch his father again. Greg was never close to either of his parents. His mother was especially distant. But Lewis was so clearly trying to reach out to him, that Munroe's crime seems a double sin: denying Greg not only of his father's life, but his father's friendship.

"That would make sense to me, dude, but Mel says that your dad hid them behind a painting."

"A painting, that's odd." The room has several paintings of various sizes and subjects. There is also a framed, antique document with something Latin written on it. The paper reminds Greg of that bizarre incident this morning with Patrick. "Do you remember much Latin?"

Jack starts peering behind each picture, trying to be careful not to damage anything. "That's a weird change of subject. Why do you ask?"

"Something my cousin Patrick said this morning before he left. He said took me aside after breakfast and say --- let's see, what was it again --- oh, yeah, 'es vos meus frater?'"

Frustrated Jack gives up on one wall of pictures and moves to another. "I think he was asking something like 'are you my brother?'"

"Weird."

"I think it's this one," Jack says peeking behind the one of Greg's grandfather. Greg helps him lift it gently off the wall. Sure enough, there is a manila envelope taped to the back. Jack opens it to discover the paperwork for an offshore account. "Holy shit: this account has ten million dollars in it!"

"Are you kidding me?"

"No dude; whatever Mel had on your dad must have been pretty damn big."

"The bastard; we shouldn't give it to him."

"Yeah, I'd like to keep it and tell my old man to go fuck himself. But that's not an option; we both have too much to lose." Jack folds the envelope and stuffs it into a pocket. Looking up, he sees a glass enclosed cabinet. "Those are cool."

"I suppose; I've never been into guns. They're all antiques, though; I know that much. A couple date back to John Halloran and colonial times."

Greg notices Jack staring at the guns, as if the collection has given him an idea. It bothers him, but he decides to say nothing. He is more interested in getting out of this room ---- and especially put the sordid matter of Mel Waite behind them so they can work out the other complications in their lives.

****

Complications seem to be everywhere these days. For an exhausted Eve King one of these is coming home after a long day at the office to find her husband sitting alone in the living room. The lights are out and the shades are drawn. He is silently nursing a scotch and soda, staring straight ahead. It reminds Eve of that terrible scene, earlier in the year, when Ben told her the news about Mel's embezzlement. Worried, she drops in the chair across from his and looks directly into his eyes.

"Sweetheart, what's wrong?"

"It may be over soon," he says trying to stay calm.

"What may be over?"

"I got a call from Pembroke this afternoon. They are convinced that Mel is in New Hampshire."

"Are they going to arrest him?"

"I hope so; we lost another big account today so it may not matter much. Barry is still pissed at me for not letting him network at the Gabler party --- of course he is nowhere near as pissed as I am at Mel."

This has been such a tough time for Ben. Eve wishes she could do more for her husband. Instead, she reaches over and gives him a supportive kiss on the forehead. "We'll make it work." Ben nods, still worried but grateful for her support. Eve picks up her briefcase and reaches for his, which is sitting closed on the floor next to the sofa. "No, no," he says suddenly. "I'll take care of that."

"Okay," Eve shrugs not thinking much of it. After all, it is *his* briefcase. He can put it away when he's ready. But there is a reason he is delaying, something that he has inside the case: Ben King finally went into that gun shop on Daniel Webster. Now he must decide what to do with his purchase.

****

Throughout the day, darkening clouds gather one by one, stitching themselves together. By early evening, they have become a quilt of gray and black covering the sky. The result is a world that looks and feels sadder than it really is. Eventually, drops fall thick and heavy to the Earth and Manchester's sidewalks become nearly empty of people. There are few signs of life, mostly from the glow of street lamps and the occasional car or city bus.

Mabel Baxter is trying to stay dry. She is standing at a bus stop on Elm Street, waiting for her ride home. A stocky woman in her late forties, Mabel is wrapped in her rubber rain coat holding a big golf umbrella. It has been a long day. Mabel is the assistant manager of a boutique on Merrimack Street. A delayed shipment of merchandise finally came in today. She and an associate had to work late getting them inventoried for the all-important Christmas season. It was exhausting, tedious work and she is anxious to get home.

From the bus stop, Mabel can see the Verizon Arena a couple of blocks away. It's quiet there tonight, but the Monarchs have a big game tomorrow. She isn't a hockey fan, but Mabel's husband has season tickets. When there is a concert or a game the arena is lit as bright as a star. Tonight it is as dark as the sky.

Across the street is Veterans Memorial Park. It is here people from southern New Hampshire come together for all sorts of festivals and concerts. The four acres can fill quickly on some days, like when a popular local band performs on the covered stage. Normally it would be empty on a rainy night like this one. But Mabel can see a man strolling up to the park's centerpiece fountain. He stands there, wearing a long dark coat and holding an umbrella, staring at the statute of a union soldier from the Civil War. The sight seems odd to her. Mabel has admired the statues surrounding the fountain many times, but never on a night like this.

Another man strolls toward the fountain, dressed in a hooded coat, trying to look as casual as possible. But it is obvious that he is here for them to meet. She can't see many details through the rain but they shake hands. The men are too far away for Mabel to know what they are talking about, but the meeting alone is suspicious. *Where is that damned bus?*

The rain starts to fall a little faster and the wind blows a little harder. The two men seemed to have agreed to something and walk toward Elm Street. Mabel pretends not to notice them.

Then she hears the shot.

Hit, one of the men falls into the other's arms. The scene is shocking. Mabel turns to see another man, at the far end of Veterans Park, run off. *Oh, my God!* One of the men cradles the other in his arms, looking around in panic. He sees Mabel. "Help me!" he screams. She pulls out her cell phone but is frustrated to see the charge is dead. *Damn!* Frightened, Mabel is about to run across the street when her bus finally appears. At the moment the door opens she says to the driver, "That man, in the park over there, he's been shot!"

TO BE CONTINUED IN BOOK TWO

Book One Discussion Guide

This guide has been created to facilitate book clubs and their members in discussing *Faraway Hill: Book One.*

- Before reading this book, had you heard about the DuMont Network or the TV series "Faraway Hill"? If so, what did you know about them?
- What do you think of the author's used of soap conventions in telling his story?
- Do you get the feeling that Faraway Hill may be a real place?
- The trilogy has characters of mixed sexualities: along with straight people, there are bisexual, gay, lesbian and even transgender individuals. This group is commonly known as the GLBT community. Are you part of this community? If not, do you know anyone who is? Can you relate to a world of mixed sexualities?
- Karen St. John is the ultimate hometown-girl-makes-good story. Is there someone from your hometown or high school that went on to a more glamorous life?
- Like many people, Greg Halloran does some compartmentalizing. He doesn't considering paying for a prostitute's services to be adultery. Do you think he's right or wrong? Why or why not?
- Ann seems to be one of those people who never quite fits in. Have you known someone like this? Do you consider yourself as such a person?
- Did you expect Lewis' murder, or was it a surprise? Did you correctly predict who the assailant was? If not, who did you suspect?
- When Ann discovers her mother's deception about her paternity, she (temporarily) cuts ties to her. Would you have done the same thing in her shoes? Why or why not?
- Karen is clearly unstable, yet somehow remains very clever and logical in her actions. How do you think she manages to do this?
- Greg is obviously torn between Julie and Jack. Whom do you think he should chose?
- Did you expect Lorene's relationship with Vivian? Why or why not?
- Were you surprised at Joe Westbrook's revelation? Would you have believed him if you were Jack? Have you ever known someone who went through a similar transformation?
- Towards the end of the book, Julie discovers the truth about her husband's relationship with Jack. What do you think she should do?
- Karen's announcement stuns her sister. Do you think she'll do as Eve fears, and tell Julie their secret?
- The book concludes with a mystery: a shot is fired in a Manchester park. Who do you think pulled the trigger? Who do you think was shot? Give reasons for your theory.